Praise for *The Girl from the Hidden Forest*

"From first page to last, Hannah [...] [...] nting and heart-stirring. *The Girl from the H[...]* [...]y steeped in atmospheric suspense and exquisite romance. With prose that flows with a rare poetic beauty and rich details that expertly evoke Regency England, this is a reading experience to treasure. Fans of Julie Klassen and Michelle Griep will be captivated by this standout historical tale."

—Amanda Barratt, Christy Award-winning author of
Within These Walls of Sorrow and *The Warsaw Sisters*

"Once again, Linder has crafted a beautifully haunting tale, full of prose both elegant and evocative, capturing the essence of the Regency period while delivering a thrilling story. The chemistry between Eliza and the enigmatic Felton Northwood is palpable, and their shared quest for answers only intensifying the bond between them. As the mystery of Eliza's true identity and the events that shattered her life comes to light, readers are treated to a tale that is as deeply moving as it is suspenseful. *The Girl from the Hidden Forest* is a must-read for fans of gothic Regency romance and historical mysteries."

—Misty M. Beller, *USA Today* bestselling author of
the Brothers of Sapphire Ranch series

"Simultaneously tender and haunting, Hannah Linder's *The Girl from the Hidden Forest*, draws you into a Regency world shrouded by danger, mystery, and suspense. Fans of Joanna Davidson Politano and Crystal Caudill will love this book."

—Amanda Cox, Christy Award winning author of *The Secret Keepers of Old Depot Grocery* and *He Should Have Told the Bees*

"*The Girl from the Hidden Forest* showcases Hannah Linder's gifts as a rising star in Regency fiction. Romance, suspense, mystery, and history intertwine and immerse you in a Gothic storyworld you won't want to leave. Well done!"

—Laura Frantz, Christy-Award winner of *The Rose and the Thistle*

"*The Girl from the Hidden Forest* by Hannah Linder is a swashbuckling story of adventure and romance that had me turning pages to find out what happens next. With likeable characters, plenty of action, a romantic setting, and surprising plot twists, this is a story you won't want to miss."

—Ann H. Gabhart, bestselling author of *In the Shadow of the River*

"What a captivating novel! *The Girl from the Hidden Forest* kept me enthralled from the first page to the last. Hannah Linder's expertly woven romantic suspense twisted and flipped all my expectations until the heartily satisfying conclusion. The conflict, motivations, and character growth displayed in this story were all believable and beautifully drawn. I can't wait to read what this author writes next."

—Jocelyn Green, Christy-award winning
author of *The Metropolitan Affair*

"With its lush, Regency setting, intriguing mystery, and toe-curling romance, *The Girl from the Hidden Forest* is one of my favorite reads this year. Eliza and Felton's story left me turning pages far into the night, and Hannah Linder is now one of my favorite go-to authors. *The Girl from the Hidden Forest* is a unique and stunning tale to savor."

—Tara Johnson, Christy and Carol finalist of *Engraved on the Heart*

"Danger, mystery, and sigh-worthy romance—Hannah Linder delivers all this and more in *The Girl from the Hidden Forrest*. Deftly crafted, it's page-turner you won't be able to put down. I highly recommend it."

—Ane Mulligan, award-winning author of *By the Sweet Gum*

"Hannah Linder weaves a spellbinding tale of danger and romance from the first page of this story. With prose reminiscent of fairy tales of old, Linder's deft hand will take readers through twists and turns to a satisfying conclusion."

—Karen Thornell, Regency author of *Edward and Amelia*
and *To Marry an Earl*

"Raised by a kind but haunted man called Captain, Eliza has taken comfort in fairy tales, imaginings, her faithful dog, and the deep forest that isolates them. But eventually, when she is forced back into the real world—the intimidating world of the wealthy ton—Eliza's persistent childhood nightmares take on life, and memories of something horrible begin to return. Hannah Linder sweeps us into a fairy tale for adults, where dreams and nightmares, imagination, and reality blend and hearts beat fast with unexpected but piercingly sweet first love. Poignant and lyrically beautiful, *The Girl from the Hidden Forest* will keep you mystified until the satisfying end."

—Denise Weimer, multi-published author of *When Hope Sank*
and The Scouts of the Georgia Frontier Series

A REGENCY NOVEL

THE GIRL
FROM THE HIDDEN
FOREST

HANNAH LINDER

BARBOUR
PUBLISHING

Other Books by Hannah Linder

Beneath His Silence
When Tomorrow Came
Garden of the Midnights

The Girl from the Hidden Forest ©2024 by HANNAH LINDER

Print ISBN 978-1-63609-833-3
Adobe Digital Edition (.epub) 978-1-63609-834-0

All scripture quotations, unless otherwise noted, are taken from the King James Version of the Bible.

This book is a work of fiction. Names, characters, places, and incidents are either products of the author's imagination or used fictitiously. Any similarity to actual people, organizations, and/or events is purely coincidental.

Cover Design: Hannah Linder Designs

Published by Barbour Publishing, Inc., 1810 Barbour Drive, Uhrichsville, Ohio 44683, www.barbourbooks.com

Our mission is to inspire the world with the life-changing message of the Bible.

Member of the
Evangelical Christian
Publishers Association

Printed in the United States of America.

DEDICATION

To everyone still living in daydreams.
I hope you find your story.

CHAPTER 1

Balfour Forest
Weltworth, Northumberland
May 1812

Something was wrong.

Eliza Ellis tramped down ferns and growth as she hurried for the only place in the world she wanted to be. The only place she knew.

Her short-legged beagle trotted after her, panting as if this were merely another stroll on another late eve.

But it wasn't.

Tonight was different. Captain was different. Would her father still be home when she returned? How many times had he left her already, all in the space of a fortnight, only to come back with the scent of ale on his breath?

He'd never drunk before.

When the stream came in view, flanked on each side by mossy rocks, she claimed the one she'd always dubbed the Lady's Throne. She used to sit here with a scepter made of twigs like a queen from Captain's stories.

What she wouldn't do for one of them now. To be back in her father's arms, young again, nestled where his heartbeat thrummed in her ear.

Instead, she was alone. All she could think of was the way he kept looking at her. As if something had changed—only it hadn't. How could it?

They were safe. They were always safe because they protected themselves. No one could hurt them or frighten them, not if they stayed where the trees were tall and the air was quiet and the world was the woods.

Oh, Captain. What is the matter? She pulled her knees to her chest and hugged them close, lulled by the rush of the stream. If she bent near enough, she could leak her tears into the swirling motion and drop her whisper into the blue-tinted waters.

If only they could whisper back.

But they only carried away her sorrow, as they always did, to some foreign place beyond these trees. Captain said if a person followed this stream, sometime or another it would open into an ocean. What must the ocean look like? Endless water, frothy waves, blue meeting blue. Pirate ships and giant white masts and ghosts of fabricated mermaids. Why couldn't she have been a mermaid? She might have danced with the fishes and ridden upon the whales and—

A snap.

Eliza swiveled on her rock and reached for her growling dog. "Merrylad, here." The last thing she needed was her brave little beast raising his hackles against some vicious varmint. "I'll have none of your barking, hear?"

Another snap. Closer.

Merrylad ripped from her hold and woofed. He braced in front of her, as if he had no desire to sprint away and chase down some frightened hare or white-tailed deer, as was usually his pleasure.

A brush of unease fluttered her chest. She scanned the trees as evening shadows wove around them.

Nothing seemed amiss.

Nothing stirred.

Whatever had disturbed the quiet had apparently scampered up a tree trunk or burrowed into the moist needles and ground.

But the flutter increased until her heartbeat turned into hammering. "Come, Merrylad." She stood, brushed the residue of moss and dirt from her dress—

Something white flashed to her left.

Merrylad yowled.

A face appeared, half hidden behind a pine tree, close enough that unfamiliar eyes met hers.

No, no. She lurched forward, pumped her legs so fast her muscles began to scream. No one was supposed to be here. Not ever. Captain would die if he knew, but it wasn't her fault.

Footsteps pounded behind her, closing in quickly, as fast as the evening darkness.

God, please. The prayer raced. Why was he chasing her?

Faster, faster, but the footfalls were gaining. One or two yards and she'd reach the path. Then the cottage. Then Captain—and he'd know what to do.

"Stop right there." The voice chilled the air, but she didn't listen.

A few more steps.

Almost there.

She threw herself into the old wooden door, Merrylad pushing at her legs, and swung it open. Just as quickly, she forced it shut and locked. "Captain?"

She pivoted, took in the entire room in one swift glance.

Empty.

"Captain?" Panic crawled up her throat, too big to swallow, like a boulder she couldn't breathe past. "Captain!"

The door jarred, followed by a loud kick.

Help me, God. She scooped Merrylad into her arms, flung herself into a corner, and sank to her knees like the frightened maiden in all her books. *Help me, help me, help me.*

Because in the nineteen years she could remember, there'd never been anyone in these woods. No one but her and Captain. Safe and alone. Protected.

Until now.

Felton Northwood winced as his shoulder slammed into the unmovable door. This wasn't going to work. Too sturdy to break down.

And there wasn't time.

The old man was gone for now, but what if he changed his mind? After all, there'd been a bottle in his hand when he nodded his agreement. When he'd stumbled out the cottage door, less than an hour ago, he'd been wiping tears with the back of his sleeve. "Do it quickly."

That's all he'd said.

Felton intended to, if only there was a way inside this infernal cottage. He gave the door one last shove, groaned, then hurried to the window instead.

Near darkness stared back at him. Evening was falling fast. In a few more minutes, these woods would be black—and if the gathering clouds from earlier were any indication, there would be no moon.

Maybe it was better this way. Then he wouldn't have to see her face again.

Not yet.

With his hands on either side of the window, he hiked up his leg and pressed his Hessian boot to the glass. He shoved it through, glass splintering, and waited to make certain a musket rifle wasn't about to fire down on him.

He didn't imagine the young chit he'd found at the stream could handle a gun.

But then again, he never imagined she could run like the wind either.

He kicked out the last shards of glass and climbed through. The room made his skin raise in bumps. This was insanity. He had no right here. Not when the place was still scented with an old man's cheroot and a young girl's dying flowers. . .and the faint, lingering aroma of the last meal they'd shared together.

The last meal they'd ever share.

But he had no time for that now. He'd come, and he was doing what was right. What was right for him. For his family. For their name—or at least what was left of it. But was it right for the girl hovering in the corner?

With every step he approached, her breathing grew faster. The dog growled. Their outlines became more distinct in the shadows, until he could make out her eyes for the second time today.

"I am not here to hurt you, so there is no need to be afraid."

She didn't answer.

"But I am taking you out of here. It can be as easy or hard as you wish to make it." He took one more step, reached for her—

The dog sprang forward and seized his hand with vicious teeth. Pain flared.

Deeper, deeper, until his fingers were wet with blood, even as he pried the animal off him. He combated the dog's second attack with his foot. One kick, then two until—

"Stop it!" The girl arose from her shadowed corner and snapped her fingers. "Merrylad, down."

Whimpering, the dog scuttled behind her.

Then she faced him, shorter than he'd realized in the woods, with hair that draped well beyond her elbows. She said nothing. Only waited.

More than ever, he didn't want to touch her or frighten her.

But he had no choice.

With his bleeding hand curled at his chest, he grabbed her forearm with the other. "Leave the dog here. We haven't room for him. I've a horse tethered out—"

She drove her foot into his shin. Twice. Then she twisted, her fingers groping for his face—but he never let go.

Instead, he jerked her into his arms and darted for the door. He fumbled with the latch as her nails clawed at his cheek, as the dog charged again and seized his ankle.

Fierce fighters, these two.

Something else he hadn't expected.

He threw the animal off and raced outside as the girl kicked and pounded him with her fists. He swung her onto his saddle.

Only then, when he'd climbed behind her and spurred the horse away from the cottage, did her shoulders finally cave. The dog's barking faded in the distance. One small, stifled sob escaped into the night air. A bothersome sound.

If anything less was at stake, he would take her back.

As it was, he had no choice.

No, no, no. This couldn't happen. *Captain, no.*

She was lost in another nightmare. Deep blackness, coldness, the need to run but the inability to move her legs.

She was trapped.

Again.

Only this time, it was real. Captain wasn't next to her, framing her cheeks with both of his wrinkled hands. "Hush, love. Ye're only dreaming again, see?"

How quickly the terror always dissipated under his warmth. The strange things would go away, the shadowed faces, the leering voices—half human, half beast. She would escape the suffocating devils of her dreams.

But there was no escaping this.

Because a devil had her in his arms, trapped against his chest, with his bloody hand the only thing she could fix her eyes on. She didn't dare look up. Not even when the veil of blackness lifted, when the first shafts of morning came darting between the trees.

Please, please. Soon the trotting horse would reach the edge. The boundary she'd never crossed. The line between everything she knew and everything she didn't. Why couldn't she move? Why couldn't she fight her way free?

She'd done it a hundred times. How often had she been kidnapped by villains and ruffians and desperate madmen? There was always fog, screams, and that one quick moment when she triumphed against her oppressor and broke free.

Nausea swirled in her stomach. Captain was right. She pretended too much, and what good had it done her?

She was weak. She could no more break free than she could bring to life Captain's tales.

"You don't remember me, do you?" His words jarred the silence. How strange, hearing a voice she'd never heard before. "But then again, I cannot own to remembering much of you either."

Remember her?

She'd never seen him before in her life. How could she have? For as long as she'd known, there had only been the cottage. The trees. The stream. Sometimes she had other memories, things she didn't understand, but they were more story—or nightmare—than anything else.

"We shall talk when we reach Weltworth."

As if talk could make sense of this. As if anything the blackguard had to say might stop her terror and bring her home again. How far did he think he could take her before Captain caught up with them? Didn't he know he'd never get away with this? That she'd flee, one way or another, the second his back was—

"You'll do well not to seek escape." As if he sensed her thoughts. "We've many a village ahead of us, and unless you should like to sleep on the ground between here and Monbury Manor, I suggest you be sensible."

"Let me go."

No answer.

"Please." Bile edged up her throat. "Please, I beg of you."

Again, nothing. He urged the horse faster and flexed his wounded hand until the dry blood cracked. "You named the dog?"

What?

"Well, did you?"

"Yes."

"Fine name. Teach him to fight too, did you?"

She lifted her gaze. The trees were thinning. The wild shrubs were fewer. In the distance, open countryside appeared like foggy brushstrokes of an unfinished painting.

"The road is up ahead."

Captain would die. Maybe she would too.

"A few minutes more and we shall be on our way to Weltworth."

Then her beloved forest would be gone.

He should have thought this through. He should have waited for Lord Gillingham to make up his own mind, weigh the consequences, and make the decision himself. But what if the viscount had decided against sending for her? Where did that leave Felton—and his family?

Exactly where they'd been for the last fourteen years, that's where. That was no place Felton intended to stay. For anyone's sake.

The hours stretched by in silence, the only noise the clomp of his horse's hooves and the loud warbles of unseen wrens. But the girl?

Not a sound.

He'd expected tears or questions or demands for freedom, at the very least.

But she just sat there, trapped in his arms, as still as the Grecian statues outside Lord Gillingham's manor. She was her father's daughter, truly.

He just didn't know how to tell her.

The road wound onward through quiet Northumberland countryside, paralleled by stone fences, without sight or sound of another horse or carriage. A few more miles and they'd reach the village of Weltworth. Then what?

He didn't know. He needed to think. Mayhap it was foolish to take her there, to think that she wouldn't enlist the help of villagers and try for an escape. But what of his food supply? By tomorrow, they'd be out of provisions. Besides that, his hand needed a sight more than mere water and bandages. How much longer could he handle the reins with this swelling?

Oh well.

The devil with his hand.

The risk was too great and he had no intention of losing her now, not after fourteen years of needing her to wash the blood and dirt from his family name. Had she any idea what her absence had cost him? All of them?

When Weltworth was long behind them and the widening road grew dim in the dusk, he turned his horse into a dense patch of trees. He pulled her from the saddle. "We shall camp here for the night."

No protest. Not even the slightest indication she'd heard him.

He tethered his horse to a sycamore, unfastened his saddlebag, and went to work with his tinderbox. Gads, but he was hungry. Although he'd eaten half a loaf during their ride—of which she'd refused even a bite—his stomach churned for something more substantial.

Unfortunately, it was looking like the rest of that loaf would have to suffice. At least until he could trust her in a village.

"Hungry?"

Again, she gave no reaction.

He snapped a couple more twigs, blew until the small flame enlarged, and sprinkled in a few dry leaves. "Well, I am. Sit down with you."

Without a word, she lowered herself to the ground on the other side of the fire.

For the first time, he had a chance to look at her. To *really* look at her. To see the eyes, gray and doe-like, blinking so fast he suspected tears. Her hair was much the same as it had been before—dark blond, gleaming—only without the perfect ringlets of her childhood years.

And her mouth. He saw Lord Gillingham in the grim line, but he saw her mother in the trembling corners. Beautiful, this creature. Even as she was, in the stained cotton gown and brown pinafore, as plain as the forest he'd stolen her from. Had she been hidden out there all these years? Alone with that mongrel of a man?

He cleared his throat and looked away. If he were better at words, this wouldn't be so difficult—and explaining the truth would already be behind him.

But he wasn't.

And heaven help him, but he didn't know how to say anything or how to soften the blow or how to ruin her life in a way that wouldn't hurt so much.

He grabbed the loaf of bread from his bag. "I am taking you to Monbury Manor, a three-day ride from here." Peeling away the linen one corner at a time, he focused on his meal instead of the woman across from him. "To meet your father, Lord Gillingham."

Silence.

He took a couple of bites, chewed long, swallowed hard. Then, folding the bread back into the linen, he added, "Eat the rest of this, for I shall not have you making yourself ill—"

"My father is Captain Jasper Ellis."

"I'm afraid not. No one is quite certain who, in truth, your Captain Ellis is."

"He knew this would happen."

"What?"

"All these years. . .he knew. He warned me. He expected someone would come looking for him, but it wasn't his fault."

"What wasn't?"

"The mutiny. The shipwreck. The loss of cargo and—"

"I don't know what you're talking about." He pushed to his feet. "This has nothing to do with Ellis' success or failure on the sea—or anything else he's told you all these years."

A pallor stole the pink from her cheeks.

"It has to do with you. And you alone."

~~~

Nothing made sense. He had no right to lie to her this way, to tell her things untrue, to pretend Captain was anything but what he'd always promised he was.

16

Her father.

The man she needed, the man she loved, the man she cried to when the nightmares grew so devilish she couldn't bear them. How could he be anything less than her own flesh and blood?

He had her heart. She had his. They depended on each other because they had no one else and the rest of the world had forsaken them. Captain said so.

She believed him.

From across the fire, in the flickering orange glow, the young stranger unwound his makeshift bandage. Pink, swollen knuckles. Bloody teeth marks. Merrylad had never hurt anyone in his life until yesterday.

She hadn't either.

But she wanted to hurt this man. She wanted to say something, do something, that would force him to set her free. How could this happen to her? What would she do? What if Captain never came and she was dragged to this Monbury Manor and—

"I suppose you are quite proud of this." His voice was not unkind, but the smile curving his lips seemed more sardonic than anything else. He retied the knot on his bandage. "But then again, it is not as if you asked to be kidnapped, I suppose."

"Why did my father not come?"

"What?"

"If this lord you speak of is truly my father, why has he not come for me himself?"

"He could not find you."

"Then how have you?"

He pulled off his navy tailcoat, shook off the dust, and walked around the fire's edge. Then he stood above her. Held her eyes. Outstretched the coat. "The night grows cold. Put it on."

She told herself to deny the coat. Or anything else he said or offered or touched.

But in the end, she pulled the heavy tailcoat around her shoulders and wished to heaven it could scare away the chill inside her soul.

If only she were back at the Lady's Throne. Or falling back into the pages of a book. Or stirring the steaming kettle at the cottage's stone hearth, with Merrylad at her feet and the branch outside tapping the window.

She didn't want to cry. She wouldn't. Captain wouldn't want her to. But even though she crammed her eyes shut, tears pushed past her eyelids.

"Goodnight, Miss Gillingham."

Her chest ached with the hurt and confusion those words inflicted. Because it almost seemed as if she'd heard the words before.

***

A noise, faint and quiet. One he shouldn't have noticed—probably wouldn't have—if the pain in his hand had not kept him in and out of sleep.

Felton sat upright. He must have been out for longer than he realized, because last time he was awake, the fire was still burning and crackling. Now it was only embers.

He couldn't see a thing.

Again, a rustling sound stabbed the silence. Like footsteps or—

His horse snorted, then the animal broke into a gallop and shot past him in the darkness.

Felton scrambled to his feet. "Stop!" Blast her, the little vixen. He groped for his flintlock pistol and darted after her. "Stop!"

She was too far ahead of him. He'd never catch her, and she'd never hear him.

He aimed upward, fired.

The gunshot boomed across the quiet trees, leaving the scent of gunpowder swirling around his face and watering his eyes.

Another snort, this time louder, followed by the stampede of hooves on ground.

And a scream.

Felton sprinted into the blackness. If anything happened to her, if she'd fallen, there would be no redeeming himself. Or his father. The whispers and speculations would only be worse until—

He spotted movement in the corner of his eye. A hobbling shadow.

With a new burst of speed, he sprang in her direction, whacked through a dead bush, and gained on her within seconds. Breathing hard, he caught her elbow and swung her against him.

She gasped at the impact. "Let me go." Pounded at him with her fists. "Let me go. Let me go. Let me go—"

"I have no intention of doing anything, Miss Gillingham, aside from bringing you to Monbury Manor."

"I won't go."

"You haven't a choice."

"I'll run away."

"I care very little what you do, so long as you stay long enough to meet my one demand." He circled her wrist and yanked her back toward the smoldering ashes of camp. "But we have no time for that now. Our main dilemma, at hand, is how we intend to get anywhere without a horse. You might have at least handled the reins instead of letting him throw you."

"'Twas your gunshot that frightened the—"

"Are you hurt?"

A pause, then a quiet, "No."

"Well, you deserve to be. Now go put on my tailcoat and sit over there. If I cannot find the deuced animal in the next hour, you might as well prepare yourself for a long journey ahead. The next village is not for another four and twenty miles."

She said nothing in return, as seemed to be her way, and Felton marched back into the wooded darkness. The cool night air pushed away some of the tension in his gut. That had been too close. This whole thing was. . .ludicrous. If anyone knew what he was doing, Lord Gillingham included, they would have his neck.

Well, they would find out soon enough, and any repercussion would be no price at all.

Because Eliza Gillingham knew what no one else in the world did.

She knew what happened that night, those fourteen long, wretched years ago. She knew how to clear his father's name from the filthy stench of murder.

And she was going to do just that, whether she liked it or not.

Because he'd been living in shame long enough.

They all had.

Eliza kept her pace with the fast, longer strides of the stranger who had yet to impart his name. Not that she wanted to know. She didn't. She would rather think back through Captain's stories, choose the most odious character, and call him as such.

Nonsense, that.

But it was easier to think of stories—ones with familiar, happy endings—than the unknown of her true life. What was her true life anyway? Who was she?

Not that she doubted Captain.

Never.

But there was something. . .a niggling sensation every time this stranger spoke certain words. Like *Lord Gillingham*. And *Monbury Manor*.

And *Miss Gillingham*.

"I should have taken my chance with you at Weltworth." From beside her, the man swept a sheen of sweat from his forehead. "At this rate, we shan't be in Poortsmoor until dark."

The walking bore no effect on her. After all, she'd been running and ambling through Balfour Forest for as long as she could remember—and despite the slight throb in her ankle, this was no different.

But the hunger pains, which had been cramping her stomach since daylight, grew more intense with each step. Why hadn't she taken the bread when he'd offered it last night?

"You favor your left foot."

"It is nothing."

"Even so, we shall have a doctor take a look when we reach Poortsmoor. I'll not be presenting you to your father injured."

"He is not my father."

"For his sake, I wish you would not say that." He massaged his bandaged hand. "At least not to his face."

What was she supposed to say?

"As for this captain you are so fond of, suppose you answer a few questions for me."

"I cannot."

"Why?"

"Because I am true to him, despite the things you tell me."

"Very noble of you, Miss Gillingham, but terribly naive. Have you ever considered he might be the one who. . ." The words trailed off.

A dull ring of alarm went off inside her chest. "Who what?"

"How much do you know of your mother?"

"Only that she died shortly after Captain returned from sea. There was no work for him after the clipper went down. Not after his own crew deserted him and the cargo of spices from Northeastern India was lost."

"So he took you to the forest."

"Yes."

"To live alone."

"Yes."

"You were lonely?"

Lonely? Yes, she'd been lonely. She'd lain awake at night, dreaming of faces, and she'd sat by the stream wishing it could talk back to her. How many times had she devoured the books Captain brought home for her? Or pored over a new edition of *La Belle Assemblée* and imagined herself among the illustrations? Or wandered away into the forest, pretended the trees were friends, and told herself she was entering a ballroom instead of more woods?

But she'd been happy in the forest.

Restless sometimes. Maybe even a bit curious and sad some days—but always happy, because Captain was everything she needed and they had no fear of the cruel world without.

The stranger's eyes were upon her, studying her.

Heat crept along her cheeks. She didn't look away, though. Not this time. Instead, she kept her head up and stared back into the deep green eyes.

He looked nothing like the rogues from Captain's stories. Not with his wind-tousled blond hair. His cleft chin. His strong face, strong jaw. Why did he seem almost approachable? Half boy, somehow, even though he was very much a man?

"You look at me very strangely, Miss Gillingham."

She looked away.

"Remember me now?"

No, she didn't. She'd never remember him, and she didn't want to. All she needed was to find a way to escape, to make it back to Balfour Forest and the cottage and Captain and Merrylad and—

"Someone's coming." He snatched her arm before she had a chance to react. "Say one word or make one wrong move, and I shall see you regret it."

"I cannot see that I have anything to lose."

"How about your captain's life?"

Her heartbeat sped faster as he pulled her closer to the center of the road—just seconds before a six-horse mail coach came in sight.

The dusty coachman jerked on the reins, his whip flurrying in the air, as if he weren't quite certain what to do with himself. "What the deuce, fellow!" When the horses halted, he ripped off his continental hat and cursed. "Get out of the bloomin' way 'fore I run the both of you down. I've a schedule to keep, I 'ave, and there be no time for dallying."

"We've no time for it either, good man. How about a ride?"

"Not a chance. Full of passengers already, we be. Now get a move on—"

"Up top then. And think not that we shan't pay either. There's fifty pence for you if you let us on. Besides that, is it not your Christian duty to aid a young man and his bride who have met with mishap on their honeymoon?"

Eliza's jaw slackened as his arm fell around her shoulder.

The coachman uttered another oath. "Bloody fools. On with you then—and mind you don't be losin' the mail."

No sooner had they climbed to the top of the luggage and mail than did the coach lurch back into motion, dust rising in their wake.

"You did well, Miss Gillingham." With his hand clinging to hers, as if in fear she might fall, her kidnapper's lips spread with a grin. "And I'm certain you can forgive the small lie. Matters of romance seem to soften even the most disagreeable of sorts."

"It was terrible to say." Her whisper was almost lost in the roar of the wind and wheels. "And what you said of Captain—"

"I meant every word of it." The grin was gone. His grip now intense. "I am taking you to Monbury Manor and will do most anything to ensure that happens. Whether you want to go or not matters little to me. Your captain means even less. Is that clear?"

Tears climbed her throat.

When she didn't answer, he took his gaze elsewhere, his brows lowered, as if as much fear and burden were weighing down his own thoughts. What was he talking about? What was happening—or *had* happened?

And in the name of heaven, what did it have to do with her?

※

Poortsmoor was the sort of place Felton had visited once and counted as too many times. The timber-framed buildings were sooty and sagging. The air carried pungent smells of dead fish and brine. Even the villagers, as they moped about the street in approaching dusk, seemed haggard and woebegone.

But Eliza Gillingham stared as if they had just entered Grosvenor Square. Her gaze roamed from one side of the street to the other. Then up. Then down. Then back and forth again, as if she'd never seen such a place in her life. Had she really never been out of those woods?

"To the apothecary first." He took her elbow. "Then we shall find lodgings and something to eat." If she didn't take the food he offered this time, he'd force it down her throat himself. Last thing he needed was the girl fainting of her stubborn hunger.

He could be just as stubborn, though.

She'd eat.

From the middle rungs of a ladder, a scruffy lamplighter doffed his hat. "Jolly evenin' to ye, me lady." Slurred. "Won't ye be so kind as to blow a poor lonesome chap a kiss?"

Her only answer was to draw closer to Felton's side as they continued past the oil streetlamp.

"Well, a pox on you then, woman. Just because ye got a neck-or-nothing young blood of the Fancy walkin' the street with you don't mean ye can't speak to those of yer own station."

Felton backtracked until he stood beneath the lamplighter. With his eyes meeting the man's glassy ones, he seized the ladder. "I've smashed in more faces than you've lit lamps, sir, and would have no qualms in drawing the cork of a drunk man." To add realism to his threat, he jerked the ladder until the man wobbled and cursed. "Now if you've a mind to say more, climb down and do so man-to-man, eh?"

Blubbering, the fellow clambered higher up his ladder and, with shaky hands, resumed lighting the oil lamp.

Any other day, Felton would have hauled him down and forced fisticuffs. He'd done more for less, after all, in his own village. How many times had he left Lodnouth with bloody knuckles or a leaking nose?

"Disgraceful." His mother always looked at him the same way, with sad eyes and sallow cheeks pulled in a frown. "Disgraceful, my son, that you should go to the village and deign yourself to fisticuffs with mere servants and fishermen."

In younger years, he'd defended himself. He'd explained all the things they'd said against his family. The insults. Insinuations. The filthy rumors that clung to his name and suffocated any pride he might have had. What did it matter, at this point, if he did disgrace himself?

It was not as if any of the society circles still cared for them. Invitations for balls or tea or dinner parties had long since stopped coming exactly fourteen years ago. Even Miss Haverfield, the squire's daughter, was not permitted to taint her reputation and court a despicable Northwood son.

But maybe all that was about to end.

Felton took Eliza's arm again and found the tiny brick apothecary shop. The paunchy old gentleman made quick time in washing Felton's hand, applying leaves of cleavers, and wrapping the wound in a clean bandage. He also thumbed over Eliza's ankle with the advice it should not be walked on heavily over the next couple of days. He'd have probably frowned to know the distance she'd walked already.

When they left the apothecary shop, they headed straight for a two-story stone building with ivy twisting around each window and dangling over the arched doorway. The windows were smudged, but a warm glow of candles brightened their panes.

She steeled herself before they entered. Even her pulse raced in the hand he held.

"This is Dalrymple Inn. I stayed here once with my elder brother before he went off to university." He pulled open the heavy wooden door. "You've nothing to fear. Not unless you are devising an escape."

She straightened her shoulders and marched into the dimly lit inn.

He followed in her wake, caught the faint trail of a pleasant scent. Rose water? Had that devil of a captain gifted her with perfume to ease his own guilt? Why now, after all these years, had the man finally decided to approach her true father?

Had the captain not come to Lord Gillingham's manor just days ago, she'd still be well hidden. Had Felton not been in the Monbury Manor library, one room over, he'd have never heard the heated exchange.

"What do you mean you know of my daughter's where-abouts?" Lord Gillingham had a voice of his own. Low, quiet, yet intense enough that when he spoke, 'twas human nature to shrink and tremble in response.

But the old captain did no such thing. "She is safe and she is well and she is happy."

"Who are you? Where is she?"

"Safe," he said again. "And she will remain so if she stays where she is."

"I want her back. I want to see my daughter."

"That is yer choice because I am making it yer choice." The words had seemed wobbly. "For her sake, not yours. A child—a woman—deserves freedom."

"Then bring her to me."

"Ye make yer choice so quickly?"

"There is nothing to decide. She is my daughter. She is the only thing I have left of my Letitia—"

"Then think of yer wife, yer lordship, and think of her carefully. Think of what happened to her in the end. Think of a murder ye had no way of stopping from an enemy ye didn't know ye had. Then think o' that same enemy unleashing that anger on your daughter."

Silence had reigned for the space of many heartbeats.

"I shall return in a fortnight. Ye have until then to make yer choice."

But it was a choice Felton had made for the viscount. He'd followed the strange old captain from Monbury Manor to the quiet woods of Balfour Forest, where he'd taken the fate of many people—both his family and hers—into his own hands.

He stole glances of her now, as they paid the proprietor for a room and meal, then took the two bowls of mutton to a quiet table in the corner.

Despite her earlier refusal to eat, she now spooned away at the mutton with her eyes closed, as if hunger made her savor every swallow. She was lovely, this girl. Lovelier than he expected. Even Miss Haverfield—whom he'd always worshipped for her beautiful golden curls and alabaster skin—did not exceed the simple fairness of Miss Eliza Gillingham.

He forced his gaze into the steaming mutton. The old captain had talked of unseen enemies, of danger that might return after all these years. But if little Eliza had truly been there when her mother was murdered, couldn't she expose such an enemy now? Before any harm came to her?

Of course she could.

Heaven help them all if she couldn't.

———— ❧⚜❧ ————

The bedchamber door clicked shut.

Heat raced along the back of Eliza's neck, then up to her cheeks, as she faced the stranger whose name she still did not know. Nor want to know. Why did he look so different from any villain she'd ever imagined? Where was the jagged scar cutting across his cheek, or the missing teeth, or the black and wicked eyes?

But this was real. Things weren't always as she'd imagined them, and the man before her was no character she'd played and frolicked with in the forest trees.

Coldness crept into her blood. She backed to the farthest wall, rubbed her arms, and watched as he lowered his candlestick to a washstand. Beside the bed. The only bed. "You told them we were wed."

"Getting to be a convenient Bansbury tale, do you not agree?"

"You should not say such things," she said. "This is not right."

"You are very scrupulous. An attribute you did not learn from your captain."

"Do not speak of him that way."

"How shall I speak of him?"

A shudder passed through her. So many lies, so many accusations. Nothing made sense and maybe she didn't want it to. If Captain had lied to her all these years, if she wasn't his daughter, mustn't there be a reason? Something noble? Something good and right, from which she could draw all her respect and love for him?

The stranger jerked the counterpane from the bed. "I shall take this and sleep by the door. We are two stories up, so I do not advise jumping out the window."

The window. Glass breaking, falling, crimson fluttering and fluttering and fluttering. . .

"What is the matter?"

"N–nothing." She hurried to the bed and slipped into the scratchy bed linens. She drew them to her neck, but even when she closed her eyes, the ferocious half-human beast roared and screamed at her.

She would not go to sleep. Not tonight. She hadn't the courage to face the nightmares already closing in. The nightmares she'd battled a thousand times.

The nightmares only Captain knew how to comfort.

CHAPTER 2

Monbury Manor
Lodnouth, Northumberland

They had arrived.

Even when her kidnapper jumped down from the rented post chaise and offered his hand, she did not move. She kept her eyes out the window. *Dear Savior, help me.*

Because she didn't want to be here. She didn't want to walk alongside this man up the gravel path. She didn't want to pass beneath the shadow of those tall nymph statues. She didn't want to reach the door of the manor itself, with its fluted Greek columns and its endless glistening windows—as beautiful as anything she'd ever dreamed of.

Only it wasn't beautiful now.

The stranger faced her in the carriage doorway. "You care nothing for the man inside this manor. Mayhap you hate him."

"I hate no one."

"Then of the same mercies you would bestow a hurting animal, be merciful to your father." He outstretched his hand. "Now come."

She placed her cold fingers in his bandaged one. She shouldn't have. Not when this very hand had ripped her from everything she knew.

But even a touch as despicable as his brought her comfort.

And courage.

"You will remember him, I think." His voice was soft. Reassuring, almost. "You were five when you left."

She stopped three feet from the massive stone steps. "Who are you?"

"An enemy at current. Maybe someday a friend."

"What is your name?"

"Felton Northwood. Perhaps you remember?"

Her heartbeat worked faster, and even when he tugged her toward the first step, she didn't move. "And your advantage in bringing me here?"

"A question for another time."

"I wish to know now."

"I do not think you do."

From the top of the steps, the double entrance doors swung open simultaneously. An older gentleman emerged, dressed in tan pantaloons and black tailcoat, with eyes that rushed to hers and stayed. Tears welled, but he didn't move.

No one had to say he was her father.

She knew him.

She knew the thick, wavy hair, now sprinkled black and white, with sideburns down his firm cheeks. She knew the tight lips. The powerful eyes. The giant set of shoulders she once rode upon.

Dear God, how can this be? She turned around, the prayer aching through her, faced the post chaise down the drive. If she had more strength, she would run for it and dash away and never look back.

"I knew what you had done, Northwood." The deep voice filled the air with tension. "By all that is holy, you had no right to do this."

Felton said nothing. No defense. No explanation. Why had he brought her? What could he possibly want so much that he should be willing to bring her this hurt?

"Eliza."

The name, spoken so huskily, turned her back around. Her own tears blurred her father's face—but even though she could no longer see him clearly, she felt years' worth of pain and suffering and longing emanate from him.

Longing she was doubtless supposed to fill.

Pain she was brought to end.

"I should not be here." She pivoted a second time and started to run, but Felton seized her before she'd gone halfway down the drive. When he whirled her back around, the entrance doors were still open.

But Lord Gillingham was gone.

Felton grabbed her shoulders and yanked her close. "You belong here."

"No—"

"You remember him. I saw it on your face. You knew him—"

"No, it is not true!" She struggled against him, shook her head. "Let me go. I shall escape if you do not release me. I shall beg Lord Gillingham to send me back."

"You do that, and I'll come after you."

"No."

"Wherever you go, no matter how far, I'll find you. And I'll bring you back. And you *will* stay, if I have to stand guard outside of this manor every night of my dashed life."

Her breathing faltered under the passion that leaked out of him. "What do you want of me?"

"I want your memory, Eliza Gillingham."

"I have no memory of this place. I have no memory of anything."

"That is of little matter. I only need your memory of one night." His fingers loosened and he backed away from her face. "The night your mother was killed."

———

Felton strode to the blue-paneled door of a house three times as small as Monbury Manor. The walk between the two homes, however, took him no more than twenty minutes. 'Twas a path he walked often, for Lord Gillingham was always offering a book or two from his library or beating Felton at another game of chess.

Doubtless it would be a while before the viscount would wish to do either.

In the end, though, he would be glad for what Felton had done.

Even if there was a risk, was it not right for father and daughter to be reunited?

"Master Northwood, you must 'urry! The family be already on their second course, they are, and—oh, let me take that for you." The young, high-pitched maid took his gloves, then helped him from his greatcoat. "Mrs. Northwood, she's just been in a terrible state since you left. You ne'er said a word. But I says to them, I says, 'Master Northwood be strong and he can take care of 'imself, he can.' But they says to me—"

"Thank you, Dodie. I shall explain." In the name of George, why could his mother not employ a maid less talkative? He hurried from the quaint foyer and headed straight for the light green dining room, where he found the white tablecloth-covered table crowded with colorful dishes.

His mother and father sat on opposite ends, and there were three empty chairs where their sons belonged.

"Mamma, Papa." Felton dropped into the seat closest to his father. "Forgive my absence these past days." No sense avoiding the inevitable. "I had urgent matters to attend to."

"I was worried." His mother dropped her fork and leaned back in her chair. Was it his imagination, or had her face gone whiter in the few days he'd been away?

"A boy must venture off sometimes," Papa said. "After all, I did the same a time or two when I was your age, I did—"

"You might have told us." She grabbed her napkin, dabbed both eyes. "A mother endures horrid things. Imaginations of her son lying beaten and bruised in some heaven-forsaken village alley or worse."

"Er—yes, yes. You are right, Martha. Best to make apologies, Son, and then we shall speak of it no more."

Felton rose from his chair, bent next to his mother, and pressed a kiss to her cold cheek. The act warranted him a smile, if not a teary one. She was beautiful, his mother. Even after forty-six years of age and many years of illness, her skin was still smooth, her lips still full and shapely, and her chestnut-colored hair still just as perfect and shiny as it must have been in her youth.

"Off to see a few good mills, did you, Son?" The older man, smaller than Felton in both height and frame, stabbed his fork into roasted fowl decked with watercresses. Contrary to his wife, his bronze skin radiated with health, and his voice boomed loud and strong against her frail one. "Nothing like a good fight, eh wot?"

"Richard."

"I'm sorry, my dear. I did not mean it, of course. Fights are, er, rubbish and that sort of thing." He glanced back at Felton, who had claimed his chair again. "If not there, pray, where did you go?"

"To retrieve Eliza Gillingham."

The room stilled.

His mother's glass, which she'd raised to her lips, clinked to the table.

Felton was tempted to stare down at his empty plate or reach for his own fowl to distract his hands. But instead, he took turns looking from his father's face to his mother's.

Both stared back without expression. Maybe without hope too. Didn't they realize what this could mean for them?

"She is bound to remember. We have always thought so." Felton rose, put distance between himself and the table. "If anyone can set things right, she is the one who—"

"Richard, tell him he should not have done this."

"Your mother is right." Of course Papa would fail to see reason. Had he ever gainsaid his wife in his life? "The matter is over and done with. There is no sense in bringing it all up now when the hurt—"

"The hurt continues, and I for one do not wish to live in it one moment longer." Fury kicked his blood into faster motion. "You may be fine with walking about the village hearing people whisper about the bloody woman murderer—but I am not. You are innocent, and I have every intention of making every last fool in Lodnouth see the truth."

"But it will all start over again." Tears were already leaking down her cheeks. Had she always cried so easily? Had she always been so

33

weak and frail and worrisome—or was this just another thing taken from him fourteen years ago?

Papa circled around the table and scooted back her chair. "Let me help you upstairs, my dear. You appear most unwell. You do not feel faint, do you?"

"No, Richard."

"Just say the word, and I shall hail Dodie for the smelling salts."

"I do not need them. Just help me upstairs, and I shall lie down." Leaning heavily on her husband's arm, she shuffled to the door and glanced back only once. "Felton?"

"Yes, Mamma?"

"A wife endures horrid things too. Imaginations of her husband finally being free, of his guilt being over after all these unbearable years."

"That is what I am trying to give you, Mamma. Can you not see?"

"You are a good boy, Felton, but I can only bear so much pain." Her voice quivered. "I fear I cannot live through yet another disappointment. God knows I cannot bear it all yet a second terrible time."

<hr />

The door was locked.

Felton Northwood had forced her through the imprisoning double doors of Monbury Manor, down the entrance hall, and up the giant, sweeping stairs that smelled of linseed oil.

He'd said nothing until they reached a glistening mahogany door. One he swung open with fervor. One that chilled her soul when he urged her inside. "As most of your five years were spent in this nursery, there is no doubt you shall be comfortable."

Then he'd yanked the door shut.

And locked.

How many hours had she been trapped here? 'Twas a dungeon, and she the innocent hostage—only there was no one waiting outside the door to break her loose, unlock her chains, and carry her off to safety like the hero in all her books.

She'd paced from the sash window, to the neatly made trundle bed, to the mantle, to the bookshelf. The walls were closing in. Suffocating her. If she didn't escape this room, she'd...what? What could she do?

Every part of her shivered. She went to the trundle bed, climbed onto the downy coverlet, and pulled her knees tight against her for lack of anything else to hold. *Merrylad, Merrylad.* If she crammed her eyes shut, she could see him. If she tried hard enough, she could hear his excited moans or feel his wet black nose or sense his contented smile.

And Captain.

She shook so hard the bed creaked, as if to voice her soundless sobs. Fear choked her. Too much fear. The woods, the woods...she was never supposed to leave the woods. By this time, he must be out of his head. Searching for her. Praying for her. Weeping for her, like she'd seen him do over that one strange page in his Bible. *Why hasn't he come, God?*

The brass doorknob rattled.

Eliza sprang from the bed just before the creaking nursery door came open.

An older woman entered—clad in a blue dress, white fichu, and wrinkleless apron—with a key ring clasped in her veiny hand. "You must be Miss Gillingham."

"No." She held the woman's daunting stare. "Miss *Ellis*."

"Pardon?"

"I am Eliza Ellis...and should like to be called such."

The woman's smooth gray brows rose. "I see. May I see your left wrist?" When Eliza hesitated, the woman snapped her fingers. "Come, come. Your wrist, child."

Moving one step closer, she held out her arm and winced when the woman snatched her hand and bent over it.

"The scar is from the day you played in the garden. A rose thorn pierced your skin, but you were senseless enough to hide it until the infection grew so grave the doctor had to cut it out." She released Eliza's hand. "I am Mrs. Eustace. Housekeeper. You may have changed greatly in your absence, but as I never pretended with you as a child, I see no point in doing so now. I will call you Miss Gillingham—not Miss Ellis. Understood?"

"I want to see Lord Gillingham."

"Precisely why I have come for you. You will have dinner with him now, and though I regret presenting you in such attire, there is little choice until a wardrobe can be arranged." The housekeeper's lips formed a smug smile. "If you will follow me."

No, she didn't want to follow. Or see Lord Gillingham. Or stand face-to-face with a past she hadn't known existed. What would she say to him?

Perhaps it didn't matter, as long as she persuaded him to let her go.

She kept pace with the housekeeper's fast footsteps as they hurried down the long hall, back down the stairs, and through several more rooms until they reached the dining room.

If she could have hidden herself in the blue folds of the housekeeper's dress, she would have. She stood facing a long, rectangular table in a red room full of gilded-framed paintings.

All of them seemed to look at her, as if they were alive, as if they had eyes.

But only one pair blinked back.

Lord Gillingham rose at the head of the table, much taller indoors than he'd seemed outside. "Thank you, Mrs. Eustace. You may leave us now."

The woman disappeared. The doors clicked shut.

Eliza wished to heaven there were trees she might climb and escape in.

"You must be hungry, Eliza." His hand swept the lavishly spread table. "Won't you sit?"

She remained standing.

He nodded, as if he'd expected as much. "A bedchamber is being prepared for you now. You always cared for pink, as did your mother, so I have requested new drapes and bedding."

"I want to go home."

"You are at last."

"I want to go back to the cottage." Her knees nearly buckled. "You cannot keep me. I want to return to the forest and to my. . . my father."

He took the words without flinching, sank back into his chair, and shook open his napkin. "I am your father, Eliza." Deep, guttural. "Will you eat with me?"

No, she wouldn't. She'd never eat again if he kept her here. Let them lock her in that room upstairs and guard every door and bar every window. She'd only die. Then Captain would come and bury her body back in the forest—

"I understand, Eliza." He stood. "I fear I have no appetite myself." Were those tears in his eyes again? He was gone before she could tell.

But it didn't matter if he had tears. Or if he loved her or didn't. If she'd rode on his shoulders as a child or only imagined she had.

Because she wasn't staying.

Cupping her mouth, she escaped out a different door and ran until she found the entrance hall. She flung herself outside into a world growing dim with dust. The gate was already closed at the end of the drive, but she raced toward it anyway and grasped the iron bars. *Help me, Savior. Please.*

Danger awaited in the world out here. Cruelty reigned beyond the trees. Captain said so. If he *had* taken her from this place, his only reason must have been for her good and protection. What else had he ever cared for?

Help me.

All the sobs Captain would have told her not to unleash came blubbering out. She sank to the ground and wrapped her arms around the cold iron bars. There was no way out. There were no streams to whisper to or trees to lean against or soft mosses to wiggle her toes in. She was a fool to think she'd ever been lonely in her beautiful forest.

She'd never been alone until now.

"How is she?"

Lord Gillingham's head remained bent over his rosewood desk. He scribbled more figures into his ledger.

"My lord?"

"How do you think she is?"

Felton took a step closer to the desk. "This is best, I assure you. With time and patience, she shall learn to—"

"To what, Northwood? Be content with a father she despises?" Lord Gillingham slammed his quill into its inkwell. "Let us not pretend, shall we? We are both quite aware of your reasons for bringing her here."

"It was the only way."

"For who?"

"For my father. For my mother. For you and—"

"No, I hardly think so. This is not about any persons you just named—but rather, as it always has been, about yourself." The older man rose from his chair, and the voice so often low and deep grew even gruffer. "This is about Felton Northwood and his own ungodly pride. He is so worried about what the world thinks of him, of his own social standing, that he would do anything to remedy his image."

The muscles tightened around Felton's jaw. "That is untrue."

"Is it?"

"Are you trying to tell me you would not have sent for her? That after all these years of looking, you would not have decided upon your own daughter's return?"

"That was my choice to make."

"Then I offer apology."

Lord Gillingham blew out air, as if the words meant nothing, and sank back into his black Sheraton chair. "What have you come for? I am busy, as you can imagine."

"I wish to see the girl."

"No."

Felton planted both fists on the desk. "My lord, with all due respect, I cannot accept such an answer. I only wish to speak with her."

"I'll not have you badgering her with your frightening questions. She needs none of it. She is afraid of this place and she is afraid of me, and she is doubtless even more afraid of you."

"Upon my honor, I shall speak nothing of that night."

"No."

"But—"

"You will leave now, Northwood, before I lose my patience."

Felton clamped his mouth shut before more rebuttals could escape. Besides, the viscount had never asked anything of him. Wasn't it Felton's duty to respect his wishes now?

"I will leave, my lord, but ask permission to return tomorrow morning."

The man's eyes raised to the ceiling, as moist as they'd been yesterday when he'd first seen his daughter. After several seconds, he nodded. "You may return with the morn."

"Thank you, my lord."

"And Northwood?"

"Yes?"

"She is a great likeness of Letitia—her face and eyes—is she not?"

"She is indeed, my lord." Of everything Felton could remember of the late Mrs. Gillingham, her daughter far exceeded. Truly, if Letitia had been beautiful, Eliza was beauty itself.

But she was still a mere child raised in an uncivilized forest. She knew nothing of the world. She knew nothing of the delicacies and graces most ladies wore like a pair of gloves.

His sights were on Miss Haverfield anyway. Always had been. He had every intention of keeping them there.

―――⚬⁂⚬―――

Captain was here.

Eliza froze at her bedchamber window. Far below, the familiar

39

figure made a five-foot leap from the courtyard wall. All day she'd waited. All day she'd paced the floor of this new chamber, denying Mrs. Eustace's meals, praying, hoping against hope there would be a sign of him.

So much so that when she'd finally heard Merrylad's woof, in the shadowy fall of evening, she'd almost dismissed it as her wishful imagination.

Until she'd heard it twice.

Now, she backed away from the window and hesitated at the door. It was unlocked. She knew because she'd pried it open over and over today, glanced down the empty hall, and debated her chances in making a run for it.

Maybe she would have had the wrought-iron entrance gate not been locked.

But Captain was smart. Of course he would come through the courtyard, where there were boxwoods to hide behind and less chance of being seen.

Now to get there herself.

She peered out into the hall, spotted a humming chambermaid with an armful of bed linens. Before the girl could glance over, Eliza eased the door back shut, waited, and tried to breathe. What if she didn't get there in time? What if someone else had heard the bark and Lord Gillingham sent servants after them—and they were gone by the time she could find the courtyard?

The humming grew louder as it passed by her door. Fading, fading, fading.

Then silence.

The chambermaid was gone.

With another glance into the hall, Eliza forced air into her lungs and darted in the opposite direction she'd heard the chambermaid going. Along the hall, around two corners, and down a small, carpeted stairwell with a smooth banister. She'd memorized the way to her bedchamber last night.

Just long enough to find her way back out today.

At the bottom of the stairs, she rushed through endless rooms until she reached a quiet corridor, with sash windows looking out into the dusk.

Hope flared at the sight of the courtyard. If there was time, she would have followed the corridor until she reached a door.

But there was no such time. Not when Captain was waiting for her.

She fumbled for one of the window catches, unlocked it, then carefully lifted the sash from the windowsill. Scarcely a creak.

Good.

Mayhap no one had heard.

Sucking in air, she climbed through, landed on all fours in soft grass, and ran for the boxwoods. Their giant shadows hid her until she reached the section of wall where Captain had made his leap.

Her heartbeat picked up pace. "Captain?" Moving forward, she went up and down the wall, along the path, and around each of the cone-shaped boxwoods. "Captain?"

Another excited woof reached her ears, and little Merrylad came bounding from the left with flopping ears.

She swooped the animal into her arms. "Merrylad." Burying her face into his fur, she nuzzled back and forth as a thousand comforts soothed her fears. "Merrylad, my sweet." But where was Captain?

He hadn't left. He wouldn't have. He had come for her, just as she'd known, and he was preparing the way to bring her home.

Please, Captain. She lowered the dog and hurried to the left, from whence Merrylad had come. When she stepped out into the open, though, she halted.

Tears stabbed her eyes as she watched the unlocked wooden gate creak back and forth, back and forth, back and forth.

As if someone had just pushed through. In a hurry. Before she'd have a chance to see them or speak with them or run into their arms.

As if Captain hadn't come to rescue her at all.

"What'ee doing?"

Eliza swiveled, her hand flying to her throat.

Standing in the middle of the stone path stood a gangly young woman, both hands on her hips, with a mass of frizzy brown hair framing her face.

Heavens, her face.

Eliza took one step back, but she couldn't look away even if she wanted to.

Because the woman's eyes were wide-set and bulging. One focused on Eliza while the other gazed somewhere to the right, and her nose was long and deformed. Even her mouth seemed too tiny for her face. "What's the matter with'ee?" The creature hobbled forward, as if her hips didn't quite work together. "Ne'er seen someone very oogley before?"

"I—"

"Oughtn't be out here."

"I'm sorry, but I—"

"Peoples died for less. People die all the time. Did'ee know that people die all the time, Miss Gillingham?"

Her throat tightened. She shook her head, but it seemed to amuse the woman and her head rolled sideways with a laugh.

"Funny, funny. Did'ee know what a funny girl'ee are?" Then the humor faded, and the twisted features grew tight and somber. "Get'ee back to yer room. Back to yer room. Hear me?"

Eliza's gaze dropped to Merrylad. "My dog."

"I shul watch him for'ee."

"No, I must watch him."

"But I can do it." Closer. "I do lots of things. Lots of things. Ask Mrs. Eustace and Mr. Cott because they know I do lots of things. And I love dogs. Do'ee believe me that I love dogs?"

Eliza spared one last glance at the gate. What were the chances she could find Captain if she ran through it now?

She didn't know and she was too confused to make the decision. Instead, she lowered next to Merrylad and swallowed him up in her arms. "I will not leave him."

The girl appeared hurt, as if Eliza had both called her a liar and ruined something vital, though heaven only knew just what. She said nothing more, merely curtsied awkwardly and tottered back down the stone path.

Eliza waited until the girl was gone before she finally stood. If she was going back inside Monbury Manor, Merrylad was coming with her.

And if Mrs. Eustace or Lord Gillingham didn't like it?

Let them order her to leave. That is just what she wanted to do.

⁓ ∾⅋∾ ⁓

Felton swooped off his beaver hat and handed it to the butler. "The groom said Lord Gillingham was gone."

"Early this morning, Mr. Northwood. Off to Bath to attend a ball Lord Afford has arranged for the Tories."

"I say they invite the Whigs too. Let the two parties fight it out like real men, yes?"

The butler's lips threatened with a smile. "If you say so, sir."

"Where is the girl?"

"You will refer to her as Miss Gillingham." This came from Mrs. Eustace, as she swept down the entrance hall with her keys jingling, prune-faced as ever. "That is her proper name and that is what all are expected to call her."

"As you say, Mrs. Eustace." Felton gave an exaggerated bow, to which she responded with a curt nod. "Now, if you shall bring her down to the drawing room, I should be most grateful."

"There has not been ample time to prepare a wardrobe, and therefore she is unable to receive visitors."

Didn't the blasted woman know he'd already seen the girl in plain cotton and pinafore?

"Besides that, she is not in the best of temperaments."

"Throwing things through windows, is she?"

"No." Mrs. Eustace raised her chin. "But she has refused to eat unless I relent and allow that beast of a dog back into her bedch—"

"Dog?"

"Yes, a noisome creature who she—"

"Which chamber?"

"What?"

"Which chamber is she in?" When the housekeeper did little more than raise her voice to say she would not permit a young gentleman to visit a young miss in her chamber—and her without proper attire, no less—he pushed past her and found his way upstairs without assistance.

He checked the nursery first.

Empty.

Then he moved to another guest room, one he'd stayed in himself a time or two, and tapped twice before he swung it open.

Another wrong guess. He pulled the door halfway back closed—

And froze. Almost missed her, so small did she appear, huddled in the corner of the room with her thin arms looped about her knees.

A chasm of pity opened inside him. She'd been crying?

Her face lifted higher and wet lashes blinked up at him. Why didn't she speak? How much better it would have been if she had been throwing things through the window or stomping back and forth or screaming at every person who penetrated her sphere.

He entered and glanced at the untouched plate sitting next to her. "You had better eat that, Miss Gillingham, lest I force you."

"I shall never eat and you cannot make me."

"Can't I, though?"

More tears. How young she looked, how desperate, like a frightened bird in a gilded cage. Were the consequences not so grave, he would have unlocked the cage, set her free, and let her fly back to that forsaken forest she seemed to love.

"Why am I here?"

The question again. The one he'd waited a lifetime to ask but couldn't seem to get past his lips. How to say such a thing anyway?

He knelt in front of her on the floor. "Lord Gillingham has been to see you?"

She shook her head no.

"He is as frightened as you are. Surely you must see that."

"I see many things, but I understand none of it."

"You will in time." He lifted the silver-rimmed plate, full of plum cake, brioche, and eggs. "Suppose you eat as we talk."

"Not until Merrylad is returned to me."

"The dog?"

She nodded at the same time he flexed his sore hand. The pain was dull now, if not nonexistent. No thanks to her vicious little devil-dog.

He handed her the fork. "When did your captain arrive?"

He'd suspected she would ignore him, or avoid the question, or lie that she hadn't seen him at all. But she only sighed. "Last night."

"You spoke?"

"No."

"He is coming back?"

"I hardly think so. It almost seems as if. . .he knew this would happen. That I would be here. And that he wanted me to stay."

"He does."

Her body stiffened. "He knew. . .about you?"

"I spoke with him while you were gone from the cottage. That is why, of course, he was nowhere to be found when I came for you."

She bolted to her feet.

He stood with her. "Now that I have made a matter clear for you, suppose you make one clear for me. Who is Jasper Ellis, and what do you know of him?"

"I know everything of him, none of which I am prepared to tell you."

"You are a fool."

"Not in this concern."

"That man has hidden you in that isolated forest, kept you from your family, lied to you. . .possibly even murdered the woman who birthed you. Does this mean nothing to you?"

"How dare you say such wretched things about—"

"How dare you ignore them, Eliza Gillingham." He forced himself to take a step back, to push down the rage surging like flames. "I see this conversation is entirely futile. The man has bewitched you." He set her plate back on the floor, left the room, and half ran back down the stairs.

Of all the insufferable, manipulated fools.

Or maybe he was the fool. For thinking he could waltz in some long-forgotten witness, clear his father's name with the snap of a finger, and end this never-ending shame as quickly as it was forced upon them.

Perhaps there'd be a blood stench on him for the rest of his life. That's what Papa would say. Not that he ever talked about it anymore. Mamma would argue that it was best forgotten too. Even Lord Gillingham would rather look to the future and pretend the past didn't exist.

But Felton couldn't stomach defeat.

And he wasn't giving up until his name was bloodless.

"You *will not* enter this house and do as you please, Felton Northwood." Mrs. Eustace met him at the entrance door, hands fisted. "If you cannot respect the wishes of those in charge—namely myself, at the moment—then you may consider yourself unwelcome on these premises."

"Give her the dog."

"That matter is none of your concern."

"Give her the dog by tomorrow, or I will come and return the little beast to her myself." Felton took back the hat the butler held his way and bowed again at the rigid woman with her rigid bun and her rigid rules. "Good day to you, Mrs. Eustace."

Felton Northwood had only been gone an hour when another tap sounded on the door. Without waiting for an answer, it pushed open and the tall frame of Mrs. Eustace filled the threshold. "You were always prone to getting your way, Miss Gillingham. The dog may stay."

Eliza stood from the edge of her four-poster bed, as relief unwound some of her anguish. "Pray, where is he?"

"For now, locked in the potting shed. He may sleep there at night, for I shall not have him in the kennel bothering his lordship's hunting dogs. Is that understood?"

"Yes, but I wish to see him."

"Not in the house. Any visiting will be done out of doors. Is that clear?"

"Very. May I go now?"

"If you must. You shall find Minney in the kitchen, and she shall direct you to the dog's whereabouts, as she will be the one seeing to the dog's feeding and welfare."

Eliza murmured thanks and approached the door, but Mrs. Eustace stopped her in the hall. "One thing, Miss Gillingham."

Eliza glanced back.

"I shall have you speak no ill word of that child's face. It is a disgrace enough to have a deformed servant in the house, let alone an addled one, without you going about mentioning it."

A disgrace?

"I have done my best to persuade his lordship to dismiss her. As it is, however, he will not permit such a thing. The least we can do is keep her as hidden as possible and mention it never. Do we understand one another?"

As if the young woman's face were any fault of her own.

But Eliza only nodded. "Yes, we do."

* * *

These were the times she was happiest.

Felton leaned back in his armchair, took the meerschaum pipe his father handed him, and placed it between his lips.

From the chaise lounge, placed strategically under the light of a wall sconce, his mother removed the seal on her newest letter. She read it first quickly, smiling some, laughing here and there. Then she read it again and paused every so often to relate the news of her youngest son. "Wellington had them storming Badajoz. Our Hugh says it was a glorious victory."

Papa leaned forward with a pipe of his own. "That is southwestern Spain, very close to the Portuguese border, is it not, dear?"

"I hardly know." Nor did it seem to matter to her. She smiled and smoothed the paper again, as if touching the ink he'd written with made him feel close. "But can you not see him, lined up with the British and Portuguese, a brave soldier at so young an age? A fine painting that would make."

"Yes, yes, if you care for paintings of soldiers toppling down hills and blood trails and shells exploding—"

"Richard!"

"Very sorry, dear. I am only thinking of your own good, for I do not wish you to romanticize our son's position. This is war, you know. Bloody affairs and all that. No pleasant thing."

"I did not say it was pleasant." Mamma folded the letter and set it aside, as if the warming pride of seconds ago had turned bitter. "I am the only one in this family who discouraged him from joining Wellington's troops, if you remember."

"I remember, dear."

"I have never understood why he should wish to enlist in the first place."

Didn't she? Didn't they all?

Papa rose from his chair, settled next to his wife, and took both of her now-trembling hands into his. "Let us talk of it no more, my dear. I can see you are growing upset. We shall keep Hugh in our prayers and think on happier things, hmm?"

Felton left the parlor before he had to witness another ordeal of tears from his mother. They were right for each other, the two of them. His mother should like to pretend her youngest son was off playing tin soldier, and Papa would rather dismiss the danger than speak of it.

They were always like that.

Pretending all the time.

As if they didn't know Hugh Northwood would rather take his chances in the heat of the Peninsular War than stay here in Lodnouth fighting an invisible battle.

One they'd already lost fourteen years ago.

One Felton was left fighting alone.

***

Blackness and then red. How coolly, how silently, the curtains fluttered. Back and forth, here and there, brushing against her face and blinding her. Why could she not escape?

But the harder she fought, the more there was red. She was tangled. She was trapped.

And then came the beast.

First there were claws, ripping through skin and red, shredding her flesh with each painful grab. Then she saw the eyes, yellow, luminous, lost in a face half-human and half-fur. "You don't understand," it roared. "You don't understand what happened."

Her throat cried with an answer, a plea, but it went unheard.

Because the beast attacked again. Glass shattering. Red flying. Falling, falling, falling...

Eliza jerked upward and cupped her mouth with her hands. "Captain." She groped around the bed, waited for the sound of his footsteps hurrying toward her or the feel of his cool hands brushing back her hair.

But the room was still. No one came running to assure her the nightmare was gone, to scare the beast of her dreams back into the dark cells of her mind.

One, two, three. She forced air in and out in rhythm to the numbers, just as Captain had always told her to do. *Four, five, six.*

But for all her counting, there was no regulating her breaths. She untangled from the bed linens, staggered to the window, and hurried it open.

Fresh night air blasted her sweating face. *God, help it go away.*

Because without Captain, the nightmare's presence still lingered in the confines of this bedchamber. The beast was yet here.

What am I going to do? She could not stay. She would not stay. Somehow, she must discover a way to return to the safety of the forest, where all danger was set at bay and Captain could pacify her nightmares. Back where she wasn't friendless because she had the trees, and she wasn't alone because she had her stories. Back where she could imagine anything on the mossy rock by the stream.

But what if Felton Northwood was right? What if she had been a little girl who had witnessed a murder all those long years ago?

After all, she'd remembered her father. Was it possible she would remember a murderer too?

Or perhaps she knew him already.

In her beast.

CHAPTER 3

The woman in the mirror did not belong to Eliza.

Maybe to one of the illustrations in the magazines Captain always brought her. Or in one of the books she was always reading. Such ladies were born for fine gowns and perfect ringlets.

But not Eliza. She was born for the plain cotton dress whose hem was stained from roaming the dewy forest. She was born for the brown pinafore, with which she would cradle newly picked flowers or ferns or some injured bird.

"Pretty, pretty."

Eliza jerked from the mirror and grimaced at the young woman who entered her chamber.

Minney smiled in a way that made her features less menacing. "What'ee think of such fine things? I wish I could be wearin' them."

Eliza ran both hands down the muslin gown with white-on-white weaves. The movement made the ringlets sway at her cheeks, made her feel like the lofty queen she'd once pretended herself to be. Maybe she shouldn't have done this. She shouldn't have agreed to wear such fancy things—

"Ye were made for them." Minney circled to one side of her. "Wait 'till his lordship be seeing'ee now. Won't be runnin' away next time, will he?"

Is that what he'd done? Run away from her?

Minney's eyes softened. Almost as if she understood Eliza's discomfort and fears—and knew the fears herself. Doubtless the girl's eighteen years had been difficult. With a face so ghastly, pain must have been her greatest companion.

But her face, upon each encounter, *did* seem less terrible. Perhaps Minney was slow-witted, even frightening sometimes, and very strange.

But there was a tenderness about her too, as she coddled and spoke to Merrylad, or as she entered Eliza's chamber every now and again with simple smiles.

"What are you doing here?"

Both Eliza and Minney jumped as Mrs. Eustace marched through the open bedchamber door. "How many times do I have to order you, Minney Bradshaw, to stay in the kitchen where you belong?"

The girl sank her chin to her chest. "I was helping, I was."

"You were doing no such thing. When are you ever a help to anyone?" Mrs. Eustace waved her hand out the door. "Back downstairs before I'm of a mind to take away your supper. You should be grateful you have a roof over your head. Most masters would have thrown you out the second your father was dismissed from here."

Minney's head snapped up. "Ye leave my papa alone! Ye say one word about him, one word about my papa. . .and I'll. . .I'll. . ."

"Back to the kitchen."

"I won't go! I won't go. Not when 'ee say things about him. My papa. No, I won't go."

Mrs. Eustace marched forward, seized the girl's elbow, and jerked her toward the door. "Cook needs help," she said in a kinder tone, as if in hopes the girl would relent. "You like to help Cook, do you not?"

Minney whimpered something, jerked free, and took off running down the hall.

With a heavy sigh, Mrs. Eustace turned back to Eliza. "The child is demented and belongs in Bedlam."

More like hurt and alone, like the red fox who had lashed out at Eliza once when she'd tried to mend his wounds.

"Anyway, since I see the maid has helped you on with your new dress, follow me downstairs. You have a visitor."

Captain?

But no, even as the hope sprang to her mind, she pushed it back.

As if Captain would visit a place like this. As if Captain would visit her at all.

He'd already had his chance once.

He hadn't cared enough to take it.

———— ✦ ————

If she were a man, Felton could make her do anything. A few blows, a few threats, talk of duels and bloodshed, and a man would start relenting.

But a girl?

Not so simple. He must use his brains and not his strength. Considering the fact that he'd never been able to convince Miss Haverfield to even speak to her father about him, his persuasive powers were less than effective.

A footman parted the drawing-room doors. "Miss Gillingham to see you, sir."

Doubtless, Felton was the last person she *wanted* to see—but she came through the large doorway nonetheless, shoulders back, head erect in a way that was most elegant and graceful.

Dear mercy. She was more Letitia than even Lord Gillingham seemed to realize.

"Why are you here?"

He blinked against a question so bold and crossed his arms over his chest. "Be seated, won't you?"

She glanced down at a damask chair but never sat. Instead, she mimicked his stance by crossing her hands over her own chest and said nothing.

Felton studied her. The shiny hair pulled into a chignon. The long curls framing her face. The new dress and the way it made her appear smaller, somehow, and so unlike the running child he'd first found in the forest.

But the eyes were the same. Young, frightened, timid—yet with enough resolve to make it impossible to get his own way.

He would, though. Eventually.

"You look lovely." Flattery wasn't the method he'd intended to use, but the words slipped out before he could rethink them. "What would your captain think if he could see you dressed so?"

"He would think I was just like them."

"Them?"

"The cruel men and women who care more for wealth than for the human soul."

"Quite a speech. Quite a hatred too."

"Not hatred, Mr. Northwood. The truth. If you knew what they did to him, how they ruined any chances he might return to the sea—"

"And I suppose he was not at fault."

"Could you sail a ship after your crew forsook you?"

"No, I could not. I prefer to keep my feet on dry ground anyway." With one finger, Felton loosened his cravat from his neck. "Did he always sail?"

"Since he was a boy."

"Family?"

"No."

"A wife?"

A blush suffused her cheeks. "Of course. My mother."

"And her name?"

She looked away. "We do not speak of her much, for I fear he loved her greatly."

"I see." Only he didn't see. He didn't see anything. "You give me very little to go on. Did he ever speak of Lord Gillingham?"

"Why must you always question me?"

"And why must you always deny me answers? If your captain is as guiltless as you seem to think, what is there to hide?"

"He has nothing to hide."

"Prove it."

Her eyes held onto his and waited, as if by staring into him she might learn whether or not he might be trusted. He hardly knew himself what she'd find. After all, if there were any evidence linking

Jasper Ellis to Lady Gillingham's murder, Felton would have no hesitation in hunting the man down and praying for a hanging.

But Eliza must have believed in the old man greatly because she nodded. She sank into the damask chair and clasped her hands. "There was a Bible."

Felton took the chair opposite her. "Yes?"

"He never spoke much about his past. He only ever told me stories. . .things that weren't real, of course, but I loved them anyway."

With nothing else to do in that forsaken forest, why wouldn't she love the old man's tales?

"But the Bible. . .well it always seemed strange to me. He read aloud from the pages every day, but sometimes at night, when he thought me to be asleep, I would see him open it again and cry over the pages." She gripped her hands so tight her knuckles whitened. "One day I was curious, so I opened the Bible when he wasn't looking and found the last page smeared with teardrops."

"And?"

"Twenty-two names were written there."

Names, names. What could that mean?

"I do not remember most of them, and some were so smeared from the tears I could not read them at all."

"Who were they?"

"Dane Brough was one. And the other was something Gastrell. . .John or James, I think, but cannot be certain which."

Felton stood. "'Tis a far cry from what I am looking for, but I shall look into it nonetheless."

She too rose. "Captain is innocent of any suspicions you may have."

"He is not innocent of hiding you all these years."

"Perhaps he had a reason."

"Perhaps he also had a reason for murdering your mother."

The wide gray eyes turned upon him, now cold, half heartbreaking in the way they filled with tears. "You would not say such things if you knew him better. He could have never murdered my. . .this woman."

"Would you have remembered if he had?"

The question went unanswered. Without a word more, Eliza Gillingham escaped the room and left him standing with more questions than he'd arrived with.

◆◆◆

"Went to see the Gillingham child again, uh, didn't you?"

Felton guided his chestnut mare closer to his father's horse as they rode the animals along a quiet riding path, close enough to the ocean that the breeze was salty and strong. "I do not think I shall answer that on the grounds you shall relate the information to Mamma."

"Tut, tut, I shall do no such thing."

When the usual chuckle did not follow, Felton glanced at his father to see his lips pinched tight. "I say something wrong, sir?"

"No, no. I was only thinking."

"Of?"

"Of what you must think of me—and what I would have thought of myself twenty years ago. You must see me as quite the ridiculous old fool, fussing over your mother the way I do, bending to her wishes, and all that sort of thing."

"You only try to make her happy."

"Yes. Yes, that is all I have ever endeavored to do, I think, for there is very little else in life that gives me pleasure. But it is more than that even."

"Oh?"

"Your mother, she is…well, she is different. Not like other women. I suppose you know, by this time, she was not born into so high a social status as myself."

"That was no reason for your father to disinherit you."

"No, but we have done splendid for ourselves besides. After all, I'm a richer landowner than my brother ever thought of being—and he inherited everything." Papa cleared his throat, urged his horse around a hole in the road. "I guess what I'm trying to say is that your mother is, well, she is not strong anymore."

56

Felton's heart stuttered at the tone. "But she will get better."

"I think not."

"These years have been a strain, but when everything clears up and you are no longer whispered about, she will gain health and—"

"Son, she is dying."

Felton jerked on the reins of his horse. He curled his fingers around the leather reins and waited until he could trust his own voice. "She cannot die."

"The doctor says a matter of months."

"The man is a fool."

"Maybe."

"I'll not have him step foot in our house again if he intends to talk such nonsense and—"

"Felton."

He didn't look up into his father's face but kept his eyes on the reins instead. "Sir?"

"Let us think on cheerier matters, eh? We shall discuss this never again."

"Yes, sir." The horses continued their walk, the afternoon heat grew warmer, and the rest of the ride was spent in meaningless conversation.

For once, Felton was glad for his father's evasive nature.

He could not have spoken of Mamma anymore if he'd wanted to.

***

There was no reason to be afraid. Indeed, if there were ever a place she should have felt safe, it ought to be here. The church.

But as she followed Mrs. Eustace down the narrow aisle, with people and hats and colors on every side of her, an enormous pounding started at her temple.

"This way." Mrs. Eustace paused at a box pew, slid in first, then motioned Eliza to follow her. "I presume you have outgrown your bothersome habit of crawling to the floor every Sunday, have you not?"

Eliza glanced around the vaulted sanctuary. Had she ever seen so many people at once? What a sound it made, a buzz almost, as countless people chattered and laughed and exclaimed.

She'd only ever imagined such noise before. She hardly knew herself if it was beautiful or terrifying.

From the other side of the aisle and a few box pews toward the front, a familiar pair of eyes snagged hers. Felton Northwood. Was that a smile upturning his lips?

She looked away lest she find herself returning it. What a terror that would be. The last thing in the world she should ever wish to do was bestow civility to such a rogue.

But a few seconds later, she glanced at him again.

He was no longer looking at Eliza but had turned to the box pew behind him to speak to a golden-haired girl with a stovepipe bonnet. She must have said something amusing, because he laughed, nodded, and leaned closer to her when he spoke. Was this his lady friend?

"Do not stare, Miss Gillingham." The housekeeper's gloved hand patted Eliza's knee. "One would think you have never been out of doors before. Do try to keep your mouth from gaping, won't you?"

From the front of the church, a man in a black cassock ascended the three-decker pulpit. Felton turned back around in his seat. The noises died into silence. The service began with song.

A strange sensation chilled the length of Eliza's arms.

So this was what it was like to be amid people. To feel, if even for a second, as if she belonged in a world she'd only read about.

'Twas a good feeling almost.

When the service concluded, Mrs. Eustace ushered her out of the box pew and into the full aisle, where everyone made a slow shuffle outside. They'd no more than made it to the vestibule when a hand touched her arm.

"You will ride home with me."

She eased out of his touch. "And if I refuse?"

"I wouldn't, if I were you." Felton's determination left little room for argument, and after explaining the change of plans to a frowning

Mrs. Eustace, he guided her outside and helped her into his high-perch phaeton. "Ever rode in one of these?"

"No."

"They're named after the son of a Greek sun god. Seems the ol' boy Phaëton was not so good at driving his sun chariot—and thus, the name of our vehicle." The carriage lurched into motion, and sweet-smelling morning air breathed on their faces.

My, but this was strange. Riding this way in a carriage with a gentleman, after a pleasant morning of church. How many times had she imagined such a scene in her head? If she imagined now, she could pretend it was a normal thing. That it happened every Sunday, and that the gentleman sitting next to her desired her company—not her memory.

But such thoughts were no better than one of Captain's stories. They were falsehoods, after all, and would end before she'd have a chance to get truly attached to them. Besides that, she would be leaving Monbury Manor soon. Just as soon as she had enough courage to find a way home.

"What think you of church?"

"It was. . .well, sort of lovely."

"I suppose you've never been before."

"Never."

"Do you pray, Miss Gillingham?"

"Of course I do. Surely you do not think I was without faith in the forest."

"I was not certain. You were quite without everything else."

The phaeton rattled onward, the horse hooves clomped the dirt road, and the silence grew nearly uncomfortable. Where were the questions he was always badgering her with?

"Your family." Eliza stared at the rolling countryside as it passed. "I did not see them with you today."

"My mother is ill."

"I am sorry. And your father?"

"By her side."

"That is very commendable of him. Do you have siblings?"

"Yes. My elder brother Aaron is off to Cambridge, while my younger brother Hugh is with Wellington's army."

"I see." She hesitated. "And I. . .I never had any siblings?"

His eyes moved to hers, then glanced back to the road just as quickly. "Yes, a brother. He only lived a few short weeks after birth."

"Did I ever hold him?"

"I think not. You were but four at the time."

"You remember me well?"

"Some." His voice softened with a smile. "I used to chase you when our parents would enjoy an evening of battledore and shuttlecock."

"Then we were friends?"

"I never quite viewed it as such. I was four years older, you know."

She should have stopped asking him questions. What did anything matter at this point? Even if she used to belong to the Gillingham family, she didn't now. After all, despite the fact that his lordship had seemed heartbroken to see her again, he had fled from her presence and still had not returned.

But then again, hadn't Captain forsaken her too? Where did she belong in all of this? She was a stranger to both worlds. A stranger to everyone. A terrified damsel on a mountaintop of ice, too high for anyone to reach her and too insignificant for anyone to care. Why had there always been a rescuer in all of her imaginings?

No one was here to rescue her now.

"I would not be opposed, though, to becoming friends now." As if he'd read her thoughts. As if he knew her loneliness. As if somehow, in all her confusion, he could offer a balm she desperately needed. Or was he merely after what she knew?

"Well, Miss Gillingham?"

"If you were my friend, would you take me back?"

"To the forest? No."

"Would you tell me where Captain is? Would you help me see him?"

"You don't understand—"

"No, I don't. Why is it so important that I must remember who murdered my mother these many years later? Why must I be here? Not even Lord Gillingham is glad of my return, and Captain will not come for me, and I remember nothing of any such night—"

"You will remember. You must."

"But why?"

"Because fourteen years ago, my father was accused of that murder. His dashed watch fob was discovered near the body—a mere coincidence, considering we'd been over and played games only a week before. He must have dropped it then, and while no one could prove he'd killed Lady Gillingham, no one could prove he didn't." His jaws tightened as he urged the phaeton faster. "And the reason my box pew was empty today was not just because my mother is ill or my brothers are away."

"What are you saying?"

"That even if mine had been the last box pew in the church, no one would have dared sit there."

"Why?"

"Because Northwood is a bloody name, Miss Gillingham—and you're the only one who can cleanse it."

The library felt like the forest all over again. Quiet, alone, with wooden shelves towering on each side of her in likeness to trees. The only difference was there was no cottage hidden somewhere in the books.

And no Captain.

How easy would it be for her to hurry out to the stables, mount a horse, and ride away from here? Would anyone try to stop her? But what if she couldn't find her way back? What if Captain, for whatever reason unbeknownst to her had allowed Felton to take her in the first place, made her return?

If only it made sense, then she'd know what to do. Captain's love was never something she'd doubted. It was just there, unchanging, confirmed every time he looked at her or smiled at her or told her stories. If she didn't have that, was there any point in returning to the cottage at all?

No, she must not think that way. She must be patient. Just because Captain had not come for her yet did not mean he wouldn't.

She would wait until he did.

At least until she discovered a better plan.

With Felton gone and Mrs. Eustace not yet returned from church, she settled into a chair next to the unlit hearth and started on the poems of *The Lady of the Lake*. If only she could live in the pages of such a book. She'd nearly finished the first canto when she heard loud voices from somewhere in the house.

Taking the book with her, she left the library and followed the distinct voice until she found Mrs. Eustace standing at the foot of the main staircase, damp with sweat, bun askew, and arms flailing as she ordered a footman to ride for the doctor. She turned upon Eliza with a frown. "Well, as you can see, I have met with great catastrophe on my way home. Did you not think to wonder about me when I never returned?"

"I did not realize—"

"You have the mind of Minney." Mrs. Eustace winced as she lifted her shoulder up and down, seeming to test the level of pain. "Leah!"

From the top of the stairs, a young maid leaned over the banister. "Mrs. Eustace?"

"Prepare a basin of warm water and hurry it to my attic bedroom. And set out my other dress. Be quick about it too! I am in no temperament for your humming and dawdling." She turned back to Eliza. "I had not made it a mile from the church when a wheel came off the carriage. Unfortunately, we were going fast enough that the carriage upturned and rolled once—and Mr. Eads, who was driving, quite busted his head open."

"How terrible. Is he—"

"We waited alongside the road for an hour before someone happened by. A pony cart, no less, and with Mr. Eads being injured,

I was forced to walk alongside the entire way back."

"Is your shoulder injured?"

"Everything is injured, I think. Leah!"

The girl appeared again. "Mrs. Eustace?"

"For heaven's sake, where is the butler?"

"Gone to see his ailing sister, methinks."

"Of all the times. Well, finish up there and then hurry down to greet the doctor upon his arrival. Direct him to Mr. Eads' room above the stables. Clear?"

The girl answered and disappeared again.

Mrs. Eustace turned to Eliza once more. "Did you see anything as you left church this morning? You remember, of course, where we left our carriage."

"Yes, but I saw nothing. Why do you ask?"

"It is just that when I was coming out of church, I thought I saw a figure lurking thereabouts. I had supposed him to be a servant, one who had missed services, but when I approached the carriage, he was gone." She shook her head. "I hardly know what I am saying. Perhaps it was nothing."

"I am certain it was." After all, who would wish to harm the housekeeper of Monbury Manor?

The woman was unpleasant, true.

But certainly not unpleasant enough to risk killing.

***

If Mamma could see him now, she would have another crying spell.

Probably need smelling salts too.

But time was of the essence, and Felton had already asked both Papa and the vicar if they'd heard the two names Eliza had given him. Both had smiled, shaken their heads, and seemed unfamiliar with even the sound of them.

Which could mean only one thing.

If Mr. Brough and Mr. Gastrell had ever been anywhere

about the village of Lodnouth, they were not cricket-playing or churchgoing fellows.

The Jester's Sunlight, the closest establishment to the village port, wore its age like an elderly woman trying to cover her wrinkles with white makeup and rouge. Indeed, this newest job of yellow paint did nothing more than highlight the fact that the walls were old and weathered, the bowed window was missing some glass, and the chimney was so black that heaven help a chimney sweep who tried to clean such a mess.

Sidestepping a raggedy man lying with his feet in the path to the door, Felton entered the building and blinked against so much smoke. Ghastly smell, this. Half body odor, half dead fish. . .and something else he couldn't quite identify. Almost a flair of sweetness, but it wasn't like anything he'd ever inhaled in the kitchen back home.

In one corner of the room, a group of dirty fishermen crowded around one table where a mismatched pair arm wrestled. A cheer went up when the bigger man won.

Felton approached the bar.

"Weel." A red-cheeked, round-faced woman sidled next to him. "Ye just dinnae know what sort of birkie might walk in, eh, Swabian?"

From the other side of her, with his head hung over a dented tankard, an older man only nodded.

"Dinnae be talkin' much, that man. Calls him Swabian, we do, 'cause he lost his foot sailing aroond the southwestern coast o' Germany. And ye know what else?"

"What?"

"Fell in love, he did, with a Swabian lassie what nursed him. Talk has it he has ten or twenty bairns runnin' aboot that Bavarian coast." The woman threw back her head, let out an uproarious laugh, and clapped Felton by the shoulder. "Enough blether from the likes o' me. What'll ye have to drink?"

"Nary a thing."

"Och? Weel then, ye can be talkin' with Swabian here for company, ye can." With a smile and unseemly belch, she left the space between him and the Swabian empty.

Felton closed the distance between them. "I am Felton Northwood."

The man did not so much as look up. "Names don't matter."

They did in some circles.

"Faces don't matter neither."

"Perhaps this will." Felton fished out some coins and slid them next to the man's tankard. "I need some information."

"And I need a bloody new leg and a barque of frailty."

"I'm looking to learn about two men."

"Told you before. Names don't matter. Better to forget them anyway."

"Dane Brough and J. Gastrell."

The man's head raised. Old, bleary, liquid eyes narrowed on Felton's face. "What do the likes o' you want with them?"

"I believe we have a mutual acquaintance."

"I believe you don't."

"What?"

"Dane and Gastrell. . .they're both dead."

"Who are they?"

"Don't matter really." The face turned back to the tankard. "Not now."

"I was hoping they might tell me something about a Captain Jasper Ellis who—"

"Ellis." Swabian spoke the word with a slight ring to his voice. He shoved the tankard away. Wiped his mouth with a shaking hand. Glanced back up at Felton with moisture swelling to the brim of his eyes. "He is alive?"

"Yes—"

"Healthy?"

"Yes, but—"

"Where?"

"Where what?"

"Where is Ellis?"

Felton took one step back. "I came with the questions, fellow, if you remember. Now if you can tell me what you know of Captain Ellis—"

"Don't know the man." Swabian looked up to the wooden beams of the ceiling. "And I wouldn't visit his bloody grave if I did."

This was the second time around, and she wanted to sit with him now no more than the first time.

But when Eliza entered the dining room, just hours after Lord Gillingham's return, she found herself lowering into a seat along the magnificent table.

"You look well, Eliza."

She kept her gaze on her lap. If Captain had seen her in such a dress, with her hair done just so, he would have lifted her off her feet and given her a laughing spin. That was the way of Captain. Smiling. Pleasant. Simple, sort of, and never less than approachable.

But the man across from her now was different. He made her want to hide, or look away, or run.

"I must apologize for my absence. The last thing I wanted was to leave." He reached for his goblet. "However, I wondered if the distance would be best for both of us."

What did he wish her to say? That in the week he'd been gone, her love had transferred from Captain to him? That time, so quickly, had remedied everything and they may now play the part of father and daughter?

She dipped her spoon into the white soup but couldn't eat. "F—Felton Northwood says there are things I must remember."

"Has he been troubling you?"

Had he? She hardly knew. "If I remember such things, will I be free to go?"

Silence.

How very long it lasted, until she had no choice but to lift her eyes to his.

But his gaze was not on her. He stared down into the amber

liquid of his goblet, lips grim, cheeks paler than they'd been before. "You are my daughter," he said at last. "Not my prisoner."

Was there any difference?

"Nothing is required of you, and if Northwood persists in this, he will no longer be welcome at Monbury Manor."

"Did I..." Her throat dried. "Is it true I saw my m—mother killed?"

"Northwood and many others have convinced themselves you did—but I for one pray you did not." He took a long drink, wiped his mouth, and lowered the goblet with a soft thud. "I saw your mother the next morning, upon my return from Brighton, and have fought the terrors of that image every day of my life. Heaven knows what such a thing would do to a child."

A shiver passed along her spine.

"If you could forget such a thing, Eliza, I shall not be the one to ask you to remember it."

Felton sat in the grassy sand, leaned back, and watched as two schooners made their way to the Lodnouth port. His lungs took in the salty air, thick with the scents of fish. Why had he ridden here anyway?

No great fascination could be derived in watching ships come and go. Or hearing the fishermen curse and yell from the docks. Or seeing endless waves rush back and forth to the creamy-sanded beach.

But at least here he was staying out of trouble. Heaven knew if he spent time in the village, he'd end up in another fight—and for Mamma's sake, he'd do well to avoid such things.

He plucked a brown, brittle blade of grass. From what he'd heard, Lord Gillingham had arrived home four days ago. Still no word from the man. Any other time, the viscount would have sent a servant over to invite Felton for chess or reading or dinner at the very least.

But no, nothing. Apparently bringing home the viscount's daughter was no great way to stay in good favor with the man.

Felton ripped the grass-blade in two. That was all he needed. The one friend who wasn't afraid to sully his name by entertaining a Northwood—and now he was done with Felton too.

And Eliza.

He lingered there a moment, smiled despite himself, and shook his head. She was something of her own, the little chit. Some part bashful, some part brave, but mostly just beautiful. All week long, he'd been seeing her in that box pew. The way she'd almost smiled at him. That hushed, delighted sound in her voice when she'd told him how lovely she found the service.

She deserved this life. She needed this chance. Why shouldn't she be a part of the world she lived in? That cur of a captain had kept her isolated for so long, but in time, she'd see the lunacy of such a life and the truth about the man who raised her.

Maybe she'd remember the truth about fourteen years ago too.

From farther up the beach, a sixsome came ambling down the beach. Each of the gentlemen carried picnic baskets, while the ladies strolled beside them with parasols and reticules. Did the slender, blue-dressed figure belong to Miss Haverfield?

Felton scrambled to his feet. He brushed the sand from his breeches and raked his windblown hair back in place—just as the girl turned to look at him. 'Twas Miss Haverfield indeed—complete with golden curls, clear blue eyes, and a cunning grin he could never quite resist.

He'd no more than smiled back, however, when she turned away her head. She spoke to the gentleman next to her—a tall bloke with a bright red Brutus haircut—and gave the grin Felton was always enjoying to the ugly gent instead.

Who was the man anyway?

He'd never been at church before, at least not that Felton had ever noticed. But then, he had been a bit preoccupied as of late. Had he missed a new courtship between Miss Haverfield and this stranger? Then why had she still been laughing and smiling at Felton only last Sunday?

Not until they were nearly in front of him, a few feet closer to the water, did some of the group glance over.

The girls frowned and raised their brows.

The gentlemen, one by one, tipped their hats.

But Miss Haverfield did not deign herself to look his way again. Was he good enough to speak to at church or alone sometimes when they'd take secret rides together, but not in front of her own friends?

When they'd passed farther up the beach, some of the girls leaned closer as if in whispers. One or two of them glanced back at Felton, realized he still watched them, and swiveled back around just as quickly.

As if he were some sort of repugnant, stinking, filthy fool of a man. As if he carried murder in his veins. As if the audacity that he would show his face—that any Northwood would show his face—was indecent and unhuman and inconsiderate to the helpless villagers of Lodnouth.

Felton kicked at the sand and walked back to where he'd left his horse. Someday it would not be this way. Someday people would look at him and not see the terrible thing they thought his father had done. *Christ, please.*

He leaned his head into his horse's neck, closed his eyes, and tried to keep back the hurt that chipped away at his soul. *Please guide me to find the truth. I want it to end.*

―――❧―――

Eliza unlatched the door of the potting shed and hesitated. Minney would doubtless scold her. After all, the girl's one great pride was being the first to greet Merrylad and let him loose every morning.

But Eliza had awakened long before the dawn, having been plagued with nightmares so real she'd been crying by the time she shook herself awake. She had no intention of going back to sleep after that. She'd already been clawed by the beast enough for one night.

As soon as she entered the dark building, Merrylad lifted his head from the pile of rags under the window. He came to his feet, shook his head and body, then came trotting to her.

She took a seat at the wooden workbench and table. "Good morning to you too, sweet. Sleep well?"

He stared up at her, made a happy-sounding groan, and nuzzled closer between her legs when she rubbed both ears.

"That's my boy. I missed you too."

The door, which Eliza had left cracked open to allow in more light, made a slight whine.

"Hush now, Merrylad. 'Tis naught but the wind." She smiled and traced her finger along his wet nose. "You are as skittish as I. Comes from reading far too many books—"

The door slammed shut.

Eliza jumped to her feet and placed her hand over a pounding heart. "The wind," she said again, more to herself than to Merrylad. She edged around the table and grabbed the knob of the door.

It wouldn't open. Had it jammed?

With both hands on the knob and her foot on the wall, she gave it another hard yank. Still nothing, as if it had been locked from the outside. But surely not.

Glass shattered behind her.

Eliza whirled, just as a flaring torch fell through the broken panes of the window. Merrylad scampered back and barked. Flames devoured the dog's makeshift bed, started up the leg of the table, and pushed smoke into the shed so fast she couldn't see beyond the window.

"Fire!" She pounded the door again. "Someone. . .fire!"

A bucket. Hadn't she seen a bucket in here?

She moved to the left wall and seized an old wooden bucket. No water, but it was filled to the rim with dark soil. Gasping, she emptied it on the flames.

But it was too late.

They were already eating away at the workbench, table, and wooden tools that were littered across the surface.

"Merrylad, here." Back to the door. More pounding. More barking. "Fire! Help!" Over and over, until the smoke choked her voice, until her eyes stung and watered.

God, please. She saw herself at the cottage hearth. Nestled by Captain's knees. Listening to his soothing voice while the fire crackled and sparked. How many times had she imagined beautiful dancing maidens in those warm flames? Or fancied the tiny sparks were magic fairies?

She slammed her body again. The impact took her breath. The fire was growing. If someone didn't hear her, if they didn't come soon—

The door jerked open and she toppled into someone's arms. "Mercy, miss." The older man swung her off her feet, ran farther into the garden, and settled her onto a dewy iron bench. "Sit here now, miss, and let me help you."

"My dog—"

"Right here, miss." The wrinkle-faced man tugged Merrylad to her, then disappeared. Shouts echoed in the distance. Talk of fire and water and buckets.

Her limbs shuddered, and she lifted Merrylad to her lap. His hair smelled burnt. A little longer in there and they'd both have been little fire fairies themselves.

"Ye almost died, Miss Gillingham?" Minney appeared, eyes soft with sleep. "The gardener, Mr. Cott, he saved'ee. He's sending for the doctor now and men are working on the fire. Why there be a fire, Miss Gillingham? You cause that fire to kill'eeself?"

Merrylad squirmed from her arms and ran to the girl's feet.

Minney lowered and rubbed him with pale and crooked fingers. "Ye did try to kill'eeself. I know'ee did."

"No, that isn't true." Eliza stood on shaking legs. "Someone locked the door. They broke the window and started the fire—"

"I don't care if'ee wanted to kill'eeself. When we was still in Cornwall, my mamm killed herself. Then we moved here. Papa did it too. He had to 'cause they…well, he just had to. People die all the time. I don't care if'ee die too if'ee want to—"

"Minney." Mrs. Eustace marched toward them and snatched the girl's arm. "Take the dog and find another suitable place to make him a bed. And do stay out of everyone's way. Is that clear?"

With a muttering answer, the girl hobbled to do her bidding.

"And you, Miss Gillingham." Mrs. Eustace's eyes went up and down Eliza's length, as if searching for injury. "The gardener relayed everything to me. Are you all right?"

"Someone locked me in."

"Preposterous."

"It is true. They locked the door first and then started the fire—"

"If you overturned a candle, Miss Gillingham, I should rather hear a confession than some ridiculous, fabricated story. Heaven only knows what you were doing out here at the break of dawn anyway." Her gaze dropped to Eliza's feet. "And without shoes, no less. Do you want to shame your father—and all of Monbury Manor in the doing?"

"All I want to do is go home."

"To that savage forest? I think not." Mrs. Eustace grabbed Eliza's hand. "Come now. Let us get you inside and I shall have a maid bring out the tub and kettles of warm water. You reek of smoke."

"But Merrylad—"

"He will be quite safe with Minney. You may also abandon all these nonsensical ideas of someone trying to harm you. Your imagination, I see, is still getting the best of you, even after all these years."

The locked door was no imagination. Nor was the fire.

Which meant only one thing.

Someone had tried to kill her.

CHAPTER 4

Well, mayhap he had not lost his one friend after all.

Felton took the path to Monbury Manor with a bit more cheerfulness in his step. The servant had arrived an hour ago with a request for "young Northwood's presence," and Felton had immediately set off to obey.

It was about time too. How long had it been? A week now?

When he reached Monbury Manor, he walked faster until he passed the gate and reached the entrance doors.

The butler greeted him and took his hat. "Lord Gillingham awaits you in the saloon, sir."

"Thank you. I can find it myself." He made quick time in reaching the room, but paused in the doorway before he made himself known.

Lord Gillingham stood at the ornate mantel, hands behind his back, staring up at the large portraits of one ancestor after another. He lingered longest on the largest painting—the only portrait ever done of the late Lady Gillingham.

Felton cleared his throat.

With neither smile nor frown, Lord Gillingham stepped away from the mantel. "You wasted very little time in arriving."

"You wasted quite a great deal of time, I daresay, in sending an invitation."

"I have been busy."

"I see."

"In short, I did not wish you bothering my daughter."

A flare of irritation shot through him. "With all due respect, my lord—"

"Never mind, Northwood. Do come in and take a seat, won't you?"

Felton approached and sat on the olive-green couch opposite the viscount. They sat staring at each other, eye to eye, in a way so intense that to look away would have been a blight on either's manhood.

Lord Gillingham's lips started upward. "You are a dashed determined boy, Northwood."

"Should I apologize?"

"By no means. Though it irks me, I fear I cannot help but admire it too." The viscount leaned back into his striped green couch. "How long do you suppose it's been since there's been a ball in here?"

Felton glanced around the spacious room, with its elaborate baroque ceiling, Turkish rug, and green furniture and walls. Even the chandelier, though unlit, made the room seem alive and pensive. "Since before. . .well, before my dancing time, no doubt."

"What say you to a ball now?"

"What?"

"In honor of Eliza's return. I thought perhaps the dancing and gaiety would encourage her."

"Or frighten away any wits she has left."

"Trying to make my decisions for me again?"

"No, my lord." Felton leaned back too, though his muscles tightened with tension. "You asked."

"So I did."

"Is that why you sent for me?"

"No, it is not. She is asking for you."

"Who?"

"My daughter, Northwood. You do remember, of course? The one you kidnapped and brought here without my knowing—"

"I apologized for that." Felton came to his feet. "And if I am to be insulted for it again at every turn of the conversation, I should take my leave now."

"Sit down, Northwood." When Felton made no move to obey, the viscount's eyes went back to the portrait of his wife. "You must forgive a friend if he lashes out upon you. One usually only does so when one is hurting."

"Then you must forgive a friend too if he does something unwise and imprudent."

"We have been over it already. I'm quite ready to go back to chess and book reading if you are."

"Indeed, my lord."

"Good." The viscount rose and shook Felton's hand. His grip was warm, settling. "Stay here, and I shall send in Eliza. She has never asked me for anything—but she entered my study today and requested to see you."

Why would she do that?

"It seems there was an accident. The potting shed took fire today, and Mrs. Eustace seems certain Eliza was the cause. By any account, it seems to have upset her even more than she has already been. Perhaps you can pacify her fears?"

"I shall do my best."

"I am sure of it." The viscount smiled. "You do your best in everything. Likely such a manner will one day be the salvation or death of you."

Of all the people, why should Felton Northwood be the one she needed to see?

She didn't know. Maybe it didn't matter. But all day long, through her quiet meals and lonely hours of learning needlework with a maid, her mind kept leaping back to him.

Now, she stared at him from the saloon doorway, her heart skittering faster for reasons unknown.

He closed the distance between them. He didn't say anything at first. Not his usual commands or questions and such. He only took both of her hands and pulled her to one of the couches.

Then he sat next to her, still holding her hands, and watched her with eyes that made her already feel as if he believed her. Maybe that was it. The reason she'd needed him. Of everyone else she knew, who would believe what she was about to say?

"I think someone is trying to kill me."

"What?"

"I think someone is—"

"Yes, I heard you." His grip tightened. "His lordship mentioned a fire, but nothing like this."

"He only knows what the housekeeper has told him. That it was an accident."

"And it wasn't?"

"No."

"You are certain?"

"I was locked in. Someone broke the window and threw in a torch."

"Did you see anyone?"

"No, I saw nothing."

Felton released her hands and stood. He walked to the mantel, rubbed his jaw, then glanced up at the portrait of a familiar woman. "We were warned of this." When she didn't answer, his face turned to hers. Regret flickered in eyes that were deep and green. "Your captain came to his lordship and spoke with him. Something about the danger in bringing you back. . .about you meeting the same fate as your mother."

He'd brought her here anyway? Knowing of such a risk?

As if sensing her thoughts, he grimaced. "Some kind of a devil, aren't I?"

"Captain knew the danger too." She squeezed her hands together. "And he let me come here?"

"He was thinking of your happiness."

"My happiness was with him."

"Such a life is meant for no one. He knew that, I think, and that is why he wished for you to be returned."

Wasn't that a choice she should have made on her own? The world out here had wounded Captain and taken so many things from him. If he wanted nothing to do with a life out here, neither did she.

Felton sat beside her once more. She sensed that he might have reached for her hands again, but he must have lacked courage because he only stared down at them. "I will talk with Lord Gillingham and make him aware of the situation. We shall keep this from happening more than once."

"It already has."

"What?"

"Happened more than once, I mean. Mrs. Eustace saw a man by our carriage on the Sunday of her wreck. I imagined someone had caused it purposely, as if to hurt her—but I fear it was me they wished to hurt. Indeed, if not kill."

"I'll not let them." Felton's eyes bored into hers. "I brought you here and have every intention of keeping you safe."

"But why should anyone wish me harm?"

"Why do you think?"

A ghastly flash of the beast entered her mind, clawing, roaring so loud she almost shook her head against the sound. Who else would taunt her?

He'd stayed in her mind so long. The one who had murdered her mother. The one who had terrified her every dream.

She should have known he would come out of the darkness one day.

She should have known he would want her dead.

<hr />

"Is she asleep?"

"Not yet." Papa one-handedly fidgeted with the top button of his banyan outside of his wife's chamber. "Dear me, can you do this, Son? The buttons they make these days."

Felton grabbed the candlestick from Papa, set it on the hall-stand, and popped the velvet button in place. "Sleeping in the guest chamber again?"

"It makes your mother more comfortable. Besides, all the coughing and such is a bit rough to sleep through."

"She will recover from it soon."

Papa raised one brow but did not argue. He only smiled. "Off to Bedfordshire with me, then. Goodnight, Son."

"Goodnight." When his father had taken the candlestick and headed downstairs, Felton slipped into his mother's dim chamber.

Only a candle burned, the glow as weak and feeble as the white-faced woman in the bed linens.

He sat on the edge of the four-poster bed. "How goes it, Mamma?"

A smile brightened her watering eyes. "Well, I see you have avoided any fights today."

"How is it you know that?"

"No bruises."

"Perhaps I am a good dodger."

She chuckled, coughed, and turned her face into a damp pillow. "Another letter arrived from our Hugh. Won't you be a good boy and read it to me?"

"Didn't Papa already?"

"Yes, but a mother likes to go to bed with such things. It is in the drawer."

Grabbing the candle, he pulled open her drawer and found the letter. He scooted next to her on the bed, read it aloud, and handed over a handkerchief when she cried at the end.

"Very gallant all of it is, my son. . .but I only wish he would have never left."

"He will come home soon, I'm sure."

"And Arthur too."

"Yes. Him too."

"Promise me something, Felton?"

"If I can."

"Promise you shall never leave me. A mother needs her children. A wife needs her husband." More tears came, as she sucked in shallow breaths and leaned into his shoulder. "You never did stop believing in your papa, did you? All those years ago. When the constable came. . .when people threw eggs at our house, when the other children told you your father had killed a woman."

"Papa would never kill."

"No. There is too much goodness in him. I knew that the moment they told me what had happened. I knew without asking him questions or seeing the watch fob or even looking into his eyes. A wife knows these things. She feels them."

"We all believe him, Mamma. We always have."

"Do you think...do you suppose this child you've brought back..." The sentence lingered without answer. As if it meant too much to be spoken aloud.

"I do not know, Mamma." He grasped her hands. "But in the name of mercy, I pray she can."

_____ ෴ _____

If she could keep her mouth from falling open, maybe Lord Gillingham would not realize the disbelief his words imposed.

"All that to say, the decision is yours. Say the word and I shall dismiss the idea immediately."

She grasped the stairwell banister halfway up the stairs, where he had stopped her on her way to bed. All those evenings came flashing back to her. The ones where she'd slipped into her one silk dress, blue but stained, and wandered off into a quiet section of woods. No music played except the wind. No people except the trees. No ballroom floor except the needles and dry leaves of the forest ground.

But she'd danced just the same and pretended it was real. She never dreamed one day it could be.

"Eliza?"

She took one step down. "A true ball?"

"Of the most modish kind."

"With dancing?"

"Indeed."

"And lemonade?"

The questions seemed to amuse him. He half laughed. "Anything you wish."

"I am sorry. I did not mean. . .well, it is just that I've only read of such things. I never thought I could go to one."

"You shall do more than go to one, Eliza. You shall be the most remarkable person there. It will be, of course, in your honor."

What had she ever done to deserve such a thing? Why would the man gift her with this when she'd only ever shown him unkindness?

He must have misread her thoughts because he shifted on his feet from the bottom stair. "I have frightened you, have I not? There need be no ball, not until this ordeal with the danger is over and you are settled in—"

"Please, I should like the ball."

For a second, that same look came over his face. The one Captain always wore when she'd done something good, or surprised him, or just kissed his cheek.

She drew in air. "There is but one thing."

"Yes?"

"I—I cannot dance."

"That is nothing at all. I shall send for a dancing master right away, and by the time the ball arrives, you shall be dancing cotillions and quadrilles with the rest of them."

"Thank you, my lord."

"You are welcome. I shall leave you to retire to your chamber." He started to turn, but hesitated. "Eliza?"

"Yes?"

"Two things I must tell you and you must forgive me if they are distressing to you."

She waited, watched his eyes raise with difficulty to hers.

"I shall do anything I can to protect you. If you go anywhere outside of this house, a manservant shall accompany you. If anything alarming or unusual occurs, you must come first to me." His voice tightened. "And if you ever wish to call me Father, you are at freedom to do so. Goodnight." He walked away, tall and poised, and she couldn't keep from staring at his wide-set shoulders.

She used to ride on those shoulders, she remembered, and hold onto his ears with her fingers. She used to call him Father too.

She just wasn't certain if it was something she could ever do again.

⎯⎯ ✦ ⎯⎯

The next evening, Felton sat before Lord Gillingham in his study, made his move, and leaned back in his chair.

"I will never understand it." Lord Gillingham steepled his hands. "No, Northwood, it will never make sense to me."

"What?"

"How you can waltz in here, make your moves, and corner me like this without so much as a strategy."

"Skill, my lord."

"Deuced luck, more likely." They fell into silence then, as they usually did, and Felton went to counting every tick of the longcase clock. *Thirty-one. Thirty-two. Thirty-three.* Why couldn't the man take a chance, for once, and play his game on instinct instead of well-thought tactic?

"By this time, you are usually off to the library to find a book."

"The very thing." Felton was quick from his chair. "Go on with your pondering, my lord, but watch that you mind that bishop and rook. A few wrong moves and the queen will be mine."

"I need no counsel from you. Out of here before you disturb me further."

Grinning, Felton made an exaggerated bow and quit the room. He found the library and was just pushing open the door when—

"Oh." A book fell from Eliza's hands, making a quiet thump on the Persian rug. "Mr. Northwood...I did not know you to be here."

"Chess." He nodded in the direction of the study. "In the other room."

"I see."

"And you?" He moved before her, retrieved the book, and placed it back into her hands. "What are you reading?"

81

"Nonsense really." She slid it back into a shelf. "Things a silly romantic girl might read—not a fine lady."

"What do you know of fine ladies?"

"Quite a lot. I spent my whole life reading about them. Enough to know I shall never be one."

"Tell me the difference."

"What?"

"The difference between you and one of these *fine* ladies you speak of."

Pink touched her cheeks, and she looked away. "Now you mock me."

"No I don't." He followed her to the other side of the room, where she perused another line of shelves without ever pulling out a title. "I am just curious as to the requirements of a fine lady. What can they do that you cannot?"

"Needlework, painting, writing good letters and invitations."

"Trivial things, if you ask me. Go on."

"And. . .dancing."

"You cannot?"

The pink intensified. "No. I can run and climb trees—but I have never danced in my life."

He grabbed her hand. Then the other. "I shall teach you."

"Oh, no. Please, I—"

"Do not be afraid. I'm only half devil, you know, and just because no one else likes me does not mean you should not." He pulled her away from the bookshelf, out into the open, and shoved back a chair with his foot. "There. We are at the ball, and I am the Duke of Sussex. That is to bring you comfort in case you feel ill at the thought of dancing with a Northwood."

"But there is no music."

"Unnecessary." He positioned her at the edge of the chair, nodded, then stepped back himself. "We are joining the set. Partners face each other like this, see, at about four and a half feet apart."

"How should I stand?"

"In line with everyone else. That is the main thing, unless you want everyone whispering about you for disrupting the straight line."

"How terrible."

"Indeed. Now bow when I do—and follow me." They came together, switched places, then came together again. Her hands were warm as they spun. Soft too. Even when they parted again, the air still lingered with scents of her loose hair and fresh rose water.

"Is that all?"

"I am not a good teacher." He moved the chair back in place and swallowed. What was he doing anyway? Thinking about her hands. Her hair. If he cared for anyone's hair, it would be Miss Haverfield's, the girl he would one day win enough respect from to properly court.

Not this girl. He was trying to remedy his soiled name—not plunge it deeper into gossip by courting an untutored child of the woods.

Even if she was lovely.

"I must go." He strode to the shelf left of the hearth, however, and pointed to a line of manuals. "There are several editions here of *The English Dancing Master* by John Playford. You will find them helpful."

"Thank you."

He nodded, smiled, and left before he could persuade himself to take her hands again. How many kinds of a fool was he? From now on, they must keep only the murder between them. Not dancing. Or anything else. . .like yesterday when he'd sat too close to her and been near enough to spot every fleck in the soft gray eyes. What were gray eyes, anyway, to shiny blue ones like Miss Haverfield's?

Felton swept back into the study, told his goodbyes to Lord Gillingham, and left moments later. The path had grown dark, the moon was obscured, and a misty rain drizzled down on him. He walked faster. If he had known a rain was forthcoming, he would have taken the carriage—or at least his horse—to avoid arriving home in soaked clothes.

Mamma would say he invited death and catastrophe with such carelessness. "Do you know how many fall ill and die of colds every day?" she was wont to say. But maybe by the time he reached home, she would be abed and would not have to see his wet attire—

Something moved at the stone wall to his right. Then to his left.

Felton halted as a black figure appeared in front of him. Hooded and faceless in the darkness. Tall, looming, a mere three feet away.

"Who are you?"

No answer, but shadows moved and footfalls edged closer to him. Men behind him too. How many? Six, seven—or more?

He balled his hands into fists. If ever he needed his flintlock, it was now. "I said who are you, and what do you want?"

A fist swung from his left and smacked his jaw. He toppled back into someone's arms, caught another punch, but turned on the man and elbowed the shadowed face.

Hands grabbed him, jerked back his arms. He kicked with both feet, sent someone falling backwards, and wriggled an arm loose.

More blows showered down on him as he fought. He must have landed his fist somewhere, though, because he heard a man fall back with a groan and another doubled over with gasps.

"Enough, men." A voice, rough and familiar, eased closer. "Hold him still."

They jerked him forward, keeping his arms held out on each side, until he faced a man he still couldn't see. "What do you want?" Blood dribbled out with the words.

"The whereabouts of Captain Ellis."

What?

Seconds ticked by. The hooded man drew closer, his cape stirring in the mist, only the white of his eyes visible. That voice. Where had he heard it?

"The Swabian." Felton jerked his arms. "You're the Swabian."

At his nod, someone stepped forward and kicked a foot into Felton's stomach. He bent over, choked, as pain cramped around his lower ribs. Fingers grabbed his hair and yanked him back up.

"Where is he?"

"What. . .what do you want with him?"

"Doesn't matter. All you have to do is tell us where you found him."

"So you can do to him what you're doing to me now?"

"That and worse."

"I do not think so." Another kick to the stomach. His vision blurred. "No."

Third kick. "Where?"

"No."

"Hand me the whip." Noises, scurrying, then they dragged him to the wet stone wall and draped him against it. Rough hands pulled off his coat, then a stinging pain lashed across his back. Once, twice, again and again and again. Until he was numb with the pain. Until he couldn't see, couldn't hear, couldn't move.

His body slumped to the ground when the figures finally released him. They were gone. He groped for the wall and tried to pull himself up—

The whip came back down on his knuckles, and he collapsed. Pain disoriented everything, made the world tip and turn and spin, as if he were dancing the library floor with the girl from the woods. . . .

A face was next to his. Close to his ear. The Swabian. "Didn't want to hurt you, but there be no choice. Come to the Jester's Sunlight in three days and tell me where he be."

Felton blinked against the rain and swallowed blood. "N–no."

"Then don't count on me to stop them when they be ready to slit your throat."

CHAPTER 5

Something was happening.

Eliza pulled on her wrapper in the darkness, felt her way to the bedchamber door, and hesitated with her ear against the wood.

Whoever had been running the hall must have already reached the stairs, because the air grew quiet again. Maybe it had been nothing. Maybe the hurried footfalls had been a servant going to the privy, or a maid meeting her midnight lover—or maybe, more likely, a figment of Eliza's imagination.

She turned back to her bed but paused. Another pitter-patter of footsteps went running past her door. Even if she wanted to, she could not blame that on her imagination. What was happening? Could someone be in the manor? What if whoever wanted to harm her had snuck in and was waiting outside, sword in hand, ready to thrust it into her the second she—

No.

She would not think such things. Where was the bravery she was always calling upon in her ridiculous dreams?

Tightening her wrapper, she pulled open the door and found her way to the stairs in the darkness. She descended faster as the voices downstairs grew louder, then followed them to the candle-lit entrance hall.

Lord Gillingham was the only one she could see. He stood in the open front doorway, clothed in his nightdress, with both hands weaving through his hair. He turned, caught sight of Eliza. He seemed as if he would have said something, but someone from outside interrupted him, and he merely swept out of the way.

Then two servants hurried through the threshold.

Carrying a body.

No. Shock jolted her chest, made her legs go weak as she flattened against the wall. *Felton?*

He was torn and wet and limp, with blood soaking the white of his shirtsleeves, with mud in his hair and his face. Like a dead man.

She started for him, but a sharp hand drew her back. "Stay out of the way, Miss Gillingham," said Mrs. Eustace. "Take him upstairs and hurry off the wet clothes. Leah?"

The girl appeared from the shadows.

"Fetch bandages and water and see that the hearth is started in his chamber. And hurry!" The housekeeper turned to Lord Gillingham, who approached with eyes that seemed dazed and aggrieved. "The doctor is on his way, my lord. Is there anything else?"

"What happened?"

"We hardly know. I myself, my lord, was awakened only minutes before you. It seems the stable master heard someone shaking at the gates, little knowing it to be young Northwood and certainly not expecting to find him like this."

"Then he said nothing of who did this?"

"No, my lord."

"I see. Send a servant to the Northwoods, for they must be made aware." When the housekeeper rushed away in her night jacket, Lord Gillingham took Eliza by the arm. "I will walk you back to your chamber."

"I want to see him."

He nodded, as if he'd known, and together they made their way to the quiet guest chamber. She almost looked away from the shirtless man half under the coverlets.

But she couldn't. She only edged closer, stood over top of him, and stared down into a face swollen and discolored. "Why would anyone do such a thing?"

Lord Gillingham positioned himself on the opposite side of the bed. "I do not know. We shall know more when he awakens."

"Is he. . ." She lowered her finger to the coverlet, traced the seam that rose and fell with each of his breaths. "Is he. . .going to awaken, of a certain?"

"He is too determined not to."

Tears climbed her throat. She didn't know why. Not so very long ago, if she could have beaten him this way herself, she would have.

But this was different. This was not the man who had entered her forest and stolen her away, or kicked at her dog, or threatened her beloved Captain.

He was the one who had danced with her in the library and promised to protect her and grasped her hands only one day ago.

And she hurt for him. She didn't know why or how or if he were more enemy or friend. . .she simply hurt for him.

<hr/>

"Get back in that bed, Northwood, before I throw you back in myself."

Why was the dashed man playing the part of Mamma? Felton went to the window and jerked back the leopard-spotted curtains. Morning light stabbed his eyes, making his head throb to a faster beat. "You may go ahead and prepare a carriage for me, my lord, as I will be going home now."

"You heard the doctor."

"I've been beaten before and have mended well enough on my own without staying bedridden. Besides that, this room unnerves me."

The bed creaked behind, as if Lord Gillingham had taken a seat on its edge. "Your parents have been made aware of the situation. I asked the doctor to stop by on his way to the village with news of your regained consciousness."

Too bad he could not have stayed that way a bit longer. How much easier it would have been to endure this dashed pain.

"Also, a servant walked the path this morning. He found your coat."

As if the coat were of any importance.

Silence. Then the bed squeaked again as the viscount stood. "All right, Northwood. Let us have it."

"Have what?"

"Do not play daft with me, son. I want to know who did this to you and why."

"I told you before. 'Twas just another fight."

"Then you must have attacked a man with a whip, because you've seventeen lashes on your back. Must have made you grievously angry indeed. What did he say that was so dreadful about your father?"

Felton picked at the tight bandage around his hand. Already, a tiny line of blood was seeping through across his knuckles—and the same must have happened on his back, because the bed linens were stained where he'd lain. Every muscle hurt. Every breath seared pain along his bruised ribs.

And in three days, it would get worse.

"Well?"

Felton eased around and faced him. "I only recognized one. A man called the Swabian. They jumped on me about half a mile down the path."

"Why?"

"They want to know about Captain Ellis. Where they can find him."

"Eliza's captain?"

"Hers indeed."

"What do they want with him?"

"I do not know." He eased toward the bed. "But no good, whatever it is—and 'twould be no great surprise if they wanted to end him."

"Here." Lord Gillingham helped him with a pillow. Then, deeper, "Did you tell them?"

"No."

"And if they attempt to persuade you again?"

"No one can make me talk."

"I see." Lord Gillingham's face tightened. He shook his head. "I understand none of this."

"Neither do I—except one thing."

"What?"

"All this time, we assumed it was Eliza alone who was being hidden in those woods." Felton hesitated. "But mayhap her Captain was hiding himself."

―⁓❧⁓―

Eliza stared at the chair in the library, the one he'd moved long enough to teach her the first steps of a dance. That had been strange of him. Like something a gentle lover, with billowing cape and gallant black steed, might have done. Not a villain. A kidnapper. Or was it not always so simple as that? Were there more than the good and the bad, and instead, a bit of both in all?

She didn't know. Maybe she never would. Only that, despite everything, it had been nice when he'd touched her, talked with her, and danced with her. There'd been mischief, fun in the eyes that had no longer looked at her like a useful object.

More like a girl.

Like a woman.

She flipped another page of the dancing manual he'd recommended. He was leaving Monbury Manor soon. She'd already heard Lord Gillingham call for the carriage and order a footman to assist him back downstairs. All day she'd wanted to talk with him. Twice she'd started up the stairs, every word planned, only to come back down again without ever reaching his door.

Because Lord Gillingham had told her everything. How despite the fact that they nearly beat and whipped him to death, he spoke no words of her Captain's whereabouts. Why would he do that? Wasn't that the courage of a king? Or a saintly-hearted knight?

If anyone disliked Captain, it was him. If anyone had reason to turn Captain over to vicious enemies, it was him. If anyone should like to—

The library door creaked open. "What'ee doing?"

"Oh—Minney. Come in."

"I can come in because'ee like me, yes?"

"Yes. Of course I like you." Of late, Minney had taken just as much interest in Eliza as she had Merrylad. "What are you doing here?"

"I can go where I want to. Anywhere Papa went, I can go. Mrs. Eustace can't be telling me I can't—"

"I'm sorry. I didn't mean you shouldn't be here, only that I didn't know if something was amiss."

"Mr. Northwood, he wants to talk with'ee. I don't be letting him in though. That's what I was doing. I was standing outside this door, so's no one can get in what would hurt'ee." From behind Minney, a hand pushed the door all the way open.

A bandaged hand. My, how different he looked, with black ringing both eyes, with a cut across his nose, with lips that were swollen and bruising. A knight with dented armor, indeed.

She looked away like the same coward who could not come to his chamber hours before. "Minney, I should like to speak with Mr. Northwood. Please, let us be alone."

"But I want to stay with'ee."

"Please."

The girl sighed and left the room, clicking the door shut behind her.

With slow movements, Felton shuffled closer. The playful comradery of yesterday was replaced with gravity, intensity, as if his pain rendered him in bad temperament. "The carriage is already prepared, so I must be brief. Does anyone know of your cottage in Balfour Forest?"

"No, I do not think so."

"See that it stays that way. It seems your captain has some unpleasant foes."

"There are many who dislike him for the ship he sunk—"

"This is more than dislike, and I have every intention of determining why and how many more secrets the man has hidden."

"This does not make him any more the murderer you wish him to be."

"Maybe not. But it proves he is not the saint you deem him."

"How?"

He scowled, clutched his ribs, and turned to the door so fast he winced.

"Wait."

"So you can persuade me longer your captain is innocent of everything?"

"No." She held one of Playford's manuals to her chest. "So I can tell you. . .so I can say thank you."

Slowly, he turned. "For?"

"For letting them do this to you to keep a man safe you do not even like."

He said nothing to this, nor changed expressions, but his eyes seemed a little softer when he whispered, "You are welcome," before he shut the door.

He was no enemy, this man, no matter how different their sides and hopes.

No, Felton Northwood was her friend.

Her first friend.

⁂

"What do you mean you knew where Ellis was, sir?" asked Swabian.

Bowles stared at them in the dim light of the tallow candle. Eight men crowded closer. Silent. Wearing age and dirt and fourteen years' worth of hate on their cursed faces. The Swabian stood in front, cap in hand like a sign of reverence.

Devil of a fool. No reverence lingered between them. Never had. Only fear—because everyone in the room knew what the man standing next to him was capable of.

What *he* was capable of.

"Yes, I knew." He smiled. Most men smiled for pleasure. A kindness of sorts. Not him though. When he smiled, people fidgeted and mumbled and lost what little nerve they had to begin with. "But it served me better this way."

"Wot you saying?" Tall Postle took a step next to Swabian. "Say it out, wot you know, 'fore we accuse you of being an Iscariot—"

"My, my." Bowles pulled out his snuffbox. A handkerchief. "Talkative today, are you not, Tall Postle? Do you talk so excessively in the presence of your wife? No, no—forgive me. I have forgotten. She left you, did she not, with that Romani gypsy?"

The cellar went quieter.

A vein bulged on Tall Postle's massive forehead, but he only hung his head and stepped back again. Another devil of a fool.

"As I was saying, Ellis was useful to me. After his sins and the grave alternative if I fed him to your lion mouths, he was quite willing to dance a jig to whatever music I played. Do you follow?"

A murmur of answers. Several nods.

"Good. You do have minds after all." He tucked his handkerchief into his collar, pinched out some snuff, and slipped the tobacco under his lip. "In perfect honesty, I cared nothing for the men who went down with the *Red Drummer*. They meant nothing to me then and mean even less to me now. Besides that, there are greater complications we must attend to."

"Sir—"

"But I spent three days in the ocean and three weeks recovering from the gravest sickness I have yet to know in my life. For that, Ellis will pay. Less noble vengeance, perhaps, but vengeance nonetheless."

The men waited and watched him. 'Twas sickening the way they dropped their mouths and stopped breathing like pitiful beggars wailing for bread. Sickening, but also delightful.

Considering he was the bread giver.

"The captain was useful to me for a season, as I said before." His smile broadened and he clicked his snuffbox back shut. "But he is useful to me no more. Let us lions enjoy our prey—and having done so, we shall proceed to rip apart the other tribulations in the arena."

The dancing master was nearly finished with his lessons. The dressmaker had come and gone. Servants were already whispering about sugar sculptures and fruits and drink. Over breakfast, Lord Gillingham had told her that all invitations had been posted, and even the orchestra had been summonsed.

Because in just one week, there would be a ball.

For her.

Eliza pressed herself to the glass of her bedchamber window. Below, the view of the courtyard stirred her stomach. How many days had it been since Captain had climbed over that wall? How many hours a day did she stand like this, watching for him to do it again?

She needed him. She needed to run into his arms and smell the earth and forest in his clothes. When was the last time she'd laughed? Or taken off her shoes and ran? Or escaped somewhere—someplace magic like the stream—and splashed away a hundred cares?

But there was nothing to do with her cares here. Not in this bedchamber, by this window, enclosed in these decorated walls.

And there was no one to tell her heart to. If Captain were here, she would have told him about the ball. How despite all the fears, there was excitement too. She would have told him about Felton. How sorry she'd been for him when he was wounded, how lonely the manor seemed when he left. She would have told him about Minney Bradshaw, how ghastly she was—and yet how easy it was becoming to feel close to the girl.

Captain would have smiled. Or laughed. Or cried when she cried. He would have told her to keep her chin up, and even without telling him of her nightmares, he would have assured her the beast could always be fought.

A lump formed in her throat as she turned from the window. No sense in watching every day like this. He wasn't coming. Now what must she do? Did she force her way back to him alone?

Or did she stay?

Felton dug his heels into his horse's side. Air whipped at his face, moist with the morning fog, chilly enough to bite back some of his tension.

It had been three days.

Three days of listening to Mamma fuss over him, and chide him, and weep at him. Three days of Papa reading his newspaper and talking of everything except what had happened.

And three days of knowing that the Swabian and his men meant blood if he didn't turn over Captain's whereabouts.

Which he wasn't about to do.

He glanced down at the flintlock pistol tucked in his trousers. He never carried a gun. But this was one situation he may not live through without such a weapon.

Christ, have mercy on me.

When he entered Lodnouth and trotted his horse to the Jester's Sunlight, the door was already ajar and a skeletal fishwife was yelling curses into the building. When she spotted Felton, however, she jerked her tot out of the way and mumbled, "He can 'ave his bloomin' ale and trollops. Wot's the likes o' me care any'ow?"

The smell hit him again as he entered. Not many crowded the room this early in the morning, but five still slumped at a table—and the Swabian still leaned against the bar where he'd been before.

Felton moved next to him. "I am here."

"I can see that." Which was odd of him to say, for he never so much as looked up. "A fine obedient lad, you be. I was rightly worried you weren't going to come at all."

"I never run from anything."

"Wish Ellis would've thought the same."

Silence.

A scraping sound—chair legs against floorboards—as the men at the table approached. They formed a wide circle around Felton and the Swabian but never said a word. The same who had beaten him three days ago?

Then he'd been unprepared.

He wasn't now.

"Well?" Swabian wiped ale from his whiskers. "Go ahead and do your telling, then get your bloody bones out of here."

"I didn't come to tell you anything."

Swabian's head finally turned. His eyes moved up and down Felton's face, as if surmising the damage, then he shook his head. "You're some kind of a fool."

Felton jerked out the pistol and leveled it to the man's chest.

The men edged closer.

Someone's hand landed on Felton's back, sending a jolt of pain through the tender cuts—but he held the gun without wavering. "I came for one reason and one reason alone, fellow. No one does to me what you did three days ago."

To his left, a man chuckled.

Another hand clapped down on his shoulder.

"And if you intend to kill me, you might as well try it here because I'm not telling you anything. My blood will not be the only blood spilt on this floor."

Swabian stared. Said nothing. Then, with a shake of his head, he turned back to his foamy tankard. "Go sit back at your table, men."

For a second no one moved.

Seconds ticked off in Felton's head. His heartbeat thrummed to his finger, the finger pressed and waiting against the trigger.

But he never had to shoot.

One by one, the men turned back to their table, sat down without muttering anything, and resumed drinking their ale.

Something wasn't right. Why were they backing down against one man?

But he had no intention of staying to find out. Stuffing his flintlock back into his trousers, Felton strode through the still-open doorway, mounted, and galloped his way out of Lodnouth's lifting fog.

There was more to find out about Captain Jasper Ellis. Much

more. And somehow all of it was linked to the night Lady Gillingham was pushed from her bedchamber window.

He just didn't know how.

Yet.

⁓⸎⁓

I don't want to go in. Eliza reached for the door, curled her hand around the knob, then withdrew.

Coward. Isn't that what a coward would have done?

Not a girl in one of her books. Not the girl she oft pretended she was. Wouldn't Captain be disappointed if he knew the courage she lacked?

But this door. For days it had been bothering her, flashing into her mind, summoning tears, carving its way into the granite of her never-changing nightmare. Because sometimes she remembered things. A piece of furniture. A painting on the wall. Or the familiar old voice of an elderly servant. All things that came and went, a faint tickle of familiarity, like a fog that lifted and settled back again.

Why couldn't she pass this door without staring? Without sickness hitting her stomach?

She reached for the knob again. She shouldn't be doing this. She should be sitting in the library with a book. Or outside watching Minney play with Merrylad. Or in her own chamber, allowing the maid to help assist her into a gown as they waited for the dancing master's daily arrival.

Not roaming the house this way.

Not prying open a door she had no right to intrude.

As she pushed it open, the hinges yawned into the quietness, as if she'd just awakened the room from slumber. Dust motes stirred as she closed herself inside.

A massive bed with tied curtains at each corner. A dark wood armoire. A bedside table, a hearth and chair, a looking glass, a dressing table.

And a window.

Her eyes were drawn to it, forced there, where the heavy red drapes hung limp and dusty. *No, no.* She almost turned and fled. The sickness took her breath. Screams split her ears, the screams of her nightmares. Why were there always screams? Were they hers or someone else's? Or both?

Her heartbeat thumped louder and harder with each step she took toward the window. This. . .could *this* be the place?

She'd never thought it to be real. Never wanted it to be real. Captain had promised they were only nightmares, that it would always be gone the next day, that none of it was true.

But it was.

Everything was true, but she didn't understand.

Nausea surged through her. She touched her hand to the white windowsill. Then to the glass no longer broken. Then, with shaking fingers, to the curtains that had so long suffocated her.

But she never looked down from the window. She couldn't. Not again. Because whatever was down below she hadn't the strength to see again.

***

"So they invited you."

"All of us." Felton took back the red-sealed invitation his father handed him. "He invited all of us."

"Tut, tut, as if your mother and I would attend such a ball."

"I think you should."

"Then you go, Son, but I have not stepped foot in that house in fourteen years. Too many chances I might drop my watch fob and take the blame for any—never mind. No sense talking about it anyway. Lord Gillingham means well enough, I suppose, but—"

"But what?"

Papa leaned deeper into his parlor chair and turned another page of the *Gentleman's Magazine*. "Hmm, looked at this meteorological journal yet, Son? Why, it says here more dry days than showery—"

"You are afraid."

Of course he was. He always was. Even now, his eyes never left the magazine. "You think I enjoy being whispered of as the murderer?"

"What are whispers? To what end must we avoid them? You have scarcely left this house in fourteen years. Not even for church. Is this not greater injustice to the Northwood name than the slander of the ignorant people who—"

"Felton." From her chaise lounge, Mamma finally looked up from the two letters she'd been reading from Aaron and Hugh. She hugged them close to her chest. "You should not speak so to your father."

"Someone must say it."

"Felton—"

"Mamma, I must be heard. They have already taken our dignity. They have already slandered our name. Are we to hide away with our heads bent like frightened dogs?" He needed to stop. He needed to leave his father alone and bend to his mother's frail command and pretend—pretend as always that everything wrong did not exist. Hadn't he said it all before?

Felton crumpled the invitation and tossed it into the hearth. "Never mind. I shall attend alone—"

"No, Felton." His mother laid aside the letters. Her head lifted. "He is right, Richard, and we are cowards if we do not show our faces."

"But your illness—"

"I am not so weak that I cannot stand alongside my son and defend our name."

A swell of pride tightened Felton's chest, as Papa lowered his magazine. A sheen of moisture filled his gaze as it turned upon Mamma. "By Jove, you're right. The both of you."

Eliza yanked off one slipper. Then the next. How cool was the courtyard grass, damp with the evening dew, as soft as the moss back in the forest.

Let Mrs. Eustace find out. Let them all find out. It did not matter and Eliza no longer cared. What were these people to her anyway? Mrs. Eustace was as cruel as the world Captain had always warned her about. Minney was mad. Lord Gillingham was elusive. Why did he go to such pains to avoid her? Even when he did see her—in quick passing down a hall or for a few moments during breakfast—he had trouble meeting her eyes.

And Felton.

She ran to the farthest tree in the courtyard, the one closest to the gate, and grabbed a low-hanging limb. She didn't care for him either. Sometimes, for a moment or so, she imagined she did.

But she imagined too much.

She was making him some noble hero in her books, or the mysterious stranger in her dreams, or the brave knight in so many stories. He was none of those. Was he?

Everything was his fault. She would not be here were it not for him, for his incessant desire to nudge the ghosts of a long-ago murder. Ghosts that kept her from sleeping. Ghosts that made the nightmares worse, so wretched she feared to close her eyes because the beast grew larger. And larger. And larger.

Ever since she'd entered that chamber.

Her mother's.

Higher and higher she ascended the tree, until she settled on a limb that draped over the courtyard wall. The gate was locked, but how easy it would be to climb to the top of the stone wall. Then jump over. Then run and run and keep running until there were no more servants or manor houses or nightmares—

"They said I would find you here."

She jumped.

From near five feet below, Felton Northwood dangled both her slippers from each hand. And grinned. "They just did not tell me to look up."

She gathered her dress tighter around her legs and fought a rush of tears. What a savage child he must think her. How he must laugh at her. The silly little fool who was more animal than lady—

"What is it?"

She looked back over the courtyard wall, but the tears came faster. He was the last person she wished to shed her tears before. Why couldn't he have been Minney? Minney would have understood. She would have known that it'd been three nights since Eliza had slept, or that the ball was in two days and she was still stumbling through the dances like a fairy with broken wings.

"Come down here."

No, she wouldn't. He was always telling her what to do. Why should she listen?

He yanked off his tailcoat, undid the knot of his necktie. Then he grabbed the lowest limb, ascended quickly, and paused one branch below her. Yellow bruises still hung below his eyes and chin, but the cut across the bridge of his nose was nearly gone. "You are crying."

She swatted the tears back off her face.

He edged closer. "Something has happened. Someone has tried to harm you again—"

"No."

"Then what?" Softer now. His eyes probed her face. "If anything is wrong, you must tell me. Have they taken your dog?"

She shook her head.

"Then Lord Gillingham. He has said something to upset you."

Another shake of her head.

"Perhaps Mrs. Eustace—"

"No, it is not her. It is not anyone." The breeze stirred the leaves around them, stirred at her hair she'd refused to let the maid fix into curls and a chignon. "It is me. . .the nightmares."

"What nightmares?"

"I can't sleep anymore. I'm afraid to."

He pulled himself to her limb, closer than he should have been, and touched her shoulder. Ever so slightly, he guided her to face him. "You never told me about this."

"It does not matter anyway. I never see the face."

"Then it is of that night?"

"I think so. I didn't know for sure. . .not until three days ago when I went into. . ." Why couldn't she speak the words?

"No one should have brought you in there."

"I went on my own."

"Why?"

Did it matter? No, nothing mattered. Not even the nightmares mattered because they didn't tell her anything and they only hurt her more.

"Eliza."

With one hand, she rubbed at each eye. More tears still escaped.

"Eliza, tell me the nightmare."

"I do not want to."

"You must."

"But it tells us nothing. Don't you see? I cannot remember who killed her."

"Tell me."

How could she put it into words? She'd only ever told Captain once or twice, in younger years, in the middle of the night when the horrors had still had their hold on her.

But this was different.

"Come, Eliza. Tell me."

"It is always so dark."

"Yes."

"And I'm standing next to a window, but I cannot get away. Something red is always wrapped around me. No matter how much I fight, I can't get loose."

"The curtains."

She met his eyes. "You know about them?"

"I've been in your mother's chamber too. Mostly looking for answers that were not there. Go on."

"Then someone comes. It is always the same. He's. . .he's like a beast or a lion, with a mane around his head, only he's part human too."

"Who does he look like?"

"I do not know. I can't remember. It's too unclear."

"But it must be someone you know. It could come to you."

"It never has before."

"But you have never been here before, this close to everything that might jar back your memories." He leaned closer. "Then?"

"He claws at me, I scream, and he shoves me through a window. I wake up before I hit the bottom."

He said nothing to this, only took his gaze away from her and scanned the world five feet below them. Then, slowly, his eyes came back to hers. Gentleness shone, a gentleness she didn't have to imagine. "How long since you've slept?"

"Three nights."

He nodded and kept her gaze. "The nightmare may be our key to everything."

Our. As if it were something they were doing together. A common purpose. Something that didn't just make her useful to him, but pulled her nearer to him as a friend with the same hope.

She just didn't know if that hope was hers.

Or if she'd ever want to see the beast's face for what it really was.

The next morning, Felton dismounted his horse in front of the stone, gothic-styled church. According to the addlepates in the village, most no one had heard of Jasper Ellis, and the ones who had knew nothing about him. Or so they said.

Oh well. If they couldn't give him answers, he'd find someone who could. The vicar, Mr. Warburton, would sooner lose his hand and foot than withhold truth. After all, wasn't he always saying it possessed the power to set one free?

"If you are looking for Mr. Warburton, he is quite indisposed."

Felton paused halfway up the stone steps and turned to see Miss Haverfield at the bottom. White dress with no wrinkles. Red pelisse with glistening silver buttons. Gold curls peeping out from a straw hat trimmed in flowing red ribbon.

The picture of a perfect lady.

Felton started back down the steps. "I didn't see you when I arrived."

"I was sitting in the carriage under the shade tree. Father is in the parish meeting with the other churchwardens. Some dull business about road maintenance and repair."

"You may not think it so dull were the roads to get muddy and impassable."

Her smile widened, and she tilted her head in the way he'd always found so flattering. As if he were amusing her. Or she were amusing him. "So the roads have been to blame for keeping you away so long."

"Away?"

"Yes." She switched her basket to the other gloved hand. "I have ridden to the cove numerous times, yet you have never been there."

"Then we simply must have missed one another." He stood before her now, on the bottom step, close enough that her ribbons brushed against him with a gust of wind. "I have taken many rides at the cove myself."

"Looking for me?"

"Not entirely."

"Why not? You used to."

"That was before I saw you strolling with that unfavorable-looking, red-haired brute."

A trilling laugh left her lips. "Why, you are the drollest boy, Mr. Northwood. Could you truly mean dear Mr. Scrope, who has left Oxford for the gallant purpose of escorting his sisters to visit me?"

"Am I to understand there is no courtship?"

"Oh, but am I to understand there is a bit of jealousy?"

From the top of the stairs, the doors parted and the squire, the bishop, and several other well-tailored gentlemen exited. They all spared Felton a brief nod, if not a condescending one, then hurried on by him.

"Come along, Penelope," said Mr. Haverfield. "If we are to deliver your baskets to the poor without being late for tea, we must waste not a moment."

"Yes, Father." She too must have noted the cool, disapproving ring in her father's voice, because her smile seemed apologetic. She curtsied. "Good day, Mr. Northwood. I trust you will enjoy those rides we spoke of."

Was that some sort of message?

"Penelope!"

"Coming, Father." With one last smile and a half-teasing flash of her eyes, she hurried back for the carriage her father was already climbing into.

Felton shook his head and scaled the stairs. She may be a perfect lady, down to every coyishly framed word, but she was as unreachable as the stars in heaven. Did she enjoy playing games with him? Why, for once in her life, could she not speak plainly and be in earnest—like the crying girl he'd climbed in a tree with yesterday?

She had beheld him without pretense. She had spoken to him without riddles. She had been real. . .inexpressibly real, in a way he'd seldom known anyone to be in his life.

But Eliza Gillingham would never fit into the world he intended to make for himself. Nor anyone's world, for that matter. She was something different. Something strange. Something he couldn't understand and maybe didn't want to.

"Mr. Northwood, how very good to see you." Mr. Warburton met him in the vestibule, grasped his hand, and upon hearing Felton wished to talk, urged him into the nave for a seat. "Now, how might I be of service to you, my son?"

"I do not wish to take up much of your time, Mr. Warburton, but I should like to inquire about a man named Jasper Ellis."

"The Captain?"

"Yes."

"Oh, oh, yes. The Captain indeed. I remember the unfortunate fellow and have prayed often for his soul. Is he yet alive?"

"Yes, sir. What can you tell me of him?"

"Only sad accounts, my son. He came to me but once, in the middle of the night, and I have never forgotten him since. What can I tell you of him?"

"Who he was, why he came to you." Felton studied the vicar—the long face, the intent eyes, the sad slant of lips so often mumbling prayer.

They stayed silent now, though, until finally Mr. Warburton glanced away. "When a man comes to me with such brokenness, as this man did, I cannot soon break his confidence."

"I would not ask, sir, were it not a matter of great importance."

"Importance to God, to Ellis, or to you?"

"Perhaps all."

The vicar nodded. "Then it is right I should tell you. I daresay, you would likely find out elsewhere anyway, for it is quite the tragic thing when a clipper of twenty-four men goes down."

"In the sea?"

"Yes, with but two survivors."

That explained the names in the Bible. "But I thought that crew committed mutiny."

"Would to heaven they had, my son. May God rest their souls, as the sea has rested their bodies."

"What caused the wreck?"

"Only what has already been forgiven."

"Meaning?"

"Meaning Ellis came to me a very tortured man. He carried many lives on his conscience. Lives that might not have been lost had he not been. . ."

"Not been what?"

"This can be of help to no one now." The vicar rose. "There are many a man who would like to hold such deaths against Ellis, but God has forgotten all. I think it would be best were we to do the same."

Felton walked alongside the man until they reached the vestibule again. He placed his hand on the door, but hesitated to open it. "One last question, Mr. Warburton, if I may."

"Yes, of course."

"Ellis brought many sins to you that night."

"He brought them to God, my son, not me. That is where he left them."

Felton stared into the man's eyes. "Was the murder of Lady Gillingham among those sins?"

"No." The vicar folded his hands, as if in prayer. "He came to me just one night before the death of Lady Gillingham, and may I say, I do not believe such a burdened man could have murdered anyone. That is why the blood of twenty-two men weighed so very much. Indeed, had I not stopped him, he would have ended his own life right here in this church—for not only did he bear such guilt, but many were seeking revenge on him."

"Then he was in hiding."

"Yes, I gathered as much from what he had said. Sad story. Very sad. I will pray that he has at last found peace and rest in the merciful kindness of the Lord."

He would need such prayers, of a certain.

Felton thanked the vicar, jogged back down the stone steps, and mounted. Sometime between when the ship went down and the night Ellis visited the church, some connection had been forged among him and the murder and little Eliza. But what? What did one have to do with the other? How had he ended up with the child?

The vicar said the man could have never murdered.

Eliza vowed the same.

Which meant either Captain Jasper Ellis was an innocent man— or he was just cunning enough to convince everyone he was.

CHAPTER 6

Eliza stiffened in her bed as the tiny knock came again. Her candle was still aglow, so she hurried out of bed and slipped on her ruffled wrapper—something Mrs. Eustace had warned her to do, above all else, lest someone see her in her nightgown.

She'd never worn a wrapper at the cottage. Why did it matter so much now?

Before she reached the door, it came open on its own. Lord Gillingham stood before her, hair disheveled, a brass candlestick in one hand, and something pink draped over his shoulder. "Eliza." Teary. Why were there tears?

She took a step back as he took a step forward. "M—my lord." What was he doing here so late?

His bottom lip trembled, but he offered a smile. "I am glad you are not yet asleep."

"No." She glanced at the book on her bed. "I was reading."

"Business kept me in Lodnouth all day. I've only just returned. May I speak with you?" When she did nothing but nod, he inched two steps forward.

She didn't back away.

He lowered the candlestick to the stand and, with unsteady hands, unfolded the pink silk. A dress, one more lovely than she'd seen in her life, with a net overlay and pink flowers embroidered on the hem. "Your mother's. She wore it on the last ball we ever attended together. . .just days before we lost our little Thomas."

A sensation worked through her as he laid the soft dress into her hands. Something of her mother's. Something that wasn't red or bloody or broken, but beautiful. Why did it make her want to cry?

Only Lord Gillingham was crying too. The tears clung to his lashes, flooded his cheeks, as he helped her hold the dress against her. "She felt healthy that day. For weeks after my son was born, she was weak. That did not matter to her, though. She was happy just the same, and every time I came home, I found the two of you nestled on each side of her in my bed."

A faint memory stirred—a lovely woman, swallowed in soft coverlets, with a new baby in one arm and an eager little girl at the other. The woman was smiling. Whispering. Pressing soft kisses onto Eliza's cheek or stroking the baby's head or laughing at the bird who tried to get in the window.

"Two days after the ball, our little Thomas. . .he. . ." Lord Gillingham pulled the dress back and pressed it against himself, as if the touch of it brought him comfort. "My Letitia, she was just holding him like she always did. They were sleeping on the lounge downstairs. Just sleeping. When she woke up, the baby was dead in her arms, for no reason at all. . .just dead in her arms." A sob broke loose. He turned his back to her, as if in shame she should see, as if frightened he could no longer keep control of himself.

She wanted to turn her back too. Everything he said hurt. The baby dead. Her little baby Thomas, who the lovely woman had taught her to kiss, who she'd knelt at his trundle bed and prayed for.

The loss settled in the room as if it were still new, as if the pain would never go away. Why must he say these things to her?

She didn't want to remember the baby. She didn't want to remember her mother. She didn't want to touch the pretty dress or imagine the loving creature who'd worn it or see the damage her death had done to the man who loved her.

Sucking in air, Lord Gillingham turned back around. "Forgive me. I do not know what is wrong with me. I should never have come up here and. . ." His gaze dropped back to the dress. "I do not suppose you would wish to wear it now. It must mean as little to you as I do."

Maybe that was true. The dress bothered her as terribly as the man who held it. But she nodded anyway and whispered, "I will wear it for the ball."

The smile came again, as he nodded and handed it over once more. "Goodnight, Eliza."

Her throat ached. "Goodnight." *Father.*

The morning came faster than she'd wanted it to. For the first night in so many, there had been no nightmares—and if there were dreams, it was only of a family, many years ago, who had loved her and whom she had loved.

'Twas a lovely dream, one she didn't want to wake up from. Why had Captain never told her these things? Why had he hidden where she'd come from, pretended she was his own when she'd had her own family?

But no, she must not question him. Captain loved her too, loved her most. Just because Lord Gillingham had shed tears before her, made her remember things she'd forgotten, did not mean she would allow Felton's doubts to creep into her mind.

She was still Captain's daughter. The cottage was still her home.

The day passed in a half-painful, half-glorious blur. How could she have known so much was involved in preparing the ladies she always admired in the magazines? First she soaked in a hot tub. Then the seamstress altered her dress. Then the humming maid used a papillote iron and papers to style her hair, as another maid brought in lotion and powders and rosewater perfume.

By the time the prominent hour of ten o'clock had arrived, she sat before the looking glass in her chamber and stared at a woman she'd have never believed could have been herself. She touched the earbobs dangling from her ears, then fingered the rhinestone necklace at her neck. *"There are people in the world, love, who are rich and only want to be richer. They don't care none for people like us.*

Not unless we can make them more money."

Now, she looked just like the people she'd always thought so ill of. What would Captain think to see her this way? Would he tell her it was wrong—to go down there to a ball, to mingle with people who had no feeling for the human heart?

"Well."

Eliza hurried to her feet, just as Mrs. Eustace swept into her chamber. "You may go now, girls. Your end result is quite the thing."

The two maids curtsied and left the room.

"Turn around."

Slowly, she turned a full circle. Heat sprang to her cheeks. Would everyone look at her this way?

"Your father has something to be proud of in your appearance, if nothing else. Do you think you can act the lady you look?"

Indignation replaced the embarrassment. "I shall certainly try to act better than you do."

Mrs. Eustace raised both brows and a small flush dotted her cheeks. Instead of a scowl, the corners of her lips worked upward. "You have not changed a bit, Miss Gillingham. You are as impertinent now as you were as a child." She took a step back and motioned out the door. "Come in now, Minney, and do hurry up."

The girl shuffled in next to Mrs. Eustace.

"She has been begging to see you all day, so let her take a good look at you and then send her back to the kitchen. Your father will be waiting for you downstairs to escort you into the saloon. Clear?"

When Eliza nodded, the housekeeper whisked away, and Minney came closer. "Ye look pretty, pretty."

A small laugh escaped. "Thank you."

"I told Merrylad I wished I was pretty like'ee. I'd give anything if I was. That's why Mamm killed herself. Papa too maybe. They wouldn't o' done it if I was pretty like'ee."

"That isn't true, Minney." Eliza reached for the girl's face, framed both cheeks. "What God has given you less of in one place, He has given you more of in others."

"What'ee mean?"

"You are kind, Minney. You have the heart of a dear and noble fairy. What friend have I here at Monbury Manor but you?"

The sad eyes brightened. "And I'm good with dogs too. I am. Mr. Cotts says I am."

"And I say you are too."

Minney leaned forward and pressed a kiss to Eliza's cheek. Then she clung to her a second, made a wretched little whimper, and tore herself away. She fled from the room without a word more.

Eliza was left alone. To leave the small chamber. To venture the hall. To descend the mighty stairs and meet her estranged father at the bottom.

And to face a ballroom of people that were real and not imagined. For the first time in her life.

***

Felton's heart picked up speed as his father stepped out of the chamber. "Well?"

Papa was dressed finer than he'd been in years—his hair well combed and waxed, his buttons shiny, his tailcoat devoid of lint or wrinkle. But the happy glow of his face, just moments before, was gone. His hand shook as he clicked shut the door. "Where is Dodie?"

"Fetching a manservant to get the doctor."

"When she is done, tell her to get more pillows and a glass of water." He pulled off his cravat. "I won't be needing this—"

"Papa."

"I do not want to talk about it, Felton. I must find Hugh's last letter. Your mother is crying for it." He brushed past Felton without another word.

As if his wife hadn't just collapsed halfway down the stairs. As if she hadn't fainted and awakened in tears. As if she weren't weaker and closer to death every new day upon them.

Felton huffed out air and pushed his way into the room.

She was curled in a fetal position on top of the counterpane, still wearing the plume feather in her hair and the satin gown she hadn't donned in ages. Her tears dripped into the pillow. "I'm so sorry. I'm so sorry."

He knelt next to the bed, laid his hand on the side of her face, and stroked his thumb against her wet cheek. "Say nothing more, Mamma. It is not your fault."

"Your father needed this."

"He needs nothing but you."

"I am a chain to him."

"No."

"I can do nothing anymore and every day I can do less. What is wrong with me, Felton?" She moved her hand over top his. "Why must there always be such pain? For your father, for your brothers. . .for you."

"Please, Mamma. You are upset. The doctor is coming, and he shall have something to help with the pain—"

"You must go on without us. I shall not have your night ruined too."

"I will stay here."

She pushed away his hand. "No, it would only make me feel the worse. A mother's heart is always with her child, even if she cannot be present. You will go for all of us, won't you?"

"I do not want to leave you."

"For the Northwoods, Son. For your father. We have no one to defend us but ourselves, and I cannot help but think you've been right all these many years. Your father and I. . .well, we've been so timid and afraid of the tongues of so many people."

He rose again and a rush of pride went through him. "I will go then."

"My darling son." Her eyes slid closed, but a tiny smile moved her lips. "You are the courage your father and I could only ever dream of."

<hr>

Every eye beheld her. They had faces like those she'd seen in the flow of the stream. They had dresses like all the trees had worn, when she'd pretended they were her friends and danced before their leafy branches. They had colors and shapes and fans and feathers, just like the pictures she'd studied a thousand times.

Her chest throbbed so fast it made them blur. Out of so many people, where was the only one familiar?

The thick blond hair. The eager eyes. The firm jawline and half-tender smile.

Lord Gillingham patted the hand that was looped around his arm. He hadn't shown affection since her arrival, and the tense touch made her long for Captain's natural ones. "You are doing well, Eliza."

As they entered farther into the large saloon, with music already rising softly, the hum of conversation started back into the room. "Where is Mr. Northwood?" she asked.

"He will be here."

"When?"

"You needn't worry. Shall I get you a glass of the lemonade you requested?"

She nodded, even though she would have much rather kept him at her side. The second he was away from her, a round-bellied man sidled next to her and grinned. "I am Bishop Dibdins, Miss Gillingham, and may I just say what the rest of us are thinking? You are the picture of exquisiteness. We are all so very glad you are returned home, safely and soundly, and looking as perfect as your mother always did."

"A shame about her mother," said a woman, as she approached with a purple turban and dress. "We all feel a little peculiar coming here, I think, having not been invited to Monbury Manor since before her death."

Why had she allowed Lord Gillingham to leave her like this?

"Miss Gillingham, what a necklace," said another. "You must be very happy to realize such wealth is at your complete disposal."

"Oh, pray tell, but where have you been all these years?" This came from a new woman, whose dress revealed more bosom than anything else and whose fluttering fan kept swaying her long black ringlets. "I must confess I have heard the most monstrous tales. Talk of you being whisked away to some horrid little hovel in the woods. Oh, pray tell, this isn't true, is it?"

"No." The word escaped breathy. "It wasn't horrid at all."

The woman gasped. "Then you *were* taken to the woods like a common gypsy? You poor girl."

"Excuse me, ladies, gentlemen." Lord Gillingham pushed through the gathering circle and pressed a glass goblet into her hand. "I see you have met the bishop and his wife."

Both Mr. and Mrs. Dibdons or Dibdins or whatever they called themselves nodded.

"Quite impressive daughter you have here, my lord. Puts me rather in mind of her ladyship, eh?"

"She is much like Letitia indeed." Lord Gillingham made more excuses and guided her away from the pressing group. "Everyone shall dance for now, and halfway through the night, we shall all partake of the banquet being prepared."

Her eyes had no place to rest. They moved from foreign face to bright color to moving figure, over and over again. Every time someone met her eyes, she was afraid. Every time they started for her, a panic swelled.

"You are displeased."

She shook her head. "It is. . ." Overwhelming? Frightening? Where in heaven's name was Felton?

"Never mind. I shall not leave you alone again." Another small pat. "Would it trouble you were I to introduce you to some acquaintances?"

"No. I do not mind."

"Most of them are Tories, and they've come all this way from London just to attend. I know they are most impatient to meet you." She was whisked away on her father's arm, introduced to gentleman after gentleman after gentleman, then finally urged into joining the set with one of their sons.

The dance passed in a blur. Too many steps she couldn't remember. Too many times she did the wrong thing, making her partner clear his throat and blush in humiliation. What was she doing here? Why had she ever agreed to such a thing?

By the time the dance was finished, more and more ladies stared at her behind ivory fans. Even her partner, who had been charming and eager at first, made only a short response and quickly left her side. She was alone in a sea of madness. Where was Lord Gillingham?

She spotted him on the opposite side of the room, still talking back and forth with the gentlemen he'd introduced her to. She couldn't go back there. She didn't want to. She wanted to pull the pins from her hair and tear out the jeweled bandeau. She wanted to rid her skin from the haunting touch of her mother's dress and yank off the tight slippers suffocating her feet and—

There.

Everything stopped, all the insane thoughts, as her gaze latched onto the man striding into the ballroom. Felton Northwood. Dressed in black tailcoat, tan pantaloons, and knotted cravat. How quickly his eyes found hers and stayed, as he weaved around couples and pushed his way through clusters.

Then he stood next to her, eyes smiling, and made all the chaos settle down with his confidence. "Excuse me, miss, but I am looking for a young girl named Eliza Gillingham."

Her heart warmed with the humor. "I hardly know where she is gone myself."

"I think I see her still." Why did it seem when he looked at her that he saw deeper than anyone else could? She couldn't look away and she didn't want to. Such haven was here, a safety in the orbs of his eyes—but it was more than that.

She just didn't know what.

His hand took hers and squeezed. "Have you danced?"

"Yes."

"And?"

"Take me away from here. Please, I cannot bear a moment more—"

"We are just in time to join the next set. Come."

"No, Mr. Northwood, I—"

"You have had your lessons. There is no reason you cannot dance." He pulled her with him, until they took their places four and a half feet apart, just as he had taught her in the library. They bowed. The dance began, just as the other had, and she pushed through the motions with tears.

Only every time her hand landed in his, something stirred. She made mistakes just as before. She was uncertain just as before.

But he never looked away, or frowned, or blushed, or cleared his throat in aggravation. He only smiled. How wonderfully it sent a shiver through her being, in a way that dancing with a tree never had in her life.

Perhaps a ball was not so terrible after all.

⚬⚬⚬

She had eyes like none he'd seen before.

Throughout the dance, then afterward as Felton stood beside her along the back wall, he kept being drawn there. Into her bashful glances. The sweet, doe-like shape of them. The fascination and the innocent fear that was all starting to seem so dangerous and addicting.

He couldn't breathe without taking in rose water. How insufferably irritating. Was it the dress—seeing her this way, looking the lady, beautiful enough to make any other woman lacking? Or was it the fact that as she stood here, she kept her hand in the crook of his elbow and smiled up at him every minute or two?

He almost pulled away, wandered outside, and took his air from the earth and not from her. The music was making him no better than the half-sprung fools who were drooling over their lady-loves throughout the room.

Amusing, that. Him calling the rest of them fools when he was the greatest one himself. What did he think it would do to his reputation to court a child like Eliza Gillingham?

She was tormented. Stubborn. Unlearned and unrefined and

incapable of everything he wanted in a wife. He had no intention of settling for such a fate. Enough was against him already. If he ever espoused himself to anyone, it would be a well-bred, well-respected woman like—

Miss Haverfield. He pulled his arm away from Eliza so fast he almost apologized. But he didn't. Just kept his eyes pinned on the golden-curled woman who sashayed toward them, dangling her wrap from a dainty wrist and already casting a smile his way.

"Well." The blue eyes glittered. "How lovely to see you again so soon, Mr. Northwood."

He bowed.

And cringed when Eliza mocked his movements. Gads, had no one taught her to curtsy? Or told her never to—

"La, what a funny girl." Miss Haverfield's giggle escaped. "Tell me, Mr. Northwood, wherever did you find such a little creature?"

Creature?

"Or could this be the lost Miss Gillingham everyone is so delighted to see returned?" Her head tilted, her smile brightened, and she leaned forward and kissed Eliza's cheek, as if in penance for the earlier unkindness. "I am Miss Haverfield, but you must call me Penelope. Wherever did you get such a gown?"

"From my mother."

"Truly? Then you are a brave girl. I would never wear anything *my* mother wore, not with the way fashions change these days." She leaned closer. "My dear, may I be so bold as to tell you something dreadful? You must have stepped on your hem, for the net is torn. Everyone has been talking of it, but I simply could not pass by you and say nothing."

Eliza's gaze dropped to the hem. Pink burned her cheeks.

Then Miss Haverfield's amused smile turned back on Felton. She took his arm and motioned toward the formation of couples preparing for the next dance. "Shall we, Mr. Northwood?"

Dance with the squire's daughter? Before everyone? Had she forgotten him to be the rogue of a Northwood everyone despised?

If she had, he wouldn't be the one to remind her. Returning the smile, he swept away with the squire's daughter on his arm—but glanced back once.

Eliza Gillingham stood stiff and red-faced, with her torn hem and her unmodish dress and her eyes he could fall into if he gave himself half a chance.

But he wouldn't.

Not on his life.

<hr />

She needed Merrylad. Someone familiar, someone kind, who would not jerk away from her touch or whisper of her or abandon her.

A lump knotted at the base of her throat. What sort of friend was Felton Northwood? That he would leave her when she needed him most. That he would say no word of defense against Miss Penelope Haverfield's belittling sweetness. That he would, in the end, be as ashamed of her as everyone else.

She glanced at Lord Gillingham.

He'd been watching her all evening, whether proud or embarrassed she could not tell, yet now he was engaged in a conversation that had his full attention.

Good. Mayhap he would not see her leave.

With every step she hurried for the door, the lump in her throat enlarged. Some smiled at her as she passed, though their expressions lacked warmth. Others curtsied or bowed—who knew when to do which? Bishop Dibdins, from his position near the door, leaned from the wall and started to speak to her.

But she rushed past him without answer and never so much as heard what he said. The dark halls blurred, as she navigated her way outside to the stables and slipped into the smaller building of the carriage house. Why did they have to lock up such a harmless dog anyway?

Merrylad had never been locked anywhere in his life.

But then, neither had she.

She weaved her way through the darkness and carriages, then found the little room on the leftward wall. "Merrylad?"

The beagle met her as she dropped to her knees. He whimpered his happiness as she muffled her tears of unhappiness. They were lonely, the two of them. Even with everyone here and all the people she'd ever dreamed of...they were more alone than during the quiet days of the forest. What was she going to do? How long must she stay here and suffer?

From outside the room, the carriage house door creaked open. Lord Gillingham must have seen her after all, must have followed to offer another pat and smile and inquiry on how the ball seemed to her.

She brushed the hay from her dress. She would tell him everything was lovely. What else could she say when he'd been so kind?

But he'd want her to come back inside. And do it all again. And sit down at the banquet and talk with the fat bishop or dance with men who thought her unbearable—

The quiet footsteps halted outside the room.

"My lord?" Her voice faded back into silence. Her blood drained. No, this could not happen. No one could have known she'd slip out here tonight, that she'd run for the carriage house, that she'd be here alone.

God, help me. If she tried to slam the door, whoever was there could grab her. If she left it open, they'd grab her anyway. The window. Yes, the window. She whirled and pressed her palms to the splintery wood, but it wouldn't budge and—

Movement behind her.

Something hard slammed into the back of her skull and made her collapse into the musty hay. *No.* Everything black, dizzy, as rough fingers seeped into her hair.

Then a bark, a growl, and the fingers loosened with a curse.

She scrambled to her feet and ran. Gasping, she threw herself against the tall carriage house doors, but they were locked and the footsteps were already coming again. *Please.* Blood dripped down her neck, as she collapsed to her knees and crawled along the perimeter of the wall. She bumped into something round. A wheel. A carriage.

Merrylad whined.

Then silence.

A man's breathing filled the room, loud and deep, raspy. The footsteps hurried as if he'd spotted her—

She lunged up and threw open the carriage door, climbed in, and slammed it shut. Seconds later it jerked back open.

Giant hands reached in for her.

Her scream rent the carriage. She kicked at the hands, but her slipper fell off and he seized one of her ankles. Jerked her forward. Grasped her by the hair again and yanked her back out.

Pain exploded, as he shoved her body into the wall and lowered his hands to her throat. *No, no, no.* Too dark to see, but his eyes held hers. Luminous. Wide. Bulging, as he squeezed tighter and tighter and banged her head a second time. A third time. A fourth time, until she couldn't see anything and she couldn't get air and the pain dulled into numbness—

Someone shouted, but it sounded so far away.

Help.

The hands must have been gone, because she slumped to the ground and laid motionless. No one came for her. No one touched her or hurt her or helped her.

God, please. Merrylad. She dragged herself forward with her elbows, felt her way to the little room where she'd last heard his growl. She had no strength to call for him and it was too dark to see. At the edge of the threshold, she waited.

If he could, Merrylad would have come for her. He would have licked her face or whimpered or barked for help.

But he didn't.

The room was silent.

No. Please no. She curled her legs to her chest, wrapped her arms around her bloody neck, and wept. Whoever had tried to kill her should have finished what they started. How much easier to die than bear this too.

Because if Merrylad was dead, so was she.

CHAPTER 7

Felton followed the expressionless manservant into the hall. "What is this all about?"

"Be it far from me, sir. Young Curry is—"

"The stable boy?"

"Yes, sir, he—"

"What the devil does he want in the middle of a ball? He should be asleep by this time."

"I hardly know myself, sir." When they reached the entrance doors, the manservant pulled them open with a word that Curry awaited him outside.

Felton jogged down the wide stone steps, night air cooling his hot face. If he had known what was good for him, he should have stayed by Mamma's bedside instead of traipsing off to a ball he didn't belong at. True, he had danced with Miss Haverfield. The squire had scoffed and the ladies had whispered and the ugly red-headed gentleman had stiffened in indignation—all of which brought pleasure.

But his dashed temptation had gotten the best of him. Like a raging fool, his eyes had kept returning to the very place he'd left, that back wall where the beautiful little chit no longer stood. Why had she run off like that? Had he injured her by leaving her side?

Of course he had.

He'd known it was wrong all along, but he'd done it anyway. For the sake of his name. For the sake of how it might benefit a Northwood to dance with a Haverfield. For the very sake that he'd waited years to earn smiles and attention from the squire's daughter.

Had he even heard a word she'd spoken? Some sort of talk about millinery shops and what Miss Withycombe did to Miss Chilcott that caused such an uproar between the two otherwise amiable souls. Matching hats or matching gowns or matching something—the nerve, she'd said—as if one had done the other some terrible crime. What did it deuced matter if every lady in the world wore the same hat?

Dash the ball and all its rotten nonsense.

Dash every millinery shop there was.

Dash everything.

"Mr. Northwood." Young Curry, with his gangly limbs and cropped black hair, met Felton a few yards from the stable. The groom, Mr. Timbrell, came ambling after him with a lantern.

And a gun.

Unease spiked through Felton's irritation. "What goes on here?"

"The c–carriage house, sir," said Curry. "Oy didn't know what to do, oy didn't, and oy was affrighted to send for his lordship on account o' all the guests. But you be his friend, Mr. Northwood, 'nd oy was thinking you could tell him—"

"Tell him what?"

"That Curry 'ere caught a thief sneakin' about in the carriage 'ouse." Mr. Timbrell dropped the gun at Felton's feet. "I shot him."

"What?"

"Curry 'eard the noises first, and I done sent 'im down to see what commotion the likes o' that dog was into. By the time I came outside, some stranger was goin' after Curry 'ere with a knife."

The old groom's eyes moved to the carriage house, and he out-stretched his lantern until the glow barely illuminated the double, red-painted doors.

"Any idea who he is?"

"No," said both in unison. The threesome approached.

A long body was sprawled with his face down, fingers half dug into the ground, with a pool of crimson already widening on the back of his oilskin coat. "What was he doing in the carriage house?" Felton asked.

"Trying to steal one, oy'd say." Curry pried open one of the doors. "Making a terrible lot of noise about doing it though."

"Tell him about the lock, boy."

"Yes, Mr. Northwood. He done locked it too from the inside, so oy had to use the key 'fore oy could get in."

"Give me that light." Felton took the lantern and stepped into the tall-ceilinged building. The soft orange glow spread over the line of carriages, the hay-scattered flagstone floor, the stairs leading to a second story and the open door on the left wall.

Something stirred.

Then a noise, half-muffled, like—

A woman. Eliza. He ran for the sound. How had he not known? The dog. Timbrell said the dog was kept in here. Where else would Eliza have gone when she left the ballroom?

Dread throbbed in his stomach as he reached the door with a small figure curled before its threshold. "Eliza." He bent next to her, set the lantern aside, and touched her shaking shoulder.

She jumped and tried to scoot away.

"Eliza, hold still. It is Felton." He slid one hand behind her neck. Blood. The feel of it, scent of it, shivered panic through his limbs. "Curry!"

"Yes, sir?"

"Go for the doctor and make haste. Timbrell, go indoors and inform Lord Gillingham."

"Yes, sir."

"Merrylad." Her head fell onto his shoulder as he pulled her into his arms and rose. "Merrylad. . ."

"The dog is well." He hoped. He prayed. "Be quiet now and I shall take you to your chamber. You are safe. Can you hear me?"

No answer. Was she too afraid or without consciousness already?

He hurried from the carriage house, stepped over the body of the man who had hurt her, and ran for the manor with her arms dangling limp and weak.

He had failed her.

He had brought her here, promised to protect her, and failed a second time. In the name of heaven, were that man not already dead, Felton would have ripped him apart and bashed the filthy blackguard into oblivion. He'd fight the world if he needed to.

But this couldn't keep happening.

By all that was holy, it could never happen again.

***

Lord Gillingham wore the look again. The one he'd worn as he'd entered her chamber a few nights ago, with untidy hair, with the dress of his wife draped across his shoulder.

Now he sat next to her bedside. He said nothing, only stared at her, with his lips half open and torment in the moisture of his eyes. With movements so slow she might have escaped them had she wanted to, his hand reached out.

The caress settled on her cheek, brushed back her hair.

She closed her eyes. He was a stranger to her, yet it brought her comfort. Maybe only because she imagined it was Captain instead, with his twinkling eyes and his familiar smile and the laugh she missed so much it hurt.

Merrylad, Merrylad. The doctor had come and gone and told her the dog was fine. Mrs. Eustace had assured her as much. Even Minney, who'd entered for a minute or two, had promised the animal was well.

But she didn't believe them. They didn't wish to upset her, or make her sad, not when she was so injured in other ways. Why had she let them keep her here?

Everything was her fault.

She should have run away. She should have been brave. She should have done as any heroine in Captain's stories would do and forged her own path back to home and freedom.

"I am sorry." The words struck the air like a discordant note. Lord Gillingham's hand withdrew from her. "I am sorry." What did he mean? That he was regretful someone had attacked her again?

But no, it was more than that. His words meant something, something vital, only she didn't know what. Why was he having so much trouble meeting her eyes?

Too quickly, he rose to his feet. He dismissed himself without words and quit the room, and a strange silence fell in his wake.

So much of her body hurt. Her scalp where the rough hands had pulled. Her neck where the bruising now swelled. The back of her skull where she'd suffered so many strikes. Why? Why must someone want to kill her? Didn't they know she remembered nothing? Couldn't they see that if she'd known who killed her mother, she would have already told?

More tears leaked free. Always tears. She was weary of grieving. *I'm so afraid, my Savior.* Of this manor and its memories. Of Lord Gillingham and the strange way he looked at her. Of the beast and the brutal pain when he clawed, and clawed, and clawed her all over again.

Her bedchamber door creaked as it eased back open. This time, Felton Northwood leaned in.

She turned her face into her pillow and closed her eyes. She had no wish to see him. Why should she?

All her pain linked back to him. She'd been happy before he ruined her life. Hadn't he done enough without bothering her now? Why didn't he go downstairs and find the golden-haired woman he was so fond of dancing with?

Quiet footsteps padded across the floor, and his presence loomed over her. Something lowered onto her bed. A whimper. A brush of soft fur and the wet, rough scrape of a tongue against her neck...

Merrylad. More tears unleashed as she pushed herself up, wrapped her arms around the animal, held him against her, and shook. *Merrylad, my sweet. My sweet.* Without meaning to, she glanced up at the man who had delivered her dog.

He stood rigid, beagle hair on the black tailcoat, with eyes that seemed more unsure of himself than she'd ever seen them before.

As if he wished to ask how she felt but didn't know how. As if he'd been afraid for her but didn't know how to show it. As if he wished to make up for everything but had no other ideas than carrying up her beloved dog.

She didn't want to forgive him so quickly. She had no wish to count him a friend again when he had so easily forsaken her downstairs.

But she had no heart to do anything else. Something vulnerable flickered in the way he looked at her, a strong sense of caring, and it made her reach out her hand to him in silent gratitude.

He grasped her fingers, squeezed, smiled, and reached over to scratch the ear of her beloved dog.

He was forgiven for everything.

Felton stood braced in the threshold of the chamber. The one he'd only entered once. "Mrs. Eustace said you were here."

"Mrs. Eustace can go to the devil."

Felton flinched. The man by the window, with both palms against the glass, was not the same Lord Gillingham who Felton so often saw behind the chessboard. Indeed, the man was a stranger.

Perhaps had a right to be.

"I know you are aggrieved, my lord, but no one could have foreseen—"

"I did."

"What?"

"I foresaw it and Captain Ellis foresaw it, but you brought her anyway." The palms curled into fists. "And now she will perish like her mother."

"She will not. I will not let her."

"You fool."

"My lord—"

"Get out of here, Northwood."

"Not without you. There are people downstairs and the banquet is waiting, and if you do not show your face, you shall be the latest on-dit for who knows how long—"

"Get out of here!" Both fists plunged through the window. Glass shattered. Blood slashed across the viscount's hands, but he only grasped each side of the curtains and shook. "God forgive me."

For what?

Slowly, he released the curtains. He turned long enough to glance into Felton's face. "You forgive me too, my son. The day has been trying. I shall have Mrs. Eustace see to the cuts, then will join the guests downstairs." With a nod of composure, he hurried from the room.

Felton lingered longer. He didn't want to approach the window, not with the cool night air rushing in and the stain of blood still fresh on the glass.

But he edged closer anyway. He placed himself where Eliza stood tangled every night, and he fought the same terror she'd battled so many years. He knew her beast. Maybe he'd known him all along, just in different ways, and had suffered the same cutting claws.

Someday it would all be over. Eliza would remember and be safe. Lord Gillingham would forget and heal.

And Felton would be respected.

For once in his life, there would be no shame.

Three days passed in bedridden agony. If Mrs. Eustace found out Eliza had left her chamber, despite the doctor's orders, more than Minney would suffer a lashing tongue.

But Eliza would do as she pleased. She always had in the forest. How many times had she snuck out in the middle of the night, crept to the stream without candle, and sat on the Lady's Throne to watch the moonlight on the water?

The blue light flickers were moon tears, she used to pretend. She'd read in books that the moon was a man, but she couldn't believe it was so. Anything so lovely must have been a woman. A sad, lonely woman in a sphere of blackness, who shed light tears onto the earth because not even the stars would befriend her.

Captain had known of her nonsense. He'd never forbidden her from any of it, not one silly whim or ridiculous play.

Back then, she'd been free.

And safe.

In all the times she'd tramped through the forest at night, or weeded through thick growth and thorns, she'd never been afraid. Now everything was different. The shadows frightened her. The noises unnerved her. Even now, as she followed Minney up the attic stairs, a sense of foreboding sliced through her. How long was she going to continue like this?

She needed to leave. She needed the cottage, the forest, the stream. Why couldn't she make herself? Why did she stay? Was it for Lord Gillingham—because the little girl inside of her still remembered a father she used to love? Or was it for Felton?

"Are'ee sure'ee will come?" At the top of the stairs, Minney pivoted for the second time. Her twisted face tightened with uncertainty. "I wanted to show'ee for a long time, but I was afraid'ee wouldn't want to come."

She mustered a smile, despite the lingering throb of her head. "Of course I wish to see it."

"I have pretty things. Pretty things. Ye want to see all of them, right?"

"Yes."

With a comforted smile, Minney led Eliza down the narrow attic hall and showed her into a small servant chamber.

The walls were white with no windows, and the wooden-framed bed sported a colorful quilt. Above the bed, several faded ribbons were tied in bows and nailed to the wall, as if in attempt to brighten the room. On the other wall hung. . .

The tapestry.

Eliza stiffened.

"The ribbons were my mamm's. She wore them in her hair. Papa said she did. I wish I had pretty hair like'ee."

Nothing made sense, but she moved forward anyway. The tapestry was small. The ends were frayed. But the picture. . .how well she knew the picture. The faded, floral border. The birds and the clouds. The trees on each side, both bending toward the center, as if to shade. . .

The beast.

He looked the same as he did every night. Part human, standing on two feet, some skin and some fur—yet with teeth and eyes and claws of a lion.

"Ye like it, my picture, Miss Gillingham?"

She took one step back. "Where did you get it?"

"Mine, mine. Mrs. Eustace said it's mine because his lordship, he didn't want it no more."

"Where did it come from?"

"The nursery. That's why he don't like it no more. He don't like the nursery. I know he don't. Ye like the picture, though?"

How could this be? The nightmares had started in her mother's chamber. With the red draperies. The window. But why should she keep seeing the beast—who'd been hanging in her nursery at the time?

The throbbing intensified. "Minney, I—I want to go back to bed."

"I can keep the picture, right? Ye don't want it, do'ee?"

"No. . .I don't want it." She never wanted to see it again in her life. All she needed was to get out of this room. Away from this place. Away from everything. "Y–your room is lovely, Minney. Thank you for showing me." She whirled to leave.

"Miss Gillingham?"

At the door, she turned and waited.

The girl's eyes grew misty. "Ye watch'eeself. Ye watch well. People die. Some people die in this house. And other places. Miss Gillingham?"

She clasped her hands to stop the tremble that rushed through her. "Yes?"

"I don't think'ee can trust the ones'ee think'ee can."

Mr. Josiah Hodgetts.

The name stayed with Felton, as he tied his horse before the wattle-and-daub shack and hurried up the weeded path. He rapped on the gray-splintered door.

And waited.

Just like he'd waited three days since the man was killed, so there would be ample chance for the burial, so the widow and her children could mourn without any more questions. Doubtless the constable had already peppered them with enough.

But the constable wasn't looking for the same answers Felton was.

The door cracked open an inch or two, and the eye of a three- or four-year-old girl peeked out.

"May I come in?"

The crack closed again. Why hadn't he used a more soothing voice, or at least smiled to ease the child's trepidations?

He knocked a second time, and this time the door was opened by a painfully thin boy, around seven or so. "Who're ye?"

"Felton Northwood. I am come to see Mrs. Hodgetts, if you please. May I come in?"

The boy frowned, wiped snot from his red nose, and jerked back the door. "I'll get me mam."

Taking off his hat, Felton entered the room whose walls bore grime and cobwebs. The windows were glassless. The floorboards gritty. The only furniture was a couple wooden stools, an empty cradle, and a crudely built table in the corner by the hearth.

The boy motioned his sister to a pile of rags, then tested the knob on a closed door. It must have been locked. He tapped twice and whispered, "Mam? Someone's come."

No one answered, so the boy backed away and stood in front of his sister, arms crossed, as if to protect her from whatever threat Felton might pose.

Several minutes later, the door burst open. A man came out first, wearing but shirtsleeves and stained buckskin breeches, with greasy hair strung into the eyes that couldn't meet Felton's. He rushed out the door without saying a word.

Mrs. Hodgetts emerged next. Had he seen her before? Perhaps the woman who had yelled into the Jester's Sunlight at an ill-behaving husband? She was as worn and rawboned as her son, with messy brown hair cascading around hollow cheeks. Her skin was so pale the only color in her face was the blue-tinted circles beneath both her eyes. "Wot ye want wif us?"

He switched his hat to the other hand. "I am sorry to come. I am sorry to disturb you at all, but—"

"Go ahead and tell the likes o' everyone wot ye saw today." Her thin arms hugged each other. "Find out any'ow, they will, and wots I care wot they fink of me?"

"Mrs. Hodgetts, I didn't come for—"

"Don't ye call me that." Her nose wrinkled. Her chin raised. "Call me a lightskirt or the devil 'iself, but don't call me that man's name. Dead now, ain't he? Three days an' his body ain't even cold. . .and already his missus be 'aving someone else in his place." A dry laugh left her lips. "That's wot ye're thinkin', eh, mister?"

A burn of unease worked through him. Dare she talk this way before the children?

"That's right, mister. Say nuthin' like the righteous fool ye are. . .but I gots rights to do wot I do. And I'm goin' to keep on doin' it too. I'll not see me children starvin' or let them take us to the work'ouse. Already lost one child, I did. But ye fink he cared?" She stumbled toward the cradle. Hunkered down beside it. "Six weeks ago. . .that's 'ow long since the baby died. And he didn't even cry. Didn't come to bury it neither. If I 'adn't told him, who knows if he would have noticed it was gone?"

Felton glanced at the children across the room. The boy had his head down. The little girl had fallen asleep in her rags. What kind of man was their father that he should be so hated in his own household?

And what did it have to do with Eliza?

"Wot ye want?" the woman said again. "Say it and leave us. And if me husband owed ye money, ye can take the clothes we wear 'cause that's all we 'ave left." She glanced at the bedroom door. "That and scraps for the gossipmongers."

"I want to know what your husband should have against Eliza Gillingham."

"Who?"

"Eliza Gillingham, daughter of the viscount of Monbury Manor. Your husband tried to kill her." He paused. "Twice."

The woman's face stayed bent over the empty cradle. "I don't know nuthin' about that. 'Sides, the constable said he was thievin' in the carriage 'ouse."

"He was strangling Miss Gillingham to death."

"Tried it on me too, he did. He was always like that. Hitting on me—or the boy there. Are ye done?"

"No. Tell me more about your husband. Where did he work?"

"He didn't. Not towards the end."

"What did he do?"

"Be hanged if I know. Gots to where he didn't come home more'n a night or two a week. He was always there at the Jester's Sunlight. Drinkin' away my children's bread. Killin' my baby." Her voice choked, and she wrapped her arms around the length of the cradle. "Get out of 'ere, whoever ye are, and leave us alone."

"He had friends at the alehouse, didn't he?"

"Out. Get out."

"Five or six or seven of them. One called the Swabian. Men who'd beat a lone man in the dead of night to get what they wanted—"

"Yes!" She bounced to her feet and slammed her body into the wall. She hid her face. "Yes, yes, yes, he knew Swabian. And they killed. And stole. And lied and cheated and loved on their trollops, the lot o' them." Sobs escaped, half muffled with her bony hands, so loud that even the little girl awoke and began to whimper. "And they...they..."

"They what?"

"Curse the Swabian for what he did to my Josiah. Curse him for livin' and breathin' and ruinin' everything. Curse him for makin' me bury my baby."

Felton took one step closer. "Please, Mrs. Hodgetts. What did he do?"

"He gave my husband. . .opium. He put the devil in his soul."

<hr />

"How do you feel?"

Eliza sat across from Felton in the drawing room, idle needlework in her lap. *Feel?* Like a bird she'd once seen caught in a thicket, with injured wings, with little black eyes that seemed frantic and afraid. She'd tried to set it free, the little thing. She'd crooned, and smiled, and moved slowly enough so the winged creature might trust her.

But it hadn't, and she'd thought it such a fool.

Now she was the bird. The fool too—whether for trusting too much or not enough, she didn't know. Pressure hammered at her temples, but she'd grown used to the headache.

She hadn't grown used to Minney's words. How they'd stayed with her, making her half afraid every time her father spoke a word, making her tense now that Mr. Northwood had finally come to visit.

Making her sick in the bottom of her stomach.

She didn't want to believe it was true. Not of the two people she'd come to believe in. Even if she did wish to leave, to flutter her wings and fly free of the thicket herself, no part of her wished to go with the knowledge that one of them had betrayed her.

"Well?"

She swallowed. "I—I feel mostly recovered."

"Good." He tossed his hat to one chair and lowered into the one adjacent from her, but he only remained sitting a moment before he rose again. He seemed distracted today. Uneasy. Guilt-ridden, perhaps?

No, no. Why couldn't she let it go? Minney was mad. What

could she know about who Eliza trusted or shouldn't trust? No truth dwelled in such nonsense.

Felton was her friend.

Lord Gillingham her father.

She would not allow some haunting warning from a mad child make her doubt. They had been kind to her and good to her. They cared about her, both of them—didn't they? Or had Captain been right? Was there only cruelty and hurt and deceit in the people of this world?

"The whole thing is a deuced mess." Felton raked both hands through his hair. "I understand none of it."

She watched his face—the smooth features, the intense gaze, the muscle in his jaw that seemed to flex with concentration. "Yesterday I went to the home of the man who tried to kill you."

The pounding grew. "Who was he?"

"A rogue of a husband. An opium smoker too. And I have reason to believe he is one of the men who attacked me in hopes of discovering your captain's hideout."

How did that make sense? 'Twas true Captain had enemies, yes. But what would those enemies have against her? How could it possibly connect with the night her mother was killed?

"What are you thinking?" He moved in front of her chaise lounge and bent next to her. "Tell me."

"I don't think'ee can trust the ones'ee think'ee can."

Over and over.

"They have no heart, love." Captain's voice. *"Not the ones out there. Trust no one outside of these woods. . . ."*

Dare she? Could he read in her face how close she was to bolting and never coming back? Or was she only fooling herself? Did she even possess such courage?

She grasped the needlework in her hands and pushed the needle through the fabric so she wouldn't have to look at him. "It is nothing. Only. . .tell me of Minney. The servant girl."

"What about her?"

"Is she. . .is she very mad?"

"That is what's troubling you?" A smile leaked into his voice. "You need not be afraid of her. She is harmless and more child than anything else, I think."

"I am not afraid. I only wondered."

"Which is just what Mrs. Eustace does not wish to happen. She is quite afraid the child will be a stain on the lily-white reputation of Monbury Manor. As if it were lily-white to begin with."

"How did Minney come to stay here?"

"Her father was the steward many years ago. Lady Gillingham must have had something against him, though I don't know what, for she asked Lord Gillingham to dismiss the man."

"But Minney said he. . ."

"Yes. He was outraged at first. Took his daughter and left. The next week, they found him hung outside the inn window, where he had been staying with his daughter."

"How terrible. How utterly terrible."

"I remember well because it was the very next night when your mother was killed and you were taken."

"Could they—"

"No. There is no connection. The constable investigated at the time, and Mr. Bradshaw's death was indeed one of suicide. He even left a goodbye note. Minney would have gone to the workhouse or an insane asylum had not Lord Gillingham brought her back here. He has seen to her ever since."

"Very noble of him."

"Very unnecessary of him, thinks Mrs. Eustace." A smile split Felton's face. "But then again, it is well Mrs. Eustace does not always get her way, eh?"

Despite herself, she returned the smile. Only something didn't feel right. The coincidence of it all. Minney's warnings. Two deaths so close together and Lord Gillingham's unnatural desire to help a child he had no duty to care for. What would make him do that? Was he the one she shouldn't trust?

Her only security was being torn from her. She needed to leave. She must.

But the nausea in her stomach churned faster, because she knew she wouldn't. All these days, she'd been preparing an escape. She'd imagined going out to the stables in the dead of night, stealing one of the horses, galloping away before anyone could stop her, and braving the long journey home with her head held high.

In all of the stories she'd pretended of herself, she would have done just that.

Yet she couldn't. She knew she couldn't. Twice last night she'd dressed and crept to the bottom of the stairs but made it no further before she rushed back to her chamber. A child. A craven child. She was trapped like the bird, with no choice but to trust the ones in her thicket.

"Come." Felton seized her hand, startling her with the quickness of his movements. "Do you have a bonnet or something? Never mind. I quite forget sometimes you have lived your entire life in some dark and forsaken wood." He dragged her through the drawing-room doors, but she halted in the hall.

"What are you doing?"

"You said you felt well, did you not?"

"Yes, but—"

"You do not appear well. And if your ailment is not physical, it must be the lack of new air and sunshine. I intend to see you get both."

Before she had time to decide if the idea frightened or calmed her, they were seated together in one of Lord Gillingham's curricles and passing through the wrought-iron gates. Would she ever be able to escape these gates on her own?

The farther they went from Monbury Manor, the quicker her stomach settled. The road was narrow and dusty, filling the air with a light brown fog. Trees stood on each side of them. They were green, playful in the salt-tasting breeze—and sometimes along the way, they stretched close enough to touch each other and form a leafy archway.

If she could but live out here. If she could but disappear into one of those trees, climb to the top, and be left alone to dream heroic dreams.

No more disturbingly familiar manor.

No more father she didn't know.

No more strangers trying to hurt her, or bothersome warnings she didn't understand, or desperate waiting for a captain who wouldn't come for her.

No more cowardice in herself.

"The sea." Felton turned the curricle off the road and up the uneven, grassy hill. Near the top of the rise, he jumped down, left his hat and tailcoat on the seat, then opened his hands to her.

Uncertainty spread through her. Why was she more afraid of his hands helping her down than of the fact he may be the one plotting against her? But did she really believe that of him?

He cupped her elbows. She held his shoulders. Then she was in the air by his strength alone, and though her nausea was gone, a new flutter disturbed her stomach. One she couldn't understand.

Or maybe did.

"Come." Another definite command, as he grasped her hand and started off through the tall, sandy grass. Why was he always telling her what to do? Pulling her this way, tugging her that way—and yet why did she almost *want* to be pulled and tugged?

"There." At the crest of the hill, they stopped. "Look at it."

The endless line of blue met with the bluer mass of sky. How the waves glistened and rippled and lapped to shore. How wonderful all of it smelled—for though she'd always imagined the beach this way, she'd never thought about the heavy scent of salt, seaweed, and fish.

They moved down the slope, slipping through warm sand, then raced for the frothy tide.

Mischief transformed his face into more boy than man. "Take off your shoes."

A laugh spilled out. Maybe her sanity with it. She glanced up the beach, where a few miles away, vessels bobbed in the waves or drifted to and from the port. Down the beach a few feet, a shaggy man stood knee-deep in the water with a fishing pole in one hand

and a bottle in the other.

Mrs. Eustace would scold her for this, lest someone see. But what did it matter if all of Lodnouth saw her in stockings? What did anything matter at all?

She took off her shoes while Felton took off his. He reached for her hand again. Together, they crept into the ocean until the cool water swished back and forth across their ankles. He splashed the air, then tugged her deeper, then turned them sideways when a forceful wave struck their middle. Wasn't this the sort of thing she'd always wanted to happen? Standing in the ocean vast, with someone handsome and noble next to her?

Only she didn't know if Felton Northwood was noble, or if she only wanted him to be. Was it wrong to pretend such things of people, even if she didn't know them to be true?

From the corner of her eye, she saw him smile. She wanted to ask why, what thought had made him so happy. . .but she didn't.

Instead she smiled too, breathed this new air he had prescribed, and squeezed the hand engulfing hers.

You are wonderful. The thought, the insanity, made her dizzy. She should be praying for an escape. She should be figuring out what to do. She should be wishing she were at the forest.

But she wasn't. She couldn't.

If only for a moment, she was happy, and she trusted the man beside her—and all Minney's warnings were as lost whispers in the salty wind.

If only she could stay here forever. Like this. With him.

Then she'd never be alone or afraid again.

Felton watched until Eliza ascended the stone steps. She turned once, lifted a hand to him, then disappeared inside. Exactly what he wanted to do. Disappear.

"Take care of the horses, Curry."

The boy was already unhooking the tack. "Oy will, sir. Won't you be stayin' for a game o' chess with his lordship?"

"Not this eve." Nor any time soon. The boy looked puzzled, but Felton merely nodded goodnight and made fast pace in reaching the well-worn, dusky path. How much longer it seemed tonight. How quiet. As quiet as Eliza had been when he'd first taken her to the beach, when she'd stared at the water as if it were golden instead of ordinary grey-blue.

He shouldn't have taken her into the waves. Why had he prodded her to take off her shoes, to wade with him into the salty spray like unsophisticated children? What would people think if they saw?

More whispers, doubtless. More stains on the name of Northwood.

But dash it all, it'd almost been worth the risk. To hear her laugh as she did once or twice when he'd splashed her. To take her up to the sandy place he often came alone. To sit next to her and watch the different expressions come over her face.

Fondness, when she told him of the time Captain had brought home a beagle pup. Then eager interest, as he pointed at various luggers, gigs, and schooners and named every one of them. By and by sadness, when she spoke of the baby named Thomas. Or compassion, when he mentioned his mother's illness.

Then happiness. For no reason at all and only because she looked at him.

He'd responded without meaning to. Something had tugged deep inside him, a flare of intensity. . .of attachment.

This was not going to work. This was not going to happen. He had one goal, one purpose—and that was to prove that Richard Northwood did not murder the viscount's wife.

No room existed in those plans for Eliza. Maybe for her memory, her nightmares, her assistance in reaching his goal.

But nothing else.

He sprinted back home, reached the stables panting, and saddled his horse. By the time he rode to the cove, night had already fallen, and the world was aglow in moonlight.

He waited for close to an hour. Miss Haverfield had mentioned she would come. Indeed, she had practically promised she'd be here when he last spoke with her at the ball. Was it just another empty tease?

He was ready to turn back for home when he spotted a horse approaching along the water's edge. He recognized the erect posture, the flower-decked riding hat, and the riding crop held in one of the girl's hands.

When she neared, her smile flashed in the moonlight. "You surprise me, Mr. Northwood. I told you I would come yesterday, yet you never deigned to show."

"Was it yesterday? I thought it today."

Her mouth formed an O. Then another smile. "Not very flattering, that."

Had she no idea how many times he had waited at the cove, only for her not to arrive? Not long ago, this has been his only pleasure. His only diversion from clearing his father's name.

Now it was his diversion yet again.

Only from something else.

Someone else.

As if she sensed as much, she sighed and tilted her head. "I do not feel much like riding tonight, Felton." Now it was his Christian name? "Shall we stroll instead?"

"I should rather ride."

If his refusal irked her, she showed no sign. Instead, she nodded gracefully and moved her horse first. He followed behind, and as they reached the water's edge, he trotted beside her while they followed the curving beachline.

Once, a year or two ago, she'd kissed him at this very cove. 'Twas the most encouragement she'd ever given, aside from a press to the hand or a charming whisper in his ear.

How he'd marveled and grinned and been so proud of the kiss from the squire's daughter.

Strange thing, that.

All Eliza had done was smile at him this afternoon, without so much as a touch—and it had made a thousand disrupting emotions march across his chest. Indeed, it made Miss Haverfield's kiss of little importance. Made everything of little importance, for that matter.

But he could not think this way.

He had a name to think of.

A name that was much too soiled to risk soiling further.

The collars of his carrick coat stirred in the wind as Bowles paced along the secluded edge of the shore. There she went again. In the blue tints of moonlight, the black sails of the *Marywich* billowed with wind, a near replica of the *Red Drummer*, aside from the ornate carvings on her bowsprit.

Marywich wouldn't go down though.

Not with a man like Captain Sherwen at the helm. He was old, yes. But he asked no questions, drank no ale. . .and took no smokes of the opium contraband they'd be loading from India and unloading in China.

That was more than could be said for Ellis.

But Ellis was not a problem. Not anymore. Filthy devil, he'd almost been worth the twenty-two men who had perished in the Atlantic. Who else would have taken the Gillingham girl that night?

How amusing. . .the look on the drunken captain's face when Bowles had burst into the man's hidden chamber and thrown down the child. "See this, Ellis?"

Ellis had scrambled from his makeshift bed on the floor, vomit on his gaping shirt, his gaze hazy and tormented. "What. . .what is this?"

The little girl had curled herself on the dirt floor. Sounds filled the room. Stupid, whimpering child. If someone had waited for him, let him do the thinking, this would never have happened.

Now everything was going wrong. And who was called upon to resolve things?

He'd jerked out his silver blade knife. "Since you do not mind taking lives, Ellis, I thought I might bring this little task to you."

The blood drained from the captain's face. "No."

"It is the least you can do for a man who has hidden you so well, do you not agree? I shall even relieve you from your discomfort if you comply. A smoke perhaps—"

"No, no." He stumbled toward the child, tossing away his tankard. "No more. I'm finished."

"You cannot live without it."

"I'll be dead then."

"Indeed you shall if my men ever get their hands on your bloody throat."

"Let them. I don't care. Don't matter anymore."

"Good. Have one more night of rest, then, and I shall throw you out of these quarters in the morning. What sport the men shall have with you." He breathed a laugh. "I almost think it would be amusing if you lived through such an experience. If not though, it might be equally amusing to use your head on the bowsprit of our next ship."

The words didn't seem to affect the captain. He only stared, wiped his wet mouth, and waited over the child.

"Well, if you have not the stomach for it." With a curse, he groped for the child's ringlets and jerked her up. She screamed, the captain stiffened—but he sliced off a chunk of her hair before either of them could stop him.

"Don't. . .don't hurt the child." Pathetic whine. "Leave her alone."

"She has seen too much, I fear. There is no alternative but to kill her. That is, unless you wish to take her—"

"No, I be wantin' no part of it."

He slid the blade across the child's arm. Twice. Blood filled her white sleeve and her hysterics rose another octave. He raised his knife again—

"Stop it!" Ellis' shaking hands rushed into his hair and the terror made tears leak down his cheeks. "Stop it. . .please. I'll take her. I'll be doin' anything you say. . .anything, only don't—"

"Kill her like you killed our crew?" He sheathed his knife, tossed the child forward, and waited until Ellis swallowed the girl in his arms.

With silent shudders, the child buried her face into the man's wrinkled neck and clung to him. Pitiful, the two of them. Why either of them should be left alive made no sense.

But he couldn't make all the decisions. Most, but not all. The one in charge wanted the girl alive. This was the only way.

"There's a coach waiting outside. Put on this cloak and get out of here—and if I ever see either of you again, you'll both be paying for what you've done."

Now, as he left the shore in the moonlight, he fought a smile at the irony of it all. Ellis should have let it end there, the fool.

Because they were both dead anyway.

Well, almost.

CHAPTER 8

She waited for him to come again.

Like some sort of childish girl, Eliza peeked through windows, looking out to the front gate of Monbury Manor instead of the courtyard wall. What was wrong with her anyway?

Over the last three nights, there'd been no nightmares.

Only dreams.

Strange, warm, comforting dreams—of playing in the ocean and holding a strong hand and talking with a handsome prince in a quiet place. Had she been so deprived, all these years, that a few hours of attention should render her so senseless?

"There you are."

Eliza jerked from the drawing-room window at the house-keeper's tight words. She smoothed both hands down her dress. "Is something wrong?"

"Aside from the fact that you roam about this house and do nothing all day, no." Keys jangling at her side, Mrs. Eustace moved to a vase and rearranged the purple scabious flowers. "Minney tells me you have been asking about the graves."

She'd been asking Minney many things. Questions about the warning, what it meant, who Eliza shouldn't trust—and why. But the girl only shook her head and found reason to excuse herself. Why would she not say more? Too afraid?

"Well?"

Eliza refocused on Mrs. Eustace's face. "Yes, I asked about my mother's grave. I wish to see it."

"Why?"

She hardly knew herself. Only it seemed she *should*, that somehow standing by her mother's resting place would make the death more real. Not just something in her nightmares.

Mrs. Eustace snapped a stem and shoved it back into the vase. "From now on, if you have questions about something, you shall do well to ask me, not that mindless little chit. Anyway, come along. I have already related your wish to his lordship, and he wishes a word with you before you do so."

Eliza followed the housekeeper to the door of her father's study, waited until Mrs. Eustace announced her, then stepped into the room alone.

Lord Gillingham straightened behind his desk. "Eliza, do sit."

Why did every time she encountered him feel like the first? Would she ever get used to the deep voice, though always kind? Or the eyes, never harsh but always unnerving? Why did it always seem he saw her mother instead of the daughter long estranged to him?

When she didn't sit, he rose. "Mrs. Eustace tells me you wish to visit your mother's graveside."

She nodded.

"Are you certain that is something you wish to do?"

"Yes."

His gaze stayed on her as he moved around the desk. "Take a maid with you, and I shall have the carriage prepared. There were signs of rain this morning, but mayhap if you hurry, you shall be back before a decline of weather. I would go with you myself if I were not so indisposed with correspondences." He waved a hand to the letters scattered across his desk. "They are unceasing, I daresay."

Silence. The same silence that lingered over them through every breakfast meal, as they both ate and fidgeted and tried in vain to find topics to share with one another.

She thanked him and started to leave, but he stopped her at the door. He moved next to her, hesitated, then, "Your mother. . .she was always fond of pink roses. After she died, I had the gardener destroy them because I could not bear to look at them." He grasped her hand. "But when you returned, I had them planted again. Perhaps you might take a few with you. . .for her grave."

"Yes, I will." Then, tugging her hand free, she hurried from the study and sighed away the tension. How greatly he must have loved her mother.

Only why had he never laid roses on her grave himself?

By the time the carriage arrived at the churchyard, a slight rumble was already echoing from the pewter-colored clouds.

The footman helped both Eliza and Minney alight. "Shall I accompany you, Miss Gillingham?"

"No, we shall only be a moment." Eliza took the roses from the carriage seat. "But if the rain comes before we do, you must wait in the carriage. I would not have you rained upon."

The footman smiled, as if the consideration brightened his otherwise dull day. "Thank you, Miss Gillingham. That I'll do."

Arm in arm, Eliza and Minney passed through the lych-gate and into the churchyard of stone, moss-covered markers, and tomb chests. "Do you know where to look?"

"This way, Miss Gillingham." The girl quickened her pace. "Good thing 'ee brought me with ye, right? Ye'd never find it without me, would 'ee?"

"No, never."

Nearer to the rear of the church, Minney bent next to several headstones, read the inscriptions, shook her head, then moved on. Finally, she pointed to two sandstone markers, both with crosses adorning the top. "Here they be, methinks. I remember 'cause I come here sometimes. To visit Papa. Mamm's not here though. Still in Cornwall, she is."

Eliza bent next to the first grave. Tiny raindrops fell, as she read the inscription and epitaph, then left pink roses on the mound.

What would her life have been like just now if this grave were not here? If she'd always been at Monbury Manor, loved by both parents, comfortable in the ways of society? What would it have been like to have a mother? To feel that kiss, the one the woman in the bed had pressed to cheek, just as it happened in the hazy memory?

"And'ee brother." Minney motioned to the second one. "Don't'ee forget about him."

No, she hadn't forgotten. Maybe she had for all these years, but not now. She moved beside the second grave, traced her finger along the carved words. This was a part of her. The two lying here, dead to the world, were lost remains she had once loved with everything she knew.

But she had lost them.

And forgotten them.

And loved someone else. Now that someone else was lost to her too. Her dear Captain. Was that the way of life? Having, then losing?

"Miss Gillingham." The girl's bony finger jabbed into Eliza's shoulder. "Look."

Rising to her feet, Eliza scanned the graveyard. "What do you see?"

"Someone be here. I see'd them."

The drizzle turned harsher and all the gravestones took on a shiny gleam. Nothing stirred. "I don't see anything, Minney. Come, let us look at your Papa's grave—"

"No, no. Leave. Let's leave."

"But I thought—"

"Please, Miss Gillingham. I don't want'ee to stay. Something'll happen to'ee. I know it." With a panicky hold on Eliza's arm, the girl whisked her through the markers in the pelting downpour. They were near the lych-gate when Eliza looked over her shoulder.

Half-hidden behind a tomb chest, a cloaked man flashed out of sight.

Eliza's heartbeat thudded. They darted for the carriage and scrambled inside before the footman had time to help them. She would not let her imagination overtake her. Not this time. 'Twas probably someone who tended the graves. The vicar, perhaps. Maybe a local urchin boy looking to dig up a grave and loot a gold tooth or two.

Or was her imagination working against her now too, making her deny the obvious?

From across the carriage, with wet hair stuck to her cheeks, Minney's face twisted in fear and dread and all the things Eliza didn't want to admit.

Because whoever was in the graveyard had been waiting for her. As if he'd known she would come.

As if someone had already told him she was on her way.

This was an oddity.

Felton stole two glances right and left before he crossed over to the carriage house. No sign of Curry or Mr. Timbrell, but then again, the two were probably already abed for the night. Who wouldn't be two hours after dark?

Careful not to make much noise, he pulled open one red door and stepped into darkness. The door along the left wall was ajar, and a soft spill of light waited for him.

That wasn't the only thing waiting for him, either.

His heart picked up pace for reasons he didn't want to think about—let alone have. He was a fool for coming here at the hasten of a note. His secret trysts with Miss Haverfield were different. They were harmless and flirtatious and more pride-inducing than anything else.

But this. . .well, this was another matter.

And it unsettled him.

The door swung wider and the light began to move, until a small figure appeared in the doorway. She wore a dress any viscount's daughter would be proud to wear, only the hair was all wrong. Unrestricted and uncurled, it draped across her shoulders in waves that looked soft enough to stroke.

Never mind her hair, though. Never mind anything about her. "I received this." Pulling the note from his waistcoat, he followed her back into the tiny room.

"I didn't want to send it." She shut the door and motioned Merrylad back to a corner. Then she turned to Felton, eyes aglow in candlelight, with an expression he couldn't decipher. "I just didn't know what else to do."

"Something has happened?"

"At the churchyard. There was someone there. He was waiting for me."

"Did he—"

"No, he didn't hurt me."

"Did you recognize him?"

"No."

He frowned and forced his eyes to peruse the tack hanging on the wall. Not her face. "Something must be done. I have no intention of standing by as someone preys upon you. You told your father, of course?"

She bent next to her dog, left the candle on the floor, and rubbed the animal's ears.

He said again, "You told Lord Gillingham?"

"No."

"Why not?"

Nothing.

Gads, why did she keep evading questions? Why was he here in the first place—late at night, in the carriage house, as if they had something to hide?

He waved the note. "You said there was a matter we needed to discuss. What is it?"

"Mr. Northwood, I think. . ."

"You think what?"

She came back to her full height, and color flooded her cheeks. "Never mind. I am sorry to trouble you. Goodnight—"

"Eliza, wait." He seized her arm. "Wait."

"You are angry."

"Only because I am helpless. This is one thing I cannot fight, at least not yet. Now why have you not told Lord Gillingham about the man at the churchyard?"

"Because I think. . .I think he sent him there."

A cold fear unfolded inside him. He gripped her arm tighter, but only because he needed the touch. "What?"

She shrugged free of him. "I know Minney is strange, that she isn't like anyone else. . .but I believe her."

"You believe what?"

"That there's someone I cannot trust. Someone I *do* trust." Pleading eyes stared into him. "I even wondered if it were you."

The words stabbed something inside him—and it wasn't his pride. "Do you still feel this way?"

"I do not know what to feel."

"But you sent for me tonight."

"I have no choice. I've no one else."

He put distance between them as she hugged her arms. Silence stretched on. Then the tears he'd been waiting for flashed into her gaze. "I want to believe you more than anything. . .and trust you. I want to trust *him* too."

"Your father?"

"Yes."

"You can trust him."

"He knew I would be at the graves. He could have sent someone—"

"He would not have done that. He is no more the killer than my father is, and I would sooner think myself more capable of such a thing than to imagine Lord Gillingham trying to hurt you."

"I'm not imagining."

"Eliza—"

"You don't know. You don't know the way he looks at me sometimes, as if he sees someone else. . .as if I were my mother."

"Even I see your mother in you."

"You don't understand."

"No."

"And you do not believe me."

"It is too preposterous to believe."

She jerked around, covered her face with both hands, and said nothing.

He crept behind her and eased her to face him. Pried away the fingers over her eyes. Breathed in rose water before he remembered to stay away from the scent. "You are afraid."

She trembled beneath his touch. If only he could banish that fear. If only he could make everything go away. The danger, the secrets, the nightmares that plagued her.

"And I do not blame you." His thumb slid down her chin. "But these suspicions of your father. . .they cannot be true. You must forget them."

"And if you are wrong?"

"I am not wrong."

She stepped away from him and grabbed her candle. "I must go now before they realize I am gone."

"Eliza?"

At the door, she paused. "Yes?"

He didn't want to ask the question. Shouldn't matter anyway. "Do you truly think I could be the one behind the attempts to hurt you?"

Different expressions crossed her face. Hesitation, worry, then confidence with the slightest, shaky smile. "No. You are good and noble and brave, or so I've imagined you. Funny thing about me. Once I imagine something for so long, I start to believe it. I guess I've believed it of you all along."

The words shouldn't have meant a thing to him. What did it matter what she thought or believed? What was her good opinion against the rest of the world's bad opinion?

Nothing, that's what.

Nothing at all.

Only he grinned, grinned big, as if it meant much more than the world itself. For right then, it almost did.

Eliza stole back into the manor and removed her half boots at the door. They were much too loud for one attempting to not be heard.

Hurrying through the darkness, she touched her chin. Silly thing, but it still tingled warmly where his finger had rubbed. Why should it mean so much? Why had she sent for him at all?

Only she'd needed to.

She'd needed to see him after so many days without him. She'd needed to tell him what had frightened her, what she'd suspected, even knowing he wouldn't believe it to be true.

Maybe he was right. Of course he was. A father could not hurt his child that way. A father could not murder his own wife.

Not when he loved her so much. Not when he still ached for her touch and treasured her dress and hurt so much he couldn't visit her grave.

Halfway up the stairs, a bang cut through the quietness. Her heart jumped. A gunshot?

No, it couldn't be. She dropped the boots and darted up the stairs, ran for her bedchamber, and grasped the knob of her room.

Locked.

"Minney?" The word escaped, raspy. She'd asked the girl to come in secret, to wait for her here in Eliza's bedchamber so she might have help getting off her stays and dress. "Minney!"

From down the hall, a door opened and a sleepy-faced Leah rushed forward. "I heard a terrible noise—"

"This door. Can you open it?"

"Why, yes, Miss Gillingham." The girl disappeared through the same doorway, then rushed back seconds later with a key. She jabbed it in, twisted it, then swung open the door.

Eliza flew inside. Everything was dark except the moonlit curtains fluttering at the window. Had she left the window open?

"Minney?"

Something moved. On the floor. Under the window. . .the window. . .

No, no. From behind her, Leah screamed. Then ran. *No, no, no.*

She didn't want to be here. She didn't want to come closer, but she did. Just as she'd done at the other window, when there'd been a scream and her mother had broken the glass.

Shaking, she collapsed next to the girl lying face up. "Minney, can you hear me?"

The eyes were closed. The lips half-open, moving without noise. And her shoulder.

Eliza let her eyes stay there, where the circle of blood was already widening. Red, red, red. Why was there always red?

She hated red. She hated windows. She hated breaking glass and lions and claws and—

"Out of the way, Miss Gillingham." From behind, Mrs. Eustace's quick hands guided Eliza away from the body. "Over here, men."

One manservant hurried Minney into his arms, while the other peered out the window. "Looks like someone got a rope around the chimney. Used it to pulley himself up, he did."

"Well, gather more men and scour the grounds. Send someone else for the constable and doctor."

A blur of movement, a hum of voices, but Eliza understood nothing. She backed away to a quiet wall and clasped her face. Minney was going to die. She was going to die in Eliza's stead because Eliza had asked her here. She was going to be murdered, just as Lady Gillingham, just as Eliza would be, one way or another.

God, I cannot do this any longer.

She stifled a sob with her hands.

I cannot stay.

───◈───

Two days later, Eliza hovered over Minney and tucked the counterpane closer to her neck. She smoothed back the damp, frizzy hair. She reached for the hand and squeezed the cold fingers. How strange it was. That a face, once so unpleasant and ghastly, could seem so lovely now.

Minney was the injured daughter of the dreaded monster of the sea. All were frightened by her, for she bore the gruesome traits of the monster.

But Eliza had found her half drowned in the waves. When all the fish and birds and seafaring men had left her alone, Eliza had taken her into her own vessel and nursed her back to health.

She found something unexpected beneath the terrible face. She found a young and frightened and sweet and innocent child, who only needed a friend, who lacked only the kindness and compassion of others.

Eliza settled back into her chair and drew Merrylad into her lap. She banished the silly dream. Back in the forest, such a story would have comforted her—because the monster's daughter would have been strong again, and Eliza would have set her back to sea, happy and healed.

But dreams were not real. No good came from imagining them. This was not the forest, and no one was truly happy, and endings were never as lovely as Captain had always read them to be.

The attic chamber door came open, and Leah's head poked in. "Can I sit with her meself, Miss Gillingham? So tired, you look. You ought to rest."

"No, I am not tired." Indeed, the lack of sleep had been a solace. For two nights, she had evaded the beast. "But perhaps you might take Merrylad out of doors. I fear he may need out for a bit."

"Of course I will. Come along, boy."

Merrylad trotted after Leah, who had already won his trust with her small treats of food, and the room returned to silence when they were gone.

Minney stirred.

Eliza stood and grabbed the hand again. For the first time, the girl's thin fingers returned the squeeze. "Minney, sweet, can you hear me?"

She batted her eyes open, wide and frantic, then jerked up her head. "Papa?"

"Shhh, now. It is only Miss Gillingham." She brought a cup of water to Minney's lips, waited until the girl sipped it down, then helped ease her head back to the pillow. "Can you speak at all? Do you remember what happened?"

"It hurts." Tears streamed loose. "It hurts, hurts, hurts."

"I know, but try not to think of it. You shall feel better soon."

"Someone shot me."

"Yes."

"They thought I was you. I know they did. I was wearing one of your dresses. I didn't think it'd hurt. . .just to wear them, so pretty. . . I'm sorry. I'm sorry. I'm sorry."

"It was not your fault. You could not have known. And as soon as you are well, you may have any of my dresses you wish. Do you hear?"

The girl's eyes closed again and her breathing turned heavy.

Eliza returned to her chair. Exhaustion threatened her own eyes, but she forced them to focus on the ribbons above Minney's bed—not the tapestry.

She would not fall asleep.

Not in here.

Not with the beast staring her down from the old, frayed fabric hanging on the other wall.

⁓⊱⊰⁓

The tall dining-room walls, with all their ancient paintings glaring down on Felton, seemed different from other days. The table was longer. The air emptier. The clinks of silver and glass more alarming and discordant.

"I am glad you came."

Felton forked a veal olive, forced a smile. "Have I ever not?"

"Very true. You have been a faithful companion to me, Northwood, though of late you seem to be absent more than you are present."

How to answer?

"But never mind that. What say you to a smoke and game of chess after dinner?"

"Fine." Felton swallowed a bite, then washed it down with a drink of water. "How fares the servant girl?"

"The same."

"It has been nearly two days."

"You think I have not counted?" Lord Gillingham uncorked the decanter of Madeira. He poured a glass with bandaged hands. "Eliza will not leave her side. She just sits there beside the child. . . strokes her brow, reads to her, even keeps the dog present in hopes the animal's noises will bring Minney back."

"Maybe they will."

"Maybe not." Silence fell. Lord Gillingham leaned back in his chair, swished his goblet of wine, and stared into the liquid as if answers might be found in the swirl.

Tension made Felton's food hard to swallow. Eliza couldn't be right. 'Twas impossible. Of any other man, any other place, Felton might have trusted the instinct of Eliza Gillingham.

But not him.

This was a man who had laughed with Felton, so hard sometimes they were both wiping tears. Had taught him the difference between a bishop and a knight. Had read with him for hours by the library hearth.

Not that Felton had ever enjoyed the books. He'd rather run or ride or fight than read words from a page. But he'd come anyway, sat beside the older man, and read through volume after volume because Lord Gillingham was his friend.

His *only* friend.

Despite the suspicion of Felton's father. Despite what people whispered. Despite the hurt and loss of what he'd endured. Despite everything.

Lord Gillingham had believed in Felton. In all the Northwoods. He'd never turned his back on them. He'd been true and honest and infinitely good to them—and when something plagued Felton's mind, it was not his mother or father he ran to.

It was Lord Gillingham.

Even now, glancing up from his wine, the older man seemed to sense something. "It is her, isn't it?"

"My lord?"

"Eliza. She is the reason you have stayed away."

"That is not true."

"Isn't it?"

"My lord—"

" 'Tis no great shame, Northwood. It is not some mark against your manhood or dishonor upon your strength to fall for the heart of a woman."

"I have not fallen anywhere."

"No?"

"No." Felton scooted from his chair. "You know my desires were always set upon Miss Haverfield."

"Those were a boy's desires."

"And I suppose this is not?"

"No." Deep, slow. The older man's eyes held his. "No, Northwood. It is not."

"Well, I am certainly glad to hear you know so very much about it." Felton ripped the napkin from his collar and flung it on the table. "Excuse me, my lord, but I fear I shall not be able to stay for the game of chess. Duties await me at home."

"I see. Run home to your duties then."

Blood running hot, Felton turned for the door.

"And Northwood?"

He paused. "My lord?"

"If this is another matter of pride, you are a fool."

No other man in the world could have called Felton such a name without a fist landing in his face. But the anger drained out of him. A twinge of sadness, of guilt, raced into its place.

He half wondered if the viscount was right.

Instead of departing, he stopped a maid in the hall for directions to the servant girl's chamber. He clenched his fists as he made his way up the stairs. Why should the viscount's words bother him so? If there was truth in it, what did it matter? Why shouldn't he have high standards for himself and stick to them? Why shouldn't he want to be affianced to a girl from society's lap?

When he reached the door, he hesitated. Noises, faint and disturbing. Minney? Was the child feverish?

Without knocking, he pushed his way inside. The girl in the bed was motionless, noiseless—but not the girl in the chair. How strange Eliza looked, how pale, with sweat dampening the hair around her face. Pitiful sounds left her lips. First murmurs, soft and devastated. Then shouts, screams for help—

Felton raced for her and caught her face. "Eliza." He jerked her awake, shook her head until wild eyes stared back into his. "Eliza, the nightmares."

"No." Her breaths were short and panicked. "No, leave me alone—"

"Eliza." Another shake. This time he edged closer, sinking his fingers deeper into her hair as pity writhed through him. "You're watching over Minney. You're sitting in her chamber. You're safe."

"But the window."

"There is no window."

"The glass."

"No glass."

Tears leaked past her lashes and ran down her face, the cheeks colorless, then burning. "He's. . .he's going to kill me."

"I won't let him."

"You cannot stop him. No one can."

"I can stop anyone." Closer. "I can fight your beast. I *will* fight him." Shouldn't have come up here. Shouldn't be holding her this way, this close, with him inhaling her breath and her rasping in his. Like they were one. Like they needed each other's air. "You believe that?"

"I want to."

"Then do." He kissed her cheek, tasted the salt of her tears. How he longed to dip lower. To press against the moist, shaking lips. To drink of her, this girl of the woods, and forget a world that would scorn such a match.

But he backed away and escaped the chamber, still unsteady from the touch of her, still weak in the pit of his soul.

How easy it would be to love such a creature.

How easy to envision he already did.

CHAPTER 9

Eliza spooned more caudle into Minney's mouth the next morning. "Good?"

"No." The girl pushed away her hand. "No more. There be cinnamon in it?"

"Yes. Mrs. Eustace's own recipe."

"I don't be likin' cinnamon. Papa, he never liked it either."

"Well, imagine some good fairy made it with beautiful tree leaves and her very own tears. That's what I always pretended when Captain fixed something terrible." She set the half-eaten bowl back on the stand. "How do you feel?"

"I hurt. I hurt bad."

"I know."

"I wish I had Papa. I wish I had Mamm. Miss Gillingham?"

"Yes?"

"How come'ee stayed here with me? How come'ee didn't have no servant care after me?"

"Because I wanted to care after you myself. Just as the good fairy might have done."

"Why?"

"Because. . .well, because you're my friend, I suppose." She'd imagined the words would warm Minney, would make her smile or maybe laugh.

But they only made her cry, grope for Eliza's hand, and lean up—wincing and whimpering. "Miss Gillingham, ye'll die too. I know'ee will."

The words struck a chord of panic. Even with Eliza's back facing the tapestry, the beast's gaze speared through her. "Please, Minney, do not say such things."

"It is true. I know it. I know he'll kill'ee too."

He. As if the person were known. As if it were not some elusive, shadowed madman—but someone Minney knew. Maybe all of them knew.

"Leave, Miss Gillingham. If'ee leave, he cannot kill'ee—"

"Who?"

Her face turned into the pillow.

"Minney, who?" No answer. "Please, why won't you tell me?"

"I be afeared."

"Why?"

"Because. . .because he already killed my papa. And he already killed Lady Gillingham." Minney rubbed a fist under her eyes, smearing away tears, even though they only dripped faster. "If I say something to'ee, maybe he'll kill me too."

"But your father killed himself—"

"No he didn't. People only says he did. They believe it. I pretend to believe it too because I have to. I don't want to die. I don't want to die, Miss Gillingham. I don't want to—"

"Shhh, shhh." Eliza grasped the girl's face, turning her until the frightened eyes met Eliza's. "Please tell me. I would not expect such a thing of you, I would not ask it if it did not mean so much. You understand, don't you?"

"Yes. I understand. I'll tell'ee because'ee are my friend, right?"

"Yes."

"And I have to tell'ee because'ee think he's good. He pretends terrible much. But I know why he killed my papa. I know why he made us go away. When I was little, I didn't know. But I think about it. I think all the time. It must o' been because Papa loved Lady Gillingham, and even when Lord Gillingham sent us away, her ladyship still comed to see us. At the inn. She weren't supposed to do that, but he must have found out. He must have killed Papa 'cause Papa loved her."

Eliza's chest constricted. *No.*

"Papa wrote a letter to her. Then she comed to the inn. She talked with my papa, but I don't be remembering what they said. Then Lady Gillingham took me back here. I never seen Papa again because they said he hanged himself. Then Lady Gillingham died too. He must have been so jealous. That must be the reason he killed her. Isn't that why he killed her, ye think?"

"Then you're saying. . ." The words wouldn't come. "You're saying. . .my father?"

"Now he wants to kill'ee too. I knew he would. I prayed he wouldn't, but he does. Ye must o' seen him do it."

"No." It wasn't true. She'd ridden on his shoulders and been rocked in his arms, but she'd never seen him kill her mother. She would have known such a thing. She would have remembered. No one would have had to tell her, because she would have recognized her own beast and hated him.

But she didn't hate him. If anything, in a clumsy, childish way, over these past weeks she'd imagined she loved Lord Gillingham. How could this be? How was this true? All his kindness, all his tears, all his talk of loving his wife and daughter. All of it had been lies?

"The bedchamber. Just'ee go to yer mother's bedchamber, under her pillows. Look there, Miss Gillingham. Then'ee shul know."

She didn't want to know. Not now. How much easier to let the beast remain faceless, to pretend that even if Captain no longer wanted her, her true father was rejoicing to have her back.

She couldn't lose that. She mustn't.

"Excuse me." She left Minney's chamber before the girl could tell her more. She flew down the attic stairs. She sank to the bottom step and framed her face, breathing deep, torn between running to her mother's chamber or away from it. *What do I do, God?*

"I was just on my way to find you." Mrs. Eustace appeared over top of Eliza, hands on her hips. "You hardly look presentable. Indeed, you are more disgraceful than anything else. Staying up there in the hottest part of the house, nursing a lunatic who shouldn't be here in the first place."

The insults didn't matter. She hardly comprehended them.

"But all that aside, you must hurry." She grabbed Eliza's arm and hauled her up. "As surprising as it may be to both of us, you have a visitor."

<hr/>

"Mr. Penn, might I have a word?"

Stepping out of the local coffeehouse, the agent for all ships porting in Lodnouth greeted Felton with a small nod. "Morning." He checked his watch fob and continued walking. "Busy today. Very busy. Perhaps another time—"

"This will only take a moment." Felton kept pace beside him, though it wasn't a difficult feat considering the man was as rotund as he was short-legged. "I want to inquire about a ship that went down some fourteen years ago."

"Oh?"

"I don't know the name of the ship."

"Forget them often myself. What did they carry?"

"I'm afraid I don't know that either."

"Tsk, man. I told you I am busy. Come back with your inquiry when you have more answers to mine—"

"The captain was a Jasper Ellis."

"Oh?"

"Recognize the name?"

"Where did she go down? The ship, I mean." The man took another glance at his watch fob. "Dear, dear, it is almost eight. I am supposed to meet the squire and talk over—err, who did you say the captain was?"

"Ellis."

"Ellis, indeed. Now that seems a bit familiar. Sort of ugly thing, was he, with missing teeth? No, no, that would be my wife's father."

He laughed, breath reeking of strong coffee. "Now then, let me see. Yes, I remember. The ship was the *Red Drummer*. Went down about thirty miles off the coast after catching afire."

"What else do you know?"

"Not much. If there was any cargo aboard, it either burned, drowned, or was hidden from me. Everyone died but a couple men."

"The captain among them."

"Yes, seems I remember that. Odd thing, him living, when talk has it the fire was his own fault. Drunk or out of his mind or something, he was, when the tragedy occurred."

"Who was the other man?"

"Bowles something or other. Never trusted that man. I've nudged the customs officers in his direction more than once, but if smuggling goes on, they've yet to sniff it out."

"You think the *Red Drummer* was smuggling goods?"

"Hard to say. But sure as the devil, part of a broken mast washed ashore some days after the wreck."

"And?"

"The mast was black, that's what." The agent paused to catch his breath and straighten the lapels of his coat. "Only reason a ship wears black masts is to sail at night. To sail, that is, without being seen. Now does that sound like smuggling or not?" Without waiting for an answer, Mr. Penn yelled out to a hackney.

The carriage stopped in front of him, and mumbling about being late, he clambered in and rode away.

Felton wasted no time. He made inquiries twice—first to the garrulous blacksmith, then to the friend-of-everyone proprietor of the local inn. The latter of the two gave him what he needed. Directions to the home of David Bowles.

Christ, give me answers. The news ran through his brain, all the little pieces he knew, but it made no sense. Too much information. All unrelated. What did any of this mean? Had Captain been a smuggler? Then, when the ship went down at his own accidental doing, the other man Bowles had told others the vindictive tale?

No wonder Ellis had gone into hiding. Probably more than a

few angry men had gone after revenge. But still, how did he end up with Eliza? What good would she have done him? And how could the murder of Lady Gillingham possibly tie in with this?

When he reached the home of Mr. Bowles, he dismounted and looped his reins around a tree branch. The house was situated on the southern end of the village, with a well-trimmed hawthorn hedge around the perimeter of the lawn. The brick house was two stories, modest in all appearance, with two chimneys on either side of the roof and white-framed windows. Vines crept along the triangular doorway.

Felton rapped on the door. No answer. Didn't the man keep servants? If not a butler, then at least a maid of all work to greet callers? He was ready to leave when the door opened.

A thin, long-faced woman wiped wet hands on her apron. "Can I help you, sir?"

"I am looking for Mr. Bowles."

"He not be home."

"When will he be?"

"I don't know, sir. I—I never know such things." She ran a tongue across dry lips, as if unsure what to say next. Then, without looking at him, "Wh–who should I be telling him called, sir?"

"Felton Northwood. I shall return another day." He nodded his thanks and left the village. His rage mounted. Why was everything a dead end? Why did every lead take him nowhere?

Back home, he stabled his horse, then walked for the house. Next plan of action would be to talk with the man Bowles—if he could find him at home, that is. It was just possible Swabian and his men were involved in this too. A gang of smugglers perhaps, the whole lot of them. Would that explain the maid's apparent nervousness?

Perhaps Felton could have learned more from speaking with her.

"Oh, Master Northwood." Dodie rushed outside before he could open the door. "I ne'er thought you'd come. Just terrible it's been, rightly terrible, and e'eryone be cryin' and cryin' and—"

His breathing hitched. "What are you talking about?"

"Just dreadful, it is. I says to them, I says, 'Mebbe that letter be wrong', but they says, 'Go away, Dodie'. So I go away and I be watchin' for you, Master Northwood, 'cause you be knowin' always wot to do—"

"Where are they?"

"The drawin' room, Master Northwood. Hurry now, please."

He sprinted through the foyer, burst through the drawing-room doors. *God, please, no.*

His mother lay on the floor, curled in front of the fireless hearth, shaking her head against the Turkish rug.

His father bent next to her. He said nothing. No calming words of comfort. No dismissive, light-hearted change of topic. Just. . .nothing.

Fear slammed Felton in the stomach. "Papa?"

"Get him out of here." Mamma's wail. "Get him out of here!"

"Son, leave—"

"Tell me." He collapsed next to them on the floor. Groped for his mother's hand, as her tremble made its way through his own body. "Please." Choked. "Tell me."

They didn't have to.

He felt the letter, tangled between her fingers, damp with her tears. "Hugh?"

In answer, Mamma pressed the letter to her face. She bit through the paper, ripped it apart, spit it out onto the rug, and flung it away from her. "Get out of here. All of you. Get out, get out, get out. Let me die with my son. Let me die with my baby, my Hugh. . .in the name of mercy, let me die."

"Mamma, stop it—"

"Son, no." Papa waved a shaking hand. No tears glistened, but veins bulged in his forehead, and his eyes were wide and stricken. "Leave your mother alone. Please."

Felton bit on his lip so hard he tasted blood. He left the room, bumped into Dodie, ran past her and back outside. *God, no, no.* Couldn't breathe. He took the path to Monbury Manor, but only because it was alone and hidden. *Please, please.*

Bile rose through him. This couldn't be true. This wouldn't happen. Not to Hugh, young and brave and strong. Papa's pride. Mamma's baby. The letters couldn't stop because everything would stop. How would Mamma survive without the letters?

She needed them.

Papa needed *her.*

Felton needed them both. Couldn't live without them. Couldn't live without Hugh. How could this happen? In the name of heaven, hadn't they suffered enough?

He walked faster. Then ran. Then slammed himself against the stone wall and bashed his fist into the mossy rocks. *No, no, no.*

Not Hugh.

Couldn't be true. This was some mistake and the letter was a lie and somehow everything would be all right again. No Northwood could be taken down so easily. Couldn't be done.

Please help me. He sank along the stone wall and covered his face with his arms. *Christ, help it not be so. I beg of You.*

"You simply cannot imagine how pleasurable it is to see you again." Miss Penelope Haverfield smiled from the striped, wingback chair in the drawing room. She was one of the pictures come to life. The ones Eliza had studied and dreamed over in endless books and magazines.

Her hair was sunlight. Her teeth pearls. Her skin cream, eyes sapphire, lips roses. Not a hair was out of place, and not a wrinkle creased the satin of her pelisse and dress. She was everything a lady should be.

Everything Eliza was not.

Her eyes, glinting and mockingly amused, said as much. "Well, do sit down, my dear. I shall feel insufferably awkward if you don't."

"Oh." Eliza hurried into a seat. "Of course."

"I hope you do not mind my visiting."

"Certainly not."

"Good. It is only that I thought of you, poor dear, and wanted to be of help if I might." She pulled a small book from behind her reticule. "Fordyce's *Sermons to Young Women.* I presume you have not read it?"

"No." She left her seat long enough to accept the book. "Thank you. I read often."

"Do you? Why, what a surprise. From the way Felton talks, I was rather under the impression you were most naked of any sort of refinement."

Hurt nipped her. "He said so?"

"La, who knows? Someone certainly whispered the notion into my ear—but that just goes to show you, doesn't it, that things are not always what they seem."

Quiet settled into the room.

Heat suffused Eliza's face as Miss Haverfield's gaze traveled her up and down. From the hair, disheveled and loose down her shoulders. To the morning dress, crinkled and still stained where she'd sloshed some of Minney's caudle from the bowl. To her face, her burning face. Oh, why had the woman come? To scorn her? To scream, if only silently, that Eliza could never be a lady?

"I do hope we can be friends." The girl tugged at one of her white gloves and smiled again. "In fact, I cannot own to only visiting for the sake of bringing you a book. Other motives drew me." When Eliza did not prod her to share more, Miss Haverfield leaned forward. "Can you be trusted with a secret now that we are dear friends?"

"If your secret is terribly precious, perhaps you should keep it to yourself."

"La, but that's just it. I cannot bear to keep it in a moment longer, and as you are such a good friend of Felton yourself, you are the truest soul I might tell. You see, my father has finally agreed."

Eliza stiffened. "Agreed to what?"

"The courtship dear Felton and I have been waiting for all these years. Soon enough, we shall not have to meet in twilight hours, but will be free to accompany each other anywhere in the world. Is it not wonderful?"

Like wretched traitors, tears came to her eyes. Wonderful?

Yes, it was wonderful. For the girl he smiled at, or touched, or laughed with. For the one hearing his voice and knowing every word was meant for her. For the receiver of all his orders, his sweet beloved commands. Hadn't she known all along such a girl would never be her?

"My dear, you seem distraught. Surely this news can have no bearing on you." The eyes widened in anxious waiting. Then, more sweetly, "Can it?"

"No." Eliza rose. "No, it has no bearing on me at all." She half ran to the door, but stopped and turned back, book in hand. As if mere pages could teach her to be a lady. As if they could make a man like Felton Northwood want the likes of her. "And you can keep this." She tossed the book harder than she'd meant, for Miss Haverfield gasped and let it *clunk* to the ground. "I will not be needing it anyway."

She quit the room, ignored Mrs. Eustace when she reprimanded Eliza's speed, and dashed for the bedchamber that had haunted her the whole of her life. She shut herself in. Approached the bed. Wrapped her hand around the first bedpost she passed, then the second, then the third.

She didn't want to pry back the pillows.

Heaven knew she didn't.

But she ripped back the first one, then the second, and gathered together the folded letters underneath. She read the first one. *Forgive me, my Letitia.* The second. *I am sorry, Letitia.* The third. *Letitia, I wish you could forgive me.*

Then a fourth, in script bold and inky, *My daughter Eliza, I am sorry.* Every part of her hurt. 'Twas not the danger that injured her so much as the realization that Lord Gillingham wanted her dead. He had planned for her to be dead and was sorry for it, even knowing he would not repent of the act and spare his own daughter's life.

Just as he hadn't spared her mother's.

She crumpled the letters, every one of them. What did it matter if he saw? If he knew? If he followed her and ended her and tossed her out a window, as he'd done to her mother?

Captain had been right. She could not trust anyone. Not Lord

Gillingham with his pretended kindness. Not even Felton, with his pretended affection. Why had he awakened her last night? Why had he rescued her from her beast, and wiped away her tears, and kissed her with lips more soft and gentle than anything she'd known in her life? Did he kiss Miss Haverfield that way?

She might have stayed here forever. She might have made Monbury Manor her home, if only he could have been hers. If only she could have stayed close to him and dear to him. She might have been a princess and he the prince, in a story where each loved the other and both were happy.

But they didn't love each other, the two of them. Only her cruel imagination had whispered they had.

She left the bedchamber and didn't fight the beast when he followed her out. Let him cling to her the rest of her life. Let him claw her to death and hurt her more and terrorize every night of her life. She could do nothing to stop him.

Except run.

She went to her room and scribbled a note to Felton. Maybe it would never reach him. Maybe Lord Gillingham would find the note first and destroy it. What did it matter? Felton wouldn't believe it anyway. He wanted a killer, someone to shift the blame away from his precious name. But he didn't want that person to be someone he loved, or respected, or trusted. After all, what would that do to the pride he cared so much for?

Her eyes stung, ached with pressure, as she changed into a riding habit and pinned back her hair. If anyone asked, she was going for a ride.

But they didn't ask. She made it to the carriage house without seeing a soul, released Merrylad, then entered the stables.

The stable boy smiled and blushed and helped her into a saddle with not a question. He handed her the reins. "Sure oy shouldn't go with you, Miss Gillingham, for your ride?"

No. She shook her head without words, lest her voice betray her. She smiled her thanks, and it seemed to suffice, for the boy grinned, followed her to the gate, and waved her away.

Then she kicked the animal into a gallop. Wind tore loose her hair, dust billowed the air, and the soft colors of daylight blurred into a mass of green, brown, and blue.

She wept without sound or tears. *God, I'm so afraid.* Everything and everyone was lost to her. Endlessly lost.

The forest was all she had left.

Now all she had to do was make it there alive.

— ❦ —

"What happened?"

Felton took the damp cloth Mrs. Eustace handed him, waited until she left the library, then turned back to Lord Gillingham. "I could not go home like this."

From his chair by the bookshelf, the older man laid down his book and waited. As if he knew something was wrong. Something more than another fight.

Maybe that's why Felton was here. He should have come in the first place. Why had he ridden into the village like some sort of mindless, reckless fool?

He'd told himself he was going to find Bowles. Anything to distract from the grief. But instead he'd found that ugly redhead Miss Haverfield was always casting her eyes upon. All the man did was speak a few spiteful, jealous words—and next thing Felton knew, he was beating down on the freckled face.

"Who this time?"

"Scrope something. I don't know."

"The gentleman from Oxford?"

"Yes."

"Hmmm. Taking to fisticuffs with gentlemen now, I see? For one who wishes to restore his good name, you do much to sully it."

"I did not ask for lectures." Felton wiped the rest of the blood from his lip and wadded the towel. "I merely wished to get cleaned up before I returned home."

"You might as well stay for dinner."

"I cannot."

"More duties to attend to?"

"Yes. More duties."

The viscount nodded, picked up his book again, and resumed reading.

Felton couldn't move. His legs wouldn't obey him. He wanted to walk out of this library, with its deep colors and warm smell and familiar silence, and bear his grief as a solitary man.

But he couldn't. He stayed, squeezing his hands around the bloody towel.

"What is it, Northwood?" Lord Gillingham spoke without looking up. His voice was deep again. Because he knew. He always knew.

"Hugh is dead."

"When?"

"The letter came today."

Silence, but it was soothing. Like something cool and soft over something hot and blistered. Wasn't that always the way of it when he came here?

"Sit down, Northwood."

He took the seat opposite Lord Gillingham, leaned forward, and faced him. "Mamma wants to die. This is going to—it is going to kill her."

"She may be stronger than you think."

"Or weaker."

"And your papa. How will he manage?"

"As he manages everything else. Pretending it does not exist, talking of anything else, throwing himself into cares of little consequence. But if he loses Mamma too. . ." The sentence died away unfinished. A knot swelled in his throat.

Lord Gillingham nodded. "You bear many worries upon shoulders so young, Northwood."

"I can handle them."

"Yes, Northwood, I think you can. For though they be young,

they are strong shoulders indeed. You know why?"

"Why?"

"They are Northwood shoulders."

The lump grew.

"And your parents. Their shoulders are Northwood too. You have forgotten that, have you not?"

Yes, he'd forgotten. Of course he had. How long had he been carrying a burden that should have belonged to all of them? That *did* belong to all of them? Now that a new burden was upon them, should he not trust his parents were strong enough to shoulder the weight?

"Now." Lord Gillingham opened his book again. "What say you to dinner?"

He came to his feet and smiled despite himself. Why did the viscount always have the wisdom he needed? How was it the older man always knew what to say—even if it wasn't always what Felton wanted to hear? He was a tonic, Lord Gillingham. A tonic and a friend. "Yes, my lord. I suppose my duties can wait."

"I thought they could."

"Only I must speak with Miss Gillingham first. I wish to tell her a bit of news I discovered this morning."

"We have left her undisturbed today, for I hear she has quite exhausted herself over the care of Minney. Your news shall not take long, I trust?"

"I will be but a moment." Felton left the room and headed to Eliza's bedchamber. The weight in his chest had lessened.

He would be all right.

Indeed, all of them would—because Lord Gillingham spoke truth. They were Northwoods. Just because they had lost one of their own did not mean they would fall apart now. Hugh wouldn't want that. He was a fighter. Whoever killed Lady Gillingham fourteen years ago is who made him one. Who else could be blamed for this? Hugh would have never joined Wellington's troops, would have never rushed off to fight foreign battles, if there had not been a more severe battle at home.

The one that made all the ladies deny a courtship to any Northwood. The one that made them whispered of, laughed at, and scorned by every common villager. The one that made Mamma sick and Papa isolated and all of their childhood marred with guilt and shame.

Yes, this was another thing Lady Gillingham's murderer had taken from him. His youngest brother. But such a killer would pay. For everything. One way or another.

I vow it to you, Hugh. He took the last few steps two at a time. When he reached Eliza's door, he tapped quietly with a fist. A sore fist. "Eliza."

Already, his heart pumped harder. Why should that happen to him every time? As if he couldn't control his own emotions. As if she had more power over him than he did himself.

"Eliza?" He pushed open the door. Probably shouldn't have. After all, Lord Gillingham told him she'd been resting.

But when he stepped inside, the bed was empty. Unrumpled. The only chair was empty too. Had she gone back to sit with Minney?

He approached the stand by her bed. How strange it felt, being here, alone in a room she was wont to inhabit. He touched the Bible, then one of Playford's dancing manuals he'd told her to read.

Half tucked under a pillow on the bed, a flash of white on the pink counterpane caught his eye. He unfolded the paper and read the ink that seemed shaky and hurried. *My father is the one you seek, Mr. Northwood. Whether you can believe me or not, he has deceived us all. I beg you not to come after me, for I can never return now. I never want to. Thank you for the ocean. I shall always remember.*

CHAPTER 10

Felton burst into the dining room, the note in his fist. "She is gone."

Lord Gillingham froze, and the maid serving a steaming platter of beef and potatoes nearly spilled her dish. As she winced and left the table, the viscount stood, his face devoid of color. "Gone where?"

"The forest."

A groan rumbled out. "I should have known this would happen. How long?"

"I hardly know."

"I shall have my men and horses prepared and set after her at once. If we ride fast and hard, perhaps we shall catch up with her before any danger—"

"I go alone." Sweat dampened the note in his grip. The note that burned fires of doubt, of uncertainty through all the trust and respect he'd always held for this man. What had made Eliza run this way, even knowing the danger? What had so convinced her of her father's guilt? Had he been wrong not to listen to her?

"Northwood."

Jaw clenched, he forced his eyes to Lord Gillingham.

The older man stretched out his hand. "Let me read the note."

"I cannot."

"Why?"

"For the same reason I must go after Eliza alone." He left the dining room and its nauseating smells, aware that the viscount dogged his steps. At the door, he turned. Pain surged its way through their stare.

"You are not bringing her back, are you, Northwood?"

"No." How could he when she was so afraid? What right did he have to pull her into danger a second time? How could he hope to protect her when he didn't even know who to trust?

"Perhaps it is best this way," said Lord Gillingham.

"Perhaps."

"She was happy in her forest."

Felton nodded, pulled open the doors, and made it halfway down the stone steps when the viscount called out to him, "Do not bring back the note."

Felton glanced back up at him, as the older man's features contorted, and his voice lost volume. "Burn it or shred it or leave it with my daughter—but do not bring it back. I should never like to know what made her run from me."

Enormous loss burrowed into Felton's chest. If only he could have been spared the note himself.

Back in the forest, Eliza had wandered into the pines at night—catching fireflies, dancing in the moonlight, listening to the stream rush by in the magical darkness.

But this was different.

Bumps raised her flesh as the horse plodded deeper into the blackness. How quiet everything was. So quiet that every snap of a twig or flutter of wings in the air made her heart kick faster. *God, please protect me.* From the men who wanted to kill her. From the night, with all its disconcerting noises and shadows.

And from herself.

Because in all the hours she'd been running away, the hurt had been running after her. Like vicious poison, all her memories of Monbury Manor were sickened. How could she ever think upon her father without seeing death in his eyes? How could she ever remember Felton without imagining the glorious Miss Haverfield in his arms?

Eliza shook her head, dismissing the fog of approaching sleep and tired thoughts. She reached down to rub her horse. She must leave it all alone. She must be brave, and she must press on, her and Merrylad, with no thought of what they had left behind.

After all, in a few days, they would be home.

Everything would be well again in the forest.

⸻

Bowles glided his fingers down the harp-lute strings as his parlor filled with music. Only during these morning hours, when he played undisturbed from the turmoil beyond his house, did some of the pressure leave his being. He felt celestial. Like a seraph.

Or a god.

Behind him, the squeak of a door disrupted the lulling music. He cursed and turned.

"I'm sorry, sir. I—I'm terribly sorry." His maid of all work entered, hands wrung together, eyes already lowered to the rug. "I don't be meaning to come and bother you when you be playing—"

"Pray, what is in your pocket?" He approached her, amused when she stiffened, and snatched the paper from her apron pocket. "A letter?"

"Only f–from my daughter, sir. She l–lives in Devonshire, she does, and I was just—"

"Reading when you should have been working?"

"Oh no, I wasn't, sir. I wasn't truly, I—"

"Enough." He ripped the letter in two. Then in four. Then in six. "Now, Miss Reay." He stuffed the shreds back into her pocket. "What was so important you wished to bother me?"

She bent her head. "Th–the Sw–Swabian, h–he wants to—"

"Speak up!" He backhanded her face, but she never moved or cried or shrunk. He had taught her well. "He wants what?"

"To s–see you, sir."

"Now?"

"Yes."

"Then by all means, Miss Reay." He turned her for the door. "Send him in." He reseated himself at his harp lute and was halfway through the intro of a second song when the Swabian cleared his throat.

Bowles never so much as looked back. "You know I detest you coming here. I despise dirty boots treading upon my rugs."

"This couldn't be waiting for another meeting."

"Well, well. News indeed."

"The girl ran away."

"Oh?"

"Tall Postle heard from one o' the Monbury servants."

"Where?"

"The market. This morning."

"I see." Bowles positioned his fingers lower on the harp lute. "And did such a servant mention where the little girl has run to?"

"To Ellis."

A smile slid up his face. "To Ellis, indeed." He picked the strings and a melody of charming victory filled the parlor. "Then you must see that our little Miss Gillingham joins her captain as quickly as possible."

<hr />

Felton rode through Poortsmoor, then the village of Weltworth. At both inns, the proprietor had shaken his head and insisted that no such girl had stayed there.

The little fool. What had she done, ridden through the nights? Had she even brought food?

A reoccurring pain squeezed through him, as he urged his horse faster down a countryside road. She'd flown without telling him. Had she trusted him so little that she couldn't ask him for help? Had her care for him been so small that saying goodbye meant nothing to her?

She'd never forget the ocean, said the note—but he didn't care if she forgot the ocean.

He just didn't want her to forget *him*.

A sigh filled his lungs, and he dragged a hand across his chin. Never mind such thoughts. They were as nonsensical and unwise now as they'd been before she left.

This would make it only easier.

Not having to see her. Or smell rose water. Or hear the voice that sounded more like a chorus of angels than anything else. By this evening or perhaps sometime during the night, he would reach the cottage. He'd make certain she was safe. He would see to it no one had hurt her.

Then he would speak the goodbye that so obviously meant nothing to her. He'd go back to a world where his name was still in shame and his only friend could no longer be trusted.

But the truth was, he didn't want to leave Eliza Gillingham at all.

God, thank You. Her horse took his first step into a sphere she'd never imagined she'd see again. The trees were taller than she remembered. How fondly, how kindly, they all shivered as if in welcome. *Thank You, thank You.*

Feverish joy breathed through her as the cool, piney air rustled her hair. Sunlight slanted through dark green branches. Sap oozed and dripped from knotty holes. A rabbit scurried across the dry, orange pine needles and disappeared into a thicket.

Never had she dreamed what this would feel like. Coming home. Treading back over ground she'd danced on and spotting trees she'd talked to and breathing air she'd lived on.

The deeper she entered the forest, the more familiar the landscape grew. Her cares took wings and flew away. Nothing mattered because everything would be the same again. She had nothing to fear. Not here.

Merrylad barked in excitement as the stone cottage became visible through the trees. How perfect and unchangeable it always was—with its gray, round stones and small chimney and thatch roof covered in greenery.

Breathing fast and grinning, she climbed off her horse and motioned Merrylad not to make a sound. She would catch Captain unaware, while he was stirring at his black cauldron or reading from his Bible.

Then she'd laugh.

He would pause, whirl around, and blink away tears at his little girl returned. How wonderful it would be when he grabbed her into his arms, squeezed her, and turned her in circles as he'd done a hundred times over.

She tried the knob on the door and eased it open without a creak.

A smell hit her like a blow. Something pungent and rotting and sickening. No fire glowed in the hearth, no smoking cauldron, no drying herbs on the table or flowers in the pottery vase.

She gagged and covered her mouth with her elbow. *Captain?*

Merrylad trotted to the doorway of the only other room in the cottage. The door was ajar, waiting for her. How many times had she bounded through that threshold? The little bed was in there, where Captain always tucked her in and read her stories. She knew every inch of it, every stone in the walls, every plank and crack in the old wooden floor.

She didn't want to enter now. Nausea churned her stomach as she edged closer and the smell grew worse. *Savior, help me.*

She pushed at the door, but it thudded against something. Merrylad squeezed inside. She leaned her head through.

A body. Captain's body. Red on the floor planks, red on the clothes, red on his face.

She stumbled backward and covered her eyes, but the sight stayed with her. His caving, rotting features. The discolored skin. The dried slash across his neck and the hole at the base of his throat. *No, God, no.*

Bile surged through her and emptied onto the floor. He wasn't dead. No, he couldn't be dead because all this time he'd been waiting for her. He was supposed to be sitting at the hearth. She was supposed to laugh. He was supposed to spin her.

No, no, no. She raked in air, the repulsive air, and vomited again as she bumped into a wooden chair. Merrylad whined and darted from the cottage. On legs that had no feeling, with eyes a blur, she chased after him and escaped the stone walls that used to shelter her.

Now there was no shelter. No hope. No home.

Captain was dead.

Someone had killed him. Someone was going to kill her too. The forest wasn't hidden anymore, and the trees couldn't protect her, and nothing would ever be the same.

She was alone.

Bereft.

God, please. Please help me. She ran for the stream, splashed through the shockingly cold water, and climbed atop one of the mossy rocks. Her body wracked. She squeezed her knees to her chest and listened to the water rush away, rush away, rush away.

I'm going to die. She needed Captain. She needed him more than anything. She needed him to keep on living—because without Captain, she had nothing left. No one left.

Please.

All she wanted to do was die.

━━━⊱✿⊰━━━

Darkness fell over her like a shroud. No moon lit the sky or glistened in the stream, not in the way she'd always loved before.

If only the blackness could stay. If only it could hide her. If only her eyes would never see and morning would never come. What was morning?

She didn't understand. She hated morning. She hated the early sun and the pink sky and the rising fog. She hated new things. Everything new.

All she wanted was the old. The lost. The father who had raised her; the cottage that could no longer be home; and the stories long asleep, never to be whispered to her again.

Without tears, she eased back and forth on the rock. *Please, I need Thee.*

Because she couldn't think. She was cold. Cold like his body on the floor. Cold like the blood, dry and red. Why was there always red?

She hated red too. She hated it more than anything.

Help, help. She tore off her riding boots, the ones Mrs. Eustace told her proper ladies wear. The stream took them away. Then her stockings. If only it could take her away too. If only it could sweep her back to the ocean, swallow her into the waves, tug her under gently and lovingly to the place where the dead are asleep.

From somewhere near, a noise rose above the burble of the stream. Footfalls. Running footfalls.

No. She scrambled off the rock, and chilling water splashed up her trained skirt. Merrylad growled behind her, as she scaled the bank and pumped her legs into a wild run. They could not have her. They could not do to her what they'd done to Captain. She wouldn't let them put their hands on her—

"Eliza!"

She hurdled over a rotten log. How strangely her name echoed across the forest. As if she were late for supper again and Captain were calling her home. As if they were playing a game and he'd grown tired of running and laughingly shouted her back.

A hand snatched her arm and jerked her backward.

She swung both fists, kicked at him—

"Eliza." Familiar, warm, but not Captain. The hands shook her hard. "Eliza, it is me."

Felton?

She froze as he captured her face. In the darkness, she made out his outline. *Felton.*

"Are you hurt?"

How she needed him. Despite anything or anyone or any complications that had made her run. Whether he belonged to her or didn't. Whether he stayed or whether she never saw him again.

"I found the body." His grip became desperate, as his forehead pressed to hers, as his voice shook and deepened. "Eliza, I—"

Then nothing.

No words of comfort, no whisper of assurance, as if he understood there was no waning the terror. His arms lifted her off the ground and cradled her against him.

For a long time, he walked. She didn't know how far he carried her or how long it took, but he never brought her back to the cottage. Instead, he lowered her at the base of a tree, covered her with blankets, and rubbed the feet that were scratched and wet.

Felton, stay with me.

As if he'd heard her soul, he scooted next to her and pulled her head into the warmth of his shoulder.

Stay with me always.

She couldn't face morning without him.

<hr/>

Felton dropped another shovel of dirt into the hole. The face was covered, and no lifeless, unseeing eyes stared up at him.

He worked until the dim light of morning turned brighter and the silvery layer of dew melted into the earth. Sometimes he buried Lady Gillingham, with her shattered body and broken face. Other times he buried Hugh. Young, strong, brave Hugh, who would have never lost his life had the shame not been so unbearable.

But as he patted the last of dirt around the pitiful mound, he buried Captain Jasper Ellis. Tightness squeezed his throat—not because the man meant anything to him and not because he'd ever trusted the rogue.

But for Eliza.

For the way she'd looked this morning, pale in the predawn light, curled in a ball beneath the blankets he'd covered her with. Even in sleep, agony strained her face.

She didn't deserve such grief. She didn't deserve to lose everything.

Rolling down his sleeves, he took the shovel back into the reeking cottage. He roamed from the hearth to the table to the bookshelves, touching different parts of her, guilt caverning deep into his chest. Everything was his fault. He should have never taken her away from here that night. How happy she might have remained, how safe and protected, had he not marched in and disrupted her life. All for what? To find out that Lord Gillingham murdered his own wife?

He didn't know if he believed such nonsense. He didn't know if he ever could. Or was Eliza right? Was he only being fooled by a man who had long mastered deceiving him? Was that why Lord Gillingham had paid for Aaron's way to Cambridge? Was that why the viscount spent hours upon hours with Felton, laughing with him and reading with him and playing with him—all to assuage his own guilt?

Felton would find out. One way or another, friend or no, he'd expose the man who had made a wreckage of his life. He'd see justice meted out. He'd see his name restored. He'd see Hugh revenged.

He'd see peace for himself.

In the tiny bedchamber, he stepped over dried blood and lifted an old Bible from the neatly made bed. He flipped to the page Eliza had told him of and read the names. Not that they mattered now. The knowledge that Ellis had been involved in the shipwreck—indeed, had *caused* it—brought Felton no closer to having answers. If anything, it confused him more.

A note fell from the Bible.

He retrieved it and was ready to unfold it when he spotted the word *Eliza*. Had Captain written her a letter? Mayhap his last words would reveal something.

Or comfort Eliza.

He stuffed it into his pocket, glanced around once more for anything else he should bring, then closed the cottage door when he left. Would she want to stay, despite the grave, despite everything? Or would she never wish to see the place again?

Leading her horse with him, he hurried back to where he'd made camp and found Eliza awake. Leaning against the base of the tree, she stared into her lap without words or tears, the blanket wrapped tightly around her shoulders.

Felton kicked out the remains of the fire. Ashes lifted in the cool morning breeze. "We had better be on our way." He hesitated. "Unless you wish to stay."

Her eyes lifted to his and the helpless emptiness of her stare made him weak. "I cannot stay."

He nodded. He should have said something soothing, something that would have been a balm to her wounds. But nothing came to him. Nothing that would help. In silence strange and uncomfortable, he fed both dog and horses, saddled his own, then helped Eliza to her feet. "Are you hungry?"

"No."

"Neither am I." He swung her atop her mount, but her fingers stayed wrapped around his arm, tight and cold. "Felton?"

"Yes?"

"I cannot go back to Monbury either. I cannot ever go back."

His pulse sped, whether from pity or merely the intensity of her touch, he could not tell. He pulled his arm free and mounted. "Do not think of it now."

If nothing else, he would bring her home. He would keep her safe, where Mamma could fuss over her, and Papa could make her laugh, and Felton would be close enough to fight away any danger.

No one would hurt her again.

That was one thing he would see to.

"Tell me a story, Captain." She didn't want to go back. She didn't want to think. She didn't want to endure all the things that now were dead to her.

But they came just the same, as her horse followed Felton's and the forest faded away around them. She saw her younger self, in memory's haze, scrambling up on Captain's knee. *"Tell me the one about the big castle."*

"But ye always want that one."

"Because I like the part when the trouba. . .trouba. . ."

"Troubadour."

"Yes, when he gives up his lute for the sad lady." Leaning her head onto his shoulder, she'd played with the buttons on his coat. *"Why did he do that, Captain?"*

"Ye ask silly questions, love."

"But why?"

"Well, because he loved the lady, I guess."

"He loved the lute too."

"But he loved the lady more. And giving away his lute would make the lady not sad anymore, see?"

"Yes."

"If I had a lute, little one, I'd give it to ye."

"You would?"

"I'd give ye my lute and everything else I ever loved, if I thought for one second it would make ye happy." She'd laughed then, pleased at the thought of receiving some shiny lute, little understanding that he'd only meant to say he loved her.

Everything he'd ever done said he loved her.

Until the end.

Until he'd forsaken her and left her alone with the kind of strangers he'd taught her to distrust. Until he'd died without giving her the chance to see him once more. Hadn't he known that if there was danger she wanted to be a part of it? That even if someone had found their forest, she'd rather die beside him than be left alone in the world?

But she wasn't alone.

With eyes that burned, Eliza stared at Felton riding before her. His back stayed straight and rigid, as if no weight in the world could make it crumble. His horse moved steadily and purposefully, guided by hands that allowed no less, and he kept a pace just fast enough to get them to the village before dark, while slow enough that it would be no strain on her.

He was as noble as she'd ever imagined him to be. He was like a tower she could run to, a branch she could cling to at the edge of a cliff. For now, she could survive. Because he had come. Because he was here. Because she wasn't alone.

But for how long? At what point would he leave her? She couldn't go back with him, and he couldn't stay with her. There was no answer.

Except that they must be parted. Then what would she do?

As the sky turned a deep, cloudy blue and darkness slowly fell, the lights of the village finally came in sight. A leaning signpost, with *Weltworth* painted on the rough wood, pointed them on to where the dirt road turned into cobblestone.

Merrylad's bark and the steady clomp of their horses echoed into the hushed village. The buildings on both sides of them cast long shadows, deepening the dusk, chilling her until she shivered.

When they reached a brick, white-painted building, Felton dismounted. "A lodging house." He reached for her, caught her waist, and swung her to the ground. Taking her hand, he led her into the building that smelled old and decayed.

A gray-haired woman in a mobcap met them upon entrance. Her smile was all gums. "Evening there. Young and married, are you?"

"No." Felton nodded toward the dark staircase. "We shall need two rooms. Next to each other, if you please."

"Ain't got none side by side. Not wot's empty, I mean."

"It shall suffice." Felton handed the woman a pound, to which her smile grew wider and two blackened teeth appeared. "See that a chambermaid is sent up to help Miss Gillingham, and we shall need fresh water and a hot meal sent up."

"Anything you want, mister, you just ask ol' Cleda." She stuffed the pound past her fichu and gave it a pat. "Now, shall I take the two o' you to your chambers?"

Felton turned to Eliza. "I must see to the horses and Merrylad. Go with the woman, and I shall come soon."

Her heart hurt when he tugged away his fingers, but he paused before he left. He pulled something from his pocket and placed a note into her palm. "You will want to be alone anyway."

Then he was gone, and the smiling old woman took her arm, led her up the creaking stairs, and deposited her into a room with two open windows.

As moonlight spilled in, as the night air stirred dust motes, Eliza took the candle the woman had given her and settled on the edge of the bed. She shook as she turned it over and read the large, messy letters of her name.

Captain had written to her.

He had one more thing to tell her before she'd never hear from him again.

⁂

Felton led the horses behind the lodging house and entered the gray, splintery stables. Leaning against one of the stalls, a tall groom in patched clothing raised his dirty topper. "Cleda's lodger, I presume?"

"Yes." Felton nodded to a couple of empty stalls at the back. "Those are unspoken for?"

"Indeed, sir. Indeed. If you hadn't already guessed, this used to be a coaching inn, thus the spacious stables."

Felton led the horses to the stalls, pulled off Eliza's saddle first, then grabbed a brush and went to work on the animal's sweaty back. "I shall need fresh hay for both animals."

"Indeed, sir." Already, Merrylad sniffed the man's boots. "Inquisitive little dog you have here, sir. Quite inquisitive."

"Is there a place he might be kept?"

"I imagine there is some little corner we might fix up for the little pet."

"He shall need to be fed too."

"Right away, sir. I shall go and fetch something from Cleda. I daresay, she shall probably accuse me of bumming the scraps for myself. Just goes to show how little I get fed around this place." With a chuckle and a pat to the dog's head, the groom left the stables in silence.

Felton finished with Eliza's horse and moved on to his own. The question wouldn't leave him alone. The one the old woman had asked, half smiling, with eyes that imagined she had guessed the relationship of her two new guests.

Young and married, she'd asked.

Funny that he should be plagued by that now. Amidst so much going wrong, with loss so heavy on both of their hearts, why should he even think of such a thing?

Of course they weren't married. They'd never be married. Felton Northwood had other plans for his life, plans that didn't include a young and helpless and unsophisticated child of the forest who…who needed him. And looked at him with longing in her eyes. And touched him with gentleness that made him want to pull her closer instead of always pulling away.

Gads, but he was a fool.

Miss Haverfield.

Miss Haverfield.

Miss Haverfield. Beautiful, rich, perfect Miss Haverfield. Maybe if he chanted the name enough times this nonsense would leave him alone.

Slamming the brush back on its shelf, Felton strode from the hall and nearly tripped over Merrylad. Dashed dog anyway. Why was the creature always in his way?

Instead of baring his teeth, or backing away from Felton as he normally did, Merrylad wagged his tongue. The brown, dark-lashed eyes blinked up at Felton, smiling almost.

Certainly, there was nothing to smile about. Not today. Even so, he lowered before the animal and stroked one ear. "Still gloating, are you not?"

The dog edged closer and licked Felton's hand.

"I've a scar from that bite, you know—"

A moving shadow. A crunch of boots on hay.

Felton sprang to his feet, whirled, but something smacked the side of his head. His vision blackened. He hit the ground, heard a bark, as a second blow knocked the breath from him.

Eliza. Her name screamed in his head, as the tunnel of blackness ended into nothing at all.

Dear Eliza,

Ye know I'm no good with letters and such. Much easier for me to tell stories than worry wif the spelling of things. I don't know if ye'll ever be reading this anyhow. I reckon I'll probly never send it. I keep it here in my Bible wif the other names. I know I never telled ye who they were. It don't be mattering none. They just be people I had a part in destroying, and I reckon that's just something a man can't never forget. I done a lot of bad things, little girl, that ye never knowed about. Before ye came to me, I was nigh to dying inside. But ye made me want to live again. Ye and God and these woods gave me something I never thought I could have, and that's a good feeling in me agin. That's why I had to let ye go. I couldn't let ye stay here, growing as ye was, without a chance to meet the world I been always telling ye of in stories. Ye stay with that lord, love. He be yer father. He be yer blood. I'm sorry for all the wrong I done, and I'm sorry I couldn't keep ye here wif me always. More than anything, I'm sorry I'm not the father ye always thought I was. The rest of my life, I'll be wishing I was.

Yer very affect and loving Captain

All the words swam across the page. She read it again, then again, and pictured him standing in front of her. He held his cap in his hands, the little brown one she'd mended more than once, and his eyes had that crinkly, soft look again. The one that came over him just before he was about to pray or bend over her and whisper kindness into her ear.

God, I love him so. She traced the letter, as the sob that couldn't come before started pushing through her. She leaned down on the bed. She covered her mouth with both hands and tried to stop the sounds from escaping into the room. *Captain, Captain, how shall I live without you?*

He had wanted her. Right to the end, he had loved her and been true to her and thought of her. What a fool she'd been to question him. She should have remembered the lute. She should have remembered everything. *God, thank You for the letter. Thank You.*

A tap sounded on the door.

Sucking in air, she swatted away her tears and sat up. "Felton?"

"No, miss. Your chambermaid, miss, with somefing for you to eat."

She tucked the letter into her pocket and went to the door.

A young girl, thirteen or fourteen, swept inside with dark hair strung into her eyes. She blew it away and set a plate of boiled salt beef and vegetables on a stand. "Is that look good for you, miss? I've pasties downstairs, and I can bring up some milk."

Eliza shook her head, blinking hard against more tears. "No." Her voice lacked strength. "No, this will be fine." She didn't know if she could eat anyway.

"I'll be bringing up fresh water for you too, miss." The girl straightened the napkin beside the plate. "I can help you wif unfastening your stays too, but that can wait until your two friends are done visiting wif you."

Eliza's gaze snapped to the girl. "Two. . .friends?"

"Yes, miss. I heard them asking Cleda which chamber you was in as I was coming up the steps to—"

Eliza flung for the door. She slammed it shut, slid the latch. Her heartbeat throbbed to her throat as she turned around and glanced about the room. *God?*

"What be the matter, miss? I done somefing wrong?"

Eliza flung to one of the windows. Too dark to see, even in the faint moonlight, how many feet stood between her and the ledge.

The girl rushed behind her. "You not be thinking of jumping, are you, miss?"

No, she wouldn't jump. She couldn't jump. The beast would want her to jump, with the red curtains and the glass breaking and the screams. . .

A body slammed into the door. The rattle shook the room, followed by a low curse.

"Miss, you can't!"

Eliza pushed one leg out the window. Her breath came out in gasps, as she grasped the ledge with both hands and eased herself out. Her body dangled along the rough brick. The door crashed open above. The maid screamed.

Now. Air whistled in her ears as she fell. Her body slammed into the earth and pain jolted through both ankles, but she rolled forward and pushed herself behind a scraggly bush. *God, help me.* She covered her ears, closed her eyes, willed the breath to come back into her lungs. *Help Felton find me.*

Before the beast saw her dead.

Like Captain.

CHAPTER 11

"I say, fellow, you a bit bosky tonight?"

Wooden beams. Cobwebs. Then a face—thin, greasy, with a ratty topper and bulging eyes.

Felton jerked upright. Pain stabbed his temple, as the groom grabbed Felton's coat and leaned him up against a beam.

"There now. I've been dipping rather deep lately myself. That is, until Cleda catches me. The fastidious old biddy allows no ale for those in need of merriment—"

"Eliza." Felton pushed the hands away. Everything careened, but he pulled himself up and grasped the beam. "You. . .get help."

"Get what, sir?"

"Eliza. . .the woman with me. Get inside the building. Get into her room." He stumbled back to the stall and grabbed his pistol from the saddlebags.

"If you don't mind my saying so, sir, I think perhaps you should lie down until you feel a bit steadier on your feet—"

"Now!"

With a slight jump, the man grumbled and darted out the open stabledoors.

The stalls, the beams, the hay—they all spun again. If anything happened to her, if he'd allowed the danger to get past him and hurt her. . .

He staggered forward, Merrylad next to him, and gained steadiness when he made it outside and took the path along the house. The windows glowed orange, all open but none emitting screams.

Mayhap they hadn't reached her yet.

Merrylad yelped.

He jerked around, pistol drawn, and faced the bush the dog circled. His stomach tensed. "Come out with your hands up."

The shadowy branches stirred. "F–Felton?"

Relief pushed through the panic. He dropped to the bush and dragged her out by the arm. "Are you hurt?"

"No." Choked voice. She ripped strands of hair free from the twigs and wobbled to her feet. "But Felton, the men—"

"I know. Come on."

"But they'll see—"

"Come!" Hands entwined, they broke into a run and made it back into the stables without sight nor sound of anyone. He swung Eliza onto her unsaddled horse. "Hold the mane."

"But, Felton, we'll never make it—"

"Hush. Go." He hastened the horse to the open doorway of the stables, slapped the rear, and waited with his flintlock until she reached the street.

Then he swung atop his own horse. Halfway past the house, a shot rang from the porch. His horse faltered. His body left the saddle.

God, help. He hit the ground so hard his vision dipped again. He was back in the tunnel, long and dark and noiseless, but he never reached the end. He scampered back to his feet, taste of dirt in his mouth, as another shot whizzed past his head.

Pumping his legs hard and fast, he made it to the cobblestone street, where the building shadows hid him, where the shots no longer rang in his ears. He rasped in air and kept running.

Then Eliza. She appeared from nowhere when she should have already been away. Why had she waited for him? The fool. The senseless little fool—

"Felton, here!"

He pulled himself onto the horse and grabbed the mane around her shaking form. Kicking his heels into the animal's side, another wave of blackness came and went as they galloped faster. Behind them, more shots sliced the air.

But the danger never touched them, and the pound of hooves on cobblestones soon morphed into the quieter thud of hooves on dirt. The night swallowed them into blackness. The road led them into quietness.

Felton leaned his pounding head onto the top of her hair and exhaled air. *Thank You, God.* Because no horses ever followed, nor gunfire blasted, nor shouts pierced the air.

They were safe. Eliza was safe.

At least for tonight.

How long they rode she couldn't remember. Sometime through the night, she must have fallen asleep, with her head near his heartbeat and his arms closing her in.

She didn't want to awaken. She never wanted to awaken. If only she could stay where the horse rocked and lulled her and her dreams carried her into oblivion. Back to the ocean, vast and quiet, where they had played and laughed in blue, sparkling water.

She was the mermaid and he the sailor in the boat. As he rowed the oars up and over the waves, he'd dip his hand into the clear water. She would catch his fingers, glide with him laughing, and break the surface long enough to meet his lips.

She shouldn't think such things. Even in sleep, she knew that. If his kisses belonged to anyone, they belonged to Miss Haverfield. The girl with the secret. The new courtship she was finally allowed to share with the world.

How soon the mermaid would grope in vain for a hand that was no longer there at a boat that now sailed lifeless. Terribly, horribly lifeless.

"Eliza, wake up." Another command. He always told her what to do. As long as he'd known her, he'd been barking orders as fast as she could follow them.

But she needed them, his orders. She loved them almost. Wasn't that a silly thing?

The horse halted in a glen of trees along the road, and she shook her head against the cobwebs of sleep. Morning light filtered in around them, faint and golden, as he dismounted and pulled her to the ground.

She stayed against him. She searched his eyes because they searched hers, and she read all the things he never said with his lips. Not that she understood them. She didn't understand any of the messages in his eyes.

Only that they were warm, for this moment. They were still and soft and as vulnerable as she was—and she loved him for his eyes. She loved him for everything. For climbing the tree, weeks ago, and listening to her nightmare. For teaching her to dance in the library. For bringing Merrylad when she was hurt and taking her to the ocean when she was sad.

For coming after her when she ran.

For being the one she needed when she'd fathomed there was no one else.

With comforting gentleness, he led her to a patch of grass, kicked away a few twigs, and ordered her to rest.

She curled onto the soft, dewy grass. She imagined Merrylad would scurry next to her, but the dog seemed more content to follow Felton.

After rubbing down the horse with his hands, he settled at a nearby tree and pulled out his flintlock. He yawned but never closed his eyes. "Rest, Eliza," he said again, as if he'd felt her gaze.

She allowed her eyes to drift shut. She was back under the sparkling blue sea, a mermaid again, breaking the surface once more to kiss the sailor in the rowboat.

<hr>

They needed provisions. Eliza's weariness was more than just the trauma and travel—she needed something hot and substantial in her stomach.

Felton could do with a meal or two himself.

But it was dangerous. Had those men known and been waiting for them at Weltworth, or had they only followed them there? Were they being followed now?

For the hundredth time, Felton glanced over his shoulder at the empty road behind them. Every once in a while, a pony cart or a coach rumbled by them, but no dust of lone riders clouded the air.

Mayhap they were in luck. Mayhap the men had sulked in defeat and scurried back to whoever it was who had sent them in the first place.

Images crowded in. Lord Gillingham showing two ruffians into his study. Closing the door. Passing twenty-pound notes into their hands for a job too bloody to do himself.

Would to heaven it wasn't true. Surely it couldn't be true.

Turning their mount on to the smaller road to Poortsmoor, he straightened. "We stop at the village, but I think it best we stay together." After all, they'd done it before, hadn't they?

Her sigh filled the air without comment. She'd said very little as they traveled. Almost as little as the first time, when he'd snatched her from her beloved cottage and told her things she hadn't wanted to believe.

They rode into the village in the afternoon hustle and bustle, the air alive with the hum of voices and hammers and livestock. He left the horse at the stables first, then found the Dalrymple Inn.

A curly-haired adolescent scrubbed at the outside windows, while the proprietor swept a billow of dust from the open doorway. He hailed them in, seemed to remember their stay before, and ushered them into the same chamber with the promise of a meal arriving soon.

Then they were alone. Just Felton Northwood and Eliza Gillingham in a room they'd once occupied as strangers.

They weren't strangers now. They weren't even friends.

They were something else, something he couldn't place, something that terrified him more than the two blackguards looking to harm them.

Eliza turned to the window. Circles hung under her eyes, deep and heavy, and her skin wore a pallor so grave it matched the white curtains on the windows. "Tonight, you must sleep," she said.

He pulled off his dusty tailcoat and tossed it to a chair in the corner. "If those men come back, I'll not be unready a second time."

"But you are weary."

"No more than you."

"I have slept."

"There will be time enough for sleep later." He crossed the room to the washstand, splashed cold water onto his dirty face, and scrubbed away some of the dust. He patted dry with a flat-woven towel. "I want to know what made you run."

"I already know you do not believe me."

"Your turn." He tossed over the towel.

She swept her hand to her cheek, as if suddenly aware how she must appear, then moved to the washstand herself. Between splashes, she told him of Minney, of the things the girl believed and had seen that day at the inn. She told him of strange looks in her father's eye and hidden letters tucked under the pillows in Lady Gillingham's chamber.

All things that made it more real.

All things that made it hurt.

With a face scrubbed clean, she glanced back at him. "Maybe it isn't true. Maybe Minney is wrong." Her words lacked conviction. Of course they did. Both of them knew what such evidence said against the man.

But evidence was not proof. He knew that more than anyone.

"Felton?"

"Yes?"

"Whether you believe me or not, I cannot go back there."

"I know." Did she think him scoundrel enough to force her back again against her wishes? "As for believing, I hardly know anything anymore."

They settled into silence, with Eliza reclining on the bed and

Felton leaning against the door, until finally the curly-haired boy delivered their food.

When Felton resituated against the door, Eliza pulled the wobbly chair in front of him, then sank to the floor. "Our table." She settled her plate on the edge of the chair seat and something of a gleam touched her eyes.

He did the same. They prayed, then started in on the warm collop, the chopped carrots, and the chunk of coarse bread and butter. The hunger pains slowly faded as he devoured the meal.

"Your chin." With lips curved enough they might have been smiling, she pretended to wipe something from her face.

He mimicked her movements and wiped butter away with his finger. "I must be eating like quite the pauper."

"You look quite the pauper."

A laugh rumbled out. Silly, that he should laugh—or that she should laugh with him.

But she did. How startlingly the sound filled the chamber and chased away a thousand burdens. Was there ever a nicer sound? Was there ever anything more wonderful? Or healing? Or. . .so very, very beautiful?

Her cheeks colored, as if she knew his thoughts. She bit the edge of her lip and shook her head. "I should not have. . .have. . ."

"Been happy a moment?" He forked a strip of collop. "I think you should have. I think you should always be."

"But Captain—"

"Would have wanted that."

"You do not understand."

"Don't I?"

She bent her head. She lifted her fork again and forked more carrots, but tears dripped onto her plate.

How easy it would be to reach over the chair and stroke away her tears. 'Twould do no good though. She cried for the same reason he'd run to his path, and slammed his fists into the wall, and hid his face from all the world.

"Felton?"

"Hmm?"

"When do you leave?"

"Leave?"

She never looked up. More tears dotted her plate. "You need not worry for me. Captain taught me more than you think. I am not so very inept, and if you leave in the morning—"

"Leave?" His pulse quickened. "You think I intend to leave you here?"

"Where else," she whispered, raising her eyes, "might I be left?"

"Your opinion of me must be very small."

"No, Felton, I—"

"I would no sooner leave you here alone, with or without those men trying to injure you, then I would. . .I would. . ." He would have jumped to his feet and put distance between them had the chair not trapped his legs.

Her chin quivered. "Then you would what?"

"Then I would die." He nodded to her plate. "Now finish your food."

His assurance didn't stop the tears on her cheeks. They came just as quickly, as she lifted her fork and shakily obeyed his command.

But her lips wore a smile.

Dash everything, but it was the most beautiful smile in the world.

<hr />

Another new place. More of the people Captain had warned her against.

But as the bareback horse brought them closer to the Northwood abode, Eliza's chest pulsated with more comfort than fear. She relaxed in the arms that held her. Did he know she thought this way?

"Home." A murmur in her ear, soft and soothing, as he nodded ahead.

Skirted on each side by tall rosebushes, the yellow brick house was square with a hip roof. Five sash windows decorated the facade, and a gravel walkway led to a blue-paneled entrance door.

By the time Felton dismounted and pulled her down, a short and wide-eyed maid rushed to greet them with her hands fluttering. "Master Northwood, you be just the one we need. Just the one we need surely! I been in such a fluster since she came—our guest that is—but I says to Mr. Northwood, I says, 'Mr. Northwood, if a person wants to do a good deed they ought to do it.' But I just worry so that she won't like it here none and—"

"Dodie, who?"

"Why, Miss Haverfield, of course!"

Eliza's breath caught.

"What is she doing here?" Felton strode through the doorway, tugging Eliza with him. Was it her imagination, or did his hands begin to perspire? Was he so in love with her?

"She come to help, she did, Mr. Northwood." Dodie slammed the door with exaggeration. "As soon as you left and Miss Haverfield found out about the passing of your dear brother, God rest his soul, she come right over to be with Mrs. Northwood during her trialing hours."

Felton's brother had passed? Eliza glanced to his face.

He shrugged off his coat, kicked the mud from his heels, with an expression tight and strained.

Yes, there was loss there. She'd been too busy with her own grief to detect his pain. How could she be so insensitive? How had she not realized?

"Dodie, take Miss Gillingham to the guest chamber and bring up hot water for a bath."

"Felton, wait." She snatched his arm as he tried to leave the foyer.

Slowly, as if in dread, he glanced back at her. "I am not ready to speak of it, Eliza."

"I am sorry."

"Yes." He ran a hand down the side of her face. A quick touch, faint and endearing. "Go and take your bath, hmm? You look the pauper now yourself."

—◦◦◦◦◦◦◦—

"Well, this is positively lovely."

Eliza backed behind the copper tub, stripped of everything but her stained and sweaty chemise. Heat seared the back of her neck. She'd already seen herself in the mirror—the loose and unkempt hair, the dirty smudges on her face, the dark circles beneath her eyes.

Miss Haverfield smiled as she pulled the door shut behind her in the tiny, floral guest chamber. "I heard it whispered throughout the house that Felton had brought home the dear little runaway everyone has been whispering about, but I could not be certain until I saw for myself."

Little runaway? She swallowed hard as Dodie poured a second bucket into the tub, then left to retrieve more.

Miss Haverfield pulled something from behind her back. A light blue linen dress unfolded as she held it up. "What do you think? I imagined you would be in need of something suitable to wear, as Dodie mentioned you had not a valise or trunk with you." She approached and held it against Eliza. "Of course, the bust would need to be drawn in. You are quite thin, I daresay, but do not let that worry you. I have known many acquaintances who were far more unshapely than you, and not one of said girls are unmarried."

Eliza clasped the dress. "Thank you."

"Nonsense, my dear. I simply adore you. May I help you off with your chemise?"

Eliza took a step back. "No, I. . ."

"You what, dear?" Miss Haverfield laughed and, when Eliza never spoke further, shook her head with a sigh. "La, but you are strange, poor thing. It is no wonder our goodly-hearted Felton has gone to such lengths to help you. How could anyone not?"

Was that why Felton had brought her here? In pity?

"But there, I can see I have upset you. Pay no mind to me, my dear, as I am never saying the right things." Miss Haverfield swept to the door, patted her cluster of perfect ringlets, and smiled once more midthreshold. "I am glad, truly, that you are here, Miss Gillingham. I am ever so in need of a friend to confide in. I have so many, many secrets where Felton Northwood is concerned."

Dodie squeezed in with another steaming bucket, so with a wink in Eliza's direction, the beautiful Miss Haverfield sashayed away.

Mouth dry, Eliza glanced down at her unclean feet. Her ankles were swollen from the jump from the window, and she wiggled sore toes against the clean Axminster carpet. How revolting she must seem. How wild and unsightly. What a fool to imagine Felton Northwood might once look at her and see something he could desire.

She should be grateful for his pity.

And forget any imagination of his love.

***

"How are you, Mamma?"

How pale and small she looked, covered to her neck in bed linens, with puffy eyes and cheeks. Her chestnut hair stuck to the side of her face, whether from sweat or tears he could not tell.

Felton sat next to her on the edge of the bed, wincing when it creaked for fear it might upset her.

She didn't seem to notice. She didn't seem to notice anything. Her gaze remained steady on some unknown object across the room, and every second or two she moved her lips.

He didn't have to hear to understand what she whispered.

"Mamma, I am home again." He smoothed her hair on the pillow, tucked the bed linen around her frail shoulders.

But she didn't answer. Maybe she never would. Maybe he'd lost her, just as he'd lost Hugh, just as they'd lost a thousand other things so vital to them.

He eased his head onto her chest. Listened to a heartbeat so feeble it made his own pound harder. *God, do not let her die.* The prayer came again, and again, and again. Maybe if he begged enough times, God would show mercy and give her life. She deserved life, didn't she?

She'd never been sickly before.

She'd never been sad before.

Not when Aaron and Felton and Hugh were young. When they'd played outside near the rosebushes, nodded when Mamma told them not to spoil their skeleton suits, and cheered when she'd come out of doors to give them each a sugar plum. She'd smiled in those days. She'd even laughed. He remembered the sound because it haunted him sometimes, in the dead of night, when he heard her sobs drift between the house's walls.

Help me find him, Christ. The man who had done this to them. The man who had ruined his name and tried one too many times to end Eliza's life.

If that man was Lord Gillingham, so help him. . . Felton would lose control of himself. He'd bash in his face or pin him to the wall or choke the breath from him, if the one friend he trusted had betrayed him.

Slow fingers moved through his hair.

Felton raised his head. "Mamma?"

For the first time, her eyes focused on his face. A ghost of a smile crossed her lips. "Son?"

"Yes, Mamma. I am here."

"You were gone so long. A mother needs her son." Tears. "A mother needs her sons by her side."

"I had to go, Mamma. You know that."

"For the girl?"

"Yes. There was no safety where she came from, so I brought her back here. She will be protected with us."

"You are a good boy, Felton." She turned her head and closed her eyes. She murmured more, things too quiet to hear, then drifted away into slumber.

Felton left her chamber. He had three or four hours before dinner would be served.

Just enough time to find the man Bowles.

The cellar darkness hid their expressions. Pity, that. He rather enjoyed the looks that crossed their faces when he sat before them on his keg and made sport of their idiocy.

Tall Postle stepped closer into the flickering candlelight. "Next time, sir, we'll be gettin' the girl 'fore she gets away."

"You will, eh?"

"Yes, sir."

"Is that a promise?"

"He hain't got the right to give no promises." Breage, shorter and dumpier than his partner, uttered a mild oath. "We could 'ave gotten free of that place, clean free, if Tall Postle 'ere would 'ave shut up the bleedin' mouth of that hollerin' woman."

"Then your temporary confinement in Weltworth might have been avoided?"

Breage started to answer, then blew air out of his cheeks.

Tall Postle hung his head.

"This is grave news indeed. I greatly despise hearing of unwise decisions in moments of great importance." Bowles hopped from his keg. "Well, Tall Postle? What have you to say for yourself?"

"I didn't see wot good there be in killin' the old woman."

"How very touching. Anything else?"

The man's giant forehead crinkled. He breathed heavily.

"You seem as if something else is on your mind. Pray, do tell. Breage and I are very interested, I dare to say."

"I want out."

"Out?"

The man raised his face, met Bowles' eyes, and set his jaw firm. "I be done with the killin'. I be done with the opium. I be done with all of it."

"You are a brave man, my friend."

Veins bulged in his neck, and the large, calloused hands shook as they waited. As they waited for David Bowles. As they waited for punishment or mercy from the only one who could forgive his sins or cleanse him from them.

Bowles grinned. "Your courage amuses me. For what it is worth now, your wife amused me too."

The man blanched.

"Until I, let us say, introduced her to the gypsy when I was finished."

Now every vein protruded, until the man's filthy skin turned red beneath the dirt and grime. His chin shook, his arms quivered, but he only said in steely words, "I be free to go?"

"Oh yes, do not let me detain you. You are quite free indeed." He nodded to Breage. "Do bid him goodbye."

The shorter man clasped Tall Postle's hand, grim faced, and turned away.

Then Tall Postle went for the door. He moved slowly, awkwardly, each step making a scratching music against the stone floor.

Bowles reached into his boot, pulled out the knife, and flipped his wrist.

A cry hit the air. The man's back arched, but he stumbled through the door and must have made it halfway up the stairs when his mercy ran out. His body thumped back to the floor.

"Now get rid of the body and tell Swabian if Eliza is not eliminated soon I shall spill his blood along with Tall Postle's."

With wary eyes, Breage nodded and disappeared.

Then silence. The lovely silence after judgment has been proclaimed, punishment has been rendered, and the power of life and death has left his hands.

He settled back onto his keg. The thrill, the euphoria, raced through his lifeblood. Other men lived for the opium. They were slaves to it, the little fools. Others lived for the smuggling. The ships voyaging to India for the opium, then to China to sell it off, then back to England with their payment of valuable goods—all hidden in the cave at Ozias Bay and ready to be sold to English villagers.

But not him.

Not David Bowles.

He was larger, greater, more supreme than that. He lived for the moments of dominance. Like the day Bradshaw wanted out for the sake of his deformed daughter. Like the thrill in hunting him down, waiting for him in his inn chamber, and tossing him out the window on the end of a rope. The sounds still stayed with him. Along with Tall Postle's cry. And those of many, many others.

From the doorway, his maid appeared with a candlestick illuminating her face. Her face bruised. "S—sir?"

"What is it?"

"I—I thought you might want to know a v—visitor is come to see you. The one I told you about before who was asking for you—"

"Tell him I shall be there promptly. See him into the parlor and give him something to drink."

"Yes, sir."

"And Miss Reay?"

Her gaze slanted back to him. "Yes, s—sir?"

"As soon as our visitor is gone, do hurry back down and clean away the blood."

Felton lowered his teacup to its saucer when the stranger entered the small parlor.

Tall and well dressed. Reddish-brown hair. Long sideburns and narrow, serious eyes. Hadn't Felton seen him before? Or at the very least someone who resembled him?

"I trust the tea is to your taste, Mr. . . . ."

"Northwood." Felton leaned forward and placed his tea on the low table before the settee. "And the tea is fine. Thank you."

"No thanks necessary, I assure you." The man claimed a chair next to a glistening harp. "As you see, I delight in seeing my guests attended to, for though I have but a modest abode, I do take great pride in seeing it run properly."

"I will not take much of your time, Mr. Bowles."

"Go on."

"I should like to inquire about a man called Jasper Ellis."

"What do you wish to know about him?"

"His relationship to you."

"There is none, I assure you."

"Yet you were both survivors of the *Red Drummer*."

"Only barely, Mr. Northwood. I spent three days in the ocean, and after I was picked up by a cutter and brought back to Lodnouth, I spent a great deal more time battling sickness. Only when I was well did I realize Ellis had survived too."

"I understand many wished he had not."

"Indeed. Our Captain Ellis, I fear, was rather out of his head when he started the fire."

"As in too much drink?"

"No." Bowles sank back into his chair. "As in too much opium."

"I see."

"It is no small wonder the friends and family of so many men wished vengeance."

"Did you?"

A smile twitched at the man's mouth. "It is I, Mr. Northwood, who had pity on the man and hid him in one of my cellar rooms, lest the others have their way with him."

"Then you will know, I am certain, what happened to Ellis the night he disappeared."

Silence.

The man's smile widened, as if he enjoyed the question dangling, as if he took pleasure in the way Felton's heart hammered in anticipation. With a shake of his head, he broke the silence. "I fear I cannot be of help to you. Ellis was free to come and go as he wished. He did so mostly at night. On one such night, he never returned. I know little more than that."

Felton stood. Wariness spread through him as he held the man's eyes unwaveringly. "One more question, Mr. Bowles."

"By all means."

"Why did the *Red Drummer* wear black masts?"

"I fear you must be confused."

"Am I?"

"Yes." Another smile, but it never reached the cold depths of the man's eyes. "Rather dangerously confused, I fear."

"I see." Felton bowed. "Then my questions are finished. Good day to you, sir." Without waiting for the maid to show him out, Felton saw himself back through the house, grabbed his topper from the hallstand, and slammed himself out the door.

Something wasn't right. The man was lying or hiding something or both.

But Felton would be back.

Whether it was dangerous or not.

⸺⸱⸳⸲⸱⸺

Eliza followed her finger around the blue lozenge border of the Wedgewood plate. Once upon a time, Captain had told her a story about a people so tiny they swam in bowls, lived in shoes, and feasted on the crumbs that fell from tablecloths.

How quickly she would become tiny herself if there were but others to be tiny with her. To be like her, belong to her, love her.

Not look at her the way Miss Haverfield stared at her now, with that amused twinkle, as if Eliza Gillingham were some exotic varmint or embarrassing fool.

Maybe she was both.

"My dear, you must eat more than that. Although I will say, since we are quite alone"—Miss Haverfield glanced about the pale-green dining room—"this goose *is* rather dry and distasteful."

Eliza slid her fork beside her plate. "I suppose I am not very hungry."

"My dear, you must think of your figure." With a sigh, she dabbed her mouth with a napkin. "Oh, this is very vexing. Here I was anticipating a cheery meal with all Northwoods present, yet none of them have come to join their guests. How shall we entertain ourselves all evening? Do you play piquet?"

"No, I—"

"Vingt-et-un then?"

"No." Eliza clasped her hands under the tablecloth. "No, I cannot play any of them."

"You poor dear. How ever have you amused yourself these many years?" Miss Haverfield reached for a couple of iced oranges. "Never mind the games, dear. We shall find something with which to divert ourselves during my stay. If nothing else, we shall talk away the hours. I do not suppose I ever told you of the time when dear Felton and I were having one of our moonlit rides and he—"

"He what?" As if on cue, Felton strode into the dining room, eyes alighting on both of them before he scooted into his seat at the end of the table. He reached for the platter of goose. "Where is Papa?"

"He wished to sit with your mother and partake of his meal in her chamber." Miss Haverfield tilted her head, beguiling, earbobs dangling. "I have been quite devoted to your mother since my arrival, Mr. Northwood, but it is such a minuscule thing. I only wish I could do more."

"It was good of you to come." He lifted his eyes to Eliza before settling them back to Miss Haverfield. "But I can make no promises the visit will not submit you to village gossip."

"I dare to say, people are not so cruel as they were back then. Indeed, I fathom some have all but forgotten."

"Your father included?"

A laugh trilled out. "You tempt me to tell you a secret with such a question. But let us speak of it no more. As soon as you are finished with your meal, we shall take a stroll outside, and you may walk me through the garden and grape arbors."

Eliza stood, chair nearly toppling, heat rising when their attention shifted to her. "Excuse me." Without meaning to, her eyes caught Felton's gaze. She was drawn into his eyes, the deep and soothing pull, as green as the forest trees she loved so much.

He looked away. Then down at his plate. Then up to Miss Haverfield—always Miss Haverfield.

Eliza left the room and locked herself into the tiny upstairs chamber she'd been given. Evidence of his kindness. His nobility. His pity.

She waited at the window for a long time before the two of them reached the garden.

Together, arms linked, they ambled the paths. Talking. Laughing. Drifting closer as they ventured from the garden to the distant grape arbors. Wasn't it lovely?

She'd always thought so before. She'd always sighed and been happy and smiled at the stories Captain told her of two people growing in their love for each other. There had been magic in the tales. Enchantment in the touches.

But there was no enchantment in this.

Eliza pulled the lilac silk curtains over the pane. She found her bed, burrowed herself into the soft folds, and tried not to remember one day ago when she'd been held in his arms.

The arms that would likely never hold her again.

***

One thing was certain. Felton had never once imagined Miss Penelope Haverfield, daughter of the squire, deigning to aid the Northwood family. He didn't know how to feel about such a thing.

Maybe he was elated.

Yes, of course he was. Why wouldn't he be? Was this not a long-sought dream finally falling into place?

"You are quiet this evening. Might I invade your thoughts?" Beneath the grape arbor, she lifted her finger to twist a vine. The same way she'd always been twisting him. "Or am I in them already?"

She was, of course, but he had no intention of admitting it. He plucked an unripe grape. "I am merely fatigued."

"Too fatigued to ask me?"

"Ask you what?"

"About my secret." She swayed closer with her familiar apricot scent, long lashes fluttering, cheeks pinking just enough to lend a sense of shyness they both knew was untrue. "Well, Mr. Northwood?"

"All right, what is it?"

"You hardly seem intrigued."

"Don't I?"

"Very well then." She whisked to the other side of the grape arbor. "I shall not tell you at all since you have so many other things occupying your mind."

Like his brother's dead body on the bottom of the sea. Like the answers he couldn't get and the fourteen-year-old truth he couldn't uncover. Like the men trying to kill Eliza. Like his dying mother in her bedchamber upstairs.

"Felton, how could you tease me this way?" She turned to him again, eyes searching his but never seeing. She touched the lapels of his coat. "Of late you seem as if you do not care for me at all."

"Should that not be a question for your university friend?"

"He was nothing to me."

"I thought I was nothing to you."

On tiptoes, she pressed her mouth to his lips. Then, lowering slowly, releasing his coat, she murmured, "Does that seem like nothing, Felton Northwood?"

This was the second time. The second time she'd kissed him. He tightened his fist to keep from dragging a hand across his mouth and wiping it away when he should have been wanting to keep it forever.

"We had better go back inside." He took her elbow, and they started back beneath the grape arbors and through the garden paths.

He was just tired tonight. That was all.

By tomorrow, he would be interested in her secrets and eager for her kisses and invigorated by her apricot-smelling hair.

But tonight, the only scent he wanted to breathe was rose water.

_____⚬ℜ⬩℞⚬_____

Eliza jerked awake. *Captain?* She groped for the cottage wall, rough and stone and cool, but her hands met a different wall. An unfamiliar one.

Because Captain was dead.

He wasn't here to run a wet cloth over her sweaty brow, or rescue her from the claws, or tell her everything would be over by morning.

Breathing fast, she climbed out of bed and paced the chamber. Anything to awaken herself. Anything to rid herself of the beast, if only for tonight.

Someone tapped on the door, startling her.

She grabbed the ruffled wrapper Miss Haverfield had given her and slipped it on as the tap came again.

"Eliza?"

"Felton?"

"Open up."

Anchoring her disheveled hair behind her ears, she crept to the door and cracked it open. "Is something wrong?"

Fully dressed, he leaned forward with a dim-glowing candlestick. "You called out."

Had she? Shame pulsated through her, making her want to slam the door and crawl back into bed where he couldn't see or pity her.

He pushed the door open wider. "Come downstairs and I shall get you a glass of water."

"No, you needn't bother—"

He grabbed her hand and tugged her into the hall anyway.

Only then did she see the rumpled counterpane outside her door. And the pistol. "You slept here?"

He didn't answer. No, of course he wouldn't. Brave men never owned to their bravery, not in all the books and stories.

But this was no book. He should never have slept outside her door. He had no reason to watch after her this way, to sacrifice his comfort, to protect her as if she...as if she meant something to him.

Downstairs, he pulled her into a dark kitchen and poured a glass from a brass pitcher. He nodded to a chair at a scratched, wooden table. "Sit."

Then, side by side, they were seated next to each other. The orange candlelight danced between them, and the beeswax filled the kitchen with the faint, earthy scent of honey.

She circled the water glass with her hands. "I am sorry."

"For?"

"Tonight. For last night. For the night before that." She shook her head. "You should not have brought me here. You should not have to sleep outside my door—"

"I want to."

She looked up at him. His eyes were tired, sad, but fire burned in them too. She didn't know what kind of fire, or what it meant, or why it flamed.

She only knew it consumed her. Like a moth, she wanted to be closer, even conscious she would be scorched. "Felton. . .why did you not tell me?"

"About Hugh?"

She nodded.

"Because there was no reason. You had pain enough."

"You comforted mine. I should have comforted yours."

He looked away, smiled, and shook his head, but when his eyes sought hers again, moisture was in his gaze. "You have a trueness in you, Eliza Gillingham, I have never seen in anyone in my life."

The praise brought her closer. Nearer to the flame.

"You make me want to tell you things."

"What things?"

"I was nine when they first accused Papa. The constable and several men from the village came that night, with lanterns and torches, and shouted things about the gallows."

"But they set him free."

"Yes, they set him free. One week later, the same men came back. They threw stones through the windows and eggs at the walls and screamed that no woman killer should live free." The knot in his throat bobbed. "We could not go anywhere. The ladies shunned my mother. The men cursed at us. So many times, the village urchins pounced on Aaron and Hugh and me. . .beat us so bad we learned how to beat them back."

"I am sorry, Felton. So very sorry."

"I couldn't run away like Aaron. I couldn't run away like Hugh. I had to stay here. I had to make things right. I had to find the man who did this to us so the Northwood name could be clean."

"You will find him."

"He didn't just kill your mother. He killed Hugh. . .he killed so much he. . ." He shook his head, glanced up at the ceiling. "I do not know. Sometimes I wish I could just forget all of it. I wish I could pretend, like Papa, that it did not exist."

"Pretending does not make things different."

"No."

"Someday you shall be happy, Felton. This will be over. Then you can run away or stay here forever or do anything in the world you wish."

"And you?" He drew closer. He pried her hands from their death clasp on the glass and tangled her fingers with his. "What do you wish of everything in the world?"

"To be free of the nightmares."

He drew closer.

To be the mermaid in the sea.

Closer, nose brushing hers.

To kiss the man in the rowboat.

His mouth fell next to her lips. He lingered there, breathing against her, and one of his hands seeped into her hair. He waited, waited, waited.

Her heart faltered with the same thrill of dipping in and out of the ocean, and breaking the surface, and leaping with a salty splash into his kiss.

His hands seized her face. He pressed hard, quick, roving her lips, drinking her love. Yes, she was burning, just as the moth. She'd known it would burn. He was out of control, and she was out of her mind, and the flames choked her and thrilled her and engulfed her.

He pulled away and hastened to the other side of the kitchen.

She couldn't move. Maybe she'd never move again.

Turning back to her without looking into her face, he nodded to the kitchen door. "Go back to bed now, Eliza." His voice was husky. "I shall check outside and make certain nothing is astir. Goodnight." He rushed from the kitchen before she could answer.

As if she could have answered anyway.

CHAPTER 12

Morning dawned too quickly.

Eliza stood before the gilt-framed mirror in Miss Haverfield's chamber, as the woman adjusted the last purple flower on Eliza's poke bonnet.

"There. You look much better in this dreadful thing than I ever did. Indeed, you make it lovely." Miss Haverfield smoothed the collar of the matching purple pelisse. "The entire outfit is yours. What do you think?"

Eliza squeezed a finger past the straw bonnet and scratched an itch. "It is. . .very nice. Thank you."

"La, think nothing of it. What are women for but to aid each other in fashion?" She locked arms with Eliza, declared they were ready to depart, then led the way to the last place Eliza wanted to go.

The breakfast parlor.

Pressure built along her chest, and for the hundredth time since last night, she moistened lips that felt unreal to her. He had kissed them? No, she had only dreamed it.

Yet he had. She knew he had. How strange that he should have done such a thing. She knew he pitied her. She knew he wished to protect her. She knew, in some way or another, he cared for her—all things she understood and made sense of.

But she didn't understand why he kissed her.

Not at all.

The breakfast parlor door swung open before she was prepared. She didn't want to face him, not when it was Miss Haverfield he would be smiling upon, and Miss Haverfield he would be speaking to, and Miss Haverfield he would be wishing he had kissed last night.

But as they approached the quaint round table, it was not Felton Northwood who glanced up from a newspaper to greet them.

"Good morning, Mr. Northwood." Miss Haverfield curtsied, and Eliza mimicked the movement. "I do hope your wife had a tolerable night?"

"Yes indeed. Yes indeed." He stood from his chair, wiped a bit of marmalade from the corner of his mouth, and motioned to the sideboard. "Do help yourself to anything you wish, my dears. I am quite finished and must be off to sit with Mrs. Northwood."

"Of a certain. You must not detain yourself on our account." Miss Haverfield was already moving to fill her plate. "I have persuaded Miss Gillingham to accompany me on my weekly visit to the poor, so unfortunately I shall not be here to assist you."

"Tut, tut, we shall need no such assistance. You have quite done enough these past days, dear girl." Tucking his newspaper under his arm, he turned to Eliza. "Miss Gillingham." A nod, a smile, a shift of his eyes. *Miss Gillingham.*

Then he bowed and was gone.

Her mind spun. *Miss Gillingham.* The voice. The words. *Miss Gillingham, Miss Gillingham.* Images flashed through her mind— shadows moving, the tapestry, another window, a hand suffocating her mouth. *Miss Gillingham, do not scream.*

"Dear?"

Eliza jerked before she realized the hand on her arm didn't mean to hurt her. She raked in a breath and met the rounded, skeptical eyes of Miss Haverfield.

The woman frowned. "Whatever is the matter?"

"Nothing." She turned to the sideboard and stared down at blurred, nauseating food. "It is nothing. . .truly."

"Well I do hope you heard some of what I said. I was telling you of the dearest little curiosity shop in Lodnouth. We simply must go if we finish our visits before teatime, as there are so many wondrous things there. Why, once I found the most darling little pearl necklace and. . ."

The words drained away. Everything drained away. She gripped the edge of the sideboard and squeezed her eyes shut against the memories.

Only they weren't memories. They were lies. Imaginations. The result of too much pain and too little sleep—because it was not possible Richard Northwood had been there that night.

He was an innocent man.

Felton said so. Felton believed so.

No way under heaven had Mr. Northwood told her not to scream.

Felton leaned back under the shadow of the coffeehouse eaves and lowered the brim of his hat. All morning, he'd been dogging Mr. David Bowles throughout the village, and not once had the man caught on to him.

Even now, across the street, Bowles continued down the sidewalk in the late-morning sun, looking neither right nor left. He walked with speed, head erect, a stick tucked under his arm and a priggish sway to his steps. Gads, but the man was proud. Did he really think himself so superior?

Lowering his stick, Bowles halted in front of the haberdasher window, peered at something through the glass, then slipped inside the open-doored building.

Felton let air fill his cheeks, then blew it out. This was pointless. All morning had been a waste. What did he really think he would gain by following the man?

Mayhap Bowles had nothing to do with any of this. Mayhap, if Felton was going to follow anyone, it should be Lord Gillingham.

But he wouldn't think of that now. Yet another matter he tried to shove away from the recesses of his mind.

Like the kiss.

Over and over he'd been taunted with it, that senseless moment. Like a dream or a terror or a whisper, soft and faint, it had pulsated through him and forced him to relive the scene a thousand times.

How soft she'd been. As soft as he'd ever thought her to be. How sweetly and eagerly her lips had responded to his, as if whatever he felt she'd felt too, as if she—

No. The resolve again. The weak resolve. *No, I cannot.*

He pushed off the coffeehouse wall and started down the street, wiping away the sweat from his forehead. He had to keep his bearings. He had to keep his mind on the matters at hand. If there was any hope of getting to the bottom of this, he could not let himself become distracted—especially by something he'd already determined should never be.

Indeed, the kiss had been a mistake.

One he would not make again.

***

Felton. Again and again, Eliza saw his face in her mind. She saw his eyes become stricken, his features twist with disbelief—the same disbelief as when she'd confided to him the suspicions of her father's guilt.

But maybe her father wasn't guilty. Maybe Mr. Northwood wasn't either. Maybe Eliza didn't remember anything, and if she ever had seen the man who murdered her mother, the memory was too distant to ever summon back.

She squeezed her fists in her lap as the barouche jostled them onward. She wouldn't tell Felton. She couldn't tell him. Too much was unclear and indistinct. Just a voice in the dark, anyone's perhaps, begging her not to scream. Could she really swear it had been Mr. Northwood?

"This is our last stop, and then we may return to the village. I am simply elated to show you that delightful curiosity shop I spoke of." When the barouche door swung open, Miss Haverfield folded her parasol and accepted the footman's aid to the ground, baskets swinging from both arms.

Eliza followed with her own baskets. After breakfast, they'd taken the Northwood gig to Miss Haverfield's estate, where the barouche, a dozen baskets, and a wigged footman were already awaiting them.

Miss Haverfield nodded to the first of a row of cottages. "Here dwells the ill-mannered Mrs. Coote." They sidestepped a mud puddle on the path to the door. "Mr. Coote died some years back of dropsy, and his wife has been cursing everyone or giving them raging stares ever since. I positively detest coming here. But as Father says"—she rapped on the splintery door with her white glove—"one must keep up good opinions, must we not?"

In seconds, the door rattled open and a red-faced woman with grime in her wrinkles blinked up at them.

"Good day, Mrs. Coote." Miss Haverfield flashed a smile and handed over the basket of fruits and breads and a knitted shawl. "I do hope you have been doing well—"

The door slammed shut before more could be said.

Miss Haverfield shrugged, mumbled something about the oddities of the poor, then moved along to the next half-crumbling hovel, then the next after that. "You know, Miss Gillingham, you must take more care against the sun."

The third door opened and Eliza offered a basket to the thin boy on the other side.

"After all, do you wish to break out in freckles? Or worse yet, become dreadfully brown?" She twirled her parasol as they approached the next cottage. "But then again, I should not scold you so, should I? You could not have known such things, I suppose, in that wretched forest of yours. Truly, I wonder that you know anything at all."

Something dark fell over the window of the last cottage.

Miss Haverfield shooed away a pig that sauntered toward them. "Heavens, the primitivism of this place. I can hardly bear the smell."

The second window darkened too.

"There used to be a child or two running about. Not that I deign myself to village gossip, mind you, but it has been mentioned more than once that the wife disappeared with some Romani gypsy." She tapped on the door and sighed. "I doubt he shall answer at all. Indeed, if I were such as he, I dare to say I would never show my face again. But I suppose that is what he deserves for housing his wife in such a place and half starving the lot of them—"

The door eased open to a crack. "Yes?" Gruff, deep.

Miss Haverfield smiled again, said something cheerful, as Eliza reached out with the basket.

The crack widened. A hand seized her wrist. She fell through the doorway, panic striking her chest when the door slammed shut. And locked.

No, no. The room was dim, every window darkened, as Miss Haverfield's scream rose on the other side.

Then the pistol. The single barrel stared down at her. The stranger took one step back, then two, then three, as if the reality of pulling the trigger took more courage than he was prepared for.

The shot rang the same time she rolled. She scampered for the other side of the room, heard him curse as the screams outside grew louder.

Then he seized something. A chair. He raised it over his head and charged, but she darted beneath the table.

He threw it over. Bashed his elbow into her face. Twice.

Fear, pain, paralysis, as warm blood flooded over her lips. *Please no.* But he was already dragging her up, throwing her over his shoulder.

Pounding vibrated the cottage door. A man's voice shouting. Miss Haverfield's scream. Boards whining and cracking and hinges busting. . .

The man threw his foot through the wooden slats nailed in the window. He started to shove her through, wood scratching her arms, but the front door must have fallen through because he yanked her back and dove headfirst out the window.

"Stop! Stop!" The footman's shout. He raced for the window and shot a bullet toward the escaping madman.

But he wouldn't stop. None of them would. They would hunt her and terrorize her and hurt her until the beast was happy and she was dead.

Miss Haverfield fell next to her on the floor and framed her face. Blood seeped onto the white gloves. "Oh dear." Shaky and real and devoid of that usual note of mock sweetness. "Poor little thing, are you dying? Has he murdered you?"

"No." Eliza scooted back against the cottage wall, escaped the touch, and smeared the blood from her nose and lips. The metallic taste stayed in her mouth. "No. . .they have not murdered me."

Not yet.

The Northwood boy was careful. He was nonchalant and imperceptible, an expert at his task.

But not expert enough.

Bowles spared another glance past the beaver hats on display in the window. The coffeehouse across the street was devoid of any lurking figures.

Good. The boy was gone. If he played that game again, Bowles would have to teach him a lesson despite the repercussions.

Tipping his hat at the haberdasher, more to demonstrate the quality of his own hat over those for sale in the store, he quit the establishment and headed straight for the port. He strolled out to one of the docks, breathed in fresh sea air, and pulled out his watchcase. Five till eleven. In less than an hour, Monsieur d'Espernon would arrive to take the £20,000 note from Bowles's pocket.

Then the *Célestine II* would be his. Another merchant ship. Another victory.

The gray-blue sea rolled in wave after wave, splashing lightly against the poles of the dock. More things still needed to be set in place—a seamstress to prepare the black masts, a few more men to make up a crew, a date to load more contraband, another letter to his Indian and Chinese contacts.

Then the *Célestine II* would be ready to join *Marywich* and their six other ships. If only his father could see them now. What had started as a small vessel smuggling out goods from the Durham coast had grown into a full operation.

He would have been proud. He *should* have been proud. They were as ruthless, his children, as the man who raised them had ever been.

And more. Much more.

Footsteps creaked the dock, and Bowles' hand dropped to his pistol on instinct. He waited, expecting the foreign greeting from Monsieur d'Espernon.

Instead, the footsteps halted and no hail came.

Bowles turned. "Breage."

Sweat upturned the ends of the man's shaggy hair, and his cheeks blazed red despite the cool breeze. He glanced around him twice before he spoke. "I watched the 'ouse like you told me."

"And?"

"Two o' them went visitin' alone, they did, so I followed them. . . followed them right to where Tall Postle lives—err lived, I mean."

"Go on."

"While they was at the other cottages, I went inside and waited for them. This close, I was." He pinched two beefy fingers. "This close."

"That close, you say?" Bowles approached him. Seized the man's throbbing wrist. Tugged him closer. "What did I tell you, friend, about being that close?"

Perspiration dotted Breage's forehead. He mumbled something incoherent. Some pathetic, whining little sound.

Until Bowles pulled out his knife.

Then he blanched, shook his head, and pulled away at his wrist.

"Hold out your fingers, Breage."

"No, sir, no—"

"Hold them out." Bowles jerked him closer, squeezing the wrist so tight his own fingers cramped. "Now."

The man's fingers uncurled from their fist, trembling.

Then the knife blade slashed across them and blood spewed forth, dotting the wet dock boards, dripping onto their boots.

With a deep-throated groan, Breage finally jerked away. He clasped his bleeding hand to his chest and bit his lip, waiting, begging for mercy.

Bowles waved him away. "Get Amos and the Swabian and circle the Northwood abode. If she leaves again, follow her. If there is opportunity, kill her."

"Yes, sir." He turned to leave—

"And Breage?"

The man's shoulders slumped as he glanced back at him. "Yes, sir?"

"Do not fail me again, hmm? I should hate to mutilate all of your fingers at once."

The knock came again. Louder. Loud enough Eliza wondered if he'd break down the guest chamber door. "Eliza, open up."

"Please, Felton."

"Open the door."

"I cannot. Please." She could not face him now. She could not face anyone. Not with blood crusting her nostrils, not with tears, not with her legs still shaking so hard she wondered if they were strong enough to carry her.

"I want to know what happened. I have a right to know."

She backed against the wall, tore off the bonnet with the purple flowers.

"He hurt you."

Yes.

"You should have never left this house."

I know.

"Eliza, do you hear me?"

Her lips quivered without answer.

Then the door jarred, as if he'd pounded it with his fist, and his footfalls marched away.

She sank to the floor, fumbling with the buttons of her pelisse, easing in one breath after another until they finally started to regulate.

Dear Savior, when will it end?

She was losing strength. She was losing hope.

She was losing everything.

◦⦁◦

"Why will she not open up the dashed door?" Felton faced the mantel and could have run a fist through the infuriating sound of the longcase clock.

Behind him, Miss Haverfield sniffed again. "It was all so frightening, Felton. I could scarcely keep myself from fainting. To come so close, so terribly close to misadventure and death—"

"Why did he not follow him?"

"Who?"

"The footman! Why did he not stay after the blackguard and see he didn't escape?"

"But who would have protected us if he had? We most certainly could not have been left alone, not after such an ordeal. Why, I shiver to think if it had been I who had handed that horrid man the basket—"

"How injured is she?" He swallowed twice, mind reeling as fast as the incessant *ticktock*s of the clock.

A sigh filled the drawing room. "Is there nothing else important to you?"

"What?"

"You seem to care very little that my life was endangered today."

"It was not you, Miss Haverfield, that man was after. It was not you he locked in the cottage. It was not you he shot at. It was not you he struck, and it was not you he tried to kill." He turned on her. "Yes, I pity you the ordeal, but I have greater things to think of."

Pink flashed to her cheeks. "A gentleman would not speak so harshly to a woman so close to falling ill with fright."

"If you are so ill, perhaps you should retire to your chamber."

"Perhaps I shall." Indignation lifted both of her brows. "We seem to both be not quite ourselves at the moment." When he did not respond, she wiped moisture from her eyes and started from the room.

Papa ambled through the doorway as she exited. "Son, the constable has just departed."

Felton exhaled. He needed to get out of this house. He needed to ride or walk or have fisticuffs with the first person to oblige him, lest the anger explode.

"Come now, Son. Do not look so miserable. She is quite safe now."

Yes, for now. This moment. But what about tomorrow? What about the next time he was away or couldn't be near her?

Papa took out his tobacco pouch and moved for the stand. He flipped open a box and rummaged through the contents. "Miss Haverfield has been quite the guest, you know. Splendid girl. Perhaps a carriage ride—the fresh air and all that sort of thing—would do you both a bit of good. When I was young, courting was the greatest diversion to any dilemma."

"I do not wish to be diverted from my troubles. I wish to resolve them."

"Yes, well, as do we all."

Felton headed for the door. "Your pipe is in the study, if that is what you are looking for."

"Oh? Oh yes, just the thing." The box lid clicked shut. "And, Son?"

In the doorway, Felton waited.

"Lord Gillingham was here just after breakfast this morning. I thought it best to tell you he was asking to see his daughter."

Felton's blood went cold. "You told him nothing, of course?"

"Only that she was not home. That she had gone visiting with Miss Haverfield to the cottages outside of the village—"

Felton darted away before he could hear any more. He ground his teeth as he brushed past Dodie, ran through the house, busted out the front door, and raced for the path.

So help him, he'd kill Lord Gillingham. He'd tear him into a thousand pieces and stomp on the remains if he was the one who hurt Eliza.

If he was the one who hurt them all.

CHAPTER 13

"Where is he?"

The butler must have noted something amiss because the wonted smile and cordial greeting never touched his lips. Instead, they frowned. "I fear, Mr. Northwood, that perhaps another time would be best—"

"There is no other time. Which room is he in?"

"But Mr. Northwood, he is unprepared for visitors at the moment. He is. . .well, Mr. Northwood, he is rather—"

"What Mr. Kelby is so clumsily trying to say," said Mrs. Eustace, as she swept forward, "is that Mr. Gillingham is in the garden." A rare glimpse of emotion softened her eyes. "At the rosebushes, if you must know."

Felton turned back for the door and descended the steps. His palms were wet. His mind frayed. His heartbeat reckless. *God, I do not want to face him.*

The garden path suffocated him, tinier than he remembered, shorter than he wanted it to be. Well-trimmed bushes, cast-iron garden urns, rows of colors so bright his eyes ached.

Then Lord Gillingham. He sat on a bench near the rosebushes, with something pink and familiar draped across his knees. The dress. The one Eliza had worn at the ball.

The one her mother had worn.

At his approach, Lord Gillingham glanced up. He smiled. Strange, that he would do that. That even with tears on his cheeks, his expression would gladden at the presence of his friend.

His friend.

The words burned, hurt, mocked. Because he no longer could believe in them. He wanted to. He'd always wanted to.

But he couldn't.

"Do not display such astonishment, Northwood, at the sight of my tears." The smile faltered. "I am made of flesh and blood as the rest of you."

"What is your soul of?"

"What?"

"I said your soul, my lord. What is it made of?"

"Once? Happiness, contentment, the strife and joy of manhood, marriage, and wealth." His face turned back to the rosebushes. "Now it is made of whatever heaven has taken from me. It is made of her."

"Your wife."

"Yes, my wife. The one thing I can never have again—along with my daughter."

"Why did you come?"

Again, Lord Gillingham met his gaze. His features tightened, body stiffened, as if the hardness of the words finally came through to him.

Felton stepped closer, balling both fists. "You knew she ran. You knew she was afraid of you. And yet you came."

"I knew nothing of her fear."

"You knew that and more."

"Northwood, you—"

"You knew Minney's father loved your wife. You had him removed, him and his daughter, but it was not enough because she followed him. You loved her. I know you loved her. You loved her so much you could not live with such a thing and you—"

"I what, Northwood?" He stood. The dress slipped to the ground. "Go on. Finish."

He couldn't. Even if everything were true, he couldn't say the words. A spear of doubt and terrifying emptiness destroyed the anger, until he couldn't even look Lord Gillingham in the face.

"You want me to tell you I did not kill Minney's father. You want me to say I did not kill my wife."

Say it. Felton's fists tightened. He'd do anything to hear the words. Anything to make everything untrue. *Please, say it.*

But Lord Gillingham said nothing. He shook his head, picked the dress back up from the ground, and returned to his bench. He spoke without lifting his head. "It is time you leave Monbury, Northwood."

Pain rent Felton's heart.

"I think it best you do not come back."

"You don't understand." The curtains fluttered, but there was no beast. Only broken glass and the echo of the scream and the footfalls rushing away behind her.

She looked down and could not look away. Her mother. Twisted and bashed and mangled in red, red, red. She hated red. The curtains brushed her face. Red again.

Then she ran. She rushed back to the nursery, closed the door, scampered back to her trundle bed, and hugged her knees. She stared at the tapestry. The woven picture. The beast on the wall, with his frightening eyes and giant claws and wretched teeth.

Outside the nursery, more footsteps. Servants yelling. Doors opening and slamming. The nursery door creaked, and Mrs. Eustace peered in. She sighed. Maybe because Eliza had not fallen through the window like her mother. Because she wasn't dead. Because there wasn't red. Always red.

"Go back to sleep, child, and never mind the noise." A gentle command, and the door clicked shut.

Dark. Quiet.

Except for the moonlight in the window and the scratching outside. The loud, loud scratching—coming closer, rattling the window, squeaking it open.

Then a face. How strangely it stared at her through the opening, with luminous eyes, with a maddening look, with a voice breathless and threatening.

Mr. Northwood.

Mr. Northwood creeping toward her and covering her mouth.

Mr. Northwood begging her not to scream.

———————

A noise stirred in the blackness of the stables.

Felton pulled his pistol the same time he turned. He backed into the stall with his horse, breath stilled, and searched beyond the lantern glow for the silhouette of a figure. "Step into the light or I shall shoot."

"I do not doubt you would." The feminine voice, hushed and smooth, calmed the racket in his chest. "With the way you have wounded my heart, a mortal wound would be no great surprise."

He stuffed his pistol back into his trousers. "Come out, Miss Haverfield."

She entered the glow of light, fully dressed in a scarlet redingote and jockey bonnet, with a riding crop clasped in gloved hands. "Pray, do not look as if my presence so vexes you."

"It doesn't." He pulled the saddle from his horse. "It has been a long day. That is all."

"You were gone the length of it."

"Yes."

"Where to?"

The sea, where he'd sat all day in the sand and let the sun burn his face and watched the boats drift to and from the docks. Not that it had done any good. He'd left the shore with as many questions and troubles as he'd come with.

"Felton?"

He glanced back at her, went rigid as she slinked next to him. Apricot mingled with the heavy smells of horse sweat and old hay. "What are you doing out here?" he asked.

"You did not answer me."

"What?"

"Indeed, you have not answered me at all. In any respect. On any matter."

"I do not understand—"

"Oh, let us not pretend, Felton. For many years now we have endured a sort of silent attachment. And though it was not possible, through no fault of my own, for us to be together. . .still we have been true to each other."

"I fear that is a reality Scrope was never made aware of."

All coyness raced from her face. A vein bulged in her forehead, and for the second time that day, her face turned unnaturally pink. "You mock me, and I shall not stand for it."

"You have mocked me a thousand times, Miss Haverfield, and *I* have always stood for it."

"Whatever are you talking about?"

"If you do not know, there is little point in mentioning it."

"Do you know why I came out here?"

"Why?"

"To persuade you to take another ride with me. Just as we used to do before that. . .that wretched *child* arrived."

Annoyance flared. "She is not wretched, and she is hardly a child."

"She might as well be with the mind she has. Are you even aware how very little she knows? I would dare to say she had never curtsied to anyone until she came here. She knows nothing of proper etiquette. She knows nothing of instruments or letter writing or acceptable manners on receiving a guest. Indeed, she could not dress herself in mode if someone did not aid her!"

The stables stilled. Silence stretched between them.

He denied none of it because all of it was true. He knew that. Everyone did. All reasons why he could never unrein his heart. Or let himself fall. Or allow himself time, even for a second, to imagine anything at all between himself and the girl from the forest.

In the name of heaven, he ought to marry Miss Haverfield. He ought to ride with her tonight. He ought to kiss her now. He ought to find a way, somehow, to ensure a courtship blossomed between them.

"Father has given his blessing." As if she'd sensed his thoughts. "We need never hide our affections nor endure such secrecy again." Leaning closer. "It is what you have always wanted, Felton." Gaze lowering to his lips. "What we both have always wanted."

He took her shoulders with his hands. For a long time, he stared at her. The long lashes. The yellow curls. The creamy skin so unaccustomed to sun, and the lips poised, waiting, and expectant. What pride there would be in walking the street with such a lady. How people would be awed. How they'd respect, for the first time, something accomplished by a Northwood.

But she'd never look at him the way Eliza did, with eyes guileless and true. She'd never say all the things that bore meaning or draw out his hurt and make it easier.

And she'd never kiss him the way Eliza kissed him. How could she? How could anyone? Eliza's lips had been trembling and uncertain and...pure. So pure and sweet and true, as if the kiss were words and the words said she loved him.

Of course she didn't love him.

He didn't love her. Did he? Did she?

"Felton..."

He eased Miss Haverfield away from him. He squeezed past her from the stall and never so much as turned when she called his name again. "Goodnight, Miss Haverfield," was all he said.

By morning, he knew, she'd be gone. He'd just severed any chances he might have had with the woman he'd spent his whole life longing for.

What was wrong with him? In the name of heaven, what was he doing?

─────────

She knew.

Eliza leaned against the bedchamber window as morning's soft light penetrated the dewy panes. Below, two gray pigeons met on the mossy flint wall behind the house. They fluttered their wings, seemed to sing something to one another, then flew away together in unison.

If only she were a bird. If only she could fly away. If only she didn't know and couldn't remember and the nightmare had never tightened its focus.

But it had. Mr. Northwood had been there. The watch fob by her mother's body was no coincidence. . .it was evidence.

Evidence Felton had never been able to believe.

And she hadn't the courage to tell.

Behind her, someone tapped lightly on the door. It creaked open, and Dodie rushed in. "Oh, Miss Gillingham. I come to 'elp you with your stays and dress and hair and all, but you be already dressed."

Eliza touched the loose tresses on her shoulder. Mrs. Eustace—indeed, Miss Haverfield too—would have twisted them all away and filled her head with pins.

She didn't want pins today. Or bonnets with purple flowers. Not when her head already hammered, and the only thing she wanted to do was rush out to that mossy wall, sit with the birds, and feel the wind play with her hair.

Dodie went to the washstand and inspected the pitcher and bowl. "I'll be gettin' you fresh water, Miss Gillingham. Anything you be needin' you just ask Dodie. That be what I told Miss Haverfield too. I said to her, I said, 'Miss Haverfield, if ever you need water, I be fetchin' it. If ever you need more coverlets, I be fetchin' it. If ever you need tea or crumpets or lavender shortbread, I be fetchin' it right for you.' And she says to me—"

Another tap on the half-open door.

Eliza glanced up. Her heart jumped to her throat at the sight of Felton.

He leaned in the doorway, hair damp and clean across his forehead, eyes soft as they beheld her. He interrupted a second string of Dodie's ramblings. "Walk with me to breakfast, Miss Gillingham."

She wanted to tell him she couldn't, that she was not hungry and wished only to remain in her chamber.

But she had no power over his commands, so she met him in the hall and placed her hand around the arm he lifted. They walked in silence. He smelled of soap and freshness, the scent invigorating and pleasant like the early morning breeze back in the forest.

If she closed her eyes, mayhap she could imagine she was there. That Captain was alive. That the stream was just ahead, with its babbling noises and cool touch and—

"Should I pretend to not have noticed?" he asked.

"Noticed?"

"The thing you did not wish me to see yesterday. You know." He glanced at her, a grin overwhelming his face, and tapped his nose.

Understanding dawned. She looked away lest he study the swelling more closely. "Is it so very bad?"

"Not bad enough you should have refused to see me."

"I—"

"After all, I dare to say you have seen me with *my* injured face. I did not hide from you, now did I?"

"No. I suppose you did not."

"Besides." The white-painted stairs creaked as they started down them. "You are more lovely with your swollen nose than most are without one."

The words struck her. Like the kiss, only different—and all over again, she could not speak. Lovely? Felton Northwood found her lovely?

He was being kind, of course. He only wished to assuage her fears and make her smile. More of his tender pity.

"Hungry?"

She nodded, but it wasn't true. Especially not when they reached the breakfast parlor and the door swept open to the same scene as yesterday.

Mr. Northwood. Seated at the table. Newspaper in one hand and steaming teacup in the other. "Ah, just the person, Son. Sit down."

Felton waited until Eliza took her seat before he took the chair next to her.

"Miss Haverfield, I fear, has given her farewells and made a hasty departure. I arranged for the groom to take her back in our carriage."

A flicker of relief shot through Eliza, but it faded just as quickly. Miss Haverfield had been her diversion these past days. Her companion, albeit an intimidating one. What would she do now that the woman had departed? When Felton was gone, she'd be. . .she'd be. . .

Alone. She raised her eyes to Mr. Northwood as he spoke back and forth with Felton, the words droning away without meaning. His eyes smiled often. He laughed too. The sound was lighthearted and pleasant, in likeness to that of his son's.

He'd killed her mother. He must have. Nothing else made sense. Why else would he have been there that night? Why else had he climbed through her window and trapped her mouth with his hand?

She watched the same hand now, as he lifted the teacup to his lips, then lowered it to the saucer with a *clank*. He laughed again, but all she heard was his voice. *"Do not scream."*

She squeezed her hands under the table.

"I shall not hurt you, Miss Gillingham."

Yet he had. He must have. He was the beast, wasn't he? The claws, the claws, the claws. . .

"Hold onto my neck."

No, she wouldn't.

"Do not fight me. Do not scream. Please, Miss Gillingham, do not scream."

"What think you to that, Eliza?"

She snapped her face to Felton as he stood from his chair. "Forgive me. . .think to what?"

"I have errands to do in the village today, but Papa has offered to give you a tour of the grounds. We haven't much to boast of, but as you are so fond of the outdoors, it will be a pleasant diversion for you."

She stood as well and swallowed. "Please, Felton. I wish to go with you."

"Not possible."

"Felton, I—"

"Sit back down, and I shall get your breakfast. Tea or chocolate?" When she didn't answer, nearly wilted back into her chair, he decided for her. Seconds later, he lowered a cup of hot cocoa and two tiny cakes made with caraway seeds. The wafting scent stirred hunger despite her lack of appetite.

Felton returned to his seat beside her with his own plate. The meal passed quickly, strangely, the silence broken only when their forks bumped the plates or their cups clanged the saucers.

Then Felton stood again and pulled the napkin from his cravat. "Good day to both of you. I shall return in time for dinner at the very least." He started from the room—

"Felton." She burst from her chair and caught him at the door. She circled his arm with her hand. "Please, take me with you."

She hadn't meant to lean so close to him. Or whisper in his face like this.

But instead of drawing away, he leaned forward. His lips brushed her forehead and he whispered back, "I shall return soon. Do not worry. Papa shall keep you from any harm."

Then he hurried away.

And she was alone with the man from her nightmare.

Felton threw the saddle over his horse's back and tightened the girth. Gads, but it was haunting him. The look on her face, the desperation in her eyes, as if she were communicating something vital she couldn't speak aloud.

Which was nonsense, of course. She was safer in his home than anywhere else, and she knew better than anybody why Felton must leave. If anyone was going to find the man trying to destroy her it was him.

Even so.

He turned the stirrup iron and grabbed the candle, preparing to mount, but hesitated. This was nonsense. There was no reason he should stay or give in to her frightened whispers like some sort of fool.

But he unsaddled his horse anyway. He jogged back to the house and reentered the breakfast parlor, where she sat at the rounded table as stiff as a corpse.

Papa turned the page of his newspaper. "Forget something, did you, Son?"

"Yes."

Eliza turned in her chair. Moisture brightened her eyes.

"Come, Eliza, and if you plan to wear a bonnet, you had better fetch it now."

She jumped from her chair and a small laugh escaped. "Where are we going?"

He grabbed her hand. "Just come and do not ask questions." Together, they hurried outside into a world of singing birds and playful breezes. He prepared the gig while she denied need of a bonnet, and they journeyed the quiet road with not a word spoken between them.

Yet she leaned so close to him. After a time, as the sun heightened and cast sunrays onto the dusty road, she slipped her arm around his. Why would she do such a thing? If anyone passed, they would whisper and gasp. Didn't she know such affection between an unwed gentleman and an unwed lady was unseemly?

No, she didn't know. She didn't know anything. In some foolish way, he hoped no one ever taught her. He hoped she stayed just as she was today, without her bonnet and without decorum, clinging to his arm as if she needed him, a wild and unlearned creature of the woods.

His wild creature. 'Twas not true, of course. She wasn't and likely would never be. A hundred reasons stood in the way of such a match, and if he cared anything for his name he would end his maddening downfall.

But she felt like his. Like they belonged together. Like he couldn't keep living if one day she left. Or cast her smile upon someone else. Or died at the hands of the beast in her dreams.

Please, God, let me protect her.

They crested the grassy hill in the jostling gig, and the first sight of the ocean changed her face. "Oh Felton." How quickly all the shadows flitted away. How beautifully all the lovely thoughts in her head made her eyes shine and lips smile and voice turn breathless.

He hopped to the ground, then reached for her. He pulled her into him and might have repeated his last mistake, lowered his mouth in another damaging kiss, if she had not grabbed his hand and started running. They raced down the sandy hill, stopping only when they reached the water's edge and the foamy waves wet the tops of their black boots.

"Let us go in, Felton. Please." Like reckless children, they took off their shoes again and waded into the warm water. He held both of her hands. She laughed and tugged her fingers loose every so often to brush the wind-tossed hair from her face.

Then they climbed back to the shore, laid next to each other on the sand, hands still entwined. Above them, the sun shifted in the blue, cloudless sky, and the hues of morning slowly morphed to hues of afternoon.

His lungs took in the air, salty and warm and hinting of rose water every time the wind gusted.

She told him stories of nonsense. Sometimes he listened with interest, pained at the tears in her voice, knowing her heart still longed for the one she had lost. Other times he didn't hear at all, just listened to the cadence of her voice, soothed by the enthusiasm of her imagination.

He loved her.

He was a fool in a thousand ways, but he could not help himself. He wanted to be a fool. Let the righteous residents of Lodnouth stroll by and find them this way, a shocking tale, another reproach on the Northwood name—only this time it didn't matter. Nothing mattered but now. But this.

But her.

He rolled his head and cut off her story with his lips. Every nerve exploded, as his sandy hand framed her jaw, as he dragged his kiss to the corner of her mouth, her cheek, her nose.

She sat upright, hair fluttering around a face blushed in color. "I am afraid."

"Why?"

"I am afraid for you to kiss me."

"I am afraid of it myself."

"Felton, I—"

He leaned up and stilled her words with a finger to her mouth. Her trembling, moist, perfect mouth. He shook his head. "No more. We must return home now."

She nodded and stood, brushing the sand from her wet dress, grabbing their boots. Partway up the hill, in sight of the gig, she stopped and glanced back. "I wish I could keep it forever."

If only they could.

***

Bowles slammed his window shut against the night air, grabbed the letter from his nightstand, and slipped in bed. The wood frame creaked as he turned on his side, positioning the letter so the tallow candle's glow would illuminate the words:

She remembers just as I told you she would. It is only a matter of time before she knows everything and we are all ruined. You must act quickly. If I am brought back into this shame, yet again, think not that I shall go alone. We will both hang, dear brother. Remember that.

He closed his fingers around the letter. Crumpled it into a ball. Tossed it across the tiny chamber, where Miss Reay would see it come morning and hurry it away.

His blood surged with heat. 'Twas not the image of the gallows that so bothered him. Or even the pressure of finding and eliminating this troublesome Eliza Gillingham whom he should have killed many years ago.

'Twas the tone. The voice in the letter. Telling him what to do, ordering him about with a lack of respect so great it made him want to load his dueling pistol, ride to the Northwood home, and end the only sibling his father had left him.

But he wouldn't.

He would do as he was told.

With so much at stake, he had very little choice.

———— ✦ ————

The next morning, Felton never came for Eliza. She remained in her chamber until the octagonal mantel clock struck nine, at which time Dodie swept in and chattered as she helped Eliza dress for the day.

"Oh no, Miss Gillingham," said the girl, as she pulled the shift over Eliza's head. "Master Northwood rode out early, he did, and ne'er said a word to me when he should come home."

"When does he usually?"

"Usually what, Miss Gillingham?"

"Come home?"

"Oh me, who can know?" Dodie laced the stays with expert speed. "Why, I was just tellin' Mrs. Northwood the other day, I says to her, 'Mrs. Northwood, Master Northwood be gone all the time anymore.' And she says to me, 'Dodie, you be mindin' your own matters, you hear me?' So that's what I be tryin' to do all the time. Mind my own matters."

A smile started at Eliza's lips. Dodie and Minney, perhaps, would make well-suited friends.

When her petticoat and muslin gown were donned, her stockings fastened, and her boots tied, she moved to the round mirror above the washstand and allowed Dodie to run a comb through her tresses.

The reflection of herself stared back at her, a girl she hardly knew. Where was the child she'd seen in the ripples of the stream so many times? The laughing little thing who carried no care in her eyes, nor frown upon her lips, nor pale shade of fear in her cheeks?

Alas, but she was gone. She was buried in the forest somewhere, like the corpse of a once-happy fairy, now cold and spiritless and rotting in the hole of a tree.

Like Captain.

She looked away before she witnessed her own pain and trained her features to remain stoic, lest Dodie should notice. The last thing she needed, or wanted, was more pity.

"There. You be all finished, Miss Gillingham. Oh—and 'ere." Dodie dug into her pocket and fished out a small paper. "I ne'er read this. I ne'er so much as looked at it, on account of me tryin' like Mrs. Northwood told me to mind my own matters."

Eliza glanced over the elegant invitation. *Miss Eliza Gillingham is invited to attend a private ball at Jaxhill Hall, Friday evening, September eleventh, at six o'clock.* Signed, in lovely script, by Miss Haverfield.

"What it say, Miss Gillingham?"

She placed the invitation on the mantel. "Did the Northwoods receive this too?"

"Yes, Miss Gillingham. But I ne'er read it either."

Eliza smiled, nodded, and headed for the door.

"Miss Gillingham?"

"Yes?"

"You'll be going to breakfast, won't you?"

"No, I think not. I should rather roam outside for a bit." With a parting smile, Eliza hurried her way through the hall, down the stairs, to the foyer, then outside. She circled the house quickly, nearly running until she reached that mossy flint wall she'd been admiring from her window.

She perched there, dug her fingers into the soft moss, and let her gaze take everything in. The wide, short bushes. The three towering trees. The small garden, very unsymmetrical and lacking ornaments, but pleasant in its simplicity and color.

She imagined a little boy scurrying about this very yard. Running, leaping, cackling in the bliss of childhood—with eyes and smiles like Felton, only younger. How he must have ordered about his little comrades in those days. How he must have ordered her about too. What had she thought of him as a child? Had she smiled at him often? Or been happy when he came to visit? Or pretended with him, as all children do?

She was still pretending. Pretending he loved her. Pretending she loved him.

But the kiss?

No, that had been real, unexpected, and frightening. She didn't know why she should be afraid, or how such a tiny thing could tremble the core of her being, but it had. Heaven knew that had she been given the choice of air or his lips, she would have suffocated in such a kiss. She would have lived and died in that moment and regretted nothing.

But then she had remembered. She had pulled away because it hurt too much to love him that way and not tell him.

She couldn't tell him. How wretched that of everyone in the world, she should be the one to uncover the truth that would destroy him. He would hate her for such a truth. She knew him well enough, knew his heart so that his anger and denial and disbelief were already expected. How could she do such a thing to him? How could she look into his face and tell him his father had been her kidnapper, if not her beast, all those long years ago?

God, I am so afraid. The same two pigeons she'd seen before flew together from one tree to the next, then soared to the roof of the house. *Please help me. Please guide me.*

Only then did she notice movement. On the second story of the house, two windows from her own, a white curtain stirred.

A face stared out at her. Too indistinguishable with the glint of the sun, but distinct enough her skin began to crawl with unease.

Protect me too. With the voiceless prayer, the white curtain pulled shut. The face was gone.

Whoever had been watching her had stopped.

For now.

~~~

Felton's clothes still reeked of the Jester's Sunlight as he urged his horse faster on the dusty road for home. He'd lingered at a lone table half the day, ignoring hard stares, until the Swabian finally arrived.

The man was a blackguard. A filthy, rotting, useless fool of a man. All he did was stand there, nursing his dented tankard, shoulders hunched, silent to all of Felton's questions. Indeed, not once did he speak. Had he no conscience? Did the life of an innocent girl mean so little to him?

Once or twice, he'd shaken his head, his frown so grave and eyes so wretchedly sad they might have been interpreted as a second of pity.

Or regret.

Then his buffoons had joined them and circled them, just like before—but this time Felton left without argument.

Not that he hadn't wanted to fight. Just that in his temperament of late, he might have ended up bashing one of them in so badly they'd bleed and die on the tavern floor planks.

'Twould be no great loss, that was for certain. One less fiend to victimize Eliza.

Up ahead, just before the road turned off to the smaller, gated road to home, waited a buggy along the stone wall. Orange evening light spilled over the scene and illuminated dust floating about a gentleman's postured form.

Felton reined in his horse and tipped his hat. "Mr. Haverfield."

The squire frowned, his gaze skewering Felton the way it always did. With disapproval, with disgust, with a righteous indignation as if he were handling unpleasant business with a farm hog or a thieving ragpicker.

Or the son of a woman killer.

"I shall be brief, Mr. Northwood. I have been waiting for you here today because I did not want to trouble your household with a visitor."

Or be seen at the Northwood residence, more likely.

"For many years now, I have disapproved of your interest in my daughter. I mean no unkindness, but she is far superior to you in every sense. The thought of such a match displeases me, to say the very least."

Felton curled his fingers tighter around the leather reins. "Say what you have come to say, Mr. Haverfield."

"I permitted a courtship out of my better judgment and was also so benevolent as to allow her a visit at your home, in the event she might be of some comfort to your ailing mother."

"What should I do in return for such generosity?"

"Do not mock me, Mr. Northwood. I received a weeping and brokenhearted daughter back to my home, and I demand to know why. You have teased her and tempted her heart and persuaded both of us into giving you a chance. Was it so great a trophy to win my approval? And now that you possess it, are you so foolish as to no longer want her?"

"I owe you no explanations, with all due respect."

"You do not know the meaning of the word *respect*. You or your family." The squire leaned forward, forehead tightening. "To think that *you* would dare reject *her* is inconceivable to me. This only further proves what I have been warning her about all these years. You are no good, Northwood. You are of ill repute and reckless and your blood is tainted as black as your father's. I want nothing to do with any of you." He seized his reins and turned his buggy back onto the road. "One more thing, Mr. Northwood. My daughter, despite everything, is still fool enough to want you. She has invited you and that Gillingham girl to my home." His lips pursed. "Do not come."

Felton's horse pranced as the squire cracked his whip and the buggy lunged forward. Hurt mixed with fury, and his fists itched for the satisfying crack of knuckles against cartilage.

"Sorry, Mr. Haverfield." He spoke the words to the empty billow of dust. "You may expect the Northwoods whether you want them or not."

The drawing room was quiet. She should have been afraid as she sat rigid on the scroll-end sofa, with Felton's father in the wingback chair next to her. They'd taken dinner together in a rather uncomfortable quietness, little speaking, both eating sparsely.

He had insisted she join him in the drawing room, where he had settled into his chair and lit his pipe. The faint, spicy scent of tobacco filled the room, as pleasant to her now, somehow, as it had been when Captain had always smoked.

Without meaning to, she sank deeper into the sofa and sighed.

"I say, you see that painting?"

She glanced over to the profile of the older man's face.

He wore a smile as he pointed with the stem of his pipe to a silver-framed painting above the hearth. "Aaron on the left, Hugh in the middle, Felton on the right with that rascally dog in his arms."

Of the three children, only the eldest brother wore a skeleton suit. The other two wore loose white gowns, with bowl-shaped haircuts, hair curled and eyes babyish. A smirk curved Felton's lips, as he held the speckled dog in his arms and leaned against his brother.

"How he loved that dog." Another puff. Another smile. "Carried it with him wherever he went, he did, until the poor creature was injured by a handful of village ruffians, years later."

"They. . ." She hesitated, licking her lips. "They killed his dog?"

"Yes. And Felton near killed them for it too. Likely would have had his brother Aaron not been there to drag him off." Mr. Northwood shook his head. "Always the fighter, that one. Poor chap. He'll be the. . ." He cleared his throat, yet tears still rang in his voice. "He'll be the death of his mother yet, you know."

"I am sorry." Words she shouldn't have spoken, shouldn't have felt, but they came anyway. "For your wife. Her illness, I mean."

Mr. Northwood looked at her. For the first time, his eyes did not hurry away, as if he were frightened or unnerved or ashamed. They stayed locked on hers, teary, more remorseful than threatening. "Dear girl." Whispered. "*I* am sorry."

Sorry. The word echoed back. *Sorry.* For climbing through her nursery window and stealing her away? For pushing her mother through the window? For trying to kill her, even now?

When she didn't answer, he nodded, as if he had expected the lack of response. Pressing the pipe back between his lips, he stood, muttered something about seeing to his wife, and ambled from the drawing room.

Stifling a yawn, Eliza curled deeper into the sofa and framed her face with her hands. She stared at the painting, into the young and happy faces, and wondered how the man who loved and nurtured his own children could kidnap and injure another.

But like all her questions, no answer was forthcoming.

She understood nothing at all.

"See, there she be. Just like I told you, Master Northwood—"

"Shhh." From the doorway of the drawing room, Felton waved the maid away with his hand. "Go and see to Mamma."

"But Mr. Northwood still be with her—"

"Well, go and murder that dashed mouse I've been hearing running about the halls at night. And if you cannot kill the mouse, find another duty to occupy you."

"Yes, but—"

"Dodie." He gave her a look, to which she bit the edge of her lip, nodded, and rushed away to do his bidding.

Felton entered the drawing room with a curious rhythm thumping his chest. Nearly an hour. That's how long Dodie said Eliza had been here, curled on the scroll-end sofa, both hands under her cheek. No wonder the maid could not disturb her.

He couldn't either.

Like an addled fool, he lowered to the floor, arms on his knees, and watched her. Twilight spilled in from the windows, blue and strange, while flickers of a nearby wall sconce danced on her cheeks.

Her cheeks. Flushed and warm and sun touched. Her lashes, dark and wet, as if she'd fallen asleep with tears. Her lips, barely parted, moist, pink, kissable, lovely.

He swallowed and shook his head. He shouldn't be here. He should have told Dodie to nudge Eliza awake, help her back to her chamber, and see her safely in bed for the night. Why had Eliza fallen asleep here anyway? Had she been waiting for him?

He would have been home in time for dinner had Mr. Haverfield not accosted him. After that, his blood had been boiling too fast for the proper etiquette of dinnertime, the stifling confines of his house, and another anguishing visit to his mother's chamber.

He'd gone to the cove instead. He rode and rode hard, letting the cool evening wind tug away his tension, letting the salty air reach deep in his lungs and soul. He forgot about Hugh. He forgot about Mamma. He forgot about Eliza's beast and Lord Gillingham's guilt and the name he couldn't make proud no matter how much he tried.

Help me, my God, had been his prayer. *Help everything.*

With a soft noise, Eliza stirred, then squinted open her eyes. She blinked, jerked upright. "Where am I?"

"The drawing room."

She swung her legs off the sofa, the pink of her cheeks burning to red as she patted at her disheveled hair. "I don't know how I. . . I mean, I was just sitting here and. . ." Her sleep-softened eyes lifted to something above the mantel.

He followed her gaze. The painting. "Sitting here and looking at me, were you?"

"Yes. I dreamed of you too."

"Another nightmare?"

The question had been posed in jest, but she rubbed her arms without answer and said instead, "You did not come to dinner."

"No."

"I wish you never left. The house is strange when you are gone."

"There is nothing here that will hurt you."

She looked away, shivering a second time.

"You are cold. Come." He stood, put her hand on his arm, and led her back through the house in darkness. "The stairs. Watch your step."

They ascended in silence. Near the top, she must have missed a step because she stumbled forward, and he caught her.

Then he flattened against the wall, and his hands threaded into her hair on impulse. He pulled her closer and held her tighter. As if to hide her. As if to protect her. As if to keep anyone from ever tearing her away from him. What was he doing?

This was madness, but next thing he knew, he was kissing her again. Longing opened up inside him. Precious longing. Longing to hold her like this forever and longing to always be the one who claimed her lips and longing to keep her safe and happy and. . .

"Felton." A murmur against his lips. "Felton, let me go."

The desperation in her voice kicked him. He dropped his arms. "What is wrong?"

She started away from him, but he caught her arm.

"Eliza, please."

"No, Felton. Let me go—"

"Eliza." Framing her face, he stared down into features only faintly distinguishable in the darkness. "Tell me what troubles you."

He felt tears on his fingers. "I cannot."

"The kiss?"

"No."

"Me then."

"No, Felton, please—"

"Please nothing. I shall not let you go until you tell me." His breathing came faster. "The nightmare. You have remembered something, haven't you?"

"I wish there were no nightmare."

"Eliza—"

"I wish I remembered nothing. I wish I had seen nothing. I wish he had killed me too so I would not have to. . .have to. . ."

"Have to what?"

"Something wrong, Master Northwood?" From the top of the stairs, Dodie appeared with a candlestick. The yellow light invaded the darkness and exposed the terror on Eliza's face.

He released her. "No, nothing is wrong."

Eliza scampered up the stairs and flew past Dodie. Seconds later, her chamber door slammed shut.

"My, but she be terrible upset tonight, Master Northwood. What be wrong with her?"

"I do not know." He shook his head, but a cold fear raced through him. "I do not know."

CHAPTER 14

Over the following days, Eliza seldom left her chamber. Once or twice she took her meals downstairs, and sometimes throughout the day she went out of doors to visit Merrylad.

But she had succeeded, for the most part, in avoiding both Felton Northwood and his father.

Until today.

Felton had already knocked three times. One to remind her of the ball tonight. Another to tell her what time their carriage would depart. And yet another to deliver the dress, which he'd instructed Dodie to take from his mother's wardrobe and alter to Eliza's size.

Now, four hours before the ball, she held that same dress against her. The fabric was smooth, silky, a shade of green more like the pine trees in the forest than anything else. A metallic trim decorated the neckline, hem, and sleeves—and if she'd seen this gown in a magazine, while nestled at the edge of the cottage hearth, she would have smiled and said it was lovely.

It didn't seem lovely now.

She didn't want to attend the ball, and she didn't want to see Felton. She didn't want to spend the evening close to him, dancing with him, accepting the graciousness of his smiles and kisses, all the while knowing she was about to upend his world.

She couldn't tell him.

She wouldn't.

In the dream, she had. She'd written another note and placed it in his hands, then watched as he'd unfolded it and scanned the words.

Then the dream had turned into a nightmare. A new nightmare. Not of the beast clawing her or shoving her out of the window with the red curtains.

But of Felton. He'd raced to the very same window, with the red billowing around him, and plunged through the panes. The shattered glass had pierced and cut her, made her bleed again, but it didn't matter because he had jumped. He was dead. Two bodies lay broken and mangled and bloody outside the window she hated—

"Oh, Miss Gillingham, look what else I found." Dodie entered and grinned with pride as she held up two white, elbow-length gloves. "I says to Mrs. Northwood, I says, 'Miss Gillingham will be lookin' ne'er so pretty as tonight.' And she says to me, 'Dodie, does she have gloves?' And I says to her, I says—"

"It is all so very kind of her." Eliza smiled and draped the dress across the bed. "The dress, the necklace, everything."

"She says she be wantin' you to look just perfect, Miss Gillingham."

"I wish I could thank her myself."

"She don't be wantin' to see nobody. Just Mr. Northwood and her son, she says. A mother needs a husband and son, she says."

"Yes."

"Now you be sittin' down right here, Miss Gillingham, while I be fixin' your hair. Master Northwood just rode off to get a surprise for you, he did."

"A surprise? For me?"

"Well, he ne'er did say it was a surprise. But I says to him, I says—"

"Do tell me, Dodie. Please."

"Well, he got a letter this mornin' and can you guess who it was from? Why, Lord Gillingham, that who it be from. And he says for Master Northwood to come right away, on account of a little maid called Minney who wants, says the letter, to see you more than anything at all."

Beside him in the rig, Minney fidgeted with a blue, faded ribbon. She tied it and untied it but never once lifted her head and spoke to him.

Felton glanced up at the silver-colored sky. "Looks like we may need to utilize the hood before we get there."

No answer.

"We could certainly use a bit of rain, hmm?"

Still nothing—except the only thing raining was the girl's eyes.

Felton pulled on the reins. "What is it?" When she didn't look up, he turned to face her and tugged that distracting ribbon from her fingers.

"Ye give that back to me!"

"Not until you tell me what this is all about."

She smeared more tears from her pallid cheeks. "I only can tell Miss Gillingham. She's my friend."

"I am your friend too, and if you're in danger at Monbury, if Lord Gillingham has—"

"No." She rattled her head. "No, no, no. Ye don't know. None of'ee know."

"Know what?"

"The terrible thing I done. Terrible thing. I can't even be sleepin' good no more because'ee all think he. . .that he. . ."

Aggravation spiked. "That he what? Who, Minney?"

"Lord Gillingham." She wilted on the word and puckered her lip. "He came in my room when I was hurt. I was frighted but he ne'er hurt me. He told me e'erything. How Papa ne'er loved Miss Gillingham, and she ne'er loved him. Not even a little."

"What?"

"Do'ee not see, Mr. Northwood? All the things I thought be wrong. All wrong, wrong, wrong."

"Anyone can claim innocence, Minney."

"But he had the letter. That be how I know."

"What letter?"

"My ribbon. Give me back my ribbon."

He sighed, handed it over, and hurried the gig back into motion. "When we arrive at the house, I want you to go inside and tell Eliza everything you have just told me. You understand?"

"That be why I came. She be my friend. Merrylad too. Can I see Merrylad?"

"Yes, if you wish."

When they reached the house, he helped her inside then returned to the gig and headed back for Monbury Manor. More questions needed answers.

Many more.

Felton burst through the study door and slammed to a halt.

Three heads swiveled his way, two surprised, one glowering. From behind his desk, the viscount stood, knuckles coming down on the stacks of paper. "Am I to understand there is an emergency, *Mr.* Northwood?"

Felton stiffened against the *mister*—and the tone. "No." He backed out the door. "Forgive the intrusion. I shall wait."

Less than five minutes later, the door opened again and two brown-coated men filled the hall, both as haggard and dirty looking as the hats they returned to their heads. Monbury tenants? Or killers? They each slanted a look at Felton, then hung their heads and disappeared.

Felton returned to the study and closed the door behind him. "My lord."

"You are not welcome here."

"I have come for the letter."

"If you are already convinced of my guilt, the letter will persuade you of little."

"It persuaded Minney."

"Yes." A humorless smile turned up the viscount's cheek. "It convinced Minney." He stood behind the desk, unlocked a drawer, and pulled out a faded stack of letters. "Letitia wrote to me often when I was away—and I was away too often."

"I remember."

"Trips to London, to Bath, to Brighton. There were many nights a woman might have suffered loneliness. Might have longed for companionship with someone closer than an oft-faraway husband." He lifted the first letter. "But not my Letitia. There was nothing between her and Mr. Bradshaw. Minney was a fool to imagine such a thing."

Unless the viscount was a fool for denying it.

"Shortly before another trip, Mr. Bradshaw had been acting strangely. He made mistakes. He seemed ill almost and was found sleeping one morning under the table in the dining room—with an empty bottle of laudanum."

Laudanum. The word processed. *Opium.*

"My wife and I consulted about the matter, and though we hated to release a man who had been our steward for so many years, we had no choice. Mr. Bradshaw left the premises with his daughter the same day I departed for my trip."

"And the letter from Lady Gillingham?"

"I never received it. Not until I was home, however, and she was already dead. It was lying on her writing desk, ready to be posted the next day, no doubt." He handed it over.

Felton unfolded it and read:

My dear Phillip,

As always, I am empty without your presence. You have been gone only two days, yet the distance between us seems so great. I speak not only of miles. Perhaps I have only myself to blame, and if I have pulled away from you these last months, you must forgive me. I wish we could speak of it. How much easier to pen such a thing than to say it to your face, for it brings me as much sorrow as it does you. I wish this pain was

*not upon us. I pray, someday, I may see the happy light enter
your eyes again and we might laugh as we used to you—you, I,
and our dear Eliza.*

*On another matter, there is much I must relate to you upon
your return. Mr. Bradshaw, who situated himself in an inn in
town, sent a most alarming letter my way. I felt it my duty to
attend to his plea, as the letter explained some sort of danger
his daughter would be in if I did not. We talked only a few
short moments, but Mr. Bradshaw told me many things I have
not the liberty to expound upon in a letter. A decision must be
made. As always, I will defer to your judgment, and you may
handle it all as you see best. In any event, I have taken little
Minney back home with me until your return.*

Do hurry back, my dear Phillip. Eliza sends her love.

Yours Eternally,
Letitia

Felton sucked in air. "Why did you never show this to anyone?"

"The constable read the letter the same day I discovered it, but
as both Mr. Bradshaw and my wife were dead, we had no way of
uncovering what decision she spoke of."

Relief trickled in, mingling with guilt, making his hands sweat.
"Minney was wrong."

"Yes."

"You could have told me."

"Perhaps I thought," he said, voice deepening, "some of the faith
you have always had in your father should have been lent to me."

Yes, it should have. Hadn't he known all along the man was
innocent? Hadn't he sensed it beyond everything? Then why had he
lashed out anyway? Why had he accused and insulted and damaged
the only friendship he had?

"As for the letters upstairs. In my wife's chamber." Lord Gillingham
placed the letters back into the drawer, slid it closed, and locked it
again. "After reading her words, I felt inclined to answer with my

own. Even if it was too late."

"And the sorrow between you?"

"The death of our son." His lips thinned. "She knew me well. She knew the reason I left so often. I avoided her and Eliza those last months because I. . .because I. . ." He rubbed a hand down his face. "Because I was a coward. I had too much hurt of my own to be able to support theirs as well, and as it happened, my absence cost more than distance between us. It cost us her life."

"You do not know that."

"If I had been here that night, where I should have been, she would not have been killed. I could have protected her." Tear-moistened eyes met Felton's. "Her and Eliza both."

"I am sorry."

"Yes."

"I am sorry for the things Minney said," Felton admitted. His throat worked up and down. "I am sorry that I believed them." All pride, any facade, fell away. He stood open and exposed and bare before a man who had always understood him and cared for him.

The name had never mattered to Lord Gillingham. The whispers had never meant anything. Not even the chance of his father's guilt, that incriminating watch fob, had stopped the viscount from being there for a boy who needed him more than anything.

Who still needed him.

Tears burned at the back of his eyes when Lord Gillingham turned his back. Not that Felton blamed him. Nor could ever blame him again.

Felton deserved to remain unforgiven and more.

He bit the edge of his lip, nodded his understanding, and left for the entrance hall. He was just taking his hat from the butler when a voice stopped him.

"Northwood?"

He steeled himself as the butler opened the door, letting in a gust of rainy air. "Yes, my lord?"

"What say you to a game of chess tomorrow night?"

Warmth pounded through him, scaring away the chill, offering balm to the fears that had already reared inside him. His friend, even still.

"I shall be here." A smile crooked his lips as he put on his hat and stepped into the downpour. When he swatted at his cheeks, he wiped away more than rain.

His friend indeed.

———⚬⚭⚬———

Eliza backed away from the foyer window, pressing a gloved hand to her stomach. The same flutter again. The one she awoke with after a nightmare, or the one that slammed her when she realized, yet again, someone was trying to take her life.

But there was no danger now.

Just a young man, dressed in black tailcoat, breeches, and stockings, who was making a mad dash from the carriage to the front door.

She moved backward another step before he burst inside, the cool mist of rain blowing in with him.

Slamming the door shut, he turned to look at her and froze. His expression altered, eyes widening, as he beheld her.

She nearly bolted. "It is. . .your mother's dress."

"I know."

Of course he knew. Wasn't he the one who had arranged for it? Yet she could think of nothing else to say to him. Not with the memory of his kiss and the intensity of his stare all swirling together and making her mindless. Why didn't he say anything? Why couldn't she?

"Come." Another command. Of course.

She looped her arm around his and together they hurried for the carriage. Once inside, as the vehicle started moving, she pulled her paisley shawl tighter around her against the chill.

Felton removed his wet hat. "Minney told you?"

"Yes."

"Did you believe her?"

"Should I?"

"Yes." A smile worked at his jaw. "I was a fool to ever think otherwise."

Perhaps Eliza had been a fool too. She'd trusted words without a memory.

A dull throb started in her temples, and she turned to the window so she might not have to see his face. She had a memory now. One he probably wouldn't believe even if she did tell him.

Which she wouldn't.

Couldn't.

Or should she?

"Eliza."

Tiny bumps pebbled her skin, as his gloved fingers landed upon her chin.

"Look at me." A whisper. "Come now. Look at me."

Slowly, painfully, she turned from the window. How easy it was to look at him. To look *into* him. To plunge, like the mermaid, into the green sea of his eyes and never want to surface.

"Tell me."

Was she so obvious?

"Tell me everything."

"I do not know everything," she said. "That is what frightens me."

"Do you trust me?"

"Felton—"

"Answer. Do you trust me?"

"You know I do."

"Then tell me what makes you so strange these last few days." His thumb eased back and forth along her jawline. "Tell me why you can scarcely look at me."

As if some harsh fisherman had dragged the mermaid from her sea, Eliza cast down her eyes. She turned back to the carriage window and lost the touch of his fingers stroking her face.

His sigh filled the silence.

Soft colors of countryside blurred out the rain-streaked window, more from tears than the motion of the carriage. The quivers in her stomach increased.

She would have done anything in the world not to lose a moment so tender.

But if she had given him what he asked, she would have doubtless lost it anyway.

———— ❦ ————

The man was a demon.

Bowles lifted his glass goblet to his lips and sipped at the fortified wine. The liquid burned as it slid down his throat—almost as much as it burned to watch such a ridiculous fool move his fingers along the twenty-seven strings of such an instrument.

The harp was perfect and meant for perfection. Not inept abilities. Situated in the corner of the ballroom with the eleven musicians, the gilt body and soundboard reflected light from the chandeliers. Vines and a cherub motif were engraved in the wood in testament to its power, elegance, and beauty.

No one appreciated beauty more than he did.

Or elegance.

Or power.

Downing the rest of his Madeira, he forced his gaze to travel the rest of the room. Gentlemen were already nudging for invitations to the ladies. Mammas were already giggling and whispering to their unattached daughters. Guests were pouring in and disrupting the arabesque-patterned chalk art on the wooden floor.

And then her.

He knew more from her face—the same innocent eyes and curls—than the fact that she entered the room on Felton Northwood's arm. Miss Eliza Gillingham. A child turned woman, no thanks to him.

Woman, indeed.

He smiled despite himself, as the shawl slid off her shoulders and slender arms became visible between glove and sleeve. He wondered if there were still scars. Or if she remembered. Or if she ever flinched at the sight of a knife.

The music all died in the memory of her screams. My, how she'd screamed. The sound was elating. He was used to the grunts of men—the curses, the husky pleas, the shouts of pain as their mercy ran out.

But a child was different. *She* was different. The way she'd looked at him and succumbed to him and feared him had been more helpless than anything he'd ever witnessed in his life.

More pleasing too. Infinitely more pleasing.

Leaving his empty goblet on a footman's tray, Bowles spared the glorious harp one last look before he made his exit from the ballroom. His absence would doubtless be unnoticed, and there were too many chances the child would recognize him, even after all these years.

'Twas good, even so, he had come. Like the harp, some things were too beautiful to be touched by inept hands.

If anyone killed Eliza Gillingham, it would be him.

***

Something was amiss.

Felton tugged Eliza back an inch or two as an overly round couple squeezed by them. He caught their faint murmurs—"The audacity of showing his face. . ."

"Upon my word, are we without scruples? To allow them residence in our village. . .all of us knowing that the father. . .scandalous to say the least. . ."

Indignation started low in his gut as the couple wandered too far away for him to hear.

Other eyes flicked their way. Faces half disappeared behind ivory fans, as they leaned close to each other and whispered. The room was on fire, smoldering with judgment and rumors and self-righteous assumptions.

And he was the burning sacrifice.

He bit the inside of his cheek so hard he tasted blood. He should have known. He should have expected the womanly slap of revenge, the pride so hurt it must hurt his in return. Didn't she know he had suffered enough?

Eliza's fingers tightened around his arm. She glanced up at him, questions in her eyes, questions to which he had no words to answer.

Dash them.

Dash them all.

'Twas not right Eliza should be here. That she should be isolated with him, the object of everyone's condemnation, when she'd been injured so much already. In the name of heaven, what was wrong with people? Why couldn't they leave Eliza alone? Why couldn't they leave him alone?

Then she swept through the open ballroom doors. Miss Penelope Haverfield, the source of the fire. She wore a peach-colored gown brocaded with white flowers, and a circlet of pearls in the gold of her hair. She found his eyes from across the room and smiled, teasingly and mockingly.

"I should have never brought you here." The words grounded out past tight lips, even as Miss Haverfield and two gentlemen started for them.

"It does not matter."

No, it didn't. He was used to village urchins throwing eggs at his house. He was used to the elders of Lodnouth crossing the street to avoid him. He was used to hearing harsh whispers and trying the rest of the day to unhear them. What was once more?

Miss Haverfield, on the arm of Mr. Scrope, curtsied before him. "So very glad you could come, Mr. Northwood." The cool gaze moved to Eliza. "Miss Gillingham."

Eliza curtsied without hesitation. She was learning.

"My father's dear acquaintance, Mr. Fransham, has begged me to make introductions." Miss Haverfield flicked her wrist at the silver-haired gentleman, whose dark eyes ogled the length of Eliza. Longer than they should have.

Longer than Felton would stand for. "Excuse us—"

"Miss Gillingham, you are exquisite." Mr. Fransham stilled her with a hand to her elbow. "Forgive my impudence, but I have so long been presenting cases to unsightly judges that a picture so lovely as you quite rids me of composure."

"Mr. Fransham is a barrister," explained Miss Haverfield. "And a very good one at that. He is quite acclaimed in both London and Cheltenham. Indeed, across England, perhaps." She tilted her head at Felton. "He is certainly *thought* very *well* of."

The jab inflicted nothing. He tugged Eliza in the other direction—

"Miss Gillingham, can I persuade you to dance?"

"She is not dancing." Felton glared at the man's hand. "And get your hand off her."

"I say, sir, you cannot mean to imply that such a divine creature is not going to dance at all. Furthermore, I asked the lady and shall wait for her answer. Not yours."

"You have the only answer you are going to get."

"But surely—"

"And if anyone dances with her, it shall be me." At the gasp from Mr. Fransham, the frown from Miss Haverfield, and the continual glare from Mr. Scrope, Felton led Eliza away from the trio and escorted her into a forming set of three other couples.

Music began, lively and rhythmic, pounding in his ears and bringing a frightened flush to Eliza's cheeks. They bowed, took hands, then stepped twice as he bent his head to hers. "I shall tear the man apart if he so much as looks at you again."

"Oh, Felton, he only—"

"But I admire him for one thing." His voice lowered as they circled to the tune. "His bravery."

"Bravery?"

"To say what I have wished to say all evening. That you are. . .lovely."

She was the princess in all the stories Captain had ever told her. She shouldn't smile. She shouldn't laugh, even for a second, when she tripped in the dance and Felton threw a grin her way.

She shouldn't be happy.

Not now. Not among the people Captain had always warned her of, with whispers against Felton swarming the room, with the beast trying to kill her, and with the wretched secret still screeching to be told.

But none of that mattered. None of it meant anything. She envisioned away the people, the danger, the secret—until the only thing she was conscious of was him. Felton Northwood. Strong. Noble. Good. Everything she'd ever imagined him to be and more.

Then the dance was over. He walked with her to some secluded window, and the clash of moonlight and candlelight made movement on his face. He leaned closer to her, his smell clean and scented of bay leaves. "I imagine they are angry we are so enjoying ourselves."

She glanced across the ballroom. More than one pair of eyes watched them with raised brows and taut expressions. "Why do you suppose she invited us?"

"For sport."

"How do you mean?"

"I do not doubt but that she has gone about visiting and stirring old stories, until the Northwood shame is the latest on-dit again. Tonight is my punishment."

"For?"

"Unwinding myself from her finger." He nodded toward the plush ottoman on the other side of the ballroom, where Miss Haverfield sat with a pinched look on her face. Her eyes flashed their way before she turned back to Scrope and tilted her head with an exaggerated laugh.

A flair of envy prickled Eliza. "Why should you wish to be?"

"What?"

"Unwound."

He glanced down at her. Not with a smile, nor a word, nor even a change of his stance. But something stirred in his eyes. Something sincere and soft and exposed, as if to say he. . .

Loves me. A thousand reasons said it couldn't be, that he didn't and never would, but she couldn't believe them. She knew it was true.

For this moment, for now, he *did* love her. She owned his heart. She was the princess, the mermaid, the fairy—and he the noble rescuer who had entered her forest and changed her life.

But now wasn't forever. The beast would ruin this too. No matter how long she tried to keep it from him, it would be there still. Lingering between them. Unspoken but real—and the longer she hid the truth, the more hurt she would bring on him.

And the more danger she would bring on herself.

She had to tell him. She had to get away from the Northwood house. She had to get the memories free from her mind, out of the nightmare, into words before it ate her alive and. . .

"You are shaking." His brows furrowed. "What is it?"

"Nothing." She could not tell him here. Not until tonight. Not until they were alone.

"Stay here. I shall get you something to drink. Lemonade?"

"Hmm?"

"Lemonade to drink?"

"Oh. No. I am really not thirsty, I only—"

"Quite enough, Mr. Northwood." Mr. Haverfield's voice turned Felton around. The squire blinked hard. "You have succeeded in making a spectacle of me in my own home and you have dishonored me even further by insulting my guest."

"Your guest?"

"Mr. Fransham—"

"The dashed man should learn to pursue ladies his own age." Felton's muscles bunched beneath the tight tailcoat. "And I did not insult him. He insulted me."

"I will not stand here and debate this with you, Mr. Northwood.

I am asking you to leave."

"With pleasure." Felton bowed, nodded, laced his fingers with Eliza's and pulled her away. Not until they were back at the carriage, with the creaking wheels carrying them back toward home, did she force herself to look up at his face.

His jaw was tight, fists on each knee, and he shook his head as if to rid his mind of the night's humiliation. "I could have beat the devil out of him for what he did tonight."

Pity flooded her, as she pulled her own fingers into fists. Her words came out breathy. "Felton, there is something I must tell you."

CHAPTER 15

"What is it?"

The carriage was too dark to see her face. Moonlight only made the shadows deeper, until little else was visible but her glowing eyes. Her stricken eyes.

"Eliza, what is it?"

"You are angry at all of them. The people tonight. The ones who whispered."

"Yes, I am angry. They are prattling gossipmongers who are more interested in keeping an innocent man in scandal than admitting the truth."

"Maybe they believe it."

"Believe what?"

"That he killed her. My mother. And the watch fob—"

"What are you saying?" Impatience rolled into a pierce of anger. "Come, Eliza. What are you saying?"

"Promise you will not be—"

"Tell me!"

"He was there." Breathless. Half sob. "He was there, Felton. I remembered as soon as I saw him. He climbed through my nursery window. He told me not to scream. He made me put my arms around his neck when he climbed back out and he kept telling me over and over not to scr—"

"Enough." Everything blurred. Her face. Her eyes. He scooted to the edge of the carriage seat and smacked his fist into the door, until the window glass rattled. A knot swelled in his throat and he

269

could not look at her. "You lied to me about Lord Gillingham, and now you are lying to me about my father."

"I am not lying, Felton, I—"

"You were wrong. I believed you, and you were wrong." He raked a vicious hand through his hair. "Think not that I will believe this too."

"It is true."

"My father killed no one."

"But he was there—"

"No, Eliza, he was *not* there." He faced her and grabbed her shoulders. "You must stop this. Stop it, I say. I will not have you bring this hurt on my family. I will not have more lies. I will not have more accusations just because you. . .because you. . ."

"Because I what?"

"Because you want to end the danger so badly your mind will tell you anything."

"It is not true, Felton." More tears. They wracked the shoulders he clung to. "I remembered before the nightmare. I remembered his voice. I remembered what he said to me. Ask him. Ask him if he took me. Ask him, Felton, please—"

"My father is not a murderer." He grasped her face, pulled her close enough he felt her uneven gasps of air chill his cheeks. "Eliza." Choked words. Shaking words. "Eliza, you do not know what you are doing. You are wrong. Just like you were wrong about Lord Gillingham—only worse."

"I am sorry."

Sorry. The word pulverized him. She was destroying them. Destroying Mamma for the second time. Destroying Papa after all these years of pretending the accusations didn't exist and hiding from them.

Destroying Felton. His name. Any pride he had left. What would happen when she told? Would it all start over again? Everything they'd barely lived through the first time?

And she was sorry.

He pulled away from her and groped in the darkness for the

carriage door. He flung it open. Thick fog swirled in. "Driver, stop!"

"What are you doing?" She snatched his arm, but he jerked from her touch. "Felton, please—"

He leaped out when the carriage was still moving and shouted the driver on. Moist wind slashed through him, cold and biting from the earlier rain, and the carriage door flapped back and forth as the vehicle picked up speed again.

Eliza must have stilled the carriage door and leaned out herself, because his name rent the air. The sound faded, drowned out by the wheels churning mud and despair ringing his ears, until finally he heard no voice at all.

Except the one in his head.

He was there. Her weeping lie devoured him as quickly as the fog. *I remember. He was there.*

***

Another hour was gone.

Eliza turned her face back into the pillow in hopes the soft fabric and feathers would muffle her cries. She needed to stop. Captain would want her to stop. He would croon for her to be strong and brave and determined.

But she didn't know how to be determined, or what to be determined about. What now? What did she do? Where did she go? Back to Lord Gillingham whom she'd run from? Back to the cottage where the dead body was buried in the forest floor?

One thing was certain.

She couldn't stay here.

Felton's face, his accusations, his anger, rushed back at her. Another nightmare, doubtless. Another hurt she would carry with her for years to come, as sharp as Captain's death or the beast's claws.

I am sorry. The words again. Over and over and over, because she didn't know what else to think or how else to make it better. *Felton, I am sorry.*

She knew it changed nothing. She knew his love would be cold now. Even the death of his affections, the end of his kisses, would have been a tragedy she could bear.

But to lose his friendship too?

More tears spilled forth, and she curled her knees to her chest. She wrapped her arms around them. No, she could not bear to lose his friendship. To lose his smile falling carelessly upon her. Or his fingers snagging hers when she felt lost or alone. Or his orders. His wonderful orders. What would she do without those incessant orders?

She needed him. Loved him. Depended on him.

He was all she'd had left.

God, let the nightmare be wrong. An empty prayer because she knew it was true. The memory was too clear. *Let it all go away somehow. Let Felton not hurt like this. Let him not despise me for what I have told him.*

But that was an empty prayer too.

He already did.

A small tap came at the door and Eliza jumped. She peeled back the bed linens, shivering against the chill. "Wh–who is it?"

"Dodie, Miss Gillingham." The door creaked open, and the girl slipped in, clad in nightgown and stockings with a candlestick in one hand. "I be sorry to wake you, Miss Gillingham, but do you not be 'earin' it?"

"Hearing what?"

"Why, Merrylad, of course, Miss Gillingham. Why, I just said to the stable boy the other day, 'You make sure that dog is locked tight at night, see, so he don't be causin' no trouble and wakin' the 'ouse.' And he says to me, he says, 'Why, Dodie, I always keep him locked in the 'arness room, I do.' But tonight, the little thing must be runnin' about near e'eywhere cause I been 'earin' him barkin' and 'owlin' loud as you please."

Eliza swung out of bed, palming the tears from her cheeks. "My wrapper. . ."

"Oh, 'ere it be, Miss Gillingham." Dodie grabbed it from the back of the chair in the corner, opened it up, and helped Eliza into it. "You be needin' shoes."

"Never mind." Eliza peeled off her stockings. She'd gone without shoes most of her life. Why bother with them now?

"Shall I go with you then?"

"No, Dodie. I will see to it."

"How about I go be findin' some milk for the thing? Might calm 'im down from whate'er be upsettin' him so."

Eliza nodded, tried to offer a smile, and accepted the candlestick Dodie gave her. Then she hurried through the quiet house, her bare feet nearly soundless, and eased her way outside into the blackness.

The moon was gone now. What time must it be? Late enough to be early, doubtless. Why would Merrylad be awake at such an hour? And barking?

Halfway to the stable, another bark froze her. Her blood flow quickened. A bark of pain. Or danger. Or both.

She broke into a run and followed the noise around the stable. The flame of her candle extinguished in the fog, casting her into deep blackness. *Merrylad.* If anything happened to him, if another animal harmed him. . .

She turned the corner of the stable and stopped. "Merrylad?" In answer, his fur brushed against her leg and relief clasped her trembling heart back into place. She bent next to him, rubbed his ears, scratched his neck, and pushed her nose against his wet one. "What is it, love? What are you doing out here?"

"Entertaining me."

Eliza jerked at the voice. She pushed back to her feet, panic gashing through her, the lightless candlestick slipping from her fingers.

A shadow moved closer. He backed her into the brick wall of the stable and stood close enough Merrylad growled. "Charming little pet you have there, Miss Gillingham."

"Who are you?"

"Do you not know?"

"No." She raked in air but couldn't exhale. *Scream.* She needed to scream. Why couldn't she scream?

The shadow moved like lightning. A crack, a thud, then Merrylad hit the ground and didn't scamper back up.

"No!" Eliza dove to her knees, groped for him, but something cold and metal rammed into her temple. The blackness deepened. She must have landed over top of Merrylad, because for a brief second, his fur tickled her face and his smell and warmth drained away some of the terror.

Then a second blow.

Pain flittered through her, as the blackness blurred into colors, the colors into red curtains, the red curtains into blackness again.

"You will know me." A roar in her ear. "You will."

Then she heard nothing at all.

———— ❧❦❧ ————

Felton turned in bed for the hundredth time. Not that he wanted to sleep. He didn't. He had too much to figure out and too much to determine.

Like what to do about Eliza.

And her lies.

Too restless to remain under his coverlet, he jerked it back and walked to the hearth. He stoked the small fire, then sat before it on the floor and watched the flames lick the air. *God, what do I do?* A prayer he'd prayed a thousand times. *What do I do?*

He wanted to hate her. He almost did. He wanted to run like Hugh to the battlefronts of France or hide like Aaron in the university books and lessons.

But he couldn't. He'd never been able to. He'd been forced to stay, chained to it somehow, and every day the wretched chains grew heavier.

He worked his jaw into a clench. By all that was holy, he needed the truth. He needed it to be over. He was tired of defending his father, his name, his family, to every dashed fool in Lodnouth.

He never imagined Eliza would be among them.

Sighing, he jabbed the poker into a log—perhaps too violently, because it shifted and a flock of tiny sparks besieged the air. One of them landed on his forearm. The pain was dull next to the hurt pressing into his soul.

Eliza, why? He'd trusted her. He'd told her everything. He'd invited her into his home and deeper than that—into his heart.

But she'd forsaken his confidence and betrayed them. She'd spit on the Northwood name just like the rest of the world.

For that, he could not forgive her.

Not when his father was an innocent man.

<hr />

Mayhap if she kept her eyes closed, they would leave her alone. Cold, uneven stone jabbed into her cheek, and she eased the musty air into her lungs. Pounding filled her head. One breath in. One breath out. One in, one out. In, out.

"She be young." An old, solemn voice. Sad almost, as if the reality of her age had an effect on him. "Very young."

In, out.

"Yet much older than the last time she was in our clutches, is she not, Swabian?" The same voice from the stable. The one that made her stomach knot. "Breage, go and relocate the *Célestine II* to Ozias Bay."

"But sir, we have not a crew—"

"We do not need a crew. We will not be sailing." Footsteps scraped the stone floor, and a door closed as if the man called Breage had left.

Her panic escalated. Her breathing faltered, caught in her throat again, but she crammed her eyes tighter shut and tried to regulate it. *In, out. In, out.*

"What are you planning?" The Swabian. "You don't be thinking of taking her there—"

"What I think, good man, is not any of your concern."

"Kill her now." The words held pleading, as if death were a

kindness. "Let Breage be doing it, and we can get rid of the body before morning and—"

"Swabian." A second of stillness.

Then, low, "Yes?"

"How old are you?"

"I. . .don't be knowing, sir. Sixty-two, sixty-three, mayhap."

"An old man."

"Yes, sir."

"Old men are prone to malady. Or accident." A long pause, as footsteps edged closer to her. "Or death."

"You don't have to be threatening me, sir. I've always done as you said before. Not going to stop now."

"How very faithful of you. I am touched." A hand swept down Eliza's cheek. Then into her hair. "Go and get me a rope."

Every nerve jerked, and she clamped down a scream, one second before he fisted her hair and pulled her head from the ground.

"Stand up." He yanked her to her feet before she had a chance to move. Slammed her backward into a moist wall. Kicked an empty keg out of his way and let it roll. "Now, the rope?"

From behind him, the old man produced it.

"Hold forth your wrists."

She thrust them forward, and as the coarse rope wound them together, she glanced around her. Some kind of tiny cellar room with kegs lining three of the walls and no window. *No window.* The words processed. *No window. No escape.* Everything was dark, except the yellow light of a candle on one of the kegs and another candle in the hand of the old man.

"Do come here, Swabian."

Her eyes jolted back to the man before her. His brooding eyes, his lifting smile—the amusement skittering over his expression and making her weak. She flinched when he ripped the sleeve off her arm. Then his long, cold fingers caressed her skin, while the Swabian stood back and watched.

"No scars." A whisper. He ripped the other sleeve. "You healed very well, Miss Gillingham. Do you remember now?"

"Sir—"

"Shut up, Swabian."

"But she was only—"

"I said shut up!"The man turned and backhanded Swabian, until he stumbled back and cradled his cheek.

"Now go and see that Breage does not endanger us with any more mistakes. If anyone sees that ship, we shall all be quite imperiled."

"Yes, sir."The older man disappeared, and the room plunged into deeper blackness with his absence.

Vomit crept up her throat. "Who are you?"

He shoved her to the back corner of the room. A rat scurried out of their way.

"Please. . .tell me."

"I should think *you* could tell *me*. Did I leave no impression on you at all?" He forced her down behind several dirty kegs. "Lie still, and do not move. On the chance someone should pay me a visit, I do not wish for a screaming chit to be discovered in my cellar room. Understood?"

"What. . .what are you going to do with me?"

"Kill you." He draped an old, rancid-smelling blanket over top of her. The darkness stifled her but didn't stifle his words. "A pleasure I was denied fourteen years ago, but shall not be denied again."

***

"Have you been to see your mother this morning?"

Felton tossed two letters upon Papa's desk. "No, I have not." He grabbed another stack. "Are these all unanswered?"

Papa stepped into the study, brushing toast crumbs from his marmalade-stained cravat. "Yes, yes, quite unanswered."

"Why?"

"Got away from me, I suppose. Time, that is. So much on my mind these days."He walked behind his desk and tapped the ledger.

"I have been keeping up with this, though. I am not entirely inept."
His father chuckled, as if it were some amusing joke that correspondences were not being attended to and marmalade was on his cravat
and the entire household had been falling apart for fourteen years.

"I say, Son, why so glum? Did you not sleep well last night?"

"No." Felton turned away from him, walked to the window, and
jerked back the calico curtain. Morning sun glowed bright and yellow
against the pale pink sky. "No, I did not sleep at all."

"I hardly did myself what with your mother's coughing. Poor dear."

"How is she today?"

"The same, I suppose. In a trifle better temperament though, if
you care to go up and see her."

"I will." He let the curtain drop. "Just as soon as I take breakfast."

"Miss Gillingham has not."

He frowned at her name. "Not what?"

"Taken breakfast. You might go and see if she should like to
join you. I fear she doesn't especially care to take breakfast with me."

"Has she been so obvious?"

"What do you mean?"

"Never mind." Felton started toward the door, but halted when
Dodie filled the threshold.

The girl's face seemed ashen. "Mr. Northwood. Master Northwood."
Even her voice was an octave or two higher. Nearly a shriek. "I be
sorry to bother you, but what with the milk she ne'er came for and
the chamber empty like it be and Merrylad—"

"What are you saying, Dodie?" Felton pulled her into the study.

"Just this, Master Northwood. I think she be gone."

"Gone where?"

"I don't know." The girl fluttered both hands at once and tears
sprung. "I says to Miss Gillingham, I says last night, 'I be gettin'
milk for the dog.' And she says to me something, but I can't 'ardly
remember what, and I waited and waited but she ne'er did come.
I guess I falled asleep in the kitchen whilst I was waitin' because
Cook woke me up sometime this mornin' and I just forgot about

e'erything until her chamber be empty like it was." She puckered a trembling lip. "Oh, Master Northwood, e'erything be my fault! I just know something be wrong."

"You are not to blame." Anxiety clamored in his brain, searching for a possibility, demanding an explanation. Had she run back to the forest? To Lord Gillingham? Had he so frightened her last night that she should flee his home alone while they slept?

Papa cleared his throat. "Er, I better go see to your mother." Quickly—too quickly—he squeezed past Dodie and left the room.

But Felton hadn't time to think on that now. "Dodie, go and check her chamber again and see if she took anything with her. Mayhap she left a note."

"Yes, Master Northwood."

"I shall visit the stable and see if she took a mount." He hurried outside, checked with the groom to see if any horses were missing, and fought an urge to punch something when the man shook his head no. What could that mean?

He spotted Merrylad in one of the stalls, a blanket wrapped about him. "What is wrong with the dog?"

"Nasty wound to the head. Found him out back, I did, this morning. Couldn't hardly walk straight, poor thing, and had a bit of bleeding to the nose."

Out back. Felton made his way there and surveyed the area, looking for anything amiss, half expecting to find her sitting with her bare feet in the grass and her hair draped over her shoulders.

But she wasn't. His pulse hastened. Dread needled through him as he paced back and forth along the back of the stables until—

Something caught his eye. Something bronze in the dewy grass.

He picked it up, clenched it in his hand, stifled back a groan when he spotted large boot prints. Dodie was right. She was gone.

And she hadn't run away.

She'd been taken.

———— ❧❧❧ ————

Somewhere next to her feet, a rat scurried by and chattered. She clamped her hands over her mouth to keep back a noise. She couldn't scream. She should have before at the stables. Maybe that would have made a difference.

But not now, not if she wanted to stay alive.

She wasn't certain she wanted to.

Savior, help me. The fear cramped through her, as suffocating as the revolting blanket. *Help him not to hurt me. Please. Please, God.*

He must have been her beast. Strange, that Mr. Northwood's voice had jarred her memory while this man's face brought back nothing.

Except the terror.

Was he the one who had pushed her mother from the window? Was that why he'd hunted her down? Why he'd wanted, all this time, to kill her?

And her arms. He'd stared at them, stroked them, looked for scars as if they ought to be there. As if the claws had been real. As if the beast really had ripped through her skin and made her bleed.

I don't want to remember. She shook and curled tighter between the wall and the kegs. *I don't want to remember. I don't want to know.*

Nothing mattered anymore. She had no one. She had nothing. Was there anyone in the world who would come looking for her? Would Lord Gillingham? Would Felton?

Even if they did, they wouldn't find her.

The beast, like everything else, would see to that.

———— ❧❧❧ ————

"Where is he?"

The heavy, balding man from behind the counter lifted one shoulder in a shrug. "I don't keep track of every person wot walks in here."

In one swift movement, Felton leaned over the counter and seized the man's sweaty shirt. "I said where is he?"

"I don't know."

Another shake. "So help me I shall—"

"All right, all right!" The man squirmed, and his flabby jowls jiggled. "He was down here little over an hour ago. Went back up to his room again, he did."

"Where is that?"

"Upstairs. First door in the hall."

Felton released the proprietor and ignored the curious glances from the Jester's Sunlight regulars. He took the stairs two at a time, turned into a hallway, and banged on the flimsy wooden door. "Swabian! This is Northwood. Open up."

"Get the bloody devil out o' here."

"Open this door, or I'll walk through it."

In answer, it swung open and the barrel of a dueling pistol stared Felton in the face. The old man's bleary eyes motioned inside. "Come in, but I can't be promising you'll walk back out."

Felton pushed into the room and turned, just as the door slammed shut.

The old man leaned back against it, unsteady, aiming the gun toward Felton's head. "Why'd you come here?" Slurred. Slow. "Why'd you come here looking for the likes o' me?"

"Where is she?"

"You should have left her in that forest."

"Tell me, or I'll kill you."

"You be in no position, Northwood, to kill anyone." Endless lines and creases marred the man's face. Grime stuck to his skin. His thin, greasy white hair and beard bore traces of yellow.

His eyes bore traces of guilt.

"Tell me, and I shall see that nothing happens to you. We can get this stopped. Whatever you're afraid of can be—"

"I be afraid o' no one. No one and nothing." Spittle flew out with the words.

"Not even the murder of an innocent girl?"

"Murder don't be bothering me. I told him to kill her. 'Twould be better than. . ." The gun wavered for a second, as if he realized he'd said too much.

Horror slammed Felton. "Better than what?"

"Whatever that devil has in his mind." Swabian shook his head, blowing air into his cheeks. "He's not like other bloody men. He don't be thinking right. He'd do anything for—"

"For what?"

"Get out of here before I kill you."

"Not until I know who has her."

"I swear I'll—"

"Bowles? Is it him?"

"So help me, I'll shoot. I got nothing to lose, boy. Look behind you."

Felton glanced behind him. A rope was tied to the rafters and dangled over top of the stained bed. The end was tied into a noose. "You do not have to do that."

"Maybe I will. Maybe I won't. It's been hanging there for three bloody weeks now, and I go to bed with it like that, trying to figure out just how bad I want to die." He stepped away from the door and pried it open with one shaking hand. "Besides, you don't be needing me."

"What do you mean?"

"All them answers you been looking for have been waiting for you—in your own house."

———

The door opened and shut.

Eliza squeezed both hands together, tensions rippling through her, and nearly screeched when the blanket was jerked away from her.

Instead of the man, a thin woman with graying-blond wisps leaned over her. The eyes were bulging and nervous, and fading bruises hung beneath them. Her words shook as she held out her hand. "Take these," she whispered.

Eliza shrunk away from the pills. "What is it?"

"Take it. H–hurry please. He be w–wanting you to have it before he..." She sucked in air and glanced behind her, as if to make certain he was not coming. "Please!"

"No." Eliza shrunk away. "No, I won't—"

"You must." The woman scooted away a keg and hurried on top of Eliza. She pressed the pills at her mouth and tried to pinch open Eliza's lips.

She jerked her head and kicked her feet against the wall, the movement sending more kegs toppling over. The woman's nails dug into her face. One of the pills slipped into her mouth, but she spat it out and rolled—

"Troubles, Miss Reay?"

The woman froze, then scrambled away from Eliza and groped for the spilled pills on the floor. She clutched them to her chest and backed against the wall. "I—I be sorry, Mr. Bowles, but sh–she f–f–fought me and—"

"Give them here."

The woman surrendered the pills. She waited, eyes closed, lips grim, as if she expected blows.

They never came. He grabbed her arm, headed her in the direction of the door, and told her to see that a carriage was waiting for him by the fall of dark.

The woman hesitated in the doorway. For one second, her gaze fell to Eliza—and a fountain of pity leaked from her stare. Without a word, she fled the room.

The beast turned on Eliza.

God, please. She scooted back, bumped into something, glanced at the half-open door, and tried to determine how far she'd get if she lunged for it.

He grinned. "Stand up."

She pulled herself to her feet, tried to keep his gaze and force the fear from her stance. She would not give him that. After all these years of being haunted by him, she would not wallow now.

The grin faltered. He stepped forward and waited, one brow lifting.

Then she realized.

He *wanted* to see her fear. Why else would he wish her to remember? Why else would he wait like this and chance hiding her when he could have finished her last night?

He wants me to shrink to him. Coldness crawled through her. *He wants me to tremble at him.* She wouldn't. She couldn't. Captain wouldn't have, and Felton wouldn't have, and the girls in all of Eliza's stories wouldn't have.

For once in her life, she would not cower to him. She would die being as brave as she'd always imagined herself to be.

"Open your mouth." He stepped closer, his fist around the pills, the grin forming again.

She tightened her lips.

His hand struck the side of her face.

She clenched her teeth against the sting but still clung to his gaze. Another blow knocked her backward. She landed on the floor and resisted the urge to stay there, curl into a ball, and wail.

She staggered back up. She took the third blow to the face without falling, though tears pushed through and blurred him.

"Now shall you take them?" Closer. "Because if this is a show of wills to you, Miss Gillingham, rest assured I shall win." He displayed the pills again in his sweaty palm. "After all, it is not as if this were a fight for your life. I should not think of poisoning you. Just a bit of opium to see that you are, shall we say, more *relaxed* when I transport you to our other location." Without warning, his fist punched.

She was on the floor again, his body over hers, his fingers pushing the opium into her bleeding mouth. "Swallow."

She gagged.

His elbow pressed into her neck, closing off airflow, until pain and darkness groped for her consciousness and—

"Swallow." He released her throat long enough for the air to rake in and the pills to slide down. He laughed as he climbed off her body. "I dare to say you shall feel much better upon our next encounter."

Then he was gone. The door slammed and locked, and she covered her face as hard sobs wracked through her hurting body. *I am so afraid, God. I am so afraid.*

Not of dying. She accepted that.

But of what he would do to her before she did.

——— ❦ ———

Felton had never asked Papa in his life.

Sweat beaded along his forehead, despite the evening chill, as he stood before the blue-paneled door and debated going inside. *Ask him.* Eliza's voice. *Please ask him.*

For once in his life, it didn't matter. He didn't want it to matter. Lady Gillingham was long dead and buried, and if the culprit in her death was undiscovered by now, maybe it was meant to stay that way.

But Eliza.

Nausea rose through him again, and he begged his mind not to think of her. Not closely. Not rationally. Because with any thought at all, he could imagine what they would do to her.

Or had already done.

Murder.

Dear God, no. A livid pain rushed through him as he turned the knob and strode into the foyer of his home. *Let me find her. Let it not be true.* Was that not the same prayer he'd been murmuring about Papa, as soon as he left Swabian?

He searched the dining room first. Dodie and another maid were clearing the table from the evening's meal, but Papa was not present.

Then the study. Empty. The drawing room. Empty too.

He took the stairs, every thump increasing the rate of his heart, until he spotted his father easing shut Mamma's bedchamber door.

"Ah, Son. Just the person. Will you be so good as to hand Hugh's letters to your mother? I must prepare her something warm to drink, along with that elixir the doctor brought over this morning."

Felton stilled his father's arm. "Papa, I must have a word with you."

"Yes, yes, in a minute."

"But Papa—"

"Come now, Son. How long do you think it takes to fetch something to drink? Go and attend to your mother, and I shall be with you in a moment." With a pat to Felton's shoulder as he passed, Papa continued down the hall.

Felton slipped into Mamma's chamber, blinking hard. He was wasting time. Time he should be riding the countryside, or beating it out of Swabian, or banging down Bowles' door—and every other door in Lodnouth until he found her.

But they were aimless. All of them. He had no idea where she was and who had her, and if answers were here in his home, he needed to find them.

Whether it incriminated his name or not.

"Son?" His mother had been resting in the bed with her eyes closed, chestnut hair gleaming on the pillows, but she glanced at him now and smiled. "I did not hear you come in."

He approached her and kissed her warm forehead. "I can only stay but a minute."

"Your papa told me." She lifted herself up an inch or two, drawing the covers to her neck. "I do hope the girl may be found."

"Yes." He moved to the stand beside her bed, pulled open the drawer, and rummaged through the letters scattered inside. "Any one in particular?"

"Hmmm?"

"Of the letters. Which one should you like to read?"

"It does not matter. They are all dear to me."

He thumbed through several, then lifted one without an address. The writing was unfamiliar. Bold and messy. He unfolded it and smoothed the creases. *Martha, you do not need to tell me how to do what you have asked. You forget I have killed more people than you have. The difference in you and I is that I take care that my killings are done in secret and my bodies are disposed of. I am not still dealing with them fourteen years later, as you are. But do not worry. She will be disposed of soon. Then you need never fear discovery again.*

He read it again.

Then again.

Everything numbed. Disbelief fought hard against the reality of the words. This could not be true. This could never be true. Not of Mamma, who nurtured him and loved him and stood by him with such conviction in Papa's innocence.

"Son?"

He flinched at the word. He took a step away from the bed and looked at her—the disarrayed hair, the white and sunken cheeks, the desperate eyes.

A woman he didn't know.

Had never known.

God? A prayer, but nothing else followed. He crumpled the letter in his fist and watched the different expressions come over her face.

First fear because she knew he knew. Then anger. Then sadness. Then just. . .nothing. Nothing at all, as she struggled upright and pushed the hair from her face. "I meant to burn that. I thought I had, only I have been so ill my mind is affected."

He dropped the letter, as if the touch of it burned him. "You killed Lady Gillingham?"

"Yes."

"You let Papa take the blame for it?"

"He would have it no other way."

"He knew?" Felton took another step back, then grabbed the edge of the washstand as the room swayed.

Then, from the doorway, "Yes, I knew." Papa closed himself into the room with a steaming teacup, his hand steady enough it did not even clink against the tray. "It was an accident. Tell him, Martha."

"Yes." A cough ripped out with the word. "It was an accident. You believe that, do you not, Son?"

"Why were you there that night?"

"I needed to speak with Lady Gillingham."

"Of what?"

"It does not matter now—"

"It does matter!"

"Son." Papa stepped forward. "Do not speak so to your mother. I shall not have you upset her."

Upset her? Felton nearly cast up the last food he'd eaten. Instead, he forced down the ire and spoke low enough that the words rasped his throat. "What happened?"

"Your mother had a matter to discuss with Lady Gillingham. She has never divulged that to me, and I leave her to her privacy."

"Papa—"

"Let me finish, Son." He handed the teacup to his wife and settled on the edge of the bed. "I followed her that night, as she had seemed troubled all evening. I was just nearing the Monbury Manor gates when she was leaving them. She was shaking. I have never seen your mother so afraid and weak."

"Richard, let us not go through it again." Tea sloshed onto the bed linens. "Please."

"We must, Martha." He squeezed her hand. "She told me there had been an argument. How Lady Gillingham had been in hysterics, and in a slight tussle fell from the window. Little Eliza saw everything."

"Then?"

"Your mother begged me to do something. She cried that she would kill herself. That she could not bring such shame on our family, not when she knew the child would understand it wrong and murder would be proclaimed." He pushed both hands through his hair. "When she asked me to go and get the child, I agreed."

An overwhelming anger swarmed him. He couldn't look Papa in the eye. Or Mamma. He let his gaze fall on the wrinkled letter on the floor, as his mind played out the scene of little Eliza being kidnapped from her nursery window.

Just as she'd told him.

"We brought the child here, and Martha promised she would only talk with the child. That she would take her for a carriage ride, explain everything, then bring her back as soon as Eliza knew the truth—that it was only an accident. Yet when Martha returned, the

THE GIRL FROM THE HIDDEN FOREST

child was not with her."

"And you did nothing?"

"What could I do? She said the child was as impossible as her mother. She said little Eliza didn't understand at all. She said there'd been no choice but to turn Eliza over to her brother, and that David would find a good home for her and—"

"David?" Felton glanced up. "David Bowles? Your brother?"

"Richard, you should not have—"

"I am sorry, my dear. Son, you must not speak of it to anyone. The relationship, I mean. What with the social difference between ourselves and her brother, we have thought it best all these years for appearances' sake not to mention the blood between them. They both wished it that way, so surely you can understand."

"I understand nothing." Heat burned his face, his neck, his ears. He faced his mother. "You surrendered Eliza over to Bowles, who pawned her off on a drunken captain who sank his ship because he was too out of his head with opium?"

"I had no choice."

"Do you even know who Bowles is? That he is suspected of smuggling?"

"Of smuggling?" Papa leaned forward. "What?"

"You tried to kill her." Felton swooped the letter back off the ground and narrowed on Mamma's rapid-blinking eyes. "You knew she would remember, so you called on your brother to get rid of her again. This time for good."

"Oh Felton." She dropped the teacup and the hot liquid seeped into the white bed linens. Sobs left her lips. She pressed her hands to her cheeks and shook her head. "Stop it. I cannot bear this. Make him leave, Richard."

"What is he saying about your brother, Martha? You said you had nothing to do with the attacks on Eliza's life. You said you knew nothing of them. You promised you were not involved—"

"I lied!" she rasped. "I lied, I lied, I lied. I lied to all of you. Now leave me alone."

Richard backed off the bed. "But it was an accident." A whisper. "It was an accident with Lady Gillingham, just like you said. . .wasn't it?"

"What do you think?"

Felton flinched at the same time Papa did.

Mamma ripped the tea-stained covers from her legs. She pushed herself higher, lifted her chin, faced her husband with a look wild and frantic. "You believed everything I told because you wanted to believe it. You knew it was not right. You knew it was not truth. But you pretended it was for so long that you believed it yourself—just like you always believed I was good enough for you, despite where I came from."

"You are good enough." Choked. "Martha—"

"Lady Gillingham found out about us. My brother and me. She knew about the opium we'd been loading in India and smuggling into China, about the silver and porcelain and silks we'd smuggle back in to Lodnouth. How else do you think my brother secured that house? How else do you think I wore such fine clothes, a mere fisherman's daughter, when you met me?"

"Martha, stop it. I do not want to hear this. I do not want to hear any more."

"I am dying now. What does it matter?" Hard coughs ripped through her, and when she moved her hand away from her mouth, blood was splattered across her fingers. "The steward at Monbury Manor. He was the one who caused all of this. He'd been working with my brother and was involved in selling the smuggled goods, but he became frightened. We knew he wanted out even before he arranged a meeting with Lady Gillingham. He must have told her everything."

Felton stepped nearer to her bed. "Then it was you who hung Minney's father."

"My brother, yes." A dull look entered her eyes. "Despite what you might think of your mother, I have only killed once. And in some ways, it was an accident. I didn't go to Monbury Manor that night to kill Lady Gillingham. She was my. . .she was my friend." Another cough. She sank deeper into the bed. "I had to convince her she could not tell. . .that everything we worked for, everything our father had taught us to build for ourselves, would be ruined."

"But she did not listen."

"No. We fought. I pushed her through the window, and the rest happened as your father said."

Silence.

She pulled the covers back over her and pressed her head into the pillow.

Papa stared at the floor. He shook his head a couple of times, wiped at his nose, then turned and left the room. Felton followed him to the door—

"Son?"

He closed his eyes, feeling his heartbeat throb out of rhythm with a pain more searing than anything he'd known in his life. "Yes?"

"You promised you would never leave me." Muffled cries. "A mother needs her sons. You know that, do you not?"

"All I know is that Eliza Gillingham may die because of you." He dragged an arm across his wet eyes. "I curse the name I share with you and Papa both."

CHAPTER 16

Bowles pulled on his wool box coat and flipped the short capes over his shoulder. He glanced out the window again.

In the moonlight, Breage was climbing to the coach box, and the pair of black horses pranced as he pulled on the reins.

Almost time.

He started back through the house, elation working through him, fighting back the smile that kept trying to resurface. He little knew himself the plans he held for Eliza.

He only knew she would crumble.

She was attempting bravery now. She knew his game, and like all worthy victims was fighting against it. But before he was through with her, she would remember. She would look at him the same way she'd looked at him as a child.

Helpless.

Pleading.

Then he would kill her. No one had to tell him when or how the job needed to be done. Not his dead father, with his slaps to David's face and his shouts that it hadn't been done right. Or his sister, with her condescending stare and her never-ending letters he was forced to obey.

He was under no one now. Not since he had learned to kill.

Everyone was under him.

From the shadowed doorway to the cellar, Miss Reay stood waiting for him, her thin hands wrung before the apron.

"What are you doing?"

"Sir, I—"

"Speak up, woman. What do you want? Have you been down there against my orders?"

"Oh no, sir." She blanched. "I n–never went down there, sir, only I—" Fearsome, rounded eyes met his. Her hands entwined at her chest. "Don't be killing her, Mr. Bowles. P–please don't be h–hurting her. She be so young and l–lovely and—"

"This little matter of mine must be of great importance to you." He raised both brows. "Indeed. I have never known you to ask for anything. What courage must have gone into the request."

Her throat bobbed up and down. "Please, sir, I—I just can't stand to know she—"

"You are disgusting, Miss Reay." He snatched her jaw, felt the frantic pulse beneath her skin. "You are slime I would detest to get on my boots, and I think I am finished with you."

"Oh no, sir! Please, I—"

"You belong on the streets."

"No, I—"

"Or perhaps back in that Durham workhouse where I found you—picking oakum until your fingers bled every day and eating so little you once told me the maggots tasted good. Or perhaps you miss a certain warden, who locked you in the chapel at night, had his way with you, and beat you nigh to death if you spoke of it? Should you like to go back to him, Miss Reay?"

"Please, please, please."

He slung her away from the door, until she banged into the opposite wall and crashed into a rosewood stand. The vase banged to the floor. Glass shards scattered.

"You realize, of course, that shall come from your wages."

She whimpered, but nodded.

"Now pick it up."

She hesitated.

"Pick it up!"

With an intake of air, she dropped to the ground and grabbed the pieces with her bare hands. He hoped they slashed her fingers. He hoped she bled.

Wiping perspiration from his forehead, he ducked through the doorway, jogged down the stairs, and lit a candle before he entered the dark room.

Eliza was sitting up now, back in the corner, with that filthy blanket draped across her shoulders. Vomit puddled on the stone floor next to her.

Well then. She had been more determined against the opium than he had realized—but no matter. She had won this battle. She would not win the next.

"Come here, Miss Gillingham."

She didn't stir at first, but at his second command, she pushed herself to her feet. She walked toward him slowly, head high, and didn't so much as flinch when he seized her arm. At least she was clever enough not to fight.

They ascended the stairs together. He caught faint, pleasant scents from her hair. Rose water? No wonder his deuced nephew stayed so close to the girl. Or woman, that is.

When they passed Miss Reay, she kept her head down and made no protest.

A sharp sound left Eliza. She stumbled.

"Whatever is the matter, Miss Gillingham? Glass in your foot?"

She limped on without further sound, and two minutes later they were seated beside one another, with Breage whipping the horses and the carriage rumbling into motion.

He removed his beaver hat, took in a second deep breath of night and Miss Gillingham's rose water. "I trust you are comfortable?"

She looked away. Not in fear, as Miss Reay. But in defiance.

Defiance he would break.

If it was the last thing he ever did.

<hr>

"My lord, she is gone."

Lord Gillingham snapped shut his book and stood from the plush library chair. Already, some of the color drained from his face. "Eliza?"

"She was taken last night." Felton had difficulty pushing out the words. "A man named Bowles. David Bowles. I am going for her now."

"I am going with you."

"I do not know what we are up against. If you were to ride for the constable—"

"I shall send a servant for the constable." The viscount pushed through the library doors and said again, "I am going with you. Where does Bowles live?"

"South end of the village."

"Mrs. Eustace"—his lordship paused and glanced up at the housekeeper at the top of the stairs—"I need you to send a manservant for the constable. Tell him to gather as many men as possible and head for the residence of David Bowles. Quickly."

"Yes, my lord. Is something the matter?"

The viscount pointed Felton to the entrance doors. "Run to the stables, Northwood, and have Curry saddle my mare. I shall meet you outside in two minutes. I must retrieve my gun."

"My lord?" Felton grabbed the man's arm before he could rush away. "There is one thing I must tell you first." His voice was unsteady. "About Bowles and how I know who has taken Eliza. About my father and mother and your wife—"

"Another time, son." Lord Gillingham dragged in air. "Now hurry. And pray."

⁂

Ropes, chains, and cables of the ship's rigging swayed and groaned in the wind. Her hair whipped in front of her face. She limped forward, walking on one side of her foot, lest the glass shard push farther through her arch.

Pain blurred everything. The moonlight on the waves. The dark wood, railings, and ladders of the ship.

The two shadows on the gritty planks. Hers and his. Alone.

"I have some business to attend to, so you must forgive me if I leave you here alone for the remainder of the night." He yanked open the lattice hatch on deck and threw the door back.

More fear attacked her. She squeezed her hands so tight they cramped, as she stared into the dark space below deck. "Why do you not kill me?"

"I told you. Business must be attended to." He pulled her around to face him. "I do not suppose you noticed our little cave, did you? Albeit dark and infested with bats, it provides a very well-suited hiding place for our payments from China. You might say, this is our own little private bay—named after one of our first coxswains, Ozias Urban." The smile again. "He met with a rather unfortunate end, I fear."

"It is a pleasure to you—killing people." People she loved. People she could not live without. Disgust lanced her grief, morphing together until it raged inside her stomach. "You killed Lady Gillingham and you killed Captain and you killed my Merrylad—"

"And many more than that, Miss Gillingham, although the pleasure of ending your mother cannot be claimed by myself. My sister had the honor of that, I fear."

"Sister?"

"Martha Northwood."

Confusion swept through her, disorienting her vision. Nothing made sense. Everything was tangled, unclear, a fog of dark and terrible truths she was not strong enough to endure. *Help me, my God.*

"And you." His fingers swept into the edge of her hair. "Do not forget I shall be killing you too, Miss Gillingham. Are you afraid?"

She shivered and turned her face away from him.

But he pulled her closer, crushed her against him, bent his mouth next to her ear. "Come now. Are you afraid, Miss Gillingham?"

No answer.

His embrace tightened. Her terror spiked.

"You can tell me the truth. You were afraid those long years ago, you know." Dragging his lips along her cheek. Panting his hot breath against her skin. "You cried. You screamed. Have you grown so strong in your woods, Miss Gillingham, that you can no longer fear me? Have I not haunted you?"

God, please. Couldn't breathe.

"Hmmm?"

Please.

Then a laugh. Harsh and ghoulish in her ear, sending bumps racing along her skin, as he pulled back and retightened the ropes on her wrists. "Let us say no more now, shall we? I fear, after the events of the day, you are quite exhausted. You must rest." He propelled her into the black hole.

She smacked below deck with a thud and felt the floor rock beneath her with small waves. She nearly lost her stomach for the second time.

"Until tomorrow, Miss Gillingham." Above, the lattice hatch door slammed back shut. "Goodnight."

"I don't be kn–nowing nothing."

Felton squeezed past the gaunt-faced woman, pistol drawn, and surveyed the foyer and sconce-lit hall. No shadowy figure loomed. "Where is he?"

"I don't be kn–nowing. I don't be knowing n–nothing." The maid circled in front of him with red-rimmed eyes. "Please, sir. Please leave. If he finds you here. . .if he knows I let you in—"

"She is here, is she not?"

"Who?"

"I do not have time to talk in circles. Where is she?" When the woman only shook her head, stuttering things that made no sense, Felton stormed the house. He stole a candle from a wall sconce and waved it about the parlor, shoving back a wave of despair when nothing looked out of place.

"Please, sir." The maid stayed behind him, dogging his every step. "Please, you w–won't be finding nothing here. I swear to you."

He swept in and out of all the ground-floor rooms, then swung open a door in a hall that led to a steep staircase. "What is down here?"

"Northwood, wait." From behind, the viscount rushed to meet him, panting. "I have checked the grounds. Nothing amiss."

"What is down here?" Felton said again to the maid.

She nearly wilted. "Nothing."

He descended the stairs anyway, the viscount behind him, and busted through a closed door. A wine room of sorts. Kegs, some in straight lines and others knocked over, as if—

"Look."

Felton swung around, his candle illuminating the find in Lord Gillingham's hands. Fabric. Ripped white fabric.

When Felton brought it to his nose, he nearly choked.

Rose water.

"She was here." He sprinted back for the stairs, ascended, caught the maid before she ran.

She wriggled in his hold, sobbing, arms flailing, hysterics rising to screams as they bumped against a stand.

"Where is she?" Every nerve ending seared. He shook her lightly, but it did no good. "In the name of heaven answer me!"

She swung her head back and forth. Writhing away. Denying him answers. Answers he needed. Answers that were costing Eliza her life—

"Let her go, Northwood."

She crumpled to the floor at his feet, and the sobs turned soundless. She covered her face, rocked back and forth, still shaking her head.

Felton took a step back and groped for calm. For sanity. *Dear Christ, give us direction.*

Lord Gillingham hunkered next to the woman on the floor. He placed a hand on the thin, convulsing shoulder. "We will not hurt you, miss. Do you understand that?"

She hiccuped.

"All we want to know is what happened to my daughter. You will not be harmed."

"He will k–kill me."

"No."

"He will th–throw me out. He will s–send me back. I can't be going b–back to the w–workhouse. To the warden. I can't be going—"

"You need not go anywhere. The constable is on his way now. I shall see that you are attended to, and if it is work you need, you shall have that too." He pried the woman's hands from her face. "There is a place for you at Monbury Manor. All I ask is that you tell me where they have taken my daughter." Emotion deepened his voice. "Please."

Her wet eyes clung to the viscount for a long time. She heaved air in and out, in and out, as if weighing the truth of his words and the consequences if she did or did not tell. Then, dropping her face, she whispered, "Ozias Bay."

Felton stepped forward and swallowed hard. "Where is it?"

"I don't be kn–nowing exactly. I heared them talk of it many times and I kn–now it be near five hours away. Near Quainford."

"I know the village," Felton said.

"As do I." Lord Gillingham stood. "I shall stay here to inform the constable, and as soon as he arrives with men, we shall be behind you."

Felton nodded, sprinted back through the house, and galloped northeast with the tick of his heart chinking away the time. Night air blasted his damp face. Deep inside, in the caverns of his soul, something caved.

Not her too.

In one night, he had lost Mamma, Papa, his name. Everything he loved. Everything he believed in. Everything he had fought for these last fourteen years of his life.

Mamma. The hurt carved deep. Mamma, with her pretty chestnut hair. Always fussing over him. Always worried for him like a good mother ought—only she wasn't a good mother.

She was a killer. She had taken a life and destroyed another, and Papa had helped her do it. He was a coward. A pitiful, disgusting coward. He'd chosen his love for Mamma over everything else in the world and swallowed the lies to keep her smiles.

Tears raced loose. Felton smeared them away and tried not to remember all the times he had fought and bled for a name that now meant nothing. Nothing but lies, blood, and filth. All the things he'd never wanted people to think of him.

He hated the name of Northwood.

For what it had done to Lady Gillingham, and for what it had taken from Lord Gillingham. For how it was hurting Eliza.

God, not her too. The prayer again. The one he kept pulsing through the madness of his brain, over and over, as if repeating the words would keep her safe and alive.

Please. He pushed away the images. Her lying beside him in the sand. Him stroking her cheek. Their lips meeting, sweet and undoing, tasting of everything good and right and true.

I'll die, God. He doubled over the saddle and squeezed his eyes shut against the harsh tears trying to push through. *I'll die if I cannot get her back.*

Morning was here. Sunbeams shone through the wooden lattice, forming crisscross shadows over Eliza's body and the rough floor. Every time the wind stirred something above deck, or the ship creaked in a wave, or a seagull squawked in the distance, she flinched. As if they were footsteps. As if he were coming for her.

She ran a tongue over her torn lip and scooted toward an old wooden cask in the corner. She lifted to her knees, cupped some of the water from the bottom, and brought it to her mouth. The warm liquid soothed away the thirst but not the fear. *Felton, I'm sorry.* She didn't know why, but the words came over and over again.

Maybe because she'd told him the truth of his father. Maybe because she knew now the truth of his mother. Or maybe because it had happened in this way. Because it ended like this.

In another world, it might have been different. If she had never been stolen from her nursery window, mayhap they would have played alongside each other, year after year, and taken hundreds of visits to the shore. Perhaps, if she had been raised like all other girls, he could have been proud of her. And wanted her. And married her.

Even now, she might have been waking up in a four-poster bed beside him. He might have stretched and yawned, she might have sighed and smiled, and somewhere in their quaint little abode a child's morning cry might have greeted them.

Her heart shuddered. She couldn't imagine now. She didn't want to. Once, in the quiet and lackluster days of the forest, such stories and dreams had sustained her. They had been her companion through many a lonely night.

But she couldn't bear them now. She couldn't bear anything. She'd couldn't bear the reality that Captain was buried in those woods she loved. Or that Felton was lost to her. Or that Merrylad was dead. Or that her father was innocent and she had run from him and there would never be a chance to beg his forgiveness and make amends.

Let him come. She stared up through the lattice door and caught glimpses of wispy clouds, white against a pale pink sky. *Let him come and let it be finished.*

She was ready to stop fighting. She was ready for the nightmare to be over.

She was ready to face her beast.

⁂

He was four hours into the morning and still nothing.

Felton rubbed both eyes with his palms and took in an unsteady breath. He'd combed the length of Quainford, asking everyone from the cobbler to the rector to the black-haired abbess outside the village brothel.

No one knew anything about Ozias Bay.

Or had even heard of such a place.

Desperation battled against the last of his forbearance, as he muttered a prayer and pushed his way into the crowd of a meat market. He grabbed shoulders, asked his question, and tried to keep

from slamming his fist into each unfavorable face when they all shook
their heads no. What had the maid done? Lied to them? Was she
so afraid of Bowles?

He fought back nausea from the stifling, bloody aroma of raw
meat and unwashed bodies. *Please, Christ.* He squeezed through the
madness to the other side of the street and picked up pace. *Help me.*

A white-haired woman, half-naked in rags and without hat or
shoes, hobbled toward him. "Alms, sir? Alms?"

He pressed several pennies into her blistered hands. "Can you
tell me where I might find Ozias Bay?"

"Alms." She brought the coins to her sore-splotched face and
smiled with blackened teeth. "Thank ye, thank ye. Alms, alms.
Thank ye—"

"Ozias Bay. Please. Have you heard of it?"

Someone brushed beside Felton. "The old woman can tell you
nothing. If you wish to know about Ozias Bay, follow me." Then he
walked on—a man with hunched shoulders in a too-large frock coat,
with a tattered bicorn hat and a limp to his walk.

Felton followed him into a cobblestone alley, where two more
beggars slept in arched doorways. Hope flared as the man turned.
"What can you tell me?"

"Keep yer voice down, gent. Ye might be fine with getting yer
bleeding head knocked off, but I just as leave keep mine to my neck,
if ye know what I mean." A smile spread onto the middle-aged,
whiskered face. "I hope ye have more coins than those ye gave away
to that old beggar woman."

"How much do you want?"

"Those be dangerous questions ye been asking."

"I said how much do you want?"

"Couple of crowns ought to do it."

Felton smacked them into the man's waiting hand. "Where is it?"

"Hour from here. No one knows about it 'cept those who favor
free-traders, if ye know what I mean. Nasty business if a customs
officer should know. Many a night, men goes out there and the

goods is sold while—"

"I said where is it?" Felton flexed his hands and towered over the man. "An hour from here. Which direction?"

"Road east of the village. Stay with it 'til ye get to the tree with two trunks. Ye'll know the place. There be a path behind it that cuts off to the sea, and if ye be following it six or seven miles, it be taking you to the bay itself."

Felton dug for another crown. "If a company of men arrives in Quainford, a constable among them, give them the same directions you gave me. Understood?"

"Two things I always do well, gent. Doing my bidding and holding onto my head." The man tipped his bicorn hat back with a second grin. "Ye'd do well, where ye be going, to hold onto yours."

<hr />

The darkness was thick and velvety.

Bowles leaned back against the damp rock wall, the cool air and his perspiration making him chilled enough to flip the collar of his box coat.

Breage spoke in tones low and monotone. A price had already been settled for the twelve tea chests, and the only detail left was to arrange a delivery place and time.

If the wretch of a man had thought ahead, he might have brought a wagon and taken the contraband with him. As it was, the only thing he'd brought was a lack of brains and a banknote.

Bowles fingered it in his pocket and leaned off the wall. "Are you quite finished?"

Breage cleared his throat. "Err—yes. Mr. Haggitt, you leave now. Have to see yourself out o' here, you will, like the note said."

"Yes, quite. No faces are to be seen, as I remember." The scratchy-voiced villager must have stepped toward Bowles, because he patted his arm first, then grabbed his hand in a clammy shake. "Jolly doing business with you, sir. Fine thing you do here. Man of guts, you are."

The praise rolled over Bowles, almost as pleasant as the music of his harp. But not quite. He withdrew from the handshake. "Go."

Seconds later, after the man's footsteps left the cave back in silence, Bowles lit a torch. He hooked it back on the iron sconce.

Wooden chests, crates, and barrels lined the perimeter of the oval-shaped cave room, and the back wall sported makeshift beds, a crude table and chairs, and the two hard-faced guards who occupied them.

Bowles flicked his wrist their way. "Lomas, Martyn—get back outside and make sure our new friend is as appreciative of our ventures as he portrays himself to be." 'Twould not be the first time a buyer had tried to cross them by bringing a customs officer on his trail. "And Breage?"

"Sir?"

Bowles removed his hat and tossed it to the empty table. Bats fluttered into motion at the movement. "I believe it is time I deal with the little matter we have been avoiding." An itch of anticipation brought on a smile. "Get her."

<hr />

The black-painted rowboat careened as they lowered it into the water. She grasped the edge, a light spray of water misting her face, and squinted against the harsh light of the afternoon sun.

"Dark down there, was it, eh?" Across from her, grabbing the oars, the man she'd heard called Breage barely smiled. No trace of remorse lined his stout face. Not like the older man from the cellar.

She took her gaze back to the ship as they sailed away from its looming shadow. In dirty yellow, *Célestine II* was painted on the bow, and the entire seaworn vessel seemed miserable against a horizon so blue and calm.

Calm. She latched onto the word and tried to grope for it. *Please, God, give me calm.* How many minutes before the rowboat reached the shore? Before they reached the cave?

Whoosh, plunk. The oars slapping in and out of the water. *Whoosh, plunk.*

Maybe if she jumped, she would have a chance.

Whoosh, plunk.

If she swam to the curved shoreline, if she ran hard up the slope...

Whoosh, plunk.

She lunged before she had a chance to reason through the consequences. Cold water engulfed her. The cut on her foot stung, as she kicked both legs and used her tied hands to bring her head above water.

A wave knocked her back down. A shout filled the air, but it was watery and deafened.

Help, Savior. The panic wracked her chest as she tried to paddle toward shore. She surfaced, then sank again. Flailed, but didn't move. Gasped in air, then sucked salt water in her nose when the coldness drew her under again. *No, no.*

The burn intensified as she gulped in more water. She was going to die. She wasn't strong enough. Not with the ropes. She couldn't escape, but mayhap that was best. The sea would lull her and rock her and suffocate her gently. The sea wouldn't claw her. The sea wouldn't laugh at her. The sea wouldn't hurt her like the beast—

A hand snatched her arm and lifted.

Then air again. She gulped it in and gagged, water spewing from her mouth, as the hands hooked under her arms and dragged her back into the boat.

He rolled her over. Hard.

More water rushed out her nose and mouth, and the terror slowly dissipated into numbness. Nothing could change what was meant to happen. He would have her, the beast. Just as he'd always wanted. Just as she'd always feared.

Please, please help me. The boat jarred, as if they'd already reached sand. Breage must have thrown the oars because they clattered to the bottom of the boat, then he pulled her with him into knee-deep water.

They splashed to shore. To the cave.

The opening was black and round against the craggy, yellow-tinted rock. At least there would be no windows. No curtains. No red.

Breage forced her one step in, but she wilted.

"Get up."

A sob rose, the weakness and fear paralyzing her limbs. "Please." The word left without sound. Just a moving of her lips, a frantic pleading as she squeezed his arm in one final attempt to escape. *Please.*

But he hauled her up anyway. He guided her through the yawning darkness, the mud cool to her feet, the air stale to her lungs—and pushed her into a rounded opening.

There, half-illuminated under the light of a torch, stood her beast. Ready to kill her.

Just as he'd been trying to do every night of her life.

Felton crouched behind a jagged boulder and darted his gaze around the bay. A ship anchored close to shore. A cave, half-hidden by the boulders on each side of the entrance.

And two men. Both tall, wearing dark clothing and Monmouth caps—and guns.

Felton pulled his own flintlock from his waist. Where was Lord Gillingham with the constable? They should have been here by now, or at least close behind.

Close behind, however, might not be enough.

He needed them now.

The metal was cold in his sweating hand, as he peered over his shoulder, then turned back to the two men pacing before the cave. He needed to bring them down without gunshots. As far as he could tell, the anchored ship was empty—but who knew how many were inside the cave. He didn't want alarming shots to bring them rushing out.

Or to endanger Eliza.

If she was still alive.

A knot stuck in his throat, but he didn't have time for that now. He slipped to a second boulder, waited until both men were facing the ocean, then darted behind yet another rock until he was closer to the cave.

Two against one. Odds that would have stimulated him before. Not now though. Not when going down would cost Eliza instead of him.

He flipped his gun around and fisted the barrel, then cleared his throat loud enough the man closest to him might hear.

Nothing.

Felton grabbed a seashell and scraped it against the rock. Twice. He heard nothing at first. No shout, no gunshot, no whisper of warning to the other guard.

Just footsteps. Crunching over grass and sand, cautious, slow, and deliberate—

Felton pounced. He brought the man to the ground in one swift movement, slammed the end of the pistol into his temple, and bounced back off the limp body just as a gunshot grazed his arm.

He ducked back behind the boulder. Hot pain sizzled through him, as he raised his gun, aimed, shot.

The other guard lost his cap but nothing else. He must have thought better about taking the time to reload, because he threw down the pistol and charged.

Felton met him head-on and smashed a fist into his swarthy face. Then another. Then another.

The man tumbled backward, but he lunged back to his feet and charged again. This time, he brought Felton down and showered two blows of his own.

They rolled together in the sand, rocks jabbing Felton's ribs, as they exchanged one punch for another. Felton was under, then on top, then under again. Pressure came down on his bleeding arm and he cried out the same time as he bashed his forehead into his opponent's.

The impact gave him enough time to throw the man off him and kick a boot into his throat, his head, his stomach.

Then Felton dropped to his knees in the sand, seized the man by the coat, and jerked his bloodied face inches from Felton's. "Where is she?"

The man's eyes rolled back, but nothing came from his mouth more than a tooth and a curse.

Felton shook him. "I said where is she?"

"I'll show you where she be." A voice from behind.

Felton whirled, stomach dropping at the pistol staring him in the face—and the short, dumpy stranger who held it.

"You be hurt, Lomas?"

Spitting out a second tooth, the man scrambled back to unsteady feet. "Martyn's out cold. Stranger here knocked him over the head. Give me that gun, Breage—"

"You just be taking care o' Martyn here." Breage motioned Felton for the cave. "Mr. Bowles, I s'pect, will be taking care o' him."

"You can run if you like, Miss Gillingham. Think not that I shall object." The silver-bladed knife flashed in the torchlight. One she'd seen before. "Indeed, it would be an expected reaction, I imagine."

Her teeth clattered. She ground them together and tried to stop her wet body from shaking, but she couldn't. Just like she had never been able to writhe from his hold. Or stop herself from hurtling out the broken window. Or escape the suffocating red curtains, flapping in the night air, the color of blood.

"You rather amaze me." He took another step toward her, grinning. "All this time I imagined you would wail as you did as a child. That we would have our moment again, Miss Gillingham, and that you would look at me in that hauntingly powerless way of yours."

Bile surged up her throat, but she swallowed it down. She didn't want to look at him. She didn't want to face him.

But she did. She caught his eyes, held his gaze, and found the ice of his stare already cutting through her. To her soul. Through her mind. All the places she'd been tortured so long he now fully inhabited—yet still, she would not look away.

He had conquered everything. Like a demon in the dark, he had manifested himself in her nightmares, determined her life, taken what he wished, and killed whomever he pleased.

But he would not have this.

He would not have the cowering child he once remembered.

With one hand, he lifted a tress of her hair. He whacked it off with his knife. "You wore them in ringlets when you were a child, did you not?" Another cut through her hair. He brushed the jagged strands from her shoulder, then eased his fingers into her scalp. "Very soft, Miss Gillingham. I am not entirely a rogue, you know. I appreciate—indeed, nearly dote on—things that are beautiful."

Her pulse sprung into madness, as his lips pressed to her neck, crawled along her skin.

Then pain. She gasped and stumbled backward, the cut on her left arm leaking crimson—just as he waved the knife again and sliced her right. He was mad. She'd known that before, only this Bowles was different. He wasn't going to plunge the blade in her stomach or shoot a bullet into her head and dump her into the ocean as she'd imagined.

He was going to cut her.

Again and again.

Until she bled everywhere and died from the claws and—

"I wanted to kill you then." The knife blade nicked her neck. Blood trickled down her throat. More pain. "But she would not let me. All my life, she and my father had dominance."

Her eyes slid shut, but it didn't stop the images. He was the tapestry. The beast. They were interwoven in the nightmare, the two of them, and her mother was screaming while the curtains fluttered.

"But they do not have dominance now, do they? No one does." Nearer, but he didn't cut again. "Do you like harps, Miss Gillingham?"

Everything numbed.

"Miss Gillingham?"

She forced her eyes back open. He had stubble on his jaw. His lips were dry. His eyes were flecked with green and blue, and hair fell over his forehead, dark and reddish and tousled.

He was flesh and bone.

A man.

Not a beast. Not a nightmare. Not a tapestry or any of the things that had haunted her. He was real, and he was wicked, but some of the torment subsided. Calm seeped into her, as quickly as the blood dripped from her arms. Strange, that she should think this now. That after all these years, she should see him like this—that it could feel so different.

That the fear would be gone.

"You look at me strangely, Miss Gillingham." He grabbed her neck, then her jawline, smearing the blood. "Pray, what is it?"

"He was right."

"Who?"

"Captain."

"How so?"

She winced when his fingers dug deeper. "He said I had nothing to be afraid of. . .when he soothed me." She raked in a breath. "After the nightmares."

"You make very little sense, Miss Gillingham. Perhaps you would care to expound." When she said nothing, he squeezed harder and screamed, "Expound!"

"All you can do is kill me."

"You bore me, Miss Gillingham."

"Go on." Tears burned through. "Go on. Do it."

"No one tells me when and how to do my killing. Martha has tried that quite enough." He threw her to the ground, kicked her against wooden chests, and grabbed another fistful of her hair.

She detected movement the same time more of her hair floated to the ground. A face in the opening. One she never thought she'd see again.

One she didn't want to see now.

Felton. A cry left her lips and the anguish cramped down on her. *Felton, no.*

She'd not only hurt him, but now she was killing him. He'd die with her. Like a fool, he'd die with her. *Felton, no.*

Because Breage was holding a gun to his head and Bowles was

already pivoting.

With the knife.

⁓⁓

"Well, Nephew, I could say I am quite surprised to see you." Bowles spread his legs. "But I am not." The knife was red, dripping—dripping with blood. Eliza's blood.

Felton's gut clenched as he roved his gaze up and down her. Fetal position against wooden chests. Slashes on her arms, blood on her face, rips in her drenched clothing.

And her hair. Littered across the muddy floor of the cave, the precious locks, some of the strands still in the fist of the man who had cut them.

Felton quivered in the center of his being. The fury scorched him. He snagged his uncle's eyes—the ones that so reminded him of Mamma—and wished to heaven he could dull them with death. "I'll kill you."

"A pleasant thought, no doubt. One that has been entertained by others, many times, without ever having come to fruition."

"Felton, no." A broken sob. Eliza pulled herself up and collapsed against stacked crates. "Felton, leave. Please."

"Very gallant, is she not?" Bowles smiled at the man with the gun. "Leave us, Breage."

"But, sir—"

"A trivial matter, I assure you. I can handle it. Now go and make certain my darling nephew did not bring more unwelcomed visitors behind him." His brows furrowed. "You did not, did you, Felton?"

"I'll kill you."

"You are very imprudent. You would kill me for what I have done to Miss Gillingham, and in the process entirely overlook what you have just stepped into." Bowles wiped the knife against the lapels of his tailcoat. He glanced to the table and chairs. "Shall we sit?"

Felton's eyes sought Eliza's again—stricken, dazed, brimming with tears. He would have died to keep her away from—

"Inconsequently, how did you find me? I do not suppose Martha aided your search, did she?" He kicked out a chair. "Never mind. It does not matter. All that matters now is that you are here, Nephew, and you should be made aware that you have a family prospering from very rich endeavors. Whether you join said endeavors or die trying to stop them is entirely up to you."

"Men are on their way."

"How many?"

"Enough."

Bowles sank into the chair. It creaked beneath his weight, and somewhere above, the flapping and scratching noise of bats echoed throughout the cave room. "I know ways of escape. I know many things, despite the fact that Martha seems to believe the only one among us with any intellect is herself. We both know, however, that is untrue." His gaze rolled to Eliza. "I leave no witnesses to my own murders."

"I don't think you heard me, Bowles. I said men are coming. More men than you can fight or run from."

"What do you expect me to do? Get on my knees and beg for mercy?" He sprang back to his feet. "On the contrary, Felton. People beg mercy from *me*. Now move beside her."

Felton hesitated, mind racing, heart pummeling the cage of his chest.

"Now!"

He shuffled in Eliza's direction, close enough that he could hear shallow breathing, and braced himself in front of her. He waited, waited, waited.

Bowles paced a half circle around them. He grinned, then frowned, then glanced back at the room's exit as if contemplating the truth of Felton's words. "My guards will take care of any men."

"One of your guards is down. The other is wounded."

"By you?"

"Yes."

"It does not matter. Breage will hold them off, and we can take sail on the *Célestine II*." He tossed the knife into a crate on the other side of the room, then sprung a pistol from his coat. "Miss Gillingham, it seems there is always occasion not to kill you. I am in need of you yet longer, in the event escape becomes arduous. Move aside." He raised the gun. "Apologies, Nephew. This one is for Martha—"

Felton dove left as the gun blasted. He crashed into barrels and crates, then whirled just as Bowles came charging at him. Hands circled his neck and cut off air, but Felton rammed his knee into the man's stomach and flew to the ground with him.

He smashed a fist into his uncle's nose, heard the cartilage crack, then seized his neck. *God, help me.* He was killing. He knew that.

Bowles kicked. Spittle flew from his lips. His blue lips. Veins bulged, and his arms flailed, and his eyes rolled back with guttural wheezes.

"Enough, Northwood." A voice behind him. Lord Gillingham, but he couldn't listen. He couldn't stop. He wouldn't stop. Not when Bowles had cut Eliza and hurt her and taken her and nearly killed her and—

"Northwood." Hands grabbed his shoulder, prying him back. "Northwood, it is over. Men, go and tie Mr. Bowles with the rest of them."

Felton stumbled away from the limp body beneath him. He staggered to Eliza, pulled her down to her knees with him, and grabbed her stoic, colorless face. "Eliza." Breathing hard. Wiping away the blood. Crying as he pushed back her wet, ragged hair.

Her eyes said a hundred things to him. Things he didn't understand. Maybe would never understand, so great was the horror of them. "Eliza, you are all right. Hear me?"

Her head lolled forward. "Felton. . ."

He swallowed her against him, soaked her blood into his clothes, and willed his body to take away the hurt. "Do not say anything. Do not talk."

Lord Gillingham bent next to them. "Northwood, is she—"

"She is alive."

"You are bleeding too."

"A mere flesh wound. Get those blankets." He stood with her in his arms and carried her to one of the makeshift beds, and Lord Gillingham draped a woolen blanket across her wet figure. *Alive.* He ran the word through his brain a hundred times, but it didn't make sense.

Because her eyes were closed. She was motionless.

If she looked anything in the world, it was dead.

CHAPTER 17

"He has been there too long." Felton stared at the bedchamber door at Monbury Manor, the candlelight and his shadow looming across the oak paneling. Tension stitched across his shoulders. "Why the deuce should it take this long?"

From beside him, Lord Gillingham finally scooted an armorial hall chair to himself and sat. He bent his head and combed a hand through his hair. "You are restless, Northwood. Sit down."

"I cannot sit."

"The doctor said she shall live."

"Then why is he taking so long?"

"Perhaps because there were many—" He cleared his throat and stood again. "I feel as if I should have been able to stop all this somehow. That I should have been able to protect her from such an agony."

The same guilt thronged Felton.

"But just as when my wife was in danger, I did not." Tears scratched his voice. "Heaven knows, I have failed them both."

"That is untrue, my lord."

"Is it?"

"If anyone should have realized what was happening"—he forced back the wave of sickness and looked away—"it should have been me." More guilt. "There are things I have not told you. Things about my father and the night your wife was killed."

"Take off that coat."

"My lord—"

"Take it off, Northwood. Flesh wound or no, I have the right to stop the bleeding before it drips upon my carpet."

"You are not listening to me."

"I have heard enough."

"I am trying to tell you that you should not have trusted us all those years. You should not have befriended the Northwoods nor believed in us because—"

"I did not believe in the Northwoods, Felton." The viscount pulled the tailcoat from Felton's shoulders. "Now roll up your sleeve."

"My lord—"

"I believed in *you*. I confess, I had as many qualms as the rest of Lodnouth about the watch fob by my wife's body. But I left justice to the hands of God and the constable, and as the latter could not find evidence to punish my neighbor, I saw no reason that I should." He ripped away the bloodied shirtsleeve around the wound. "Especially when three young boys were already being punished enough."

"It was both of them. Mamma and Papa—"

"There is no need to speak of it." He pulled off his cravat and patted at the blood. "Miss Reay has told me quite enough."

"Lord Gillingham?" From the darkness at the end of the hall, Mrs. Eustace's steps grew louder as she swept forward. Her keys jangled until she stopped before them. "Lord Gillingham, forgive the interruption."

"What is it, Mrs. Eustace?"

"A message for Mr. Northwood." Her eyes slanted to Felton's and held for a second, with a look more pitiful than anything else. "His father begs him come quickly. It is Mrs. Northwood, I fear." A pause. "She is dead."

The words tumbled through Felton. He blinked hard, met Lord Gillingham's stare, tried to derive comfort in the warm hand already pressing his shoulder.

"Go on, son."

Felton looked back to the door. Eliza. He could not leave. He would not leave her now.

"I shall be with her when the doctor is finished. You may see her as soon as you return." The viscount motioned to Mrs. Eustace. "Go and prepare a mount for him. Quickly."

"Yes, my lord." Her footsteps and keys thumped and clattered again, then died back into silence.

Felton drew in air. He pulled the numbness up and around him like a shroud and wished to mercy he could never find his way out of such a fog. He wiped his eyes. They were wet to his touch, the traitors. "I do not want to go." A rough whisper.

Lord Gillingham wound the cravat around Felton's arm, tied a loose knot, then pulled the torn shirtsleeve back over his arm. "You must."

———⸱❧⸱———

Eliza stared at the plaster rose on the ceiling above her. Pain arced through her, sharp enough she fisted the bed linens as the doctor spread a poultice over each of her cuts.

"Don't'ee hurt her." Minney circled the bed, voice fraught, eyes wild. "Don't'ee hurt her one bit."

"Just you hold that candle still, young girl." The doctor swung his queue behind his shoulder and lifted Eliza's left arm. Their shadows moved on the walls, larger than life. "I must make these tight, Miss Gillingham. I trust you shall bear it tolerably?"

She nodded with tears. She closed her eyes before they could flood her cheeks, and the next time she opened them, the doctor was finished and pressing a cup of willow bark tea to her lips.

She sipped the warm liquid down her throat, then rested her eyes again. *Thank you, Doctor.* She wasn't certain if she spoke the words aloud or only thought them.

A door opened and closed, as if the doctor had left, then a thin hand grasped hers. "I'll take good care of'ee, Miss Gillingham, because'ee are my friend. E'erything shul be just fine now. Even Merrylad be home, and I be feedin' him again and takin' good care of him too." A gentle kiss pressed to Eliza's cheek, and Minney's voice whispered into her ear, "Ye be home now, Miss Gillingham. Ye be home safe at last."

Sleep pulled her away from the bed and the discomfort and the ache of everything she had endured.

But the words stayed still, even as she slumbered.

I am home.

Felton took the stairs one at a time, gliding his hand along the cold banister. When he reached the hall, he almost turned back. *I cannot do this.*

Dodie and two other maids stood outside Mamma's door. They huddled close together, whispering, and Dodie brushed tears from her eyes.

Felton strode past them. The bedchamber door was ajar, and the hinges whined when he eased it open and entered. He shut it behind him. *I cannot.*

Papa was in the bed with her. She was draped across his arms, with the lustrous chestnut hair dangling, her eyes closed and pale lips unmoving.

His numbness prickled. *Cannot.* He took three steps forward and stood at the bedside. Letters were scattered across the floor. Hugh's letters. Letters she had held dear and read a hundred times over.

"She wanted me to read them to her." Papa smoothed the hair away from her face. Gentle. Achingly gentle because he was always gentle with Mamma. "I was so angry with her after you left. . .I refused. The first time in my life I did not do what she asked of me."

Hurt speared through the shroud he couldn't hide beneath. "Papa, do not say that."

"She must have tried to get them herself. She fell over there by the stand. She was dead before I could come for her." He held her closer, his cheek against hers, and his dry eyes blinked faster. "A terrible thing for her. To die alone in this room. I should have been holding her. I should have been holding her like this. . .to make it easier."

"You could not have known." Felton sniffed. He wiped his nose with his arm, bent closer, reached out. He hesitated with his hand over her cheek.

He shouldn't touch her. He shouldn't grieve her. Not after everything she'd done, the wickedness she'd hid from them, the lies she'd told them all this time.

But he touched her anyway. He brushed his fingers up and down against the soft skin, and he ached with the memory of her smile the first time he had recited his alphabet. Or the look on her face when he'd picked cornflowers from the garden and handed them to her. Or her laugh—the seldom, beautiful cadence of her laugh—when he'd said something childish that amused her.

"Mamma." He spoke her name, even knowing she could not hear him. He half expected the lashes to flutter open, for her to stare at him with that worried frown when she saw the blood on his shirtsleeves. "Mamma, I—" His voice cracked. He pulled away, walked to the window, wiped more tears away, and tried to still the bruising throb of his chest.

"All I ever wanted to do was please her." Papa's murmur. "And make her happy. I just. . .I only. . .I loved her. More than anything under heaven, I loved her."

Felton moved back to the bed and ran his hand, once more, down the soft tresses of her chestnut hair. "I know, Papa." He turned away with stinging eyes. "I know."

───※───

The next time Eliza awoke, it was not Minney who sat beside her. 'Twas Lord Gillingham.

He had scooted a high-backed chair next to her bed, with his chin on his knuckles, his elbows on his knees. The wavy hair, more whitened than black since she'd arrived, was uncombed and disheveled.

Shadows hung beneath his eyes, as if he'd spent these last days in as much torment as she had.

Which was not possible. Was it? Mayhap such a thing could have been true of Captain, who had known her and loved her.

But Lord Gillingham...

A lump pushed up her throat. Not only did he not know her, but the fragile relationship that had formed between them had been shattered when she ran from him and believed him a killer.

As if he sensed her wakefulness, he glanced at her. Some of the despair, the tightness of his expression, fell away as he leaned over her. "Are you thirsty?"

She eased her tongue across her bottom lip. The swelling must have lessened, and she no longer tasted dry blood.

He fetched a glass of water before she could answer. Instead of the chair, he sat on the edge of her bed, placed his hand behind her neck, and gently slid the water to her lips. When she was finished, he returned to his chair. "How do you feel?"

Feel? She felt a thousand things and nothing. She glanced back at the plaster rose on the ceiling, the intricate design, something that could arrest her attention so she would not have to look into the viscount's face. "Tell me what happened."

"You do not remember?"

She strained through the haze. The torch-lit cave, the knife slashing her hair and skin, the beast and his eyes, then Felton, the gun.

She shook her head. "Tell me...please."

"We could have never found you without Northwood. He realized first who had taken you, then rode beyond the rest of us to bring you back."

A flood of comfort raced through her. She was still hurting, still in the dark, still confused—but the reality that Felton had come for her was a stronghold. Something she could cling to. *Someone* she could cling to, in a world where she belonged nowhere at all.

"By the time the constable, the men, and myself reached the cave, Northwood had Mr. Bowles down. We had already apprehended the others outside the cave, and much work is being done now to locate the rest of the men and ships involved." His jaw flexed. "They will hurt you no longer. I suspect the gallows for all of them."

"And Felton? Is he unharmed?"

"In the way you speak of, yes." His eyes bequeathed the same pity that pulsed in her own heart. "But in many other ways, he is harmed greatly."

"Then he knows."

"Yes."

"Will Mrs. Northwood. . .will she hang too?"

"No. She is dead, I fear, already." Lord Gillingham drew the soft bed linens closer to her neck. "As for Mr. Northwood, I do not know what shall become of him. I cannot help feeling, however, that the man has taken a very grave punishment for his deeds. I myself want no part of inflicting him with further penance."

Felton. How she ached for him. For the loss of everything he had believed in. For the dousing of the fire that had given him purpose. For his name, his ruined and soiled name, the one thing he wanted more than anything else.

"Do not cry, Eliza."

She hadn't realized more tears were streaming. How many could she weep before there were no more? When would they stop? Would they ever?

She nearly started when Lord Gillingham's careful finger swiped them away. The touch was awkward, uncomfortable, and when he sank back to his chair, he could not look her in the face.

But his own nose and eyes were red too. "When you were little, I pulled you onto my knee when you cried. Or I put you on my shoulders and carried you about, pointing out silly things in the pictures on the walls, until you forgot about whatever trouble had made you sad." Slowly, almost helplessly, his gaze met hers. "I do not know what to do for you now, my little daughter."

My little daughter. Something Captain had never said to her. In all his life, had he ever called her daughter?

No, he hadn't. Because he couldn't. Because she wasn't.

The lump increased, until it burned to breathe past. "I do not deserve to be called your daughter."

"We seldom deserve what we are or what we are given." He took her hand. His hold was warm, strong, big. "I know, for I never deserved my Letitia. I never deserved little Thomas." A squeeze. "I never deserved you."

She nearly looked away, nearly had to, because the words were too much. They almost sounded as if he wanted her. As if no matter what was behind or before, she was his daughter and he was her father.

And he loved her.

The reality eased away that lost feeling. In a slow, quiet way, it settled her—like a homeless fairy who, after years of fluttering about with birds and butterflies, finally found a hole in a tree of other fairies. A place where she could belong. Truly belong.

For the second time, he squeezed her hand.

For the first time, she squeezed back.

Felton walked the path back to Monbury Manor, just as golden sunrays cut through the morning fog. Branches stirred above him, heavy with dew, the leaves more orange and red than green.

In sight of Monbury Manor, he halted. He leaned onto the rock wall, his coat sleeve drinking moisture from the moss on the stones. His other arm throbbed. *Now what?*

The loss of too many things drained his energy. He wanted to run. He wanted to sprint back down the path, saddle his horse, and ride someplace where no one would ever find him.

Or know him.

Or hear of the sordid name of Northwood and what it meant.

He ran both hands down his face, inhaled, exhaled, tried to make sense of everything. How would he face the world after this? How people would whisper. They would shame him all over again—only

THE GIRL FROM THE HIDDEN FOREST

worse this time because he had tried so hard for so many years to convince them the rumors were lies.

What a fool.

He should have seen the truth just as Papa should have seen the truth. Shouldn't he have sensed something was wrong? Shouldn't he have once looked at Mamma and felt a prick of unease, instead of the oblivious, unsuspecting warmth for her?

He didn't know. All he knew was that no matter what, he could not run. He had to stay, and he had to fight the shame, just as he'd stayed to disprove it before. Mayhap the villagers would hate him. Mayhap the urchins would run the streets and shout names to him. Mayhap he'd attended his last ball, his last of any social event, because no one would dare wish him present. Not now.

But I'm not a name. He swallowed hard, thrusting his hands into his pockets. He was more than a name. Wasn't he?

He was Felton. *Felton.* Just Felton, who had no reason to hang his head low, despite the sins of his family, because he had never committed those sins himself. What did it matter what they thought of him? What anyone thought of him?

A shiver worked through him, and he flipped his collar up against the cool breeze. God never looked down on Felton Northwood and turned away his prayers because of one night fourteen years ago. Lord Gillingham had never turned Felton away because of the evils of his family.

Even Eliza.

Dear, sweet, guileless Eliza, who should have despised him when she realized his father had kidnapped her, all those years ago, from her nursery window.

But she didn't. She wouldn't. Even knowing all the hurt and agony his family had wrought upon her, she would still look at him the same. With that tender smile. That blushful air. That sweet light that seemed to call him noble and good and strong, despite anything else in the world.

She loved him.

For Felton.

Not Northwood.

He pushed himself off the wall and walked to the manor, navigated the halls he knew so well, and found the bedchamber that made his heart hammer faster. He crept inside.

Lord Gillingham sat beside her, asleep like his daughter, but at Felton's creaking footsteps, he nodded awake. He rubbed his eyes and smiled. "I shall leave you alone."

Then the door shut, and Felton stood over top of the barefoot girl he'd once stolen from the forest. Mrs. Eustace must have seen to her hair, because the jagged ends had been evened, and the tresses now waved, clean and glistening, above her shoulders. Light bruises splotched her face. Her lip was cut. One of her arms rested above her head, and the white bandage was already spotted with bright red blood.

But she was lovely.

In a hundred million ways, she was lovely.

He bent over the bed, and it creaked when he placed his hands on both sides of her face. Then he lowered closer, closer, closer, until his lips brushed against her still ones.

At the touch, she stirred. She blinked fast, disoriented, afraid perhaps. Then the fear fell away, and whatever pulsated his heart came to life on her face. "Felton." Tenderly, preciously, as if she needed him.

He hoped to goodness she needed him. He needed her. He would always need her. Needed the way she looked at him and the way she spoke to him and the things she said and the way she said them and. . .

Another kiss. The pull of it drew him in, like a vortex, into a place where souls become one. He grasped her face with one hand. Kissed again. Breathed. Kissed her forehead, her cheek, her brow. *Eliza, I love you.*

Heart sprinting, he closed his eyes, drank of her lips once more, and then stood. He crossed the room and glanced back from the threshold.

She had pulled herself upright, with the bed linens drawn to her shoulders, her eyes filling with tears as his did. All the hurt he couldn't speak was heard, understood, and felt by her too in ways he could not comprehend. How could that be?

"Rest now." The command left his lips. He wished he had said something softer, gentler—but in answer, she only smiled.

A smile that said she loved him.

As much, if that were even possible, as he loved her.

CHAPTER 18

Eliza scooted her chair nearer to the library hearth. Flames danced and crackled, drifting sparks up the chimney, as the warmth spread through her cold body.

But it did not reach her heart. Not when Felton had not visited Monbury Manor in over four days.

She turned the page of her book and tried to read the words, but they were as senseless as the doubts pouring through her. In the last three weeks, she had grown stronger. For the first time in longer than she could remember, she was not attacked every night in her sleep. The beast had no power over her. More than just her cuts began to heal.

All through the days, Felton had come. He had sat beside her while she rested, read her books that likely bored him, and taught her chess with enough grins she felt as if she'd won, even at every loss.

But between his smiles, when he imagined she did not see, a shadow came over his face. Sometimes for only a second. Other times less than that. But the looks bore so much pain it stabbed her chest, and she bled for him.

She would always bleed for him. She was as much a part of his pain as he had become of hers. Couldn't he see that? Did he not know? How had it happened like this—feeling this way, him and her, as if they were no longer two people but one? Or had she only imagined his love as she imagined everything else?

She closed the book and drew it against her chest. Her heart thudded against the cover, and a sickening chill rushed through her veins. Was that the reason he had not kissed her since that first day? Was that the reason he was not here now? Because he sensed her own feelings and could not return them?

Behind her, the library door squeaked open. A woman slipped next to Eliza's chair, hair pulled tight from her face, with eyes that seemed ready to dart back to the floor at any second. "Miss Gillingham?"

Eliza stood. "Miss Reay."

The woman's face bore no trace of bruises. Fear still clouded her eyes, but every once in a while, as she busied herself with duties about the manor, a smile or quick flash of contentment came over her.

Eliza tried to push away the images of the woman's body over hers, the nails scratching at her face, the bitter taste of opium being shoved into her mouth.

As if sensing her thoughts, Miss Reay's gaze dropped to the library rug. "Mrs. Eustace t–told me I ought to be t–telling you about Mr. Northwood."

Eliza squeezed the book. "He has come?"

"Yes, miss. He be speaking with his l–lordship now, but he be saying to dress w–warm on account of him wishing to take you on a ride."

A ride. Anticipation made her drop the book. She must hurry, find Minney to help her into something warm, and—

"Miss Gillingham?"

She refocused on Miss Reay, and when the maid placed a thin hand on Eliza's arm, she felt the tremors.

"My daughter...she be something a lot like you." Miss Reay shook her head and whimpered. "I—I be so ashamed of myself I could die."

Pity stirred in all the places where Eliza had resented the woman. She hesitated, then leaned forward and pressed a kiss to the woman's gaunt cheek. "You were only afraid of him, as I was afraid of him." Eliza's heart soared. "But he has no hold on us anymore, does he? We are both quite free of him now."

"We know the last of them." Felton tossed a piece of paper to the untidy surface of Lord Gillingham's desk.

The viscount lifted it, perused it, then creaked back in his chair. "How?"

"Man called Swabian. He has been locked up ever since the rest of them, but two days ago he. . ." Felton sighed and rubbed his face.

"He what?"

"Hung himself in the village cage. He left the names in his boot."

"I see."

Felton slid his hands into the pockets of his tailcoat. "My lord, I. . ." His throat dried. He coughed, went to the oak stand in the corner, and uncorked the glass decanter. "I daresay, you are likely the only gentleman alive who would dare keep water in his study."

"Let us not spread the word abroad, shall we?"

Felton poured a glass and swallowed it down in one gulp.

"Good?"

"My lord?"

"The water." The chair legs scraped wood as if the viscount stood. "As you seem uncommonly thirsty, I inquired if the water was satisfactory."

"Oh. Yes." Felton curled his fingers around the glass but kept his back to Lord Gillingham. He squeezed tighter. Waited.

"Northwood?"

"Hmm?"

"You had better say what you wish to say before you bust that glass between your fingers."

"I wish to marry your daughter." The words came out fast, breathy. He turned and met a pair of piercing eyes.

"It was my understanding you wished to marry Miss Haverfield."

"No."

"Why? She embodies everything you have ever wished for in matrimony. Beauty, wealth, social standing—"

"She is not Eliza."

"Meaning?"

"I love her." Strange, how releasing it was to speak the words. To have them alive, echoing through his mind, powerful enough they sent chills up and down his arms. "I knew before, only I was a fool."

"They are only fools, Northwood, who continue in their folly." The viscount approached. He clapped his hand on Felton's shoulder. "What do you wish me to say?"

"I know I do not have a name to offer her. Not one she might be proud of. But under all that is holy, I shall protect her and care for her—"

"I said what do you wish me to say, Northwood?"

His mouth was dry again. "That you would bless such a match."

"It is blessed."

Relief filtered through him, ebbing away the strain—and when the viscount's eyes crinkled with a smile, Felton breathed out a laugh. "Thank you, my lord." He slammed the glass back on the stand, then whirled to leave.

"Northwood?"

Felton pulled the reins on his excitement and paused in the doorframe. "My lord?"

"Only one thing do I ask of the man who marries my daughter."

"Anything."

"Walk proud." The smile left Lord Gillingham's lips but glistened all the stronger in his eyes.

Felton grinned. "I will."

She could not bear this.

Eliza pulled her cashmere shawl tighter, her cheeks already chilling from the wind in her face. She did not look at him. She blinked often enough and hard enough that any mist in her eye was only from the October cold.

Not what Minney had told her.

The gig rolled up the familiar hill, and at the rise, the ocean spread out before them. Deep blue water rolling with white waves. A gray, foreboding sky. A flock of seagulls and a half-torn net washed up on the beach.

Her shawl flapped in the wind as Felton swung her down. Still, she did not look at him, but her body went colder when his touch was gone.

He was as strange as she was. He had said nothing, not in all the time they had been riding. Even now, as they descended the hill to the beach, he did not speak.

Then they stood there, close enough to the water that the mist found a home on their faces, salty and cool. They had once played here. They had once loved here.

Or so she had imagined.

But that was all it was. Another story. Another make believe. Minney had nearly said as much, as she'd helped Eliza pin back her hair and don a bonnet. *"Mr. Northwood be goin' to leave, Miss Gillingham. I heard him say so when he first arrived. I hear lots of things, don't I? He be goin' to Cambridge. His brother be there. I knowed because I heard them say so."*

She'd shaken her head and denied the words were true. She'd told herself he would not run. He would not leave. Not now.

But the moment she saw him, she doubted. Why else would he have stayed away so many days? Why else would he take her on such a ride, if not to tell her goodbye?

Goodbye. The word formed, swallowed her, pulled her under. She was the mermaid all over again, and the rowboat was sailing away. How empty the waters would be in his absence. How terrible it would be to ever surface again, knowing the rowboat would no longer be there, knowing his kiss. . .

His kiss. She lingered there, frozen by the undoing thought, and glanced at him.

He watched the horizon, intent, wind whipping hair across his forehead. She knew he felt her stare, but he kept his eyes in front of him and left the silence as it was.

She slipped her arm around his. She shouldn't have. Not now. But if the mermaid could reach once more through the water, touch his hand before he rowed away, hadn't she the right?

"There is something I must ask you."

She leaned her head onto his shoulder. "Please do not ask me. You must tell me." The warmth of his arm soaked into her, a torturing pleasure. "You are always ordering me about everything, Felton, and you must not stop now."

"Eliza—"

"Tell me to be brave, and I shall do it. Tell me not to cry, and there shall be no tears." She forced herself away from him. Just one step, but the gap seemed an ocean. "There is but one order I could never obey, and that is to cease loving you. Even after you. . .after you. . ."

"After I what?"

"Leave."

"Leave?"

She turned away and shivered. "I do not blame you, Felton. There is too much hurt for you here. There are too many whispers, and you must escape them. I am not so selfish as to wish you to remain in a place where there is nothing left for y—"

"There is something left for me." He was next to her again, pulling her back around. The shawl billowed around them. "And I have no intention of leaving."

She sucked in air. "But Minney—"

"With the morn, I am taking my father to Cambridge to live with Aaron. I shall be gone only as long as the trip." His gaze moved from her eyes to her lips, back to her eyes again. "If Minney would have eavesdropped a moment longer, she might have spared you such a tale."

Her pulse went mad, as his hands eased up her cheeks. Heat burned her face. "I should not have spoken such things."

"Which of them do you regret?"

She looked away.

"That you would never cease to love me?" His thumbs worked up and down. Soft, gentle, undoing. "I must remember to praise Minney for her folly."

"Felton—"

"Marry me." Deep, raw, a command so soft she could have died for the glory of the words. He pulled her face closer, nose against hers, then his mouth sought her own.

A thousand emotions jarred her, thrilled her, left her breathless when he pulled away.

"Marry me, Eliza Gillingham, and never listen to silly maids who might say I would leave you. . .because I will not." Another kiss. Deeper, stirring. "I shall never leave you, and I shall never stop loving you."

"Felton." She cried into yet another kiss. "Felton—"

"Do not speak. Do not do anything." He pushed back her bonnet, until the wisps of hair fluttered around her face. "Except kiss me. And love me. And go on loving me until the day we die."

Her mouth met his again in an order she would obey the rest of her life.

EPILOGUE

Balfour Forest
Weltworth, Northumberland
May 1813

Eliza tramped through ferns and growth, Merrylad two steps ahead, and took off her half boots before she climbed atop the Lady's Throne.

The stream had not changed.

Merrylad splashed through it, tongue wagging, as the water rushed through his legs and carried on to some unknown place. Captain had always told her it ended at the ocean. How many times, with a dull and lonely ache, had she wished it might take her to such a faraway sea?

She didn't wish for such things anymore. She didn't imagine she was a fairy as big as her finger, who would climb into a leaf and float away. She didn't imagine anything. She didn't have to.

Because she was happy.

Captain would have smiled to see her so happy.

From behind, footsteps crunched the forest floor, then Felton scooted next to her on the moss-covered rock. He tipped back his beaver hat. "This is where I found you."

Merrylad climbed back to the bank, shook off the water, and then came to Eliza for a rub of his ears. "Would you have been angry to know then that such a girl would be your wife?"

"No angrier than you, I imagine." His arm came around her. "Or Merrylad, I daresay."

How wonderful it was, even a year later, to press close to a man she called her husband. To belong to him. To be loved by him. To feel all the things she had only ever dreamed or read of before.

"I used to dance with those trees over there." She nestled deeper into him and pointed to a cluster of knotty-looking pines. "We had many a ball together."

"I should have brought my axe."

"You are jealous?"

"Considering they exceed me in both strength and height, do you not think I should be?"

"No." She laughed. "They are not as warm as you."

"That all depends."

"On what?"

"Whether you burn them in the hearth or not." He stood, glowing with the amusement of his own nonsense, and pulled her up with him. "Dance with me."

"Oh Felton—"

"Come now. Do not argue." He swooped her off her feet, splashed to the other side of the stream, and positioned her four and a half feet apart. "Now bow."

A laugh trilled out, echoing with the birdsongs and breeze, as they switched places, met, switched places, met again—

He never released her. He pressed her close, each of their hearts thudding against the other, sighs mingling. "Does it hurt you to have come here?"

She closed her eyes. "No, it does not hurt me. I suppose, in some way or another, this place shall always be a bit of home to me."

"I am sorry, Eliza." His embrace tightened. "I am sorry for the way I took you away and all the things you suffered because of it."

"I suffered less than I have gained."

"But Captain—"

"He would have wanted it this way. He would have wanted the nightmares to be over. He would have wanted me to see the ocean at the end of the stream. I know that now."

His hand rubbed her hair back and forth, a soothing motion, a loving one. "We had best be on our way then if we wish to be out of the forest by night. Lord Gillingham made me promise I would not have his grandchild beneath the stars and treetops."

They started back for the stream, Felton carried her across, and her hand rested on the small bump at her stomach as they ambled away.

Only once, just before she lost sight of the mossy rocks, did she turn. All the fairies and stories and dreams she'd ever had seemed to wave to her. Even the old trees, stern and tall, seemed to sway in a final goodbye.

Eliza smiled when Felton's fingers entwined with hers. She would miss them, the stories—but now she had one of her own. One that needed to be lived, not imagined.

Captain would be happy indeed.

Hannah Linder resides in the beautiful mountains of central West Virginia. Represented by Books & Such, she writes Regency romantic suspense novels filled with passion, secrets, and danger. She is a four-time Selah Award winner, a 2023 Carol Award semi-finalist, a 2023 Angel Book Award third place winner, and a member of American Christian Fiction Writers (ACFW). Also, Hannah is an international and multi-award-winning graphic designer who specializes in professional book cover design. She designs for both traditional publishing houses and individual authors, including New York Times, USA Today, and international bestsellers. She is also a self-portrait photographer of historical fashion. When Hannah is not writing, she enjoys playing her instruments—piano, guitar, ukulele, and banjolele—songwriting, painting still life, walking in the rain, square dancing, and sitting on the front porch of her 1800s farmhouse. To follow her journey, visit hannahlinderbooks.com.